I0599080

Feather & Flame
The Birdsong Trilogy: Book Two
Copyright © 2022 by Nina Lane
All rights reserved.

This book is a work of fiction. All names, characters, locations, and incidents are products of the author's imagination, or have been used fictitiously. Any resemblance to actual persons living or dead, locales, or events is entirely coincidental.

Cover design: Najla Qamber Designs

Published by Snow Queen Publishing

ISBN: 978-1-954185-19-7

FEATHER & FLAME: THE BIRDSONG TRILOGY #2

NINA LANE

Darius

"This is why I never contacted you. I still have no control around you. You want me to tell you I haven't thought of you? That would be a damned lie. Wherever I've been, whatever I've done, I haven't stopped thinking of you. You are always there."

Nell

Once, I was convinced that my feelings for Darius, my love for him, were pure and real. I fought against all his perceptions of *wrongness*.

But that was four years ago. If I still can't find pleasure in even the thought of kissing another man, maybe my feelings for Darius *have* gotten twisted and warped. Maybe they're obsessive.

Maybe they're wrong.

New York Times bestselling author Nina Lane returns with the Birdsong Trilogy, a provocative romance between two people whose forbidden love will set their lives—and the world—on fire.

There is peace even in the storm.

—*Vincent van Gogh*

PROLOGUE

Darius

IF THE GREAT white shark stops moving, it will die.

He has the same survival instinct. Now more than ever.

His camera doesn't capture the smells or the sounds. The volcano of acrid smoke after a suicide bomber's explosion. Flames eating through a building. The screams of the wounded. No frame conveys the death rattle of a soldier's voice as he lies on the ground, his chest torn open, or a woman's choked gasp when a bullet strikes her in the back.

He sells the images to news agencies, press services, newspapers, online sites. AP, Reuters, Agence France-Presse, the BBC, Deutsche Presse-Agentur. He doesn't care where they go or who publishes them. He takes assignments in Somalia, Afghanistan, Syria, China.

When he's not on the front lines, he wages a war of his own against his former captors. Through UN and NATO counterterrorism and security councils, he launches investigations into the

People's Liberation Front. He digs into the details of their financing, strategies, operations. He wants to destroy their very foundation.

He never misses a chance to get on another plane. He lives in Paris for two months, Madrid for three weeks, Beijing for ten days. He travels for eight months through the Middle East. His home base is the ground under his feet. He rejects invitations to photo exhibitions, contests, award dinners, lectures.

He takes a lengthy assignment documenting the brutal, decades-long war in South Sudan, then seeks out tribal wars, genocide, refugee camps. He shoots thousands upon thousands of frames. Millions.

He gets robbed. He's in car crashes. He's held at knifepoint. He's thrown in prison. He fights countless street battles. He falls sick and recovers. He fractures his left arm in a fall, but keeps shooting with his right. He's in a helicopter crash and a small plane emergency landing. He's bitten by insects, spiders, a snake. He's shot at, yelled at, spit on, and detained. He crosses armed borders, smuggles illegal goods in exchange for favors, escapes another abduction attempt, bribes local officials, and runs relentlessly toward gunfire, bomb blasts, the front lines.

His fucked-up psyche shuts down. He has no nightmares. His fear reached its limits long ago. He thinks there's no situation, no possible circumstance, *nothing* that can scare him anymore.

He's wrong.

PART I

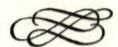

CHAPTER 1

Nell

I'VE SEEN him a thousand times over the past four years.

Though his powerful shadow eclipses every other man, I catch sight of him in the dark-haired executive striding toward a waiting taxi, the well-built jogger passing me in Central Park, the unshaven customer who orders black coffee and works on his laptop at a table by the window. It takes only a gesture, the glint of sunlight on black hair, sometimes even the quick flash of a smile, for me to remember how deeply Darius Hawke is embedded in my blood, my bones.

My imaginary glimpses of him are feeble substitutions for the reality I know so well, but they still make my heart jolt with both longing and a cascade of sharp memories. I've become so accustomed to the way he's still here and yet not here, an invisible, essential part of me, that the idea of his physical presence is impossible.

I come to a stop in the entrance hall of the New York

Public Library. Overhead lights flood the marble arches. The low hum of conversation rises from patrons and tourists, but I can't make out any words past the realization roaring in my ears.

A tall man stands on the north side of the hall, his back to me, his head bent like he's looking at his phone. The pendant light above him spills over his thick, dark hair. His shoulders are as broad as ever beneath his black peacoat, his stance solid like a pyramid. Worn jeans hug his long legs, and melting slush clings to his boots.

It's *him*.

For all the men who have unknowingly given me glimpses of Darius Hawke over the years, I've never thought those two words. Never once have I wondered if the businessman in a tailored suit or the rough-hewn worker at the diner counter is actually him because, of course, my instincts know the truth.

I would *feel* him, like an animal sensing the deep shock of an earthquake right before it fractures the surface. I would know if he was occupying the same space as me, breathing the same air.

Which is why I can't move. My body already knows what my mind refuses to believe.

For the longest moment, he doesn't move either. Then tension courses through his large frame. He starts to turn. The ground shifts under my feet. I see the movement of his body in slow motion, a revelation stripping away the layers of time.

Our gazes collide with a force that vibrates all the way down to my toes. I can't pull in a breath. If I'd ever had any illusions that he might have retreated into my past, become a heart-warming but distant memory, that notion shatters like glass hitting concrete.

Every nerve ending, every cell in my blood, every hope, wish, and dream I've harbored for the past four years now flourishes into wild, electric life.

It's him.

He breaks the spell first and starts walking across the vast marble ocean toward me.

I manage to move forward, pulled inextricably into his atmosphere. I meet him halfway, and then he's close enough to touch, but he doesn't reach for me, and I don't reach for him. Instead we just stand there, two feet of space and an infinity between us.

"Hello, Nell." His deep voice enfolds me like an embrace.

"Darius." My tongue stumbles over the name I haven't spoken aloud since before the night I confessed my love for him. "You're...you're here."

"I just got in a couple of days ago." His eyes sweep over me as if he's assessing all the changes that four years have wrought. "How have you been?"

"Fine."

I don't know what else to say. I don't know what to do or even think.

He's as strikingly beautiful as he's been in my memory—no, far more so because he's alive and in front of me, and his presence is carved into the very air itself. He radiates strength and the immutable courage of survival.

Shadows graze his strong cheekbones, and the light gleams in his thick-lashed brown eyes with their countless secrets and experiences. Aside from a few more lines radiating toward his temples and the deeper brackets around his mouth, he looks the same as he did four years ago. Big, muscular, suffused with energy.

But he and I both know that the most profound changes in a person are invisible to the eye.

"Why are you here?" I can't stop staring at him.

"For work." He indicates two thick books tucked under his arm. "And some research."

"Is this your first time back since..." My voice trails off.

Since you left. Since I wanted you so desperately, and you refused to let yourself want me back. Since my life broke wide open. Since you disappeared again.

He nods. A weighty silence falls. Had he known I was living in New York? Is that why he hasn't come back until now?

I'm sure my father has told him at some point that I've been living here since the summer after high school. Even if Darius had intended to cut himself off from me entirely, he couldn't stay in touch with my father and not hear about me. Just like he's always been on the periphery of my life, despite our complete lack of contact.

My father was the one to tell me Darius hadn't been able to find the photo album my mother once had that contained child-hood pictures of her—the only ones that exist anymore. Darius had looked for it, but couldn't find it or discover what happened to it.

I wasn't surprised that Darius hadn't told me himself, not after all communication was severed between us. I've never asked my father about him either, but his name has still come up in conversations, and he's in the public eye. I've seen his photos on news websites and magazines, and I've kept an eye out for his memoir, which still doesn't appear to have been published yet.

"I heard you graduated from art school." His gaze hasn't moved from my face. "I hoped you'd end up studying art some-where. Where are you working now?"

I swallow a tide of embarrassment. In the six months since graduation, I've discovered the massive gulf between studying art and working as an artist. Not to mention the struggle of trying to make rent payments without a steady job. If something doesn't change for me soon, I'll be forced to cut my losses and move back to Grenville.

Which was never part of my plan.

"I'm waitressing part-time," I tell Darius casually. "How long will you be in town?"

"A little over a week." He takes a slight step back. "It's good to see you again."

An unexpected tension tightens my chest. After all this time, that's *it*? A polite greeting, how are you, and goodbye?

"If you don't have any plans right now, do you want to get a coffee?" The question pops out before I can even question the wisdom of spending more time with the man who still eclipses all other men, whose existence has been like a wall between me and any potential romantic interest.

For a moment, he doesn't respond. The overhead lights reveal a faint, faded bruise on the slope of his cheekbone. The lines of his shoulders are tight.

"Just to catch up," I add hastily. "No big deal if you're busy."

"I'm not busy." He extends a hand toward the doors in an indication for me to precede him. "Coffee sounds good."

We walk out together into the gray late-March afternoon and descend the steps. The now-familiar noise of the city fills the air —horns honking, the whoosh of tires over the slushy streets, a manhole cover clanking, the hiss of air brakes. Lights of every color pierce through the gloom from traffic signs, billboards, storefronts.

I push my hands into the pockets of my green coat, acutely conscious of him beside me. He walks with the stride of a man who is guarded and self-assured at the same time. He knows his own power just as he knows the risk of unexpected danger or a sudden crisis. He is never uncertain and never fully at ease.

We go into a coffeehouse on East 40th Street. The interior is warm, a few tables occupied by people on their phones or laptops, the air scented with coffee and baked goods. Though I've been here several times before on my trips to the library, now it feels different, almost surreal. Not thirty minutes ago, I was thinking about my work schedule, an email I have to send, what to add to my grocery list.

Now I can only think about him. He'd had the same effect

when I was a child, each time he'd return from his daring adventures. Everything else just faded into the distance when he was around.

I shouldn't be surprised that it still does, though when I was younger, I'd welcomed his all-consuming presence in my life. He'd obliterated the fear and pain and reminded me that the world was an exciting place full of possibilities. He'd given me hope and safety.

But that was back when he was a living, breathing part of my life. For four years, he's been a phantom I can't shake. Even my memories of him have shaped and changed my decisions, my plans, my relationships.

Sometimes it's been good—I've taken a lot more risks both personally and in my art because Darius Hawke has epitomized the meaning of *courage*. Other times, my thoughts of him have been too overpowering, too pervasive. I've wanted him to get out of my head, to leave my heart alone. To let me figure out how to navigate my own way without him.

So why the heck did I ask him to have a coffee? I have no expectations or hopes about reviving any kind of relationship with him after all this time. But I also can't let him just walk away again, as if we're nothing more than former acquaintances.

Maybe I also need to find out if I've idealized him over the years. Maybe he's not as captivating and heroic as I remember.

One can hope.

After placing our orders, we collect our drinks and head to a small, round table by the wall.

He pulls out the chair for me and waits until I sit down. The gesture is both sweet and a little sad. Not once in four years has a man—whether a friend, a fellow student, or a date—pulled out a chair for me, and not once have I expected it.

Only Darius has ever been so courteous, and now his archaic chivalry is strangely heartbreaking. Though he has confronted the worst of the world—more than I can possibly imagine—he is still innately *polite.*

I thank him, and he sits across from me. Our knees bump underneath the table.

"So you were at the New York Art Institute." He sets his books down, then shrugs out of his coat and drapes it over the back of the chair.

"I graduated last December, a semester early."

"What made you choose New York?" He closes his big hand around the body of the mug and lifts it to his mouth.

"Mostly because of the school and the courses they offered." I drag my attention away from his fingers and the way the leather strap of his watch coils around his strong wrist. "A college in Oregon offered me a better financial aid package, and I almost took it, but it was a small, rural campus close to an even smaller town. I decided I wanted my next step in life to be bigger than that, and you can't get much bigger than New York."

There's an expression in his eyes that I can't quite read. "Do you like it here?"

"At first, I didn't." I take a sip of my caffè mocha. "I mean, navigating New York was scary, and I was intimidated by the professors and the other students. It took about a year for me to even feel like I deserved to be here. But once I started getting to know people and making friends, I finally began to feel like I belonged."

"What was your major?"

"The Institute doesn't require a major. It's a great program because I learned about so many different subjects and techniques. I focused on illustration, but I took classes on bookmaking, computer animation, woodcutting, writing, ceramics, sculpture, art history, painting, textiles…I can't even remember them all. And the professors were from all over the world, so their experiences and talent were mind-blowing. I'd never have learned as much as I did if I'd…"

Stayed in Grenville.

I let my voice fade. I don't want to bring up Grenville and risk excavating everything that happened between us there. God knows I've relived it enough in my own mind. I don't want or need to rehash it all with him.

"What kind of art have you been doing?" he asks.

"Mostly drawing and mixed-media. I've done quite a few collages."

He hasn't looked at my online portfolio or he'd know about my art. He'd have seen the digital images of the *Mother* series that I showed at my first student exhibition. He'd recognize all the ways I've conflated memories of my mother with Van Gogh's turbulent life and intense creativity. He would understand the Keyhole paintings—scenes of private, messy bedrooms and bathrooms, an office piled with papers and books, a farmhouse kitchen, all inhabited by shadowy figures and framed by thick, black keyholes that cast the viewer as the voyeur.

But he wouldn't know about the drawings of him that I've done, the ones I've never shown to anyone.

"So what have you been doing since graduation?" He leans back in his chair, still studying me. He's wearing a long-sleeved navy shirt that brings out golden flecks in his dark brown eyes. Like topaz or amber.

I tighten my grip on the cup. My pulse is beating faster than normal. I don't want to admit what I already know deep inside— that Darius is as powerful now, in real life, as he's always been in my head and my heart. I haven't idealized him because I didn't have to. He just *is*. Still.

What does that mean for me? Will I ever be free of him?

Do I want to be?

Though he's been a source of frustration and pain, I've still never wanted to know the world without him in it. I don't think I'd want to know myself without him either. I wouldn't be the same person I am now.

"I've been looking for a job." I turn my attention to my coffee. "I have an interview at an art gallery next Monday, and I've been querying publishers with a graphic novel idea."

"Winsome Swift?"

"Yes." The fact that he remembers my original character and the heroine of my work elicits a tiny glow of pleasure. "I'm also keeping an eye out for commercial work, but right now I'm waitressing at a diner and sending out as many applications as I can."

"Are you happy?"

The question almost startles me. I lift my gaze to his, struck by the intense way he's looking at me, as if he's been waiting for the answer for much longer than fifteen seconds. As if it's important to him.

Am I happy?

Despite the uncertainty of treading water after graduation, I'm proud of what I've done and the courage it took. My studies at the Art Institute changed both me and my creativity in immeasurable ways. I like my life, even the struggles, and the fact that I'm here because of me and no one else. I have real friends. I know I'm talented. I feel like I have something to offer, that I have a voice and a story.

Is that happiness?

I'm fully prepared to say, *Yes, I'm very happy* but what comes out is, "I think so."

His features tighten slightly, and he breaks his gaze from mine.

"What about you?" I force a bright note into my voice, though I already know there is nothing *bright* about his relentless immersion in war.

Though he looks the same—still the man I've known my whole life—the darkness in him feels deeper, saturated with all the recent unimaginable horrors he's witnessed. The chaos he's always chosen over everything—and everyone—else.

Is he still involved in that horrible underground fighting ring too? Did he get that bruise on his cheek from beating another man bloody?

I can't bear to ask. I don't want to know the answer.

"Have you been…" *Happy?* "…all right?" I finish lamely.

"Yeah." He rubs his thumb over the handle of his cup. "Working." A wry note undercuts his voice as he adds, "No shortage of wars to cover."

I don't want to think about what that statement means for both him and the world itself. At the Art Institute, I met and learned about artists whose work reflects the ravages of social and political turmoil, often within their own country. They've created some of the most beautiful, shocking, heartbreaking, terrible, and hopeful art I've ever seen, expressing far more than words alone ever could.

"Have you come back to the States at all?" I ask.

He shakes his head. A faint line appears between his dark eyebrows.

No, there's been no brightness in his work, but possibly there's been some in his personal life. I'm not so naive to think he's gone for four years without female companionship, maybe even a serious relationship, though it's searingly painful to imagine he might have found pleasure or even joy with another woman when he was so determined *not* to find it with me.

And yet, I'm the one irrevocably marked by him.

"I've seen your photos on news sites and magazines." I force a casual note into my voice. "I've been keeping an eye out for your book, but I never found it."

"It was never published." He twists his mouth. "The more I tried, the more I hated the idea of giving the PLF any publicity. I didn't want to tell the story or have anyone read it."

The revelation isn't as big a surprise as it probably should be. I know how hard he struggled with even the first few lines of the book, and he's always been intensely private about his life.

People know him through his photographs—not because of anything he personally reveals.

"Hey, how are your friends back in Grenville?" he asks. "Your father said Comic Castle is still going strong."

"Yes, and Fern is busier than ever." A rush of affection eases the tightness in my chest. "Did you know she and my father are still together?"

"Last time I talked to him, he mentioned it, yes. Good for them."

"He proposed to her last year, but she wasn't ready for marriage." I swallow the last of my coffee. "I think he was okay with that, though. He's a bit like a tortoise when it comes to change. Slow and prone to ducking back into his shell."

Darius smiles faintly. "But even tortoises aren't immune to change. And you're still in touch with Clover?"

"Oh, yes." I hold up the end of the green-and-blue scarf I'm wearing. "She knitted this for me as a Christmas present last year. She's at UCLA now. Simon is graduating in June, and Clover is finishing her sophomore year. They're not a couple anymore, but they're still close friends. We text and email a lot, and I see them when I go back to Grenville."

"Do you go back often?"

"Not really. Mostly over the holidays."

We look at each other for a moment that feels longer than it actually is. I have a sudden recollection of us sitting at the rickety kitchen table in the house on Dearborne Street the morning after he'd first arrived.

I'd been tense, hostile, and totally unsure of what to do and how to act around the tall, powerful man who'd become a stranger and yet was going to live with us for the next few months. Darius had been attentive, kind, and unfailingly respectful. At the time, I hadn't known, could never have imagined, everything that would happen after that morning.

"Do you still have the house at Volkov Bay?" A deep flush sweeps up my neck the instant I ask.

His eyes darken. He hesitates, then nods. "Haven't been back, though."

I avert my gaze. Though obviously if he hasn't even been in the US, he couldn't have returned to Volkov Bay, his avoidance of the beach house still feels like another determination to erase what happened between us. And yet the blistering memories still pervade my fantasies.

This was a bad idea. At the library, I should have said a polite goodbye, then turned and walked away from him again. Deliberately spending more time in Darius's presence is like letting myself stay out in the sun too long. First it's hot and lovely, and you bask in the sheer pleasure, but then you forget that your fair skin is no match for the scorching heat. You forget that the burn will hurt like hell.

"I should get going." I pat my lips with a napkin and make a show of looking at my watch. "I'd like to get home before dark."

"Where's home?" He pushes back his chair and puts on his coat.

"Brooklyn. Where are you staying?"

"Eastlake Hotel in midtown. I still have an apartment here, but a colleague is using it right now."

"Do you rent it out?"

"No. I just let friends and colleagues stay there whenever I'm not in town."

New York used to be home for him. I can't help wondering if he's seen his father—as far as I know, Conrad Hawke is still in New York—but I don't ask. From what I know, Darius's relationship with his wealthy father has always been loaded with conflict and estrangement. Not that it's any of my business.

He takes our empty cups back to the counter. I pull on my coat and pick up the two books he'd left on the table. They're heavy, thick books etched with lengthy titles about foreign policy, international politics, and terror abductions.

Our fingers brush as he takes them from me, and a jolt of heat courses all the way up my arm. I quickly pull away from him and head back outside.

"I'll get you a cab." He starts toward the curb.

"No, it's okay." I tilt my head in the direction of Fifth Avenue. "I'm actually going back to the library before I head home."

He turns to face me. The streetlight casts him in a hazy, unfocused glow. "I was glad to hear you've been doing so well."

An ache pushes at my heart. He doesn't know how or what I've been doing, not really. Getting the details secondhand from my father is vastly different from hearing it directly from me.

"Thanks for the coffee." A cold wind rustles through my coat. "It was nice to see you again."

"You too, Nell."

We move toward each other at the same time. My chest constricts the instant his arm circles my shoulders. Though his embrace is loose, the solid strength of his forearm against my back resurrects a sharp, painful longing.

His cheek brushes mine, the faint scrape of stubble against my skin, and I fight the urge to fist my hand into his coat, to let myself sink against him. Instead I inhale deeply—wool, a hint of shaving cream, *him*—and back away.

So apparently, yes. This is it. We part as polite acquaintances.

What happens next?

Another four years pass—or ten or twenty—while I catch glimpses of him on news websites and struggle not to let him overshadow every other man? He escapes into the worst parts of the world, and I don't see him again until…what? His funeral? And what will I have become by then?

"Goodbye, Darius." Before he can respond, I turn and hurry back toward the library.

The cold ices the tears filling my eyes, but it doesn't soothe the flicker of growing anger.

The last time he came back into my life, everything changed. I'd wanted it to, asked for it. I'd begged, even. I'd been desperate for my world to explode from the inside out, as if a seismic detonation was the only way my life—and I—could be different. The only way I could transform beyond the scared, troubled girl I'd been for so long.

Darius had been the key twisting into the lock of my uncertainty and fear. Opening me up.

I'd seen the possibilities of the world again and had gone after them. I left Grenville to chart my own path and live life on my own terms. I've done it, too, even if I'm still a work-in-progress.

What if this brief encounter ends up resetting me like a clock? Undoing all the effort I've put into coming to terms with our relationship?

I'm already painfully close to going back to Grenville and living at my father's house again. It would be no small irony if I take an emotional quantum leap backward as well. *Nell Fairchild, the girl who can turn back both time and herself.*

No. I'm stronger than that. I went through the looking glass and the wardrobe. I survived the hurricane and the fall down the rabbit hole. I came out the other side a different person. A woman who understands the beauty of chaos. A woman who can turn on a light in the darkness—for herself, at least.

But not for him.

My hands close into fists inside my coat pockets.

Enough.

Enough of him in my head and my heart. Enough of him affecting me in his absence. He made his choice. I wouldn't even have known he was in New York if we hadn't both been at the library. And he'd been ready to walk away from me within one minute of us seeing each other again.

Okay, world. You can have Darius Hawke. I'm banishing him from my life.

This time, for good.

CHAPTER 2

Nell

"Nell, order up!"

Glancing at the clock, I grab the plates of burgers and fries, then weave my way through the narrow diner to the couple by the window. After depositing the plates on their table and refilling their water glasses, I return to the counter to take the order of the older, sallow-faced man who just sat down.

"I don't need a menu." He waves his hand at the coffeepot. "Gimme a coffee and a piece of apple pie."

"You got it." I fill his order and make another round through the restaurant to see if anyone needs anything.

As usual, the Golden Biscuit is busy on a Friday afternoon, which I appreciate for the extra tips and the fact that staying busy keeps my mind occupied.

As the clock approaches five, another waitress arrives to take over the dinner rush.

"I'm off, Gus." I wave at the barrel-chested owner in the kitchen. "Any chance I can pick up more shifts next week?"

"Sorry, Nell." He squints at the old-fashioned calendar across from the grill. "I'll give you a call if someone calls in sick, but otherwise we're covered."

I thank him and dump my apron in the laundry bin before clocking out, collecting my bag, and heading outside.

Spring is still struggling to break through the crust of winter. The evening sky is iron-gray, and a steady sleet coats the streets with a layer of ice. Pulling my coat tighter around me, I slog through the dirty slush, swerving to avoid splashes from the cars churning close to the sidewalk. A garbage truck rolls past, the huge tires kicking up a spray of muck.

I reach my building, its old brick facade perforated with narrow windows and crisscrossed by rusted fire escapes. The lock on the security door has been broken for well over a month, and I send yet another text to the landlord telling him to please get it fixed.

I hurry up the five flights of stairs to my apartment. The stairwell smells like urine, and the corridor with its threadbare carpet and peeling paint is even bleaker than usual in the gloom.

After letting myself into my single shoebox-size apartment, I bolt the door and quickly strip out of my wet boots and coat. I shower to wash away the smells of greasy burgers and grill smoke, then sit on the sofa with my laptop.

Grateful as I am to have a job—any job—I hadn't expected to be waitressing part-time at a diner after graduating. I hadn't expected to land a lucrative job or a gallery show either, but I'd hoped for an entry-level position or at least an internship.

So far, all I have is a pile of rejection letters.

As much as I loved studying at the Institute, my recent struggles have forced me to confront the rather bitter truth that my father had been right when he'd warned me that it's tough to make a living as an artist. Freelancing is unpredictable, and the commercial and graphic design jobs are intensely competitive. While I've had a lot of support from my former professors, my applications are always one among hundreds, if not thousands.

I pull up a web browser and log in to my email. I'd told myself I would send out five more applications this week, which means more searching and writing cover letters.

I scan the contents of my inbox, clicking on a message from a Brooklyn-based graphic design firm. Though I'd been half-expecting another rejection since the job was a reach for an art student with no practical work experience, the words *We've decided you are not a match for the position* cause a sharp sting of disappointment. Every rejection puts me one step closer to moving back to Grenville.

Aside from my student loan payments and the astronomical costs of living in New York City, my apartment lease expires in three weeks. If I can't find a full-time job by then, one that pays well enough for me to cover my expenses, I'll be forced to cut my losses and start over. Like a board game that sends you back to the beginning with one roll of the dice.

I can't go back. I don't want to start over again, not when I've already come so far.

I bring up a video call app and connect to my father's office in the history department of Evergreen College. He still has his archaic computer at home, but a grad student helped him install video software on his campus computer.

He appears on my screen, looking as comfortingly familiar as ever in his tailored white shirt, the lines of his face sharpened by his neatly trimmed beard. After we exchange greetings, I update him on my job search and my recent meeting with the Art Institute career placement counselor.

"Fern said she had some potential leads for you," he tells me. "Have you talked to her?"

"Yes, she emailed me a couple of links to comic-book publishers. I sent in my resumés, but am still waiting to hear back. I have an interview at an art gallery on Monday afternoon. Pretty fancy midtown place called Signature."

"Good for you." He nods. "I know you're trying."

A strange combination of guilt, embarrassment, and appreciation rises in me. My father hadn't wanted me to attend art school, but after I'd won the Student Art Competition and scholarship my senior year of high school, he hadn't tried to stop me from sending out applications.

He'd become more receptive when I started getting acceptance letters and more scholarship offers, though he'd made it clear that I was on my own financially, and he continued to maintain I'd be better off with a more "practical" college education. While I still wouldn't change my decisions or my studies at the Art Institute for anything, I've been able to see his point a lot more clearly.

"Darius said you and he ran into each other at the library yesterday," he says.

My heart bumps against my ribs. "Yes. It was nice to see him again."

"Have you been in touch? He said you had coffee together."

"No, I haven't had any contact with him since Grenville." I manage to keep my tone neutral, even as my insides knot up.

Why did Darius find it necessary to tell my father we'd seen each other? When did he talk to him? Or was it just a text? Did he think telling my father would mitigate any hint of wrongness?

Moreover, did Darius seriously feel that having a stupid coffee with me after four years of no contact was *wrong*?

And how in the love of God am I ever going to "banish" him if he keeps showing up everywhere—my memories and fantasies, my conversations with my father, my imagination, and now my real life again?

"He said he's in New York for work," I say. *Way to change the subject, Nell.*

My father chuckles. "Illustrious work, for sure. He's been

working on counterterrorism initiatives at NATO and the UN, especially with regard to the group that took him hostage. The People's Liberation Front. It's been keeping him pretty busy."

"I thought the PLF was defeated in Krasnovar's civil war."

"Darius wants to make sure they're dismantled for good." My father shrugs. "Especially since they were designated a terrorist organization. He's gone after them pretty hard these past few years. Pushing for investigations into their funding channels and structure. Obviously he has personal as well as more civic-minded reasons."

"So what kind of work is he doing in Manhattan?"

"He's there to speak at a UN conference about the threat of the PLF and other underground terrorist groups. Didn't he tell you?"

I shake my head.

"With all his counterterrorism work, he's become sought after as a policy expert," my father explains. "He's testifying before a congressional committee later this year too."

Though I'm not surprised by Darius's renown—it's not a huge leap, considering his experience and knowledge—my pride in him is mixed with an unwelcome sinking feeling. I'd once thought he and I were the same, but he's always lived in an entirely different stratosphere. Now more than ever.

Maybe that's part of the reason he had no intention of contacting me during his trip to New York. We no longer have anything in common.

Maybe we never did.

"I should get going, Dad." I glance at the clock. "I'm going to a friend's place to celebrate the opening of her dance recital."

"Have fun, and be careful. Think you can visit anytime soon?"

"I'm not sure. I'll let you know." I deflect another wave of guilt. Though I've been on my own financially, my father has always insisted on paying my airfare for my trips back to

Grenville. He's also offered to pay my moving expenses, should I need to leave New York when my lease expires.

We say goodbye before ending the call. After putting on some makeup and fixing my hair, I head back outside and take the train a few stops to Elmhurst.

Cecily lives in a sixth-floor walk-up above a deli, and the weathered apartment door is thumping with music and noise. I knock loudly, and she opens it with a screech of delight.

"Come in, come in!" She hugs me in a wave of patchouli and lavender. "Pizza's on the way."

"Congrats on the performance." I tighten my arms around her. "I brought cheap wine to celebrate."

"My favorite kind." With a grin, she points me toward the kitchen. "Corkscrew's in there."

"I said *cheap*." I tap the twist-off cap on the bottle.

She laughs. "Well, if you want a glass, they're in the kitchen too. Or feel free to just swig from the bottle while you mingle."

I weave through the crowd, pausing to greet acquaintances and friends. The party guests are mostly fellow Art Institute students and their significant others. I open the wine and pour myself a glass. I head out of the kitchen and wander around chatting with a few people I know.

"Nell!"

I turn, smiling as Alice Adams pushes through the crowd toward me. At five-eleven, she towers over most of the other women, and her statuesque beauty has made her a favorite model for our fellow students. We move closer to the wall to avoid being in the way of the crowd.

"I've been meaning to text you, but I've had the worst week." Alice puts her wineglass on a table and digs a vape pen out of her bag. "A shipment went awry, and of course I had to deal with all the red tape trying to track it down. People are so pissy about their shit, you know? I don't care that it's expensive. Doesn't mean you have a right to yell at me about it."

"Any word on the promotion?"

"No." She sucks on the pen and exhales the smoke. "I don't care anymore. I mean, a job's a job, but I'm really just an administrative hack for a glorified moving company. The only difference is we shuffle fine arts and antiques instead of oversized TVs and oak bookshelves."

"Are they still sending you to London next month?"

"Yes." Her eyes light up. "I also managed to get some vacation time, so I'm going to stay for an extra week. Remember Jessica Barnett, from John's class? The artist who works with the London Arts Council? She told me to contact her if I was ever in town, and so I emailed her that I'm coming for a visit. I checked the Council website, and there are a few manager and assistant vacancies open, so I'm going for it. If I can get in with Jessica, I'll have a shot."

I have no doubt that Alice will *be* the shot. She's one of the most determined, fearless people I know—the only one of our class who completed three study abroad programs in Cuba, Ukraine, and Japan—and has pushed more boundaries than I knew existed with video and performance art. Her future is definitely not one of administrative hacking.

"Talk to me about you." She takes another hit off the vape. "What's going on?"

"The usual. I have a couple of interviews coming up. And the career counselor Erin is still scraping up possible leads for me."

"Did you hear that Jason joined the Peace Corps?"

There was a time when Alice's abrupt subject changes would give me whiplash, but I've gotten used to them over the years. "No, but wow. That's impressive."

"He's already started training." Alice picks up her glass, tapping her fingernails against the stem. "You ever think of doing something like that?"

I almost laugh. "No. I'm not Peace Corps material."

"Not necessarily the *Peace Corps,* but something like it. A volunteer program overseas or something."

"That's a nice idea, but I need a job that pays enough for me to at least make my rent." I take a sip of wine. "I can't afford to volunteer."

"Still, you should ask Erin what's out there." Alice shrugs. "Like, I wouldn't have thought about the London Arts Council if it hadn't been for Jessica. There's stuff beyond New York, you know. Or the US."

Considering I've never been out of the country—and only ever lived in California and New York—I can't imagine looking for a position abroad. But I'm not surprised that Alice sees possibilities anywhere in the world. Not for the first time, I wish I had some of her fearlessness.

"Text her now." She pokes me in the arm. "Where's your phone?"

I dig my phone out of my pocket. With Alice peering over my shoulder, I send Erin a message.

If you know of any overseas opportunities, I'd be interested in finding out about them too. Thank you so much for all your help.

"Good." Alice takes a healthy swallow of wine. "Lemme know what she says. Maybe you'll end up in London with me."

"Have you been there before?" I ask.

"Couple of times, yeah. Talk about expensive."

She gives me the lowdown on her London itinerary before she excuses herself to use the bathroom. I pour myself another glass of wine and seek out some other friends to chat with.

When the music and noise start getting louder, I pull on my coat and climb the stairs to the roof where the party's spillover guests are hanging out. Little fairy lights twinkle around the exhaust stacks and along the roof's barrier.

My old friend Jonah is manning a small bar from a folding table, and he waves me over. "Hey, Nell like bell. I was telling

Dan earlier about your interview with that fancy gallery. It's next week, right?"

"Monday afternoon. How did your exam go?"

"I think I did okay, but I won't find out until after the weekend." He pops the cap on a beer bottle, and we head over to two lawn chairs by the roof's edge. "I get why design theory is important, but I long for the day I don't have to be tested on it anymore."

Though I'm sympathetic—I didn't always love the theoretical discussions about art—I can't help envying Jonah's well-defined world of graduate school. He has one more year before earning his master's degree in architecture at Columbia, and already he's interning part-time with a firm in Chelsea. He won't have any trouble finding a good job after graduation.

"Have you heard anything from the graphic novel publisher?" he asks as we settle into the lawn chairs.

"They passed, but Colin told me they didn't offer a great contract anyway. Oh, he got an agent, did I tell you that? He's hoping to get into illustrating children's books."

"You could get into book illustration in a heartbeat." Jonah tilts his head back to take a swallow of his beer. "You talk to your dad?"

"Earlier today, yes." I let out my breath slowly. "But there's not much to talk about. If I can't afford to renew my lease, or if I don't have a job that pays well enough for me to find another place to live, then I have to move back to Grenville. I'm running out of time."

"You could stay at our place, if you need to," Jonah suggests.

I shake my head at him in amusement. "I'm sure the administration would frown upon me squatting in grad student housing. So would your roommate."

"Okay, but there's a bunch of people who'd put you up so you don't have to leave."

While *a bunch* isn't quite accurate, I do have a few friends who would let me crash on their sofas when my lease expires. I haven't discounted asking for temporary help, but I also have no idea how long it will take for me to find a steady job and my own place again.

Plus I don't want to take advantage of a friend, no matter how generously they offer. Given the microscopic size of my apartment, a roommate isn't an option either. And the way things are going, even paying half my rent would be a struggle.

"I have high hopes for the art gallery interview," I tell Jonah. "The manager asked me to bring my portfolio too, even though it's for an assistant position."

"What kind of art do they sell?"

"Contemporary and modern." I lean forward to pick up my wineglass from the ground beside my chair. "They're close to MoMA, which is also pretty cool."

"Text me when you're done, let me know how it went."

"I will."

That's one of the many nice things about Jonah. He's not just saying he wants to know; he really does want to know.

He's sitting with his elbows on his knees, his body angled toward mine, and I realize that we're very close. He's picking at the label on the beer bottle, and his eyelashes make little shadows on his cheekbones.

Jonah was one of the reasons I'd been able to find my footing during my sophomore year at the Art Institute. He'd moved to New York in September of that year to start the Columbia graduate program, and though we'd been a little wary with each other at first because of our past, we'd learned how to become friends. Having him close by has been a welcome source of comfort.

He looks up, catching my stare. My stomach tightens. Before I can think, question, or second-guess myself, I lean forward to kiss him.

Our lips barely touch when he jerks back and shoves to his feet. "What are you doing?"

"Oh, god." Shame crawls up my neck. "I didn't mean to do that."

"Seriously?" He paces a few feet away and back, his cheeks reddening.

"Jonah, I'm so sorry." I groan and cover my face with my hands. "I'm not...I'm a little confused."

"So you decided to try and kiss me?"

"It was a mistake." I lower my hands and force myself to look at him directly. "I wasn't thinking."

"Look, Nell, I've been over you for a long time." He spreads his arms out, his eyes darkening. "I once wanted to be the guy who'd...I don't know, get past your defenses or whatever, but only if you were into it. I sure as hell don't want to be your experiment again."

I feel like shit. When I was eighteen, I'd been genuinely convinced that Jonah might be The One to help me move forward. I'd started dating him with that intention, though of course I hadn't told him about Darius. There was no reason to tell anyone.

He was gone. And Jonah would be the boyfriend I "should" have—the good-looking, age-appropriate college student whose life was far more closely aligned with mine.

It should have been easy.

It wasn't.

And now, again, I'm sickened by the rediscovery that one stupid *look* from Darius Hawke can make my whole body come alive...and yet, I can't manufacture even a tiny spark for a smart, solid young man who should be perfect for me.

"I'm sorry." Tears sting the backs of my eyes. "I'm not trying to use you."

His mouth thins. "Aren't you?"

I can't respond. Jonah looks at me for a long minute before he turns and goes back inside.

I scrub my coat sleeve across my face and suppress the ache burning my throat.

I'd once been convinced my intense feelings for Darius, my love for him, were pure and real. I'd rejected and fought against all his perceptions of *wrongness*. I'd known to the depths of my soul that what we had was not twisted or immoral. He was not depraved and fucked-up for wanting me. I was not obsessing over a silly schoolgirl crush.

But that was four years ago. If I still can't find pleasure in even the thought of kissing another man, maybe my feelings for Darius *have* gotten twisted and warped. Maybe they're obsessive.

Maybe they're wrong.

I wipe away a stray tear and lean my head against the back of the chair. The sky is faded black. A hazy film of clouds conceals the watery moon. No matter how hard I look, I can't see a single star.

CHAPTER 3

Nell

I MANAGE to get an extra shift at the diner over the weekend—a welcome distraction from my tangled thoughts and feelings. I send Jonah an apology in the form of a fresh-baked cookies delivery from a local bakery, and I add extra for his roommate and other friends. It's not much and probably won't make him willing to see me again anytime soon, but at least he'll know I'm trying to make amends.

He's not the only person I've been unable to feel a romantic attraction toward, though he was the first. We'd started dating in April of my senior year in high school, a few months after Darius left Grenville.

Jonah had been attentive, enjoyable company...until he'd gotten impatient with my inability to let him get close to me, both physically and emotionally. Our breakup had been tense and resigned. I'd thought I couldn't muster up feelings for him only because I wasn't over Darius yet. Surely that would change at some point.

After I moved to New York, I kept other students at arm's length until I became more at ease and secure in my new life. As I slowly learned how to recognize the signs of flirtation and attraction, I'd navigated my way through several dates for dinner, movies, parties. I'd kissed and been kissed. I'd tried to do more, like I had with Jonah, but I froze up whenever a man tried to touch me more intimately.

Eventually those encounters got so discolored by frustration and embarrassment that I've found it easier to avoid any romantic attachments at all.

Jonah was the only one who'd figured out I was testing the waters and not actually seeking a relationship. He'd moved on long before he came to New York, though it had taken another few months for us to find our way to true friendship.

Now I might very well have screwed that up.

This is not the version of Nell I want to be.

I work the breakfast rush on Monday and clock out at noon, which gives me plenty of time to get ready for my interview at Signature Gallery. I shower and change into black tights, a plaid skirt, and a soft black sweater. I apply a light coating of makeup, fasten my hair into a tidy ponytail, and make sure my portfolio is organized.

Before leaving, I check my email on my laptop. A message from the Art Institute career counselor Erin shows up, linking to a few overseas volunteer art programs. She's highlighted one in particular, an organization called Global Rebuild.

Nell, this nonprofit usually needs people for construction projects, but they put out a recent call for volunteers with arts experience.

They're looking for help organizing community museums as part of the rebuilding process. Could be a good fit for you.

I scan the Global Rebuild website, which details its mission of helping to rebuild cities and towns that have been damaged by military and political strife. In addition to major construction projects, Global Rebuild focuses on repopulating decimated cities, reviving local economies, and creating sustainable infrastructures.

The organization has established programs in twenty cities—in the Caucasus, Central Europe, Africa, and South America. Most recently, they've started working in Varaz, a northern town in the Eastern European country of Krasnovar.

Because I'd researched Krasnovar after we learned that Darius had been taken hostage there, I know Varaz is an old, walled town in the mountains, overlooked by a medieval castle that was a popular tourist destination before the civil war.

I close the email and push away from my desk. Though I can't picture myself navigating a foreign city, I did make the flying leap from small-town Grenville to the heart of New York, and I've been living here for four years. It's not as if I'm a babe in the woods anymore. I'm not Wonder Woman either, but...well, I'm definitely somewhere on the "in-between" scale. Nell 2.0, ready for an upgrade.

I head out to the subway. As I'm waiting for my transfer, my phone buzzes with a text from Jonah. *Thanks again for the cookies. Good luck with the interview—you'll do great!*

Grateful, I respond with thanks and tell him I'll let him know how it goes. I take the subway to the West 57th Street gallery—a posh, glass-fronted space on the ground floor of a massive, Art Deco style high-rise. The interior is warm and elegant, the doors shutting out the chaotic noise of the street. Abstract paintings glow from the walls, and bronze sculptures sit on white pedestals.

"Nell?" A slender man in a Gucci suit strides forward, his hand outstretched. "I'm Michael Graves, the gallery manager. You're right on time. I like that."

"The trains cooperated with me." I return his smile and shake his hand. "It's nice to meet you."

"My pleasure. Come back to the office." He speaks briefly with a blond woman at the front desk, then gestures for me to follow him across the carpeted space to a smaller room in the back. "You can hang your coat up on the rack there."

I take off my coat and place it on a hook, giving the room a quick sweeping glance. His glass desk is impeccable, topped with a state-of-the-art computer. Several bold, colorful paintings of abstract figures decorate the pale green walls.

"Can I get you a cappuccino or something else to drink?" He closes the door and walks to a sidebar holding an espresso machine and mini fridge.

"No, I'm fine, thanks."

"Great. Have a seat." He nods toward a seating area by the windows.

I put my portfolio on the glass coffee table and sit on the gray suede sofa, adjusting my small crossbody bag over my shoulder. After the espresso machine finishes hissing and fizzing, Michael joins me with a frothy drink in a white china cup and saucer.

"So, you're an Art Institute grad. We see a lot of your kind around here." He sets his cup on the table and sits in the chair next to the sofa. "Not that that's a bad thing."

"I hope not. I had a wonderful experience there."

"So tell me about yourself." He crosses one leg over the other. "Where you're from, what you studied, your artistic interests."

Since I've been through a number of interviews already, it's no longer nerve-racking to talk about myself. I've also researched the Signature Gallery history and exhibitions, as well as the recent artists they've featured. We chat for a while, and I both answer and ask questions with relative ease.

"Let's have a look at your portfolio." Michael rises and moves to sit on the sofa beside me. "Artistic abilities aren't one of the job requirements—an eye for art definitely is, of course—but I'd like to get a feel for your style."

Edging away from him, I open my portfolio. "All of these are also on my online portfolio, but I prefer the physical artwork for the texture and details of the media."

"Agreed." He reaches for a pencil drawing of an old, high-heeled shoe. "Physical is always better."

He leafs through the drawings and paintings, a crease between his eyebrows. "Looks as if you mostly draw women when you're doing figure work."

My chest tightens. "It's what I'm comfortable with."

"Not comfortable with men, huh?" He flashes me a strange smile.

"I've drawn men, yes, but I'm interested in expressing the changes and growth of women. Specifically, how both beginnings and endings affect the female experience and personal stories."

"Any self-portraits?" He shuffles through a few more drawings.

"I've done some in the past, but I'd rather be on the other side of the canvas."

"Pity." He gives me a sideways glance, his gaze moving from my face to my legs. "You'd look good on canvas."

The confidence I'd been feeling throughout the interview suddenly evaporates. I have an urge to get out of there. I start gathering my artwork back up.

To deflect the subject away from me, I ask, "So what are the responsibilities of the assistant position?"

"You'd talk to visitors, answer calls and queries, perform administrative tasks." He turns toward me. "We'd prefer someone with experience, but it's more important that the right candidate has strong interpersonal skills and potential. I can see that you do."

"I appreciate your time." I push my papers back into the portfolio.

"We're also highly selective about the artists we show." He shrugs. "If we're unable to offer you the assistant position, we might be able consider your artwork...not for a full show, of course. You're talented, but since you're inexperienced, we'd have to work out an agreement."

He settles his hand on my knee.

Son of a bitch.

I start to rise, but his grip tightens and he aggressively slides his hand under my skirt. My skin crawls. I grab his arm and twist, shoving him away.

"Don't touch me." Bolting to my feet, I pick up my portfolio and cross the room.

"Cooperation is also an essential quality for success, Ms. Fairchild." Michael stands, his mouth thinning. "I'd suggest you rethink how badly you want it."

"Fuck you." I grab my coat and leave the office. The blonde at the front desk glances up as I stalk past her to the front door.

Outside, the cold air eases the heat of anger and disgust, but the pit of my stomach aches. I walk quickly away from the gallery before stopping to pull on my coat. Like any other industry, the art world is crawling with slimeballs, and I've heard plenty of stories about collectors and patrons demanding sexual favors in exchange for supporting an artist.

And while I've had to deflect unwanted advances before, this is the first time it's happened in relation to a job or my career. It makes me even sicker to think it's likely not the last time either.

I cross the street, still walking fast to put more distance between me and the gallery. I pass designer shops, weave around pedestrians, navigate puddles of slush. The glass-fronted

Museum of Modern Art building reflects the bustle of West 53rd Street.

As a graduation present, my father gave me memberships to MoMA and the Met, which gives me free admission to the museums. I show my card at the front desk and enter the well-lit, sacred space. For the next hour, I let the bright, vibrant paintings ease my lingering anger.

I love both the art and the artists—the dreamers, rebels, and renegades. The boundary-pushers, revolutionaries, and anarchists. The romantics and explorers. The visionaries who struggled, scraped, failed, cried, fought, surrendered, and fought again.

I stop near Van Gogh's *The Starry Night,* where a small crowd has gathered. I'd first visited the painting the day after I moved to New York, and I've seen it many times since. I haven't drawn my own nocturnes since I was at the institution, but Van Gogh's turbulent night is the only thing other than the actual star-filled sky that reminds me of the vastness of the universe.

At the same time, those wild, spinning stars and moon feel as if they're churning right in the middle of my chest. Like everything inside me is alive and moving. *Electric.*

Setting my portfolio on the floor, I sit down on a bench and text both Jonah and my father that the interview didn't go well. I add an upbeat message about my hopes for the applications I've sent in to several publishers.

Dropping my phone back into my bag, I wander around a few of the other galleries before the darkening twilight tells me it's time to head home.

I leave the museum and walk toward the subway station. Across the street, diagonal from the subway entrance, is the gleaming stone-and-glass facade of the Eastlake Hotel.

Where Darius is staying.

Whatever instinct propels me toward the hotel, I have no idea. It's not good or healthy for me to seek him out.

On the other hand, I've done a lousy job trying to get rid of him. Maybe I need to *tell him* I'm done with him infiltrating his way into my thoughts and dreams.

Maybe I need to hear that he's done with me, too—that he's been done since the day he left Grenville. That in the past four years, he hasn't given a second thought to the desperate young woman who'd begged him to touch her, who'd seen right down to his soul, who'd told him she loved him. I need to know that he's moved on with his life and forgotten about the girl who'd broken down his ironclad resolve.

Should I tell him the truth now—that he's been an overwhelming presence in my life for too long? That he's stopped me from even getting close to another relationship? That seeing him again has forced me to wonder if my thoughts are bordering on obsessive? That if he can also just tell me he's done with me, maybe the thread will snap and I can finally escape the only thing preventing me from being free?

He knows I spent my childhood caught in the cycles of my mother's volatile unpredictability, fearful of doing or saying something wrong. The aftermath of her suicide sent me into another dark maze of bullying and cruelty that led to cutting and my lockup at the institution. Even after I was released, I'd known that my life would be confined to the narrow path my father had dictated.

I know exactly what it feels like to be trapped. The deep knowledge of being held captive, unable to escape, was just one of the reasons I understood Darius Hawke right to the marrow of my bones.

But what's ticking me off now is that *I did escape*. I got out of small-town California, upended the "plan" of Evergreen College and library sciences. I finally acknowledged what I wanted, and I figured out a way to get there.

I've made a life for myself in New York, for god's sake—a girl who'd never been out of Grenville moved to one of the biggest

cities in the world to pursue studies and a career in the arts. I
should be the plucky heroine of a goddamned movie.

Except in a movie, the heroine would meet a handsome
young man in some cute, clumsy way, like bumping into him
while carrying a pile of packages, and they'd embark on a
madcap, romantic journey to happily ever after.

The heroine would not be haunted by memories of a man
who society thinks is "inappropriate" for her. A man she used to
call *uncle*. She would not compare every other man to him. She
would not still masturbate to fantasies of him. She would not
look up at the stars and wonder where he was in the world.

Her heart would not be imprisoned by him.

The glass doors of the hotel swish open. I enter the lobby—an
elegant, pristine space with a huge chandelier shedding a soft
glow onto the shiny marble floor leading to the reception desk.
Several people are sitting in an open room to the left, where
cushioned chairs and round tables draped in white cloth are
placed near a curved, gleaming bar.

I start walking to the reception desk when a sudden shiver
races down my spine.

Coming to a halt, I glance instinctively toward the bar.

He's there, sitting at one of the tables with a drink in front of
him. A stunning woman with long, reddish hair is next to him,
leaning closer as they converse. Her hand is on his arm.

My heart pushes up into my throat. I take a step back.

Darius turns, his gaze landing on me like an arrow hitting a
target.

CHAPTER 4

Nell

I'M HALFWAY to the front doors when he steps in front of me, blocking my escape. I stop, my gaze on his shirtfront. A hot flush crawls up my cheeks.

"Nell." He ducks his head, like he's trying to catch my eye. "What's wrong?"

"I...I'm sorry. You're busy."

"It's okay. What's wrong?"

His question twists inside me like a corkscrew. I don't want him to know something is wrong just by looking at me. He should have lost that instinct when he left, and I should be a lot less transparent.

Not to mention...what *isn't* wrong right now?

"I'm fine." I edge to the right with the intention of moving past him. "I'm going to go."

He extends his hand. A breath catches in my throat at the sudden shock of his fingers closing around my wrist.

"Come and sit down." He nods toward the bar. "I'd like for you to meet Lindsey."

I'm not at all sure I want to meet Lindsey. I glance toward the redhead, who is scrolling on her phone.

It occurs to me that in all the years I've known Darius—the twenty-two years of my life so far—I haven't met many of his friends and acquaintances. Patrick O'Hare, a fellow photojournalist and one of his good friends, had taken over Darius's teaching job in Grenville. I'd liked him and learned how to value his knowledge of photography, but after his contract expired, he'd gone off on another assignment. He's been the only person in Darius's larger circle whom I've known.

And, somewhat painfully, I admit that I'm curious about this gorgeous woman and what she means to Darius.

"Just for a few minutes," I finally say.

He releases me, and we walk to the table. I steel my spine against whatever introduction is about to take place—*This is Lindsey, my date...my colleague...my girlfriend...my fiancée.*

God forbid, *my wife.*

Darius takes my portfolio from me and leans it against an empty chair. Lindsey looks up, her eyebrows lifting.

"Lin, this is Nell Fairchild, Henry's daughter." He pulls out a chair and gestures for me to sit down.

I smile politely, deflecting a stab of irritation over being introduced as *Henry's daughter.*

"Nell, this is Lindsey Harris," Darius continues. "She's an old friend."

Lindsey rolls her eyes. "Old is a bit relative, isn't it?" She holds out her hand. "Nell, it's a pleasure to meet you. I've met your father a few times over the years. I'm pretty sure there's no one else in the world who knows more about the economics of the Roman Empire."

"He'd be thrilled to hear you say that." I shake her hand. "It's nice meeting you too."

"Come and sit." Lindsey pushes away from the table to make room, and the tablecloth slides over the arms of a wheelchair. Catching my quick glance, she smiles ruefully. "Old spinal cord injury."

"I'm sorry." I wince inwardly and sit down, slipping my bag off my shoulder and setting it on my lap. "I didn't mean to stare."

"Don't apologize." She waves her hand. "I used to be a reporter before a bad fall put an end to my Lois Lane days."

"That must have been horrible."

"It was at the time, but I've recovered and learned to live with it." She takes a sip of her drink and glances at Darius. "Tom just texted that he's running late. He should be here within half an hour."

Darius nods and turns to me. "What would you like to drink?"

"I don't want to intrude."

"Oh, stay and chat for a few minutes, please." Lindsey points to her glass. "I promise, you won't regret staying long enough to have one of these. Darius, get her a mojito."

Before I can protest, he walks to the bar and places the order. My curiosity shifts from his relationship with Lindsey to Lindsey herself.

"So do you still work as a reporter?" I ask.

"Sometimes, but about ten years ago, I opened a bookstore over on Forty-Third Street." She flicks a lock of hair over her shoulder. "That's my full-time job. I still do some freelancing, just not the dangerous kind like Batman over there."

She indicates Darius at the bar. He's wearing black trousers and a charcoal-gray shirt that fits beautifully over his chest and shoulders. His dark hair is brushed away from his forehead and he's clean-shaven, the lack of stubble intensifying the strong lines of his face.

A shadow passes over my heart. I return my attention to Lindsey. "What's the name of your bookstore?"

"Pen and Paper. It's a little independent place, and thankfully we have a loyal clientele who keep us afloat against all the online retailers."

"I'll have to stop by. I have a weakness for bookstores."

"Then we really need to be good friends." She smiles, and the last of the tension eases from my shoulders. "How long have you lived in New York?"

"Four years. I graduated from the Art Institute last December. What about you?"

"I've lived here for twenty years, which I guess counts as always." She tells me about moving to the city when she was nineteen to pursue a career in journalism. "My husband is a professor at NYU, and we met when I interviewed him for one of my first stories on the Telluride Film Festival. We've been together ever since."

"How did you and Darius meet?" I ask, as he returns with the drink.

"I was assigned as the photographer for a story Lin was working on." He sits back down. "That was over fifteen years ago."

"What was the story?"

"A contentious presidential election in Brazil." Lindsey shakes her head with a slight laugh. "It was literally less than two weeks after Tom and I got married. Since I was starting out, I had to take whatever I was offered whether I wanted to or not. I was still a newbie about foreign affairs, especially political unrest. Thankfully, Darius knew what he was doing."

She tells me about the growing protests and violence leading up to the election. I'm not surprised to learn that Darius helped her navigate an unnerving, if not downright scary, situation. The report ended up getting Lindsey a foreign correspondent position with the *Chicago Tribune,* which led to assignments on everything from the Colombian army to a Chilean mining crisis. It sounds as if she has a life worthy of her own memoir.

"So what do you do, Nell, now that you've graduated?" She reaches for her glass.

For some reason, the question catches me off guard. In a split-second, a dozen scenarios run through my head. *Peace Corps. Architecture firm internship. London Arts Council. Agent. Graphic novel publisher. Art gallery assistant. Student exhibition.*

"I'm waitressing right now." I make an effort to keep my voice breezy, as if the Golden Biscuit is just part of my bigger plan. "I'm considering volunteering with an arts organization, maybe overseas. But mostly I'm job searching, of course."

"It must be exciting to have so many possibilities open to you," Lindsey says.

"You had an interview today at an art gallery, didn't you?" Darius asks. "How did it go?"

My stomach twists. "It was fine."

Because I'm not looking at him, I sense rather than see his slight frown. Before he can ask another question, Lindsey says, "Oh, there's Tom. Excuse me just for a moment, please. He needs to confirm the use of the ballroom for an event he's hosting, but we'll be right back."

She maneuvers her wheelchair away from the table and to the doors, where a tall, bearded man is entering the hotel. He bends to kiss her in greeting before they make their way to the reception desk.

"I know a lot of people in New York." Darius settles his gaze on me. "So do Lindsey and Tom. I can ask around about job or internship opportunities if you—"

"No." As desperate as I am for an actual full-time job, I can't fathom being indebted to him for help finding one. "Thank you, but I have plenty of leads on my own."

He's silent for a second. "What happened at the interview?"

"Nothing." I glance toward the hotel entrance, wishing Lindsey would come back.

"Is that why you were upset when you walked in here?" Darius asks.

Irritation crawls up my throat. "Why did you introduce me as *Henry's daughter*?"

He blinks. "That's who you are."

I put my hand on the table and lean closer to him, lowering my voice to a hiss. "I am a lot more than that, and you know it. But you're still determined to put me into a neat little category so you don't have to actually admit that I'm an adult now. A woman who makes her own choices and has a life independent of her father. Why are you so afraid to see who I've become?"

His features tighten. "What I *see* is who you are, a bright, talented young woman who has her whole life—"

"Oh, stop it." I sit back and reach for my drink.

A heavy silence falls between us, broken only when Lindsey and her husband approach the table. Darius rises and makes another round of introductions. Tom is as kind and gracious as Lindsey, but after they both get settled at the table again, I reach for my bag and coat.

"This has been lovely, but it's time for me to head home." I push my chair back. "It was so nice meeting both of you."

"Nell, give me your number." Lindsey takes out her phone. "I'd love to get together for lunch sometime, just the two of us."

I hesitate, not certain about the wisdom of making a friend who is in Darius's circle, but I can't think of a polite way to decline. I don't really want to, either. Ever since Fern became a part of my life, I've been instinctively drawn to warm, confident women, as if I hope I can somehow absorb their strength.

I give Lindsey my number and say goodbye to her and Tom. Darius is already standing, waiting for me to precede him to the doors.

"I'll walk Nell out," he tells the Harrises.

"Thank you for inviting me to join you." I button up my coat as we head to the front of the hotel. "Lindsey and Tom are wonderful people."

"They are. I'm glad you stayed." Though he doesn't have a coat, he walks outside with me. "Let's get you a cab."

"No need, but thank you." A bitingly cold combination of sleet and snow has started to fall, covering the sidewalks with ice.

The doorman hurries forward, and Darius asks him to hail a cab. I can't afford a cab, and I don't feel right about having him pay for one, even though I know he'll insist.

"I'll take the subway." I point toward the station across the street.

He frowns. "It's getting late."

"I've been living in New York for four years. I've taken the subway more times than I can count, often much later than this."

He glances toward the curb, where a taxi has just slid to a halt. "I'd prefer it if you'd take a cab."

"I'd prefer it if you'd listen to what I'm saying." My voice comes out sharp again. I back up a few steps toward the street crossing. "I'll take the subway."

Faint irritation flashes in his eyes. "I'll pay for the cab, Nell."

"Not the point." I pause and try to soften my tone, not wanting to end this evening on an unpleasant note. "Look, I appreciate the offer, but I'll be fine. Thank you again for the drink and the company. Please go back in and enjoy the rest of the evening with your friends."

Before he can respond, I walk quickly to the street crossing. Thankfully, the walk sign is green, and I hurry to the subway entrance without looking back. But even as I descend the stairs to the underground, I swear I can feel the weight of his gaze.

Is this *it* again? The last time I'll see him?

Or maybe it's the last time he'll see me.

～

After making the two-transfer trip back to my apartment, I drop my bag on the sofa and take off my boots. The heat is wonky again, doing little to warm the air, and a fringe of ice coats the inside of my single window. I crank up the space heater I'd splurged on last January and sit down with my laptop.

There's an email from Signature Gallery telling me I didn't get the assistant job. With a snort, I fire off a sharp, pointed message to the gallery owner detailing the manager's harassing behavior and suggesting that he's likely overdue for a full investigation.

I open the email about the overseas volunteer positions again and scan the information. Even if I didn't resolve anything with Darius—and probably never will—I have the urge to *do* something.

Lindsey was right—it should be exciting to have so many possibilities open to me. I should be grabbing at them all, thinking outside the box, celebrating the fact that I can go anywhere and do anything, as long as I can reasonably support myself. My Art Institute friends are making things happen for themselves, so why can't I?

I close the laptop and change into a fleece shirt and pajama bottoms. As I pull my slippers out from under the bed, my fingers touch a storage box.

My heart thumps.

Not comfortable with men, huh?

The slimy gallery manager's question echoes in my head.

I pull the locked box out and set it on my lap. I can't remember the last time I'd looked through the contents. My hand shakes as I work the combination lock and open the box.

Inside are several photos I've kept from my senior year when Darius taught my photography class, as well as a few mementoes from my childhood. There's a carved wooden elephant he'd brought back from a trip to India, seashells I'd found on the beach at Volkov Bay, a necklace that once belonged to my mother. Underneath the items is a worn sketchbook.

I take the book out and sit on the bed to leaf through the pages. I haven't looked at the book in ages. My first year at the Art Institute, I'd been so overwhelmed by all the changes—living in New York, the dozens of new people I was meeting, navigating classes and the city itself—that I'd kept several sketchbooks as a way of rediscovering my comfort zone. I'd drawn whatever I felt compelled to—birds in Central Park, the lines of a skyscraper, a broken pencil, Winsome Swift, a Picasso painting at the Met.

Darius Hawke.

This book is filled with drawings only of him. I'd recreated his face so many times—the dark slash of his eyebrows, his penetrating gaze, the strong line of his jaw. I'd drawn him serious, frowning, smiling, and one—my favorite—of him laughing, his eyes bright with amusement and crinkling at the corners. I'd sketched his entire figure—standing with his feet apart in that pyramidal stance, sitting with his ankle crossed over his thigh, crouched with his camera lifted to his eye. I'd drawn him in every guise I could think of, in all the ways he'd filled my life.

The portraits are the last time I drew a *man*. I've painted a few male bodies in figure art classes, but not once have I been interested in including men in my work. After filling a book with Darius, I had nothing left. I didn't want another man to take his place in my art.

I close the book and rest my hand on the cover. Keeping dozens of images of Darius under my bed might be thwarting my efforts to be free of him.

The trash chute is at the end of the hallway. Trying to pretend I can't feel my heart breaking a little, I tuck the book under my arm and unbolt the door.

Just throw it away quickly. Like ripping off a band-aid.

I yank open the door and hurry out. My vision is blurry. Two steps into the hallway, I slam right into a brick-hard wall of maleness.

CHAPTER 5

Nell

ARE YOU FUCKING KIDDING ME?

His scent hits my bloodstream like a drug—eucalyptus, spice; pure, delicious warmth. My sketchbook falls to the floor. He closes his hands around my shoulders. The cold wetness of his coat seeps through my fleece shirt.

"You okay?" His grip tightens.

I nod, forcing myself to look up at him. His hair is damp, his dark eyes glittering.

"W-what are you doing here?" I stammer.

"You forgot this at the hotel." He releases me and indicates my portfolio tucked under his arm.

"How did you get in?"

"There's a note outside that the intercom is out of order." He frowns. "And the front door was open, so I assume the security lock is also broken. How long has that been an issue?"

Defensiveness stiffens my spine. "I've told the landlord."

"When is it supposed to be fixed?"

"Soon," I lie. "Not that my apartment problems are your business."

He bends to pick up my sketchbook. Too late, I realize it's fallen open. I grab for the book, but he gets it first. As he straightens, his gaze falls on the unmistakable drawings of him that fill the pages.

I snatch the book from his hands and hug it against my chest. My heart hammers, and a hot flush heats my cheeks.

Darius takes the portfolio from under his arm. "I didn't know if you needed this anytime soon."

"How did you even know where I live?" I tighten my arms around the sketchbook. "Did you call my father and ask for my address? Did you tell him I had drinks with you and your friends, like you told him about us having coffee?"

He unsnaps the leather ID holder attached to my portfolio, revealing my name, address, and cell number written on the interior card.

"Oh." My face gets hotter. "So why didn't you just call?"

"I did. Your phone was either off or dead."

Crap. "If you—"

The neighbor's door opens a crack, and an elderly woman peers out at me with a scowl.

"Sorry, Mrs. Carroll." I back toward my apartment. Maybe this is my chance to tell Darius what I need to, even if the thought of confessing makes me almost ill with anxiety.

I push open the door. "You'd better come in."

He follows me and closes the door behind him, taking in the apartment with one swift glance. He sets the portfolio on a chair and assesses the door locks and deadbolts.

I take a breath and tell myself to be gracious. "Thank you for coming all the way out here. You didn't have to, but I appreciate it. You can sit down, if you want to."

I suppose grudging graciousness is better than none at all.

He remains standing, his hands in his pockets. "How long have you lived here?"

"Since last November. Six-month lease."

"Where did you live before that?"

"I was in student housing for my first year at the Institute, then I moved to the women's residence." I toss the sketchbook onto the bed. "But that's also only for students, so I found this place a month before graduation. Why are you asking?" I hold up a hand. "No, wait. Don't tell me. You want to find out if I've always lived in such poor conditions. You're wondering if my father knows."

"No." He frowns and takes a keyring out of his pocket. "The colleague staying in my apartment is leaving in a week, and no one else has asked to use it for the summer. You can have the place, if you'd like. I'll leave the keys with you. One is for the security door, and the other is for the apartment."

I don't know whether to laugh, cry, or yell at him. I settle for being icily polite.

"Thank you, but no."

"It's in Manhattan, not far from Central Park." He takes two keys off the ring and puts them on the coffee table. "If you want to pay rent, I'll charge whatever you're paying here."

"You don't need to try and convince me. My answer is no."

He studies me, his eyes unreadable. "What happened at your interview?"

"Oh, for god's sake. Why are you interrogating me?"

"Because you came to the hotel looking for me, and it was clear something had happened. I want to know what it was."

I blow out my breath in a gusty sigh. "The gallery manager hit on me."

His anger flashes like lightning. I hold up my hand again.

"Before you start blustering, I took care of the situation," I continue. "But at the time, I was feeling shitty and the gallery was close to your hotel, so I stopped by."

My voice tangles in my throat. I'd told myself I was seeking him out to sever the ties between us once and for all, but at least one thing will be there forever. To him, I will always be *Henry's daughter.*

"You don't have to deal with assholes and slog through more interviews," Darius says. "I can help you find a job."

"Please stop. You don't get to come back after four years away and think you have a right to question me about my apartment and offer to find me a job."

He has the grace not to refute that remark, even if his features are still set.

I step back toward the window. His sheer size makes my small apartment seem claustrophobic. "Could you please sit down?"

He unbuttons his coat and tosses it over the back of a chair before sitting on the sofa. The dim lamplight reflects off his dark hair, illuminating the strands with gold. His gray shirt shifts over his chest, the buttons marching in a perfect line downward before disappearing behind his belt buckle.

My heart is racing again, as if he just turned a key and started the ignition.

I want to touch him. I can see myself sitting beside him on the sofa. Putting my hand on his chest. I can feel his arm settle heavily over my shoulders. His body heat would warm me from the inside out. I would melt against him like honey.

The desire is so sharply visceral, a throb deep inside me, that I go into the kitchenette before I do something stupid. I busy myself with the mundane task of making instant coffee, then return to place the mugs on the table.

I sit in the chair across from him and rub my palms over my thighs. The raised scar tissue on my thigh is rough under my flannel pants.

"Where are you going after you leave the States again?" I ask.

His gaze flickers to the movement of my hand. "Crimean Peninsula."

Another war. Did I even need to ask? What line of fire will he run into this time—a fight, a bombing, a violent raid? Will he ever come back?

"You weren't going to tell me you were in New York, were you?" I tighten my fingers into the material of my pants.

"No."

Though it's the answer I was expecting, the flat denial still pierces me like a needle. I look away so he won't see the flash of hurt.

After a stretch of silence, Darius lets out his breath.

"Nell." He leans forward, his elbows on his thighs and his hands linked.

My stomach tenses. Though I need him to tell me he's been done with me for years now, I'm suddenly terrified of hearing the words. Because of him, I know what love and desire feel like. Without him, I've been distant and maybe even cold. If he's gone forever from my mind and my heart, I might forget entirely what it feels like to *feel*.

"I wasn't going to intrude on your life," he says.

"Right." There's a bitter taste in my mouth. "Because you dictate what happens. You get to define my seeing you again as an *intrusion* rather than a *reunion*."

His mouth compresses. "That's what it is."

"An intrusion is unwelcome," I retort. "No one wants an intrusion. But if you'd emailed me two weeks ago and told me you were coming to New York, I'd have been…"

Happy? Nervous? Scared shitless?

"Actually, I don't know what I'd have been," I admit. "But I wouldn't have not wanted to see you. And honestly, it's a little insulting that you were deliberately avoiding me. What did you think I'd do? Throw myself at you and beg you to touch me again?"

He flinches, an almost imperceptible reaction that gives me a fresh burst of courage. He might want to act like a polite, distant stranger (*"I was glad to hear you've been doing so well"*) or Mr. Fix-It family friend, but nothing...*nothing*...can ever erase what happened between us.

"Well, I wouldn't have." I curl my hands into fists. "I'm not the girl you left behind in Grenville. I've done a lot since then. I've been on my own, fended for myself, *grown up*. I've moved on and learned things without you. I've dated and been kissed and had boyfriends who—"

He stands so abruptly that the air itself seems to recoil.

"*That* is exactly what you should be doing." The words snap out of him. "You need to focus on your life now. Not the past."

"Don't tell me what I *need*." I push to my feet to put us on equal ground. "You have no idea what I need or want, not anymore. You were the one who walked away, and yes, I understood why. I knew there was no alternative. But I didn't expect... I didn't think..."

His mouth compresses. "What?"

"I didn't think you leaving Grenville meant you would also be leaving *my life*."

"What did you think, Nell?" He spreads his arms out. "That I'd want to hover around while you were *moving on*?"

"So your alternative was to cut off all contact? Then think you have a right to run in and fix the things that are tough for me right now?"

"I only ever wanted—"

"What's best for me, which again, you don't get to decide." I pace to the windows, my skin prickling with both hot and cold. "Do you want to know what's best for me? What I need?"

I need you to get out of my head, out of my heart. I need to stop thinking about you and seeing you in every other man who crosses my path. I need to stop dreaming about you at night and wondering where you are and if you ever think of me.

The words push up into my throat, crowded and painful. He's been part of me for so long—for my entire life. What happens when you carve out an essential piece of yourself?

"I need…" I drag in a breath. My heart is racing, my mind blistering with all the sharp, intense memories of how I'd felt when he'd touched me.

Inflamed. Electric. Alive.

I desperately want to feel that way again.

All rational thought vanishes. Instinct propels me toward him, my vision a blur, his presence pulling me in like some sort of overpowering force field. I reach for him before he can back away. He puts his hands up, but there's no stopping this fierce urge to feel his body against mine again.

"I need *you.*" I grab the sides of his head and yank him down, pressing my lips clumsily to his.

He goes still, and my heart wants to explode with fear and love and pain. My entire being floods with sensations—his mouth against mine, his body mere inches away, my fingers gripping his thick hair.

A wave of dizziness spills over me. I kiss him harder, breathe him in, and move my hands down to clutch his shoulders. He's a statue, rigid and unmoving.

I smother a stab of despair, the shame of embarrassment. This is brutal evidence of the truth I haven't wanted to acknowledge—the only man who makes me want so much more will never give it to me.

Then…

He does.

He locks his arms around me so swiftly that my heart slams against my ribs. In one movement, he hauls me to him. Our bodies crash together. He brings one hand up to grasp the length of my hair, tilting my head back and slanting his mouth firmly over mine.

Wild flames explode in my blood. He takes over the kiss like a man staking a claim, his mouth moving with hot, intense pressure, his arms steel bands holding me against him.

My mind fogs with disbelief and shock. His muscles tense, urgency coiling through every tendon and sinew. His chest is a weight against my breasts, the thump of his heartbeat echoing through me with the strength of thunder.

My knees weaken. I grip him harder, twisting my fingers into his shirt. I'm drowning, falling, spinning. He moves me backward two steps, and then I'm up against the wall, his hand coming up to cover my throat, his mouth devouring mine.

I hear a low, desperate moan, barely able to realize it's coming from me. His knee is between my thighs. I'm trembling, unable to grasp a single thought, everything in me thrilling at the possessive crush of his mouth, the unyielding press of his body.

He thrusts his tongue past my lips. I gasp, melting and igniting at the same time. He tastes like dark, sexy things—chocolate, spices, amaretto. I'm starting to burn, a throb of lust curling through my lower body.

He could strip me naked right now, and I would open for him like clouds parting after a storm.

A guttural noise rumbles through his chest. Before he even breaks the kiss, I feel his retreat. I pull away first, my heart pounding and my fists still tangled in his shirt.

He lifts his head, his breathing heavy and his eyes glittering with heat. He rests one hand on the wall behind me, his other hand still against my throat. A trickle of sweat rolls down his temple. We stare at each other. The air is hot and thick.

"Goddammit." He slides his gaze to my mouth and back to my eyes. "*This* is why I never contacted you. Why I couldn't. I still have no fucking control around you."

He shoves away, scraping a hand through his hair. Slowly, I regain my balance, taking a deep breath and trying to quell the urgency still throbbing in my blood. I feel us both sliding backward into the old, agonizing impasse that has no solutions or answers.

Anger—toward him, toward myself—flares in me. No amount of physical desire and pleasure can ease the torture of being locked in that maze again with no way out.

"Darius."

He holds up a hand, his control snapping visibly back into place. "I'm—"

"Don't you dare tell me you're sorry."

His features tighten. "We're not doing this again."

"No, we're not doing it *again* because I'm a different person now."

"I'm not."

"Good. Because I only ever wanted the man you are."

A deeply pained look darkens his eyes. I feel his hardened regret start to take shape, and I turn away before he can voice it. I grab the sketchbook from my bed and toss it on the sofa.

"In case you haven't figured it out, I've been unable to stop thinking about you." My stomach clenches as I force out the truth. "I spent months drawing pictures of you, as if I could somehow conjure you back. I couldn't even draw another man. You've been the only one. And I see you in every man I meet. I dream about you at night. I fantasize about you. I've tried so hard to feel things for other men and to...to be normal, but I just end up comparing them to you, and they never win."

He doesn't move. The line of his jaw is like stone, as if he's clenching his teeth.

"I know." I hold up my trembling hands. The confession tumbles out of me like a waterfall. "My issues are nothing compared to what you deal with every day. You owe me nothing.

And when I saw you at the library, I told myself I was going to get rid of you once and for all. The problem…"

I pull in a breath. "The problem is that you're impossible to get rid of because you made me feel so good in so many different ways, and part of me wants you to tell me that you haven't thought about me at all because then maybe I can move on. But I also hate that you could just walk away and forget about me after—"

"Forget?" he snaps. He crosses the room to me in three strides.

My breath stops in my throat. He grabs my shoulders. His dark eyes blaze into mine.

"I have spent the past four years trying to escape you." His voice is low and serrated, like the edge of a knife. "I've run toward front lines, explosions, airstrikes. I've embedded with armies and fringe militant groups. I've fucked plenty of women. I've gone to the shittiest places in the world—prisons, execution sites, minefields. And every goddamned time, you've followed me. You want me to tell you I haven't thought of you? That would be a fucking lie. Wherever I've been, whatever I've done, I haven't *stopped* thinking of you. *You are always there.*"

The world spins. I grip the windowsill. My chest burns.

He shoves away from me and grabs his coat. "That's why I haven't contacted you." He opens the door. All emotion drains from his eyes, leaving them cold and hard. "You don't want to hear it, but it's the truth. I can't be anywhere near you ever again."

The door closes with a hard click. I struggle to breathe, to slow my racing heart.

Slowly I unclench my fingers from the windowsill and open my laptop to my email inbox. I click on the message about overseas opportunities and hit the reply button.

Erin, thanks for the information. I'd like to volunteer for the Global Rebuild program in Krasnovar.

Please let me know the quickest way to proceed. I'm available immediately.

Regards,
Nell

PART II

CHAPTER 6

Nell

THE MEDIEVAL TOWN OF VARAZ, one of the oldest settlements in Eastern Europe, clings like a barnacle to the side of a mountain range in northern Krasnovar. A glacial-blue lake, replenished by snowmelt, nestles among the forested hills nearby.

Once known as the country's "crown jewel," Varaz was built beneath the shadow of Bram Castle, a twelfth-century fortification that used to be one of the country's main attractions until it was closed at the start of the civil war.

Because of Varaz's cultural and historic importance, the regional government had also asked residents to temporarily evacuate during the war due to fears that the town would be a military target. Many people had initially stayed, but as the war dragged on, increasing supply shortages and economic depression had forced them to seek new lives and work in larger cities.

Though the most severe fighting had taken place in the capital farther south and around the plains, Varaz had not been isolated from the war. Bram Castle remained untouched, but the town suffered intermittent bombing that resulted in both civilian casualties and the destruction of several neighborhoods.

Since the war ended six years ago, Varaz has been struggling to come back to life. But the town's endurance over hundreds of years—through wars, sieges, uprisings, kingdoms, industrialization, natural disasters, and all the other turbulent circumstances of history—is a testament to its ability to survive.

I arrive in Krasnovar after a twelve-hour trip and a layover in Frankfurt, then take a shorter domestic flight to the city of Telina. I'm met at the airport by Brian, a friendly, bearded man in his early forties who has been in Krasnovar for the past two months helping to get the Global Rebuild programs implemented.

"We're really happy to have you," he says as he puts my suitcases in the trunk of an old Lada. "We've just gotten started in Varaz, and you're our first volunteer. Hazel and I are the only Global Rebuild staff here until we can get crews and equipment in. Unfortunately, we've run into a bunch of logistical issues and red tape. But we've been working with local construction crews, and the museum director needs all the help he can get. He's going to put you to work right away."

"Great, because I'm ready to get started right away," I assure him.

After signing up for the program, it had taken me a couple of weeks to fill out all the paperwork, put my meager belongings into storage, and make travel arrangements. With every passing day, my eagerness to start my four-week volunteer term had grown stronger.

Our drive from the airport to the Opala mountain range skims across vast fields dotted with farms and villages. Even in mid-April, a dusting of icy snow still covers the trees and grass, but the butter-yellow sun is warm through the windows of the rusted Lada.

Northern Krasnovar is beautiful—rolling hills laced with rivers and valleys that dip gently into broad, flat plains. The rugged mountains sprawl against the pastel blue sky, and to the west, dark forests smudge the horizon like paint strokes.

There are no immediate signs of the five-year-long war that ravaged the country. Like most deep wounds, Krasnovar's battle scars are hidden beneath the surface.

The mountain range borders the lowlands like the rim of a dinner plate. Brian is an adept driver, but the trip up the winding road takes well over an hour and a half.

"There's another route up the eastern face, but it's even narrower." He shrugs and guides the tin-can Lada around another sharp turn. "There were plans to repave this road, but funding got diverted to other things since so few people live in Varaz. But hopefully that will change in the next year or so."

"What's the population now?" I ask.

"Maybe five hundred, if that." He squints against the noonday sun. "It used to be over five thousand. Some people stayed through the war, but most of the residents were employed by a cheese factory that was shut down. So they left and haven't returned. With Varaz in a kind of remote location, it doesn't have the economic opportunities of bigger cities. But it's one of the oldest and most culturally significant cities in Krasnovar, which is why we're implementing the Global Rebuild programs there."

"What will it take to revive it?" I ask.

"The main goal is to bring residents back and expand the tourism industry," Brian says. "The UNESCO World Heritage Committee is voting later this year to include Bram Castle on the World Heritage list, which would be huge for tourism. There's a ton of potential for activities too—hiking, boating, fishing, skiing. The wineries in the foothills have been doing well since the war ended, so that's looking promising too. With the right investments, it could become a very attractive resort town. The process is slow, but it's definitely been moving forward."

I fall in love with Varaz as soon as we arrive at the town center. The cobblestone streets wind around the prominent Harmony Square, which features a plaza and fountain that sits opposite a masonry cathedral topped with a gleaming onion-dome tower.

Lopsided stone buildings with steep roofs line mazelike passages that twist and curve along with the natural rhythm of the mountain. Archways open into secret courtyards, and ice-frosted trees cluster around the square.

The imposing facade of Bram Castle overlooks the town like a guarding dragon. Embedded in the western face of the mountain, the fortress's thick walls are capped by turrets and round towers that mirror the highest peaks.

"It's a blessing that the old town wasn't bombed." Brian points toward the stone wall circling the town. "The newer houses were all built beyond the wall, but it's a ghost town over there now. The idea is to lure people, especially tourists, back to the historic town, which will provide revenue to rebuild the other neighborhoods."

He introduces me to Hazel, a bright-eyed, spindly woman in her fifties who is the main coordinator of the Global Rebuild program in Varaz. She shows me to my lodgings—a single-room, furnished apartment with whitewashed walls perforated by a window facing the town square and Dandelion Street. On the top floor of a three-story building, the room is smaller than my Brooklyn apartment and infinitely more charming.

"Brian's place is next to the cathedral, if you need anything." Hazel pushes the wooden shutters open wider and locks them into place. "There are a few other residents in this building, but not many. I have a house close to the Global Rebuild office. Any questions about the apartment?"

"I don't think so." I set my bag down on a rough-hewn table. "It's lovely."

"The electricity is unreliable, especially in bad weather, so be aware of that when you buy food." Hazel opens the mini-refrigerator and peers inside. "And cell signals are a total luck of the draw everywhere in town, regardless of the network. Same with Wi-Fi. Telecommunications in general were severely disrupted during the war, and unfortunately Varaz hasn't been on the priority list for a full rewiring."

She pushes her glasses back up the bridge of her nose. "It's a little frustrating, but if we need to send large files, Brian and I make a trip over to Telina to use their signal strength. Do you want to get settled in or would you like a tour?"

"Both." I smile and gesture to my grubby yoga pants and shirt. "Can you give me an hour to shower and change?"

"You bet." She points out the window to a row of shops on the opposite side of the square. "Just so you know, that building with the cross on the awning has been the town's pharmacy since the fifteenth century. You can get all your soap, toothpaste, and toiletries there. And the corner store has groceries and other supplies, like matches and battery-powered lanterns. Stock up in case of power outages. I'll come back in an hour and we'll take a walk."

Though I'm jet-lagged and exhausted, I'm also wired up about actually being here. I take a quick, tepid shower and change into jeans and a sweatshirt. I've brought two suitcases packed with both winter and summer clothing, as per the warning that spring weather in Varaz is capricious.

I'd texted my father as soon as my plane landed in Telina, but I manage to connect to the Wi-Fi and send him another message that I'm safely in Varaz. He had not been overly enthused about my four-week detour to Krasnovar—or my decision to put my airfare on my credit card –but he hadn't tried to stop me.

When he was in grad school, he'd dreamed about studying in Athens. His marriage to my mother, and my birth, had put a stop to those plans, but he's always encouraged his students to both study and work abroad if they can manage it. I think he knows

on some level that this experience will benefit me in immeasurable ways.

I pull on a coat and boots before descending the worn stone
stairs to the ground floor. Hazel is waiting in the foyer, and we
spend the next couple of hours walking around the town. There
aren't many cars, likely because there are so few residents, and
most people are either walking or riding bikes.

Scaffolding covers the fronts of many buildings, which Hazel
explains are being prepared for restoration by local workers
before the Global Rebuild construction equipment and crews
arrive. Other buildings are still vacant and boarded up, but the
inhabited houses are tidy and bright, with freshly painted shutters and window boxes.

Hazel points out the few restaurants and shops that have
opened up, the local school, a café, and the building where
Global Rebuild has set up an office. The shop signs bear smaller
English translations underneath the Krasnovian names, which
Hazel explains came from the increasing use of English after
Krasnovar became independent from the Soviet Union.

"You'll hear a mix of Krasnovian, Russian, and English," she
tells me. "Most people in Varaz know English, to varying degrees
of fluency. I studied both Russian and Krasnovian before coming
here, but then I discovered that most people prefer speaking
English so they can practice."

"How long have you been here?" I look up at an old fresco of
a flowering vine that curves around a second-story window.

"Almost three months. Arriving in the dead of winter was not
my smartest move, but I've heard spring and summer are glorious, once they actually get here." She indicates a Renaissance-
style building with three arches carved into the facade. Decora-
tive columns border the portals, and a rose window sits directly
above the entrance.

"That's the art museum," she says. "The local construction
crews recently finished repairing some damage to the southern

facade, so they're moving on to the interior now. Your first job will be to help unpack and organize the paintings and artifacts."

"Are they all in storage?"

"Yes, everything was packed away in the castle storage rooms when the war started," Hazel explains. "The museum director is out of town now, but he'll be back tomorrow. He's only gotten about a quarter of the art out of storage, but with funding from Global Rebuild and other international grants, he's hoping to have the exhibitions done sometime this summer. Museums can really serve as the nucleus of a town, so it's important to get it up and running again. Are you hungry?"

"Sure."

"Come on." She turns a corner and starts marching down a narrow passageway flanked by wrought-iron streetlamps and half-timber houses. "I'll introduce you to one of Varaz's anchors. The owners managed to stay open throughout the war."

Pernikavoy Donik, the Gingerbread House, is a warmly lit little shop that smells like a heavenly combination of cinnamon, cloves, and allspice. A glass case and wooden shelves display an incredible array of iced cookies of all sizes, some as big as a pizza and others as small as a saltine. Most of the cookies are in the shape of hearts, while others are horseshoes, clovers, stars, birds, and diamonds.

"The Gingerbread House has been in Lara's family for three generations." Hazel waves at a plump, older woman through a window opening into the back kitchen. "Gingerbread is obviously their specialty. Lara, this is Nell, the American art student I told you about."

"Nell, so nice to finally see you." Lara's wrinkled face creases with a smile, and her bright blue eyes twinkle. She grabs a piece of waxed paper and takes a large, heart-shaped cookie iced with blue and red swirls out of the case. "New friends always get cookie."

"Thank you." I take the cookie and feel my stomach rumble.

The spicy-sweet flavor melts in my mouth. "Wow. This is delicious."

Lara beams an engaging, gap-toothed smile.

"The recipe was created by Lara's great-great-great grand-mother," Hazel says. "No other bakery in the world has it. It's practically a national treasure."

"We use very old technique." Lara pinches her fingers together. "Special wood molds, very precise measurements. Whole country know about our bread."

After admiring all the different cookies, I purchase three more with the Krasnovian rubles I'd exchanged at the airport. Hazel and I leave the bakery, and she introduces me to a few more people—the bookseller, a stationery shop owner, the schoolteacher. They all already know who I am and greet me with both warmth and appreciation.

By the time I return to my apartment, it's starting to get dark. Outside the window, a tiny star appears in the sky like a guiding light.

Although I've never been to Varaz before now, never imagined until two weeks ago that I would ever travel here, I fall asleep with a strange but peaceful feeling of being at home.

CHAPTER 7

Nell

ALEXEI ROSTOV IS A TALL, handsome man in his mid-thirties with snapping black eyes and a quick, ready smile. He became the director of the Varaz Museum of Art ten years ago after completing his studies at the University of Saldem in the country's capital. He has no staff yet—which is another part of the reason the museum's reopening has been slow—and he's so grateful for my help that I'm already regretting the fact that I'll have to leave in four weeks.

During the war, the town's art and religious artifacts were moved to storage rooms in Bram Castle to keep them safe in the event of an attack. Most of it is still there, but Alexei has slowly been transporting crates back to the museum to sort through.

The work is dirty, physical, and fascinating—in the underground basement rooms of the museum, I open the boxes to reveal priceless icons, silverware, wood carvings, ancient pottery, and paintings. I check the artworks and accession numbers against the current records and put them in areas designated for cleaning and restoration or display.

Alexei, who I quickly discover has a boundless, wiry energy, hurries down the stairs periodically to assess my progress, answer questions, and see what I've unpacked. He's organizing the layout of the permanent collection and plans to put out a call for town volunteers to help with the installation. After a couple hours of unpacking, he shows me around the galleries and explains his plans for displaying the artwork.

Close to noon, as he's showing me how to use the collections software at the front desk, the door opens. A slender young woman with honey-colored hair comes in, carrying a foil-wrapped plate. Alexei lights up like a Christmas tree.

"Sofia!" He hurries around the desk to greet her. "I thought you were working today."

"I have a break, and I made *pampushki* last night." She extends the plate. "I thought you might like some."

"Wonderful, thank you." He leans in as if he's about to kiss her, then glances at me and stops. "Er, this is our new American volunteer, Nell."

"Yes, of course." Sofia smiles and gives me a little wave. "You were in the pharmacy yesterday. Welcome to Varaz."

"Thank you. It's beautiful." Even though I'm just getting to know them both, the bright energy radiating between them makes me happy.

"Sofia moved back to Varaz to work with her father at the pharmacy," Alexei explains, holding up the plate. "And she is the best baker in Krasnovar."

Sofia laughs. "The boys will not agree. They reserve this title for Lara. And I would never attempt to make gingerbread."

"Sofia has twin sons, seven years old." Alexei puts the plate on the desk and unwraps the foil to reveal a dozen fluffy, golden-brown buns that look and smell heavenly. "You have eaten *pampushki?*"

I shake my head, and he urges me to take one. It's delicious—a soft, yeasty bread that Sofia tells me is a recipe from her Ukrainian grandmother. She promises to make me a batch of my own soon, then leaves to return to the pharmacy. Alexei walks her out, ducking behind the door to—I hope—give her a quick goodbye kiss.

"Did she grow up in Varaz?" I ask when he comes back inside.

"Yes, she moved away for college and then to marry." His expression darkens. "Her husband was killed in the war when the twins were just babies. She then came back here to be close to her father."

"I think I've seen her boys playing in the square. Dark hair, lots of energy?"

He smiles affectionately. "Jacob and Tomas, yes. They cannot be missed. They are like two comets. I wish one day to ask Sofia to marry me and to adopt the boys as my own. But first I must finish the work here so I can provide better for them all. I hope by next year, we can be a family."

For all of their sakes, I hope so too.

Alexei and I get back to organizing the artwork. Later in the afternoon, we walk to the mostly deserted neighborhood tucked up against the mountainside. The city wall ends about a mile away since the mountain itself provided a natural defense for this part of town. The hilly streets twist and turn around sharp corners and boarded-up, half-timber houses.

Shading my eyes from the sun, I look up at the castle embedded in the mountain above the town, like a huge ship moored on the rocks. "When will the castle be opened again?"

"We are hoping in summer," Alexei says. "Very expensive to upkeep, and the town administration does not yet have the funds. But if it becomes a World Heritage site, we will gain much attention and, one hopes, international aid."

He unlocks the door of a little stone building that once served as the parish church for this neighborhood. Now dusty and deserted, the Holy Trinity Church is being renovated as part of the town's revival process, with plans to reopen it as a place of worship and as a repository for some of the museum's religious artwork.

Alexei shows me around the nave and alcoves. Boxes and crates fill the aisles—having been transported from the castle—and we get to work. Close to five, his footsteps thump on the stone floor leading to the alcove where I'm unwrapping a small statue of the Virgin Mary.

"Nell." He says my name with a slight uptick at the end, like he's adding an exclamation point. "Come with me to dinner. A welcome to Varaz."

"I'd like that, thank you."

Since I'm filthy from opening dusty crates all day, I stop at my apartment for a quick shower and change of clothes before meeting him at the Koroleva Café just off the square. There are about a dozen tables and a long bar, where several men are drinking and talking loudly.

The owner, Ivan, greets Alexei with familiar warmth, welcomes me, and proceeds to bring us each a beer and enough Krasnovian food to feed a football team—beef soup with dumplings, cabbage rolls, potato pancakes, dark rye bread, sausages slathered with mustard, and eggplant stew.

As we eat, Alexei tells me about his childhood growing up in the economically depressed Russian city of Penza.

"My father worked in factory that made steel pipes, but he lost job when steel prices dropped." He forks another cabbage roll onto his plate. "His brother was living in Krasnovar, so my father moved us here in the hopes of finding new job. But as a Russian, he had difficult time. My mother earned money as seamstress, and my father accepted whatever work he could get. Laborer, farm worker, fisherman. My parents, they only wanted that my sister and I would get good education."

"It sounds like they succeeded."

"Yes." Affection softens his features. "My sister is teacher of primary school. Married with three children. My father is now gone, but my mother lives with my sister's family in Saldem. I visit them often. You have big family?"

"No, it's just me and my father." Although I've dealt with my mother's death—or I like to think I have—I still have to deflect a stab of both grief and anger. "My mother is gone too."

"I am sorry." Alexei creases his forehead. "It is difficult, the loss of a parent. I find comfort that my father is proud, even in afterlife."

"I'm sure he is. It sounds like you and your sister have fulfilled his hopes for you."

"And you have done so with your mother?"

It's an innocent question, but it hits me like a brick. I have no idea if my mother even had any hopes for me. If she did, I don't know what they were.

"I think so," I finally say. "So what led you to study art history?"

He follows the change of subject easily, and we talk about our respective studies as Ivan plies us with more food and beer. By the time he brings over coffee and fried doughnuts served with blackberry jam and sour cream, I'm stuffed but unable to turn down the dessert.

"Nell." Alexei works my name around his mouth as he pours cream in his coffee. "I have not heard this name before. Nell. What does it mean?"

"Nothing."

He lifts his black eyebrows. "Nothing? Every name means something. Alexei, for example, means *the great and powerful defender*."

I grin. "The *great and powerful* defender? Like the great and powerful Oz?"

"Okay, maybe it is only *the defender*." He scowls slightly. "But you see, it has history." He thumps his chest. "It gives me a shape."

"Are you a defender?"

"I have helped to defend the art of the museum. I defend my family. I would defend my country, if called upon. *Alexei* has a definition."

"I don't think Nell means anything." I add more jam to the doughnut, realizing I've never wondered about my name before. "At least, not that I know of."

"But of course it means *something*." He wipes his fingers on a napkin and takes out his phone. He shouts at Ivan in Krasnovian —asking for the Wi-Fi password, I assume. After a minute, he swipes the screen and types. "Ah ha! Nell is of Latin origin and means *shining light*."

I blink and set my fork down. "Are you serious?"

"Why would I not be serious?" He shows me his phone screen displaying the etymology of the name *Nell*. "Shining light…this is accurate, yes? You are shaped by a shining light."

He drops his phone on the table and digs a fork into the doughnut. When he realizes I'm not eating, he glances up.

"The dessert does not appeal to you?"

"No, it's delicious." I reach for my coffee. "I was just… thinking."

I am shaped by a shining light.

The website's etymology might not be perfectly accurate, but that doesn't matter. My name has meaning. I have a definition.

After we scrape up the last of the sweet, sticky doughnuts, Ivan wraps up the leftover food for us. I thank both him and Alexei profusely before walking around the corner to my building. The streetlamps cast coins of golden light onto the cobblestones.

As I unlock the front door, a faint rustling noise comes from the alley between the buildings. I peer into the darkness just as a ragged dog emerges. Large with a thick, black coat, he looks as if he should weigh seventy or eighty pounds, but he's so skinny that his ribs show through his fur. He lifts his head and sniffs the air.

I put my hand on the doorknob, not too sure about the wisdom of getting friendly with a stray, hungry dog. He pokes his nose into the icy gutter. Despite his bedraggled fur, he looks relatively young. A faint whine whistles through his throat.

I unwrap the foil from the box holding the rest of the sausages and eggplant stew. The dog's ears perk straight up, and he sniffs again relentlessly.

Cautiously, I set the open box down and back away. He descends on the food in one fell swoop, wolfing it down in a few gulps. He licks the empty box and looks at me, his nose quivering.

"Hold on, and I'll get you some water." I hurry upstairs and fill a plastic cereal bowl with water.

The dog is still there when I return, and he laps up half the water in about thirty seconds.

"I'm guessing you don't belong to anyone." I eye his neck, but can't see a collar underneath all his fur. "You look like you might be part shepherd. Do you have a name?"

He blinks and licks his chops. He's probably still hungry, but it might not be a great idea to feed him too much all at one time.

"If you come back tomorrow morning, I'll give you some more." I pick up the bowl and empty box and open the door.

He sits at the alley entrance, his ears twitching. After another hesitation, I prop open the security door. "You can sleep inside, at least."

I leave a message on the glass window for the other residents to keep the door open for the dog, then I head upstairs. When I come back the next morning, the dog is waiting at the bottom of the stairs, his dark gaze wary but hopeful.

"I guess you need a name, don't you?" I set down bowls of scrambled eggs and fresh water, eyeing his pitch-black fur. "Shadow or Coal, maybe?"

He gobbles down the eggs without a response. I wait until he's finished before risking a quick pat on his neck. He nudges his head against my palm.

"What about Raven?" I ask. "Or that might be more of a girl's name. I know! Poe. Does that sound good?"

He licks the empty bowl. I take that as assent.

"Okay, Poe." I straighten and gesture to the street. "I have to go to work, but if you come back this evening, I'll give you some dinner."

Instead, he follows me across the square to the museum and sits beside the door as I go inside. When I come back out at five, he's still waiting.

CHAPTER 8

Nell

BY THE TIME I tell myself not to get attached to Poe, it's already too late. It was probably too late the minute I shared my leftovers with him. I ask around about a lost dog, but no one has heard anything. So I keep feeding him and he keeps following me around.

Though he starts out sleeping in the foyer, a couple of days later I find him sleeping right outside my apartment door. Of course, I end up letting him inside and arrange a nest of blankets for his bed. Then I give him a bath—no fleas or any other mites, thank goodness—and brush his thick coat, which he seems to enjoy so much that I figure we're definitely bonded.

In addition to being a temporary foster dog mom, my life in Varaz eases into a routine punctuated by power outages, an unreliable hot water supply, and spotty telecommunications.

The inconveniences are easily outweighed by the joy of living in the historic town—every day, I discover something fascinating, like a thirteenth-century fresco decorating the side of the inn, or the stunning view from an old watchtower on the city wall.

Though Bram Castle is still closed, I learn about its history dating back to the twelfth-century Knights of the Teutonic Order. One afternoon I accompany Alexei up to the storage rooms, which are filled with many of the artifacts that once belonged to the region's rulers.

I wake every day before dawn and have bread and coffee by the window while Poe wolfs down leftovers from the previous night. After getting dressed, I walk to the museum, where Alexei is invariably already working, and spend several hours helping him organize the artwork for display. Brian and Hazel often stop by to see how things are going or to have lunch, and on my afternoon break, I shop for groceries or visit Lara at the Gingerbread House.

I make friends with Josef, the bookstore owner; Anna, the schoolteacher; and a young woman who works at the grocery store. Sofia and I get together for coffee several times on her breaks from her pharmacy shifts, and she tells me her story of a happy life shattered by the tragedies and violence of the war. Since she and her boys moved back to Varaz a year ago, she confides, Alexei has been their bright, shining sun. Warming their hurt places.

Sofia's twins, Jacob and Tomas, liven the whole town with their energy, and they both become my coaches for several different street games. I buy a sketchbook and walk around town with Poe, finding places where I can sit and draw the Opala mountain range, the castle, and the houses. I discover an ice cream shop whose proprietor insists on showing me the generator that keeps the freezer running even when the power is out.

I join Anna after school to teach a group of children about drawing techniques. In the evenings, I either have dinner with a friend or return to my apartment to read and sketch. Poe is content to go wherever I go and to be wherever I am—probably because I've become his source of food, but I like to think he also enjoys my company.

I text my father and my Art Institute friends whenever I can get a signal. I play chess with Josef and checkers with Jacob, join in ball games, and lose spectacularly at poker. The Koroleva Café hosts a concert with a trio of musicians playing the violin, guitar, and flute, and I learn the lyrics of several traditional folk songs. I develop a taste for pickles—a Krasnovian specialty—and discover about a thousand new ways to eat both potatoes and sour cream.

Almost three weeks pass so quickly that I'm surprised by a message from the Art Institute career placement counselor that includes links to four job announcement openings at graphic design firms and an art auction house.

Nell, send in your applications ASAP—these will be competitive.

All of the jobs are in Manhattan. Since I no longer have my Brooklyn apartment, my friends Cecily and Alice both assured me I could stay with them for as long as I needed to, or at least until I find a job and another place to live.

Though of course I've known I'd have to restart my search after I leave Varaz, the thought is more sobering than usual. When Hazel invites me to have coffee at the café, I ask her about the possibility of staying on for another couple of weeks past my May 20 departure date.

"We'd love to have you, but unfortunately Global Rebuild can't afford to pay your living expenses beyond your four-week term," she says. "Much as I wish we could. We've had to divert emergency funds to two other cities, which is why we're so behind getting the major construction equipment in. If you did stay, would you be able to swing your room and board?"

Only if I ask my father for a loan. Working in Varaz isn't an option—I don't have a work permit, and besides, the town wants to employ actual residents rather than a visiting American.

"I'll see what I can figure out," I tell Hazel, though I don't love the idea of swallowing my pride and asking my father for help. I haven't asked him for anything over the past four years, and I'm not sure I can—or want to—start now. Not to mention, I still have my credit card and student loans to pay.

No. As much as I'd love to stay in Varaz, I'll have to go back to New York and jumpstart my job search again. Maybe with the Global Rebuild position on my resumé, I'll have more of a chance.

I ask Hazel to please let me know if she hears about any employment opportunities with other US-based foundations, and I continue my volunteer work with both new appreciation and a touch of sorrow.

In such a short time, I've already discovered what I'd once only known through Darius's photographs. Though he documents war and violence, he's also taken countless pictures of people who embody strength and resilience. And Krasnovar has suffered brutally, but the country radiates an unbreakable warmth, history, and love of life.

That should make it incomprehensible that Darius was held captive here and that a civil war almost tore the country in half, but the opposite is true. I think the darkness has enhanced the light. For the people of Krasnovar, at least.

I don't know about Darius.

And now…I never will.

For a few minutes before going to bed, and if the electricity is working, I watch the static-filled, little TV in my apartment. Though the soap opera actors and newscasters speak too fast for me to understand much of anything, I pay attention out of both cultural curiosity—I'm familiar now with the biggest chocolate, car, and soda brands in the country—and an attempt to learn a new word or two.

The weather hasn't warmed up much, and since the apartment heating is also unreliable, I huddle under a couple of blankets while eating the gingerbread horseshoe that Lara drizzled with extra chocolate for me.

Tomorrow, Alexei and I are going to start drafting a blueprint for the museum's permanent collection, then in the afternoon, I've promised to join the "sheep" team in a kids' game of Shepherds and Sheep.

On TV, the newscasters—Elena and Lucien—are stone-faced and grave. I can sometimes pick up the context of a story based on the photos or videos, but when the camera cuts from the newsroom to a mob scene on a street in the capital city of Saldem, I have no idea what they're reporting.

The onsite reporter speaks in rapid-fire Krasnovian into the mic, her skin ghostly pale in the glare of the camera light. A storefront glass window shatters behind her. The crowd is yelling and throwing rocks, along with small devices that explode when they hit the ground.

A knock comes at my door. I peer through the peephole and open the door for Brian.

"Hey, I was just over at the café." He rakes a hand through his rumpled hair and shifts from foot to foot. "Did you hear what's going on?"

"In Saldem?" I gesture for him to come in and close the door. "I was watching the news, but I can't understand what they're saying."

"A bunch of fighting has broken out." He stops in front of the TV. "Or protests, I guess. No one knows for sure. A group of armed soldiers launched an attack in an area of Saldem, not far from the Capitol building. Ivan said they're tied to the old military that was run and funded by the dictatorship."

A chill runs through me. The civil war had started as a

nationwide call for democratic and economic reform against the autocratic government. When the general secretary tried to crack down on protesters with violent military force—orders that were executed by the People's Liberation Front troops—the wave had only grown stronger. A newly formed Resistance Army had thwarted the PLF's attempt to crush the reform movement, leading to a chaos of fighting and unspeakable casualties.

After almost five years of war, the Resistance Army had launched an offensive that toppled the dictatorship and led to the exile or execution of the top officials. A ceasefire was declared, and the country began the lengthy, complicated process of installing an elected president and a cabinet that has been in power ever since.

"If the attackers were part of the old dictatorship…" I swallow a rising tide of unease. "It's not the People's Liberation Front, is it?"

"They haven't claimed responsibility yet, but it's likely." Brian shoves his hands into his pockets. "Reports are that some of them were wearing red bandannas, which used to be the PLF's symbol of loyalty to the dictatorship. Everyone thought they were defeated during the war. Now it looks like they might've gone underground and spent the past five years rearming and regrouping."

My legs weaken. I sit down, staring at the TV screen. The crowd surges, their yells rising like smoke.

Had Darius known the PLF was still a threat? Is that why he'd spent so much time and effort working on counterterrorism initiatives and investigating the PLF's structure and funding operations? His personal reasons aside, had he suspected they might be planning another attack?

"That doesn't sound good," I finally manage to say.

"No, but the national military has also been building up for five years," Brian replies. "And the Krasnovian army is a lot bigger than the PLF ever was."

The news report switches to a shot of uniformed soldiers descending like ants from a convoy of army trucks.

Brian takes out his phone and swipes the screen. "Damn signal. I'm going over to talk to Hazel. You want to come?"

I nod and pull on my boots and coat. We hurry through the darkened streets to Hazel's house. Lights burn in the windows of the inhabited apartments and houses.

Hazel's TV is on, and she's also listening to the news on an old transistor radio.

"Have you been able to reach anyone at the Rebuild offices in New York?" Brian asks.

"No, though honestly, they might not even have heard of the situation yet." Hazel frowns at the TV. "I'm not too worried, but we should make contact with both Global Rebuild and the US embassy. If the Wi-Fi isn't back by morning, let's plan to head toward Telina and see if we can get a cell signal."

"Have you talked to Alexei?" I ask. "His mother and sister live in Saldem, so I'm sure he's concerned."

"No, but he might still have a connection." Hazel grabs a jacket. "Let's go."

Alexei lives in a small, whitewashed house close to the eastern city wall. He answers the door looking disheveled and slightly frantic.

"No signal." He waves his cell phone. "No landline either, and workers say they don't know when it will be available again. I must get to Telina and contact my mother and sister. Make sure they are okay."

"We're planning to go tomorrow morning, if we can't get a signal tonight," Brian says. "We can also ask around and see if anyone else needs to contact family in other parts of the country, so we can make calls for them."

We walk to Ivan's café, where the old TV mounted in the corner is blaring with the news. The place is crowded with people who don't have TVs at home, and conversation buzzes about the situation. It's soon confirmed that the attack was indeed launched by the People's Liberation Front, which tightens the knot of dread in my stomach.

Alexei quickly organizes a "check in" center to collect names and numbers for those who want to contact family members and friends. When dawn breaks and lightens the road, the three of them pile into the old Lada and head down the mountain.

Since I have a set of museum keys, I continue working throughout the day. So does everyone else in town—aside from more people stopping to talk to each other, life goes on as usual. I'm reminded that all of these people have lived through outright war, so an unexpected attack isn't out of the ordinary for them.

Alexei, Brian, and Hazel return in midafternoon with good news. We gather at the café for a late lunch as they tell us they accessed a cell signal in a village en route to Telina. Alexei was able to contact the townspeople's family members, including his own mother and sister.

He reports that they are safe and at home, so far not affected by the sudden violence. Brian sent a text to my father, assuring him I'm fine and that we've been in contact with the embassy.

"The embassy officer I spoke with said there's no cause for alarm this far north," Hazel tells me. "The military stopped the People's Liberation Front from moving beyond Saldem, and reports are that they're already retreating."

"What were they trying to accomplish?" I ask.

"Show of power." Ivan waves his hands around. "Intimidation."

"But they had to have a reason," I say. "Did they issue a statement or anything?"

"Not that we know of." Hazel shrugs. "Probably they want the release of political prisoners or something."

Ivan nods. "Many high-level officials were arrested for war crimes after the ceasefire. There are still people who support them and believe they were unjustly punished."

"And the PLF always did terrible things for publicity." Alexei shakes his head, lines etching his face. "Public hangings, ransacking defenseless villages, kidnapping. Anything to bring the TV cameras and reporters to them."

"Anything for international attention," Ivan adds.

I look at the TV, where a reporter is interviewing a man in front of a ransacked grocery store.

Had that been the reason the PLF abducted Darius and held him hostage for so long? He'd told me that the negotiations for his release hadn't "worked out," but I still don't know why or what else the PLF had demanded.

The news about both the PLF's retreat and Alexei's success in contacting family members eases everyone's initial concerns. Though Ivan keeps the café TV on, the news settles into a lot of talk, speculation, and interviews rather than reporting.

That evening, the technicians get the Wi-Fi back up and running. I hurry to my apartment and finally connect my phone. A few worried messages from friends and my father flood onto the messenger. I pull up an international call app and input my father's number.

"Nell?"

"Hi, Dad." I speak quickly in case the call drops. "Sorry I couldn't call, but the Wi-Fi has been out for a while, and this whole mountain range is a dead zone for cell signals. Did you get the text from Brian?"

"Yes, but he didn't respond to my questions so I don't know any details." My father lets out his breath in a long sigh. "Plus, I wanted to talk directly to you. What's going on? I only heard about the attack because I get news alerts about Krasnovar. None of our national news has covered it, and no one in the State Department seems to know or care."

I explain about the People's Liberation Front, then assure him I'm not in danger.

"Everything's fine," I say. "We contacted the embassy, and they said there's no threat this far north. And the PLF has already retreated from Saldem. The government says they thwarted another attempted attack and took a bunch of them into custody. The national military mobilized pretty fast to put a stop to it all."

"Still, I don't like you being in a country where there's sudden civil unrest." My father's voice bends with a frown. "What are the other Americans planning to do?"

"Stay unless they have instructions from the embassy to leave," I say. "There's been no travel advisory or anything. And I'm only here for another week or so anyway, so I'll leave sooner than they will."

"I've been...no success through official channels, so I..." Interference crackles over the connection. "...knows better than anyone...lots of people and resources..."

"Dad, you're breaking up." I raise my voice in the hopes he can still hear me. "The telecommunications seem to be getting worse, but I've been...Dad?"

Dead air. I try to reconnect, but the signal is out again.

With a sigh, I drop my phone back into my bag. At least I was able to talk to him and he knows I'm not in any danger.

Though Varaz has always been a tight-knit community, the news of the attack pulls everyone even closer together. For the next couple of days, people report what they've learned, check on each other, and ask about family members in the southern province. Alexei keeps the radio on as we continue our museum work.

The days are getting both warmer and longer. The top of the sun is still peeking over the mountains when we close up the museum in the evening. We head home in opposite directions.

Poe is waiting outside the apartment, and he trots over to greet me as I cross the street. He's already gained weight and is looking much healthier.

"Hi, boy." I rub him behind the ears. Though I don't want to think about what will happen to him when I leave Varaz, I'm grateful for his company.

"I don't have much tonight, but the leftover beef stew is all yours, if you want it." As if he'd ever turn down food. "Let's go upstairs, and I'll get it ready for you."

I step around him to unlock the door when he goes on alert—his body stiffens and his ears shoot straight up.

"What's wrong?" I glance toward the shops. The bookseller, Josef, is locking the door, and a woman is coming out of the grocery store with a paper bag. Nothing unusual.

Poe paces a few steps forward and issues a low bark.

"What's the…" I follow the dog's gaze to a black car rumbling over the cobblestone street from the walled entrance.

I don't recognize the car, not that that means much, but for some reason a shiver rattles down my spine.

"Come on, Poe." I push open the door. "I think I have some sausages too, if you—"

The car comes to a stop in front of the bookstore. The driver brakes and cuts the engine.

Every cell in my body ices over.

"Oh, no." The whisper breaks like glass in my mouth. "No."

CHAPTER 9

Darius

FOR THE FIRST time in a thousand years, I feel my heart beating.

No.

It's racing. Hammering. Punching against my ribs.

I start toward her. Wanting to run.

Nell doesn't move. The dog next to her is in guard mode, his ears back and eyes narrowed.

I force myself to stop half a block away. "Are you all right?"

She stares at me. Her disbelief is tangible. She shakes her head, a quick movement that either means *No, I'm not all right* or *What the hell are you doing here?*

Or both.

Physically, she looks fine.

No. She's fucking incredible. Like a vibrant blade of grass in her green coat. The changed picture of her has been in my head since New York. Her sparrow-wing hair is shorter than it used to be, falling just past her shoulders, the dark brown color lightened in places with strands of gold. The round lines of her features have sharpened into high cheekbones that emphasize her full, bow-shaped lips.

It hurts to look at her, that brightness as sharp as the sun.

"Nell."

The dog bares his teeth. She rests her hand on his head.

"I'm..." She swallows, curling her fingers into the dog's fur. "Of course I'm all right. What are you doing here?"

"Your father couldn't reach you, so—"

"What do you mean, he couldn't reach me?" She takes a step away, her shoulders tensing. "I talked to him two days ago."

"That was the only time he's been able to get through to you since the attack."

"But he knows I'm fine." She frowns. "Did he call you and tell you I was here?"

"Yes. He was worried about not being in contact with you, and he wasn't able to get any information from the State Department."

"Did he ask you to come to Varaz?"

"No." Tension shoots down my spine. I've known for the past thirty-six hours that she won't like my immediate reaction. "He called to ask what I knew about the situation."

"Which is?"

"Nothing good."

She shakes her head again, her eyes hardening. "So you just decided to come here."

Of course I came. I ran like hell. I couldn't get here fast enough.

"I didn't even know you were in Varaz until he told me." If I had known, I'd have been here before the attack was over.

I'd thought I wasn't hearing Henry right. The words *Nell* and *Krasnovar* had crashed repeatedly in my brain. My response was visceral. I've always been able to separate the country itself from the forces who want to destroy it, but I couldn't make any sense of this perfect girl in the war-torn country where I'd been imprisoned.

She's still looking at me like she can't believe I'm standing a few feet away.

"So you came to…what?" she asks. "Check up on me?"

My chest tightens. "I want…no, I *need* you to come with me."

"I'm not going anywhere with you."

"You have to get back to Telina." I indicate the car. "If we leave now, we'll be there in a few hours, and you can catch the next flight to Frankfurt."

Nell's eyes widen. "You came to take me out of the country?"

"I want you to be safe."

"You want to rescue me, even though there's nothing to rescue me from. You still can't get past the need to save Henry's daughter, can you?"

Impatience flickers through me. We don't have a lot of time. There's no rational reason I know that, but my instinct about violence is the only feeling I trust anymore.

"This has nothing to do with you being Henry's daughter."

"Doesn't it?" she snaps. "For your information, the US embassy officials have told us there's no danger to Varaz."

"The US embassy has been operating with a reduced staff since the war. Last year, all non-emergency employees were withdrawn because of budget cuts for embassy security. They will make every effort to avoid allocating resources to help volunteers."

"Then why haven't they even issued a travel advisory for the northern part of the country?" she asks. "And the program coordinator also said it's fine to stay, so you really wasted your time coming all the way from…wherever you were."

"I don't care what the coordinator said. You need to come with me."

She gives a short laugh. "You think I'm just going to do what you say, even though you walked away from me *again*? Even though you refuse to believe I can handle things on my own? What is it you plan to do, Darius, dive back into my life whenever you think I need help because it assuages your guilt over what we've done?"

I dig my fingers into my palms. Fight down a memory of crushing her lips with mine.

"Nell." I force my voice to stay steady and reasonable. "The State Department doesn't even have intelligence on some of the things happening right now."

"But you do?"

"I know the PLF won't back down, regardless of the cost. They are ruthless."

A shadow darkens her eyes as she appears to remember that I know the People's Liberation Front better than most people. And not in ways I'd want anyone else to suffer.

"It's a volatile situation that could explode any minute." I step toward her. "It's happened in this country before, and it could happen again now. I want to get you to safety before it's too late."

She wavers, even as her mouth compresses with determination. "I have a plane ticket back to New York on May twentieth. That's a week from now. I'm part of a volunteer team, and I can't just bail on everyone without warning."

"Given the circumstances, I'm sure they'll understand."

Nell moves toward the building behind her, the dog close at her side. "You can't do this."

"Can't do what?" I struggle against a wave of frustration. "Get you out of a powder keg?"

"You can't come in here and expect me to follow your orders without even taking my concerns into account." She spreads her arms out, regret creasing her forehead. "I don't want to disparage your efforts in coming all this way, but I have responsibilities here. To both people and this town. And yes, there was a time when I would have followed you to the ends of the earth without question, but that time is long past."

She opens the building door. I'm struck by the sense that once she walks through it, I'll never see her again.

I move forward and grab her arm. She draws in a breath. The dog growls.

"Nell, please." I tighten my grip, willing her to trust me. "This is not an isolated incident. I know how fast violence can spread. I was in this country during the civil war. The PLF has spent six years rebuilding its forces. Their leader—Balakin—was one of the top generals of the military under the dictatorship. The speculation is that he intends to recapture control of the cities and government, and there's no way he's going to stop just because his forces were driven back from Saldem. It's only a matter of time before they strike somewhere else, and I do not want you in this country when they do."

Her features are tight, her jaw clenched so hard a muscle jumps in her cheek. "Did you tell my father you were coming here?"

"No."

"Why not?"

"Because I might not have made it." I take a breath, shoving down my impatience. "Nell, I'm not leaving without you. Please. I am *begging* you to come with me."

She meets my gaze, her gray eyes sparking. For four years, I've seen the color of her eyes everywhere. In clouds, bird wings, river stones, ashes.

A charged moment passes. My heartbeat increases.

"I'm here with two other Americans," she finally says. "I can't just leave them."

A twinge of relief eases my frustration. It's not an agreement, but it's close.

"They can come with us."

She looks down as the dog paces at her feet and nudges against her leg. Nell pulls her arm from my grip.

"Look, come inside." She turns to the door, her tone clipped. "I need to feed Poe, then I'll go talk to Hazel and Brian."

I follow her up the interior stairs, letting the dog go ahead of me. Nell ushers him into the one-room apartment and takes a container of food out of the mini-fridge. Her movements are sharp, her shoulders tense. She's still angry with me, but I suspect she's also upset with herself for relenting even a small amount.

I can't afford to care right now. All I want is to get her on a plane out of here.

Outside, the darkness is getting thicker, and a layer of clouds obscures the stars. It will be safer to travel under the cover of night, but I don't like what I've heard about the movements of the PLF. The Krasnovian national military has started putting up checkpoints on the main roads to deter any potential terrorist activity in the north, but the PLF isn't executing their attack haphazardly. They have a well-planned strategy that no doubt accounts for both civilian and military responses.

I take out my phone and swipe the screen. "Do you have Wi-Fi?"

"It goes in and out. More often, it's out. We haven't had a signal since I talked to my father."

"There have been reports that the PLF is launching cyberat-tacks." I walk to the window. "How long have you been here?"

"Almost three weeks." She sets down a bowl of food for the dog and straightens to wash the container at the sink. "I only found out about Global Rebuild last month. They'd just started the program in Varaz, and they needed volunteers for both construction and to help with the museum. Since I didn't have a job and my lease was expiring, it seemed like a great thing for me to do. And it was...I mean, it has been. Until now, obviously."

"No one knew the PLF was rearming, much less planning any kind of attack. As far as I've been able to tell, the security forces

didn't even have any intelligence pointing to an armed insurrection."

"You knew." She dries her hands on a dishtowel and turns to
face me. "You've known for years, haven't you?"

"I've suspected."

"Where were you when my father called you?"

"Odessa. I'd have been here sooner, but I had trouble getting
into the country. They're starting to crack down on local travel
too." I gesture to her suitcase. "Pack a few essentials and whatever you can't leave behind."

"I need to talk to Hazel and Brian first."

"Where are they?"

"I don't know." She buttons up her coat and glances at her
watch. "They went up to the castle this afternoon. A construction
crew is doing some repair work on one of the ramparts. I don't
know when they were planning to be back, but I can check their
houses or over at the café."

"Fine." I yank open the door. "Let's go."

"*You* are not going." Nell holds up her hand. "I want to talk to
them alone. You can stay here."

"I'm going with you."

"No. First, I'll have to explain who you are and what you're
doing here, which will likely take far more explanation than you
want. Second, I don't need you arguing with them or anyone
else. Third, I will not have you creating unnecessary alarm."

Though she has a point, I have to smother another surge of
frustrated impatience. Not only do we need to get on the road
right now, I don't want to let Nell out of my sight.

I step away from the door. "If you're not back in half an hour,
I'm coming to find you."

She shoots me a glare and snaps her fingers at the dog, who
lumbers to his feet.

What's she doing with a pet? Knowing her, she won't want to

leave him behind. But even if we took him to Telina, he wouldn't be allowed on the plane.

She and the dog—Poe—go back downstairs to the square. I follow, watching as she strides toward a cross street. Poe trots close to her legs, like he's protecting her. They disappear around the corner.

I pace to the end of the block and back. The last time I was in Varaz—well over twelve years ago—the picturesque town had been bustling with tourists and residents. There were souvenir stands, cheese shops, racks filled with bright, traditionally embroidered cloth.

Now the streets are almost empty, the buildings either covered with scaffolding or boarded up, the vacant castle looming above like a massive headstone. There's an eerie silence to the night air, the quiet before a thunderstorm.

I don't like it. Ever since crossing the border back into Krasnovar, I've been on high alert. Though the checkpoints on the roads are patrolled by the national military, being stopped and questioned had brought back the gut-wrenching fear of being ambushed by terrorists. I could taste the gag in my mouth again. Feel the barrel of the gun jammed up against the base of my skull.

I shake my head to dislodge the phantoms I thought I'd defeated. Intellectually, I know the former dictatorship of Krasnovar and its strongarm military do not represent the vast majority of this country. I know the people of Krasnovar are inherently good, peaceful, welcoming, warm-hearted.

But peace is a fragile thing. I've seen it shatter with one blow. I know exactly how brutal the rogue soldiers-turned-terrorists can be. And I will do anything to get Nell out of here now.

CHAPTER 10

Nell

AS SOON AS I turn the corner, I start to shake in a delayed reaction to the shock of *him*. Right when I was coming to terms with "the end" of Darius Hawke, he's back with his overprotective streak going supernova. Only he would think it's imperative that I leave the country right this second, even though there's no indication from any other quarter that Varaz is in danger.

But despite my anger and instinctive resistance, I still have an innate, unassailable trust in him. And his demands now are quite different from insisting I take a cab in bad weather or disapproving of my apartment's lack of security.

Darius's instincts have been sharpened to blades by years of war and conflict. His resources and knowledge are vast. He sure as hell knows more about the PLF than probably anyone else except the terrorists themselves—and maybe even them. He would not have come all this way if he didn't believe, or even know for a fact, that the situation will worsen.

I am begging you to come with me.

The desperation in his eyes still burns through me. I don't want to believe him, don't want to have to trust or depend on him in any way, but I've also never seen him desperate before now. I've never known him to *beg* for anything. The fact that he is now—and of me, no less—causes a twist of both pain and fear.

I quicken my pace to Hazel's house near the Global Rebuild office. All the windows are dark and there's no answer to my knock. I try Brian's apartment next, with the same results, then hurry to the café. As is usual in the evenings, the tables and bar are crowded with patrons, and the mounted TV is blaring with news reports.

Alexei and Sofia are seated at a table by the window, and I make my way over to them. After a quick greeting and apology for interrupting their dinner, I ask if they've seen the other two Americans.

"They took Brian's car up to the castle this afternoon." Alexei frowns. "They have not yet returned?"

"Neither one of them is at home, so I don't think so."

"Is there something I can help you with?" Alexei asks.

"Nell, sit down and have something to eat." Sofia pushes another chair away from the table.

"No, I...I can't, but thank you." A sudden stab of guilt goes through me. "If you see Brian or Hazel, could you tell them I'm looking for them? I'll be back at my apartment."

"Sure, no problem." Alexei gives me a faintly quizzical look.

I turn and leave the café, my insides twisting. Suppose I convince Hazel and Brian to trust Darius, and the three of us head off to Telina and a flight back home. Everyone else would still be in Varaz—of course, since they live here—but it doesn't feel right to leave without even warning them about Darius's suspicions.

I walk back to Hazel's house again, relieved to see Brian's car pulling up to the front door. They both get out, lifting their eyebrows in surprise at the sight of me.

"What's going on?" Hazel approaches, her eyes creasing behind her glasses. "Are you okay?"

"I'm fine." My heart is hammering again. "But a...um, a friend of mine just showed up and thinks we should leave Varaz...well, the country actually...as soon as possible."

Brian and Hazel exchange glances.

"What are you talking about?" he asks.

I explain as quickly as I can—who Darius is, what he does, and why he came all this way to get me on a flight back to the States.

"Obviously, I couldn't just leave without talking to you both," I continue. "Would you come with us?"

"Come with you?" Hazel shakes her head. "The embassy hasn't given us any instructions to leave, except for telling us to avoid Saldem and the southern province. Global Rebuild is monitoring the situation and also reports that we're in a safe zone. Why would your friend think he knows something different?"

"Darius is an expert on counterterrorism measures. He's done a lot of work investigating the PLF because he knew they were still a threat. He's worked in this country. He speaks Krasnovian and fluent Russian. He knows what he's talking about and what he's doing."

"Where is he?" Brian asks.

"Back at my apartment."

They look at each other again. I stifle a sudden rush of frustration, though I don't know if it's directed at them or myself.

"I know it sounds bizarre," I say. "And yes, I'm technically only here for another week anyway, but Darius wouldn't have come all this way if he didn't know it could get dangerous."

"I appreciate his concern, but Brian and I can't leave based on nothing more than your friend's speculations," Hazel says. "Aside from the fact that we have no reason to, Global Rebuild would never allow it."

"We can't even reach the organization or the embassy right now." The irony of trying to convince them of what I'd just argued about less than an hour ago is not lost on me. "There hasn't been a signal since the weekend."

"That doesn't mean it's okay for us to go against company policy without good reason," Hazel retorts. "Global Rebuild has programs all over the world and is constantly monitoring situations. And the embassy knows we're here, so if they advise us to leave, then we certainly will. But until then, we have to stick to protocol."

"When does this guy want to leave?" Brian asked.

"Right now."

Hazel frowns. "Nell, I'm not comfortable letting you go with a man we don't know and who isn't affiliated with either Global Rebuild or any other organization. Obviously, we can't stop you, but Global Rebuild is responsible for the safety and well-being of all its volunteers. In fact, safety is the first priority. And Brian and I are responsible for you."

"Which is why you really shouldn't run off until we've figured this out." Brian looks at his watch. "I've gotta get some dinner and sleep. Why don't we plan to meet tomorrow morning and talk about this again?"

Darius will probably be gone by tomorrow—but he won't leave unless I'm in the car with him.

"At the very least, we can arrange to drive to Telina for the cell signal again," Hazel says. "If the embassy and Global Rebuild agree that it's the right course of action, then we can do what your friend suggests and catch a flight out."

It's a rational, sensible compromise.

"Okay." I nod and take a few steps away. "I'll stop at the café on the way to the museum, probably around seven or so."

"We'll be there," Hazel promises.

I walk back to Harmony Square, Poe trotting along beside me. Despite knowing that I have to do what Darius is asking—I'd be an idiot not to—I'd also meant what I'd told him. There *had* been a time when I'd have dropped everything and followed him anywhere.

I'm painfully aware that going with him to Telina doesn't mean I can let myself feel that kind of utter devotion again. What I do with him has to be for practical reasons—separated from any feelings at all for no other reason than to protect my heart.

Streetlamps throw a golden light over the square. Darius is pacing in front of the cathedral, his stride long and his body taut with leashed energy. He turns, as if sensing my approach, and crosses the street. The shadows cut across his features, making him look dangerous and sinister.

"Well?" he demands. "What did they say?"

Poe growls low in his throat. I put my hand on his head.

"They want to talk again tomorrow morning," I tell Darius.

He swears, low and sharp. "We're not waiting until tomorrow."

"We have to." I unlock the apartment door and push it open.

"Nell—"

"Darius." I turn to face him, my shoulders tensing. "Hazel and Brian are not only my friends, they're also my supervisors. They don't like the idea of me leaving with a man they don't even know, and I don't like the idea of bailing on them and everyone else in this town with hardly any warning. So you can meet them first, and we can talk rationally about the situation. They've agreed to come with us to Telina where we can hopefully get more information, but we can't leave until tomorrow morning."

Without waiting for a response, I go inside and let the door shut behind me. Even when I'm back in the apartment, Poe sticks close to my side as if he knows how badly unsettled I am.

Darius doesn't follow me in. I peer out the window to find him stalking back to his car, his fists clenched.

I pick up my phone and check for a signal again. Nothing. I take a quick shower and change into my pajamas. Before getting into bed, I look outside again.

Darius is sitting in the driver's seat, the car door open, his feet planted on the ground. He's leaning forward with his elbows on his thighs and his attention on his phone. The screen light throws his face into solid relief, like the edge of a cliff.

He'll sit out there all night, if he has to. I have no doubt.

After putting on my slippers, I go back downstairs and open the door. "Come inside."

He glances up. "I'll find a hotel or an inn."

"None of them have reopened." I wave a hand to indicate the block of closed-up buildings on the other side of the square. "The local economy can't count on tourist dollars yet, and the hotels would all end up operating at a loss if they open too soon. Just come in."

He gets out of the car, retrieving a travel bag from the passenger seat before following me back to the apartment. Poe goes on alert, his eyes narrowing when Darius closes the door behind him. I pull the dog's nest of blankets closer to the sofa, then take another pillow out of the narrow storage closet.

"You can take the bed." I toss the pillow and an extra blanket onto the bed.

"I don't need it. I'll sleep on the sofa."

An unexpected chuckle bursts out of me. "Unless you've developed the ability to fold up like a paper clip, there is no way you'll fit on the sofa."

"I'll manage fine."

"Darius, chill out." I throw him a look of slight exasperation. "You probably swam oceans and hacked your way through jungles to get here. I don't mind making the minuscule sacrifice of giving you my bed for a few hours."

Though of course he frowns, he doesn't argue again.

"Are you hungry?" I pass him to go into the kitchen and open the cupboards. "I gave Poe my leftovers, but I have bread, cheese, and some salami. And two jars of pickles."

"No, I'm okay." He drags a hand through his hair. "I could use a shower, though."

"Go ahead." I gesture to the bathroom door. "There's a clean towel in the cabinet. Soap and stuff under the sink."

He picks up his bag and disappears into the bathroom. As soon as the door clicks shut, I let out the breath knotting my chest. The only way I can handle being around him again is to be polite and practical. To pretend like the last time we were in the same room, I hadn't kissed him as if I were a dry, desiccated plant and he was a...waterfall.

A shiver rattles through me. I settle down on the sofa and pull a blanket over my legs. Darius comes out of the shower with his T-shirt still clinging to the damp parts of his torso and his pajama pants low on his hips. His arms are tanned and muscular, maybe even bigger than they were four years ago, the muscles shifting smoothly under his taut skin.

"You want me to turn the light off?" he asks.

"Sure." I put my phone on the coffee table, trying not to inhale deeply and fill my lungs with his delicious scent.

He flicks the light switch, throwing the room into darkness aside from the horizontal bars of light slanting through the wooden shutters. He climbs into bed and adjusts the pillows behind his head.

"Did you give up an assignment to come here?" I ask.

"No." He rests one arm over his abdomen. "I was covering the situation in southern Ukraine and the Crimean Peninsula, but freelance."

I shift onto my side to look at him. "You really haven't been doing anything else but working and investigating the PLF all this time?"

"Nothing else to do."

"You have nothing else to do? Isn't there anything else you *want* to do?"

He shakes his head. An old ache clenches my heart. War has always been his focus, but he's also lived through the brutality of being held captive and tortured. Wasn't that enough darkness? Hasn't he ever wanted to stop running toward violent conflict and bloodshed? To tell stories of goodness and light? To find peace?

When he left Grenville, *peace* was what I'd wished and hoped for him. But four years later, he still hasn't found it. He hasn't even looked. Maybe he doesn't think it's possible.

I look at his profile, etched against the whitewashed wall, shadows resting in the angles of his cheekbones.

After I found out about the meaning of the name Nell, I'd looked up the etymology of the name Darius—even though I wasn't supposed to be thinking about him. Derived from Persian, *Darius* means, among other definitions, "he who possesses."

He is shaped by possession. Ownership.

Maybe it was inevitable that he'd keep hold of my heart for so many years. And that I still don't know if I'll ever get it all the way back.

CHAPTER 11

Nell

I WAKE WITH A START, the broken threads of sleep slipping away. Poe lifts his head. The bed is empty, the blanket rumpled.

I sit up slowly. I'd think it was a dream—*Darius here, now?*—but my body knows the truth. I feel him, like the space inside me where he has always belonged is now filling up and becoming whole.

However, that is not a feeling I like and certainly not one I welcome.

Pushing to my feet, I go to use the bathroom and pull on jeans and a sweatshirt. I feed Poe and look out the window at the empty square. The dawn sky is charcoal-gray, a thin layer of clouds diffusing pale light over the town.

Darius's car is gone. Though I don't for a second think he left without me, my heart bumps oddly against my ribs.

No. I can't feel even the slightest need for him. Not anymore. Aside from being rattled by his unexpected appearance, I came to Varaz to start fresh, do something different, prove I could take bigger risks. To move farther away from his shadow and into my own light. Even if my time here is being cut short, I still have to hold on to those intentions.

I glance at the clock. Five fifty-three. I'd told Hazel and Brian we'd meet them at seven.

I check for Wi-Fi again, then pull on my shoes. Poe and I can head over to the Koroleva Café and see if Ivan is opening earlier than usual. As I step into the hallway, I notice the stairwell door leading to the roof is open slightly.

I walk upstairs and push open the door to the rooftop. The air is chilly, and a ribbon of orange streaks across the horizon. In the distance, lights flash in intermittent bursts, like fireworks.

I have no idea what they are, but a shudder goes through me. Clicking my fingers for Poe, I leave the rooftop and hurry to the café.

There's no sign of Hazel or Brian, but it's not seven yet. Despite the early hour, several residents have gathered to watch the old TV. Their conversation is loud, strident, and incomprehensible.

Onscreen, the news reports are shifting back and forth between reporters at various locations, two of whom are on city streets with chaos erupting behind them—looters breaking store windows, a crowd of what appears to be protesters, an armed soldier firing a gun toward the sky.

I approach the bar. "Ivan, what's going on?"

"Not good." He shakes his head, his face settled into deep lines. "New reports are of simultaneous explosions in and around Saldem and several other cities. Officials say it is a strategic, concentrated attack."

I stare at video footage of a soldier firing a rifle from the top of a building. "But I thought the PLF had been stopped."

"In Saldem, yes, but turns out that was a diversion while they were preparing for their *real* assault nationwide." Ivan tosses a dishrag into the sink behind him. "General Balakin issued a statement saying they intend to take over government buildings. They are advancing toward Telina."

Where Darius wants to go.

I leave the café and return to the square just as his car comes up the slight hill from the road leading down the mountain. I cross the street to meet him as he gets out. His features are set, his mouth a line of disapproval.

"Where did you go?" I ask.

"To see what I could find out." He closes the driver's side door. "I was stopped at a couple of checkpoints coming in. I figured they'd put up more controls if things got worse."

Tension laces my shoulders. "They have gotten worse."

He nods shortly.

"What happened?" I swallow hard. "I mean, they were just saying that the PLF had retreated."

He gives a hollow laugh. "They were never going to retreat that easily. Everyone underestimated them."

Except you.

I smother a wave of guilt. "So are the roads still open? Did they put up more checkpoints?"

"Probably. I didn't get far enough to find out." He slants his gaze to the hill. "The Krasnovian military barricaded the road at the base of the mountain. They say it's for protection because the PLF is threatening Varaz."

"I know they're moving toward Telina, but why would they threaten Varaz? There aren't even that many people here anymore."

"It's one of the country's oldest towns, a cultural and historical epicenter with a big tourism industry. Attacking Varaz would be a show of power and a long-lasting hit to the economy, which is still fragile. So the national military wants to defend it."

"I heard there've been simultaneous attacks across the

country overnight." My throat is dry. "I saw some lights flashing in the distance."

"Artillery." He folds his arms, his face dark with a frown. "I went down to find out exactly where it was coming from, but they stopped me at the barricade."

"Why is there a barricade?"

"They're putting the town in lockdown." He shakes his head. "To avoid security risks, no one is allowed in or out."

"Are you serious?" My stomach knots. "They can't do that... can they?"

"They already have. It's an official, military-enforced order. Violators are subject to arrest. Without the embassy's help, we have no choice. We have to stay here."

"But for how long?"

"I don't know. Hopefully not longer than a few days. A week at most. The government also just closed the border to Moldova. My guess is that the airports are next. Even if we did leave, we'd have trouble getting out of the country."

"When did they issue this order?"

"A couple of hours ago."

Which means we might have made it if we'd left when Darius wanted to.

Before I can say anything, he reaches out and runs his hand over my hair. Though the movement lasts less than a second, the fleeting pressure of his palm is both a comfort and a relief.

He drops his hand away from me and gets back into the car.

"The local police are going to make the rounds letting the residents know what's going on," he says. "I want to drive over to the other neighborhoods and see if I can get a cell signal." He glances at his watch. "Where do you work during the day?"

"At the museum across the square."

"I'll come find you later."

He leaves, the tires squealing on the cobblestones.

A ball of ice forms in my chest. I go back to the café to wait for Hazel and Brian.

The news reports are increasingly chaotic and alarming. The cameras show footage of buildings on fire, streets filled with fighting and rioting, and the stone-faced president saying something—Ivan translates—about a *violent coup* and a *nationwide terrorist insurrection.*

This no longer sounds "not good."

It sounds pretty fucking bad.

Within a couple of hours, everyone in town is buzzing with talk, gossip, and speculation about the tsunami of attacks happening throughout the country. The five officers who comprise the entire local police force make the rounds telling residents about the military-ordered lockdown and warning us not to leave for "our own safety."

Hazel and Brian are both concerned but not overly alarmed about the turn of events, rationalizing that the US embassy and Global Rebuild all know that we're here. Even with the embassy's reduced staff, as American workers and volunteers we have resources we can call upon for help and instructions...if we can reach them.

The technicians assure everyone they're trying to restore the Wi-Fi. Though I've become accustomed to the lack of connectivity, I have a new urgency to reach my father and tell him I'm fine. If he's heard about the attacks, he'll be worried sick.

Darius doesn't return for the rest of the morning. Alexei and I get back to sorting and organizing the museum's collection, though we keep the radio on while we work. He translates bits of information—a hijacking of a police convoy in the south, a skirmish west of Telina, another statement from the president about a defensive strategy.

To no one's surprise, there appears to be no forthcoming international support. Krasnovar is rich in forests and salt mines, but other countries don't consider it to be politically or strategically advantageous.

I meet Hazel and Brian at the café again in midafternoon, and Darius comes in just as we're sitting down. He weaves around the tables to reach us, his shoulders tense.

I make introductions warily, sensing his frustration as if it's a living creature.

"I guess we should have listened to Nell yesterday," Brian remarks as Darius pulls a chair up to the table.

Hazel throws him an irritated glance. "There was no way we were going to bail out of here with a complete stranger."

"He's not a stranger," I say.

"Not to you." She scrolls uselessly on her phone, then tosses it on the table. "It's not as if he's trained in this sort of thing."

"I want to get Nell safely home." Darius leans back, his arms folded. "That's the only reason I'm here. She wanted to talk to you first, but the delay hasn't changed the fact that I plan to get her out of Krasnovar with or without you."

"Good luck with that," Hazel mutters. "The embassy frowns upon US citizens going rogue."

The lines around Darius's mouth deepen. "The embassy should have told you to leave as soon as the attacks started in Saldem."

"Why do you think you know so much more than they do?" Hazel raises her voice a notch.

Though I suspect her belligerence comes from a place of fear, I don't like her confronting Darius and questioning his competence. I have plenty of my own issues with him, but lack of faith in his abilities has never been one of them.

"Hazel, aside from working in the field for years, Darius is an expert on international relations and counterterrorism initiatives," I tell her firmly. "I told you that I guarantee he knows what he's talking about and what he's doing."

"Does it even matter anymore?" Brian asks. "We're stuck here until the embassy or Global Rebuild can get us out."

"They're probably planning an emergency evacuation right now," Hazel adds. "We're definitely not going to try and leave without any communication. If we're not in Varaz when they come to evacuate us, it might be impossible for them to find us again."

"Keep an eye on the TV," Darius says. "When there's a disruption in cell service during a crisis, the US alerts citizens with important news via local media, if possible. I'll keep looking for a cell signal. We can't leave right now, but as soon as I find a way to do so safely, I will."

"But how will we know if the roads are even open?" Brian asks.

"That's why I need a signal. I want to contact some people and find out just how bad it is out there."

Hazel frowns. "Regardless of what you find out, traversing the country isn't a risk we should take."

"You both need to do what you think is best." Darius pushes his chair back and stands. "My goal won't change. I'm going to get Nell out of here. When I do, you can both come with us or stay here. It's your call, but you won't stop Nell from leaving with me again."

He turns and strides to the door. I feel Hazel and Brian looking at me, as if they've just sensed there is something more to my relationship with him than "friendship."

Mumbling an excuse, I grab my bag and hurry out. He's walking swiftly toward his car, each booted step ringing against the cobblestones.

"Darius."

He slows but doesn't stop. "Keep a bag packed and ready."

"*Darius.* You just said we can't leave."

"We can't leave right *now*." He stops and turns. "I could give a shit about the lockdown, but no way am I putting you in danger or risking you getting arrested. We're staying here until I know we can leave safely."

I rub my temple. My breath is burning my lungs. I don't know why I feel so guilty. No one could have predicted this course of events—not even him. He might have known something could happen, but he didn't know that it *would*.

Krasnovar hasn't even been on the international radar since the war. Before I left the US, there hadn't been any travel advisories or restrictions about Americans traveling here. Just the opposite, in fact—dozens of websites laud the country's natural and historic beauty and urge people to visit. There was no reason I shouldn't have come.

"I'm going to find another place to stay." He starts toward his car again.

"The landlord of my building lives over by the eastern wall. Considering there are so few residents, I'm sure he'd be happy to rent you an apartment. I'll give you his address."

He nods shortly. He's walking so fast I almost have to jog to keep up. "Darius, I'm sorry."

"You don't have to be sorry."

"Well, I know you went through a lot to try and help me. And I'm sorry we ended up stuck here."

His hands flex at his sides. "Forget it."

"I can't exactly forget it," I say dryly. "But even you can understand why I couldn't just leave with you at a moment's notice. It wasn't unreasonable to want to wait for a few hours."

"Nell." He stops and faces me again, his eyes dark. "I don't blame you. You are not at fault. Yes, I understand why you wanted to wait. But the shit has hit the fan, which means my job just got a hell of a lot harder."

"Your *job*?" I stare at him. "After you explicitly told me, and I quote, 'I can't be anywhere near you ever again,' suddenly I'm now your responsibility? Did someone pay you to swoop in and rescue me?"

"No, but—"

"But nothing." My blood heats. "I am not your *job,* and I'm certainly not the object of whatever hero complex you've got going on now."

"This is *reality,*" he snaps. "It's what I deal with every time I have an assignment. Just because the military has imposed a lockdown does not for one second mean Varaz, or anyone living here, is safe. And I came here to get you out of danger, not put you right back into it. Call it whatever the fuck you want, Nell, but we're in a war zone. Nothing good ever happens here."

He stalks toward the car, his spine rigid enough to break.

CHAPTER 12

Darius

NO ONE in town has a satellite phone. I'm ticked off that I didn't think to bring one. I'd been so laser-focused on getting to Nell that I hadn't taken the time to prep and strategize. *Get in, get her, get out.* That was my only plan.

I drop my travel bag on the bed and try my phone again. I haven't been able to get even one bar anywhere. The technicians claim they're working on getting the Wi-Fi restored, but all day no one has reported a signal. Likely the dead air is a fallout from the cyberattacks.

I push open the window shutter, which overlooks a view of a courtyard. The landlord quickly agreed to rent me the one-room apartment across the hall from Nell's. It's sparsely furnished, and the shower and toilet both work, making it better than many of the places I've stayed.

I unpack a few clothes. The room is small, just big enough for the bed, a sofa, a narrow desk, and a table with chairs. An attached kitchen has a refrigerator and a two-burner range. Anywhere else in the world, it would be more than enough for me.

But this isn't *anywhere else*.

After stashing my travel bag under the bed, I take the stairs to the rooftop. The view spans the distance over the town wall and down into the valley, which is covered with fields and farms bisected by the road.

There's no longer any sign of the gunfire from early this morning, though its absence could mean anything—the PLF is prepping for an attack somewhere else; they successfully ransacked a village; they're on the move. They're advancing toward Varaz.

No one could have predicted the swiftness of the raid on Saldem, but it was foolish for anyone to think the People's Liberation Front would just disappear after the war. They were too well-funded, too powerful. All they needed was time, more money, and more weapons.

Now time is on their side. Though the president deployed the national military immediately, the PLF had a head start and a planned, well-executed strategy. Their goal is to overthrow the elected government by brute force, and their concerted violent attacks are a means to their end.

It makes me sick to think this country is being torn apart again right in the middle of rebuilding. Any other time I'd head for the front lines, the resistance forces, the riots.

A dark, smoke-like feeling fills my chest.

I can't fucking stand it. Not only did I fail to get Nell safely home, now she's trapped.

The military might say the lockdown is for protection, but a few barricades and checkpoints are no match for the heavy artillery of the People's Liberation Front. The government is sending its forces into direct conflict, which means there aren't many units left to defend vulnerable cities and towns.

A movement from down in the square catches my eye. Nell is coming out of the bookstore, a book tucked under her arm. She's wearing jeans that hug her rounded hips, and a blue fleece shirt that can't hide the full curves of her breasts.

She moves differently than she did four years ago. Now she walks with her head up, facing the world instead of trying to hide from it. Her stride is longer, her shoulders back. That change was one of the first things I noticed about her in New York. After I'd absorbed the shock of her beauty. After I'd realized that her gray eyes still have the power to sear me through the heart.

But before I'd lost control.

My insides clench. Every instant of that kiss in her apartment is burned into me. Scarred with both the shame I can't get rid of...and an undeniable relief. After four years without even hearing her voice, kissing her had been like pouring water down my parched throat.

It had also been a blistering reminder of the reason I'd left Grenville. Left *her*. The reason I'd plunged back into work and refused to come up for air. If I buried myself in the world, I could smother all the urges and temptations that even the thought of Nell inspired. She'd have room to breathe and grow and move on.

Four years of hard-fought distance. Then?

Less than three days in the same city as her, and I'm shoving her against the wall and forcing her mouth open with mine.

I take a breath and push the memory aside. I'll lock myself down with fucking barbed wire, if I have to. Nothing will get in the way of her safety.

Not even me.

Grabbing my keys, I walk down to my car and drive over to the neighborhoods that spread beyond the old walled section of town. This area, once host to tourists and resort-seekers, is entirely deserted, with areas still gutted from shelling damage, invasions, and looting.

I prowl around the streets, prying loose, weak boards from the windows and looking for anything that might prove useful. The houses and buildings all contain few furnishings—overturned chairs and tables, smashed TVs, torn mattresses. Even the retail stores are empty, the floors littered with a few dirty clothes and toys.

In a former electronics store, I find an old, busted-up radio scanner. It doesn't look like it works, but I've used the same kind of conventional scanner before, so I take it with me in the hopes of repairing it.

I drive a few miles away from Varaz over the eastern route leading back down to the valley. The deserted cheese factory sits on a plot of land off the road, a good distance from the town itself. The old brick buildings are perforated by broken windows and metal doors locked with rusted chains.

After another hour of prowling around to no avail, I head back to my apartment. I'm unlocking the door when Nell comes up the stairs, a paper bag in one hand.

"Oh, hi." She climbs the rest of the way. Her cheeks are pink from the evening chill. "How's the apartment? Any issues?"

"Fine. No issues."

"Can I see it?"

"It's not much different than yours." I open the door and step aside so she can enter. As she passes me, I catch a scent of vanilla and fresh air. I follow her in and put the radio scanner on the table.

"You have a view of the courtyard, that's nice." She walks to the window, pausing to set the bag on the kitchen counter. "It should be quieter back here too, not that Harmony Square is super noisy. Here, let's exchange keys in case we get locked out or you need to let Poe into my apartment."

She pulls her keyring out of her pocket and takes off a spare key. I get the second key the landlord left in the kitchen and give it to her.

"I brought you some food to stock the fridge." She attaches my spare key to her keyring and gestures to the bag. "I figured you probably weren't in much of a mood to shop."

"You didn't have to bring me anything."

"It wasn't a problem." She opens the bag and starts putting stuff away—bread, cheese, apples. "I know you're the opposite of a picky eater, but I remembered that you like wheat bread, peanut butter crackers, bananas, and strawberry jam. Lucky for you, the grocery store had all of those things."

She keeps plucking food out of the bag, dusting off the cupboard shelves before putting things away, telling me I should make sure to check the refrigerator temperature because the electricity is "wonky." Her hair shifts around her shoulders every time she moves.

I tighten my jaw. "You can leave that. I'll take care of it."

"I'm almost done." She puts a bottle of dish detergent under the sink. My gaze skids to the curve of her hips and ass.

Goddammit.

Since leaving Grenville, I've had knockdown, drag-out fights with the fantasies boiling right under my consciousness. I haven't always won, especially at night. Raw, hot dreams have slipped past my guarded sleep. I've woken up sweaty and aching. Not knowing how to make them stop. To block them.

So I'd plunge into another dark, violent part of the world. Trying—and failing—to outrun them. Outrun her.

Now she's right here. Within touching distance.

By now, I'd expected her to be on a plane, flying far away from me.

"I'll pick up some gingerbread tomorrow." She puts the milk and cheese in the fridge. "Lara's gingerbread is amazing. It was the first thing I tried when I arrived in Varaz. The Gingerbread House is an institution here."

"I know."

"Oh, of course." She shakes her head with a small laugh. "You've been to Varaz before, haven't you?"

"A long time ago." Tension crawls up my spine. "Before the war."

"Well, then you should be looking forward to having some of Lara's gingerbread again." She puts a few boxes of pasta in the cupboard.

"Nell, I could give a flying fuck about gingerbread right now." The words come out sharp and abrasive.

Her eyes widen. I dig my fingers into my palms.

"I was just trying to…" She looks away.

"I know what you were trying to do." I step closer, my blood heating. "But this is not Grenville. We are not playing house. I know it seems like nothing has changed, that you're safe here. I know it looks like the Krasnovian military will protect the town. But that's bullshit. You saw how fast everything went to hell. I guarantee it can get worse even faster. And that it will. The only question is when."

She lifts her chin, her mouth tightening. "I am not trying to minimize the situation simply by bringing you groceries. What do you want me to do? Hide in my room until the threat passes or until you plan the great escape? I know you meant well in coming here, but I—"

"Meant well? I didn't fucking *mean well*. I came here to get you out of danger. The only thing I *meant* was to stop you from getting hurt or killed."

"I know that!" Her eyes flash like charcoal on fire. "And *I* didn't come here for a vacation. You don't need to treat me like an innocent little girl anymore. Yes, we have a history, but you are not responsible for me. I'm not your daughter or your girl-friend or your colleague or your wife. I don't even think we're friends anymore."

A blade slides into my chest, silent and bloodless. "This isn't about any of those things."

"Of course not," she retorts. "It's about you not realizing that I'm an adult who's capable of standing on her own. It's about you not wanting to admit that I've changed. And it's about you still needing absolution for what's happened between us."

I grind my teeth together. None of this is going as I'd intended. "Your psychoanalysis notwithstanding, what I *need* is to get us out of here."

"And I appreciate your efforts, but there are still parts of this situation that are within our control." She grabs her bag and hitches it over her shoulder. "I intend to follow police orders, take necessary precautions, and obey the lockdown orders. I will also do whatever the US embassy says we should do when we're able to contact them. What I will *not* do is let you make me feel like a nitwit just because I brought you a dozen goddamned eggs."

She stalks to the door and yanks it open, throwing me a cold glance. "I also intend to continue my work and friendships here, for however long this lockdown lasts. And if you want me to jump into the car with you whenever you say it's safe to leave, you'd damned well better start believing that I'm capable of making the right decision."

She leaves, slamming the door shut behind her.

All the air goes out of the room. My chest burns.

I grip the back of a chair. The walls shift and start closing in.

CHAPTER 13

Nell

SINCE MY INTERACTIONS with Darius are creating a friction like steel striking flint, I avoid him for the next couple of days—not that that's difficult. His car is gone when I wake up in the morning, and I stick to my usual routine of breakfast and walking to work. Sometimes I catch a glimpse of him when I leave the museum for lunch or stop at the café, but he doesn't spare me a glance. He's grim-faced and tense, his features settled into a permanent shield of guardedness.

Despite my own resolve not to feel anything for him, I'm unable to prevent pangs of regret, fear, and outright sorrow. When I think of how he'd filled my life for so many years, how he *was* the daring hero who showed me there was a universe beyond my anxious, claustrophobic world…and how drastically our relationship has altered since those days, I can't help but be a little heartbroken.

But even so, I wouldn't change a single thing about what I've done and how we ended up. If I'd stayed the same, I'd still be stagnating like an old rain puddle.

Aside from receiving orders about the lockdown, not much changes in Varaz. Alexei and I both make what I think is a valiant effort to continue our work "as usual," which means bringing artwork up from storage and refining the exhibition blueprints. We arrange the display cases and create mock-up wall-text labels.

None of the Krasnovian military come into town for reconnaissance or whatever, and the news reports continue to focus on major skirmishes and riots in larger cities. Every time the PLF takes a hit, a band of terrorists shows up somewhere else in another surprise attack.

The residents of Varaz, for the most part, are more angry than they are afraid—all of them have lived through the war, and none of them want to see their country overtaken by the very forces that were defeated. They speak bitterly about the violence, the sacrifices, the destruction. No one wants more of it. They are furious that the PLF has been hiding underground all these years, and theories abound about how and why they went undetected, who is funding them, how they can be stopped.

On the third day of the lockdown, the technicians finally get the Wi-Fi back up and running again. Hazel receives a text from Global Rebuild firmly instructing us not to go anywhere or risk traveling in the country on our own.

An embassy official texts that they "know we're here" and are "taking steps" to help us get safely out of the country. Alexei then informs us he heard on the news that the US embassy is now operating at "skeletal capacity" with "essential personnel only," which doesn't sound all that reassuring.

I hurry back to my apartment, stopping to knock on Darius's door to tell him about the signal in case he hasn't heard. No answer.

I let myself into my room and, after a few failed attempts, get through to my father.

"Nell?" The connection is terrible and it sounds like he's speaking in a cave.

"Dad, I'm okay. We're trying to figure out how we can leave Varaz right now, but I'm fine."

"I've been going out of my mind. I've called the State Department a hundred times. You sure you're all right? Has anyone from the embassy contacted you?"

I relay what Hazel learned and explain that Global Rebuild is also trying to help us find a safe way home. I leave out the part that we have no idea what that entails or when it will be.

"Dad, did you know that Darius is here? He said you called him."

"Yes, he...no success through official channels, so I..." The interference breaks up his voice.

"He's actually here, in Varaz."

"He's there? Right now?"

"He arrived a few days ago. He said he came right after you called him."

My father lets out a long breath. "I knew he'd do whatever he could to help, but I never imagined he'd actually go back to Krasnovar. He didn't even know you were in Varaz. I thought you might've told him in New York."

"No, I hadn't made the arrangements yet."

"Let me talk to him."

"I don't know where he is right now."

"What's his plan?"

I'm not surprised my father just *knows* Darius has a plan, even if it stings a little that he has more faith in Darius than anyone else.

"I don't know, but I'm following instructions from Global Rebuild and the embassy," I tell him. "I'll try and call you again as soon as they give us the details. How's Fern?"

He doesn't counteract my change of subject, and we talk for a few more minutes before the signal weakens and we have to say goodbye.

I put my phone on the bedside table. At my feet, Poe thumps his tail. I rub his ears, pushing aside another worry about what's going to happen to him when I finally do leave Varaz. Maybe I can ask Alexei to take care of him.

After giving Poe some food, I head over to the café. As usual, people are crowded at the bar, alternately drinking, having heated conversations, and watching the news.

Despite their anger, the townspeople are also somewhat mollified by the lockdown. No one likes being told what to do, but there's a definite relief that the Krasnovian military is taking preemptive measures to keep the town safe. Other cities and towns were so taken by surprise that they had no time to put up a defense. Everyone agrees that in that respect, Varaz and its residents are fortunate.

I find Sofia and her twins at a table near the back and join them for dinner and a tabletop game of checkers. While it's an enjoyable hour, I'm bothered by my conversation with my father —though I can't pinpoint why. It's not that he called Darius—I actually would have expected that, if I'd thought about it. It's something else.

I get home close to nine thirty, and my knock on Darius's door still goes unanswered. A glance out my apartment window shows that his car is gone. Unless he's found a way past the military barricade, there aren't many places he could go. The only other route out of Varaz is past the old factory on the eastern road, which I assume is also being guarded.

I pull on my pajamas and try to settle down with a book, but I can't concentrate. After shuffling his blankets, Poe flops down and is asleep in less than fifteen seconds.

I turn off the light, but lie awake listening for the sound of Darius's car. Shadows shift against the walls. The quiet is almost eerie, especially given the news images of the chaos breaking over other parts of the country.

The chaos that could make its way here.

I never imagined he'd actually go back to Krasnovar.

My father's words surface again.

Suppressing unease, I roll over and try to fall asleep. I'm aware that at any time, Darius could suddenly tell me he's found a way out and we have to leave *now*. Though this time I wouldn't hesitate for a second before going with him, I still have a loyalty to both Global Rebuild and the friends I've made. Even, in this short time, to Varaz itself. I would—

Bang!

I bolt upright, a gasp lodging in my throat. *What the hell...?*

Darkness gleams through the shutters. The clock says twelve thirty.

My brain is fuzzy, still clinging to threads of sleep. I must have dozed off, ruminations still swimming in my subconscious.

Another bang rattles through the apartment, like something hitting a wall. I push off the bed, clambering over a still-sleeping Poe to look out the window. The square is silent and deserted, cast in the dimness of midnight.

Thud.

I hurry to the door, pulling it open and peering into the hallway.

Crash.

The noise is coming from Darius's apartment.

Fear and confusion slice through me. *Is someone in there with him?*

I cross the hallway and knock. "Darius?"

Silence. I press my ear to the door. The deep rumble of his voice is barely audible, a stream of noise that sounds like an animal in pain.

I run back and grab my keyring from the kitchen counter. My

hands shake as I fumble to find the key that unlocks his door. I knock again and call his name.

"Darius, I'm coming in."

No answer. Another thud, like an object hitting the floor.

I push the key into the lock and turn the handle. The pounding of my heartbeat echoes in my head. Slowly, I open the door.

The room is a mess—the table and chairs overturned, broken glass littering the floor, the bedcovers torn. Items from the desk are scattered everywhere—a notebook, the radio scanner, a smashed lamp.

My vision goes in and out of focus.

Darius is crouched in a corner, wearing only a pair of pajama pants, his fists clenched and muscles locked. He's sweating, his hair clinging damply to his forehead, his eyes black and glittering. Distorted. He's here, but he's not here.

I never imagined he'd actually go back to Krasnovar.

Oh, my god.

Shutting the door, I drop the keys and rush across the room. "Darius."

No response. I get to my knees in front of him. His chest rises and falls with ragged breaths. The veins in his chest and arms throb and pulse right at the surface of his skin. The look in his eyes—a fathomless pain, darker than a coal mine—cuts me to the soul.

I don't know what to do. Should I touch him? Leave him alone? Wake him?

Slowly, I lift my hand. "Darius."

Like the strike of a snake, he darts toward something half-hidden under the sofa. I barely have time to recoil before realizing what it is.

Harsh breaths saw in and out of his lungs. He grips the pistol handle, his knuckles whitening, one finger flexing on the trigger.

My throat tightens. The barrel is pointed toward the floor.

Not for a second do I think he'd ever point the gun at me, not even in a state of delusion, but I sure as hell don't want the damned thing going off.

I put my hand on his arm. His skin is hot, the muscles hard as steel.

"No." The growl rips from his chest, guttural and cold.

He grabs my shoulder and bolts out from the corner, yanking me behind him at the same time. I stumble, bracing myself on the wall as he lunges to his feet.

Tears burn my eyes. He moves forward, the gun trained on the door now, shielding me with his body from a danger that exists only in his head.

Now, at least. Once upon a time, the danger—the evil—had tortured and almost killed him.

In one sweeping movement, he grabs a broken wooden chair and throws it at the door. The wood splinters. Another serrated noise comes from his throat. Through my blurred vision, my brain registers the long, thin scars crisscrossing his back.

"Darius." I almost choke on his name. Maybe the sound of my voice will penetrate the black fog. "Darius, it's Nell. You're having a nightmare. I used to have them when I was younger, but mine were about monsters that weren't real. Like ogres in fairy tales or beasts with fangs. I remember you once told me that if I talked about the bad stuff, that would give them less power. Make them weaker. I don't know if you—"

"Get out!" He shoots his arm to the side, knocking over an open laptop on the coffee table. His arm muscles are tight enough to snap like branches. I can't see the gun.

Shoving away from the corner, I move cautiously around next to him. "Darius, listen to my voice. It's Nell. You're not trapped anymore. You're here with me. Remember how many times we explored the tide pools at Volkov Bay? I loved finding shells and touching the sea anemones, and it was always such a big deal when we saw a little octopus. Remember how cold and salty the wind was?"

Sweat rolls down his temple. He's still breathing hard, but he's lowered the gun slightly. I touch his arm again. His muscles jump under my fingers.

Stepping closer, I slide my hand down his forearm to the gun in his grip. He jerks back, his arm coming up in defense. I take advantage of his momentary pause and wrench the gun out of his hand.

He stumbles backward. "Nell."

My name is a twisted noise of pain. His back hits the wall, and he slides to the floor. I push the gun far underneath the bed and cross to him again. He draws his legs up, resting his elbows on his knees, his head lowered and chest heaving.

"Look at me," I say. "Please."

After a long minute, he lifts his head. His eyes are still coal-black, simmering with pain, but he focuses on my face. I push his damp hair away from his forehead. My fingers tremble. Though the fear of his rejection still lives inside me, not even that can stop me from folding my arms around him and holding on tight.

He doesn't move. Heat pours off him in waves. His body is still leashed with tension. It feels as if he could break the earth right in half.

"You're here." I settle my hand on the side of his face. "You're free."

He stares at me for a long minute. We're so close that I inhale his breath every time he lets it out. The golden flecks appear again in his irises. The distortion eases, bringing him back into the here and now. He lifts his hand, brushing his thumb over the side of my neck. My pulse is still hammering wildly.

I put my hand on his chest. The thump of his heartbeat, heavy and strong, reverberates all the way through me. His eyes darken to the color of mahogany. He moves his hand to the back of my neck, the weight of his palm warm and delicious, and brings my face closer to his.

My throat constricts. The place inside me, the box where I've hidden away my everlasting but brittle, fragile love, is still locked tight. As desperately as I've longed for him, it has hurt badly to have all my wishes go unfulfilled for so long.

But now...one of those wishes blooms into wild, glorious truth.

I don't know if he moves first. I don't know if I do. All I know is that one second we're looking at each other, and the next, our lips are pressed together.

Our kiss back in New York had been so swift and intense that I'd felt as if I were trying to stay upright on a storm-riddled sea. But this time, it's light, gentle, like the whisper of a memory before it takes full shape. Then he deepens the pressure, shifting so I'm pressed more closely against him. I soften like honey, yielding to the hard planes of his body.

This.

This is what I've been missing, what I've been searching for, what I feared I would never find. But of course, he's the one who had it all along, the intangible, golden thread linking us through time and space.

I spread my palms over his damp chest, feeling both his raw strength and the heat radiating from him. He moves his hands to the sides of my neck and lifts my head to just the right angle. Everything in me surrenders, wakes up, comes to life. Even now, in the aftermath of torment, he kisses me with exquisite assurance, as if he knows exactly what I want.

He winds my hair around his hand and urges my lips apart. Our tongues touch. Sparklers burst and pop in my blood. Tension spreads in my lower body. He slides his hands to my waist and eases back against the wall, pulling me half on top of him, his arm supporting my back.

He moves one hand under my shirt, settling his warm palm

against my spine like an anchor. Delicious shivers course through me. The back of my mind fills with images of his hands gliding over my bare skin. Of me underneath him.

Thoughts of him have consumed me for years now. My dreams have blistered with explicit images of our naked bodies entwined, my legs around his hips, his erection pushing into me. I've imagined kissing a line down his bare chest, over his abs, and then taking him in my mouth. I've pictured myself on my hands and knees with him thrusting into me from behind. I've straddled him, gotten on my knees, let him bend me over the back of the sofa. There have been no rules, no restrictions, nothing forbidden.

I've wanted all that for so long that this moment is suddenly more surreal than it was before. I almost can't believe it's happening—less the kiss itself than the fact that Darius is so deliberate, so intent, as if all his perceptions of *wrongness* have slid away.

I'm pressed up against his half-naked body, the scents of sweat and maleness adding fire to my growing arousal. He tilts my head back again and increases the pressure of his lips, a low murmur of approval rumbling through his chest.

I'm sinking into a pool of swirling colors and heat. I don't want to leave. I've wanted to be back here forever. I love the sensation of his mouth on mine, his big arms holding me like I'm precious to him. Everything *Darius* fills my blood—the fire burning inside him, his relentless determination, the depth of both his courage and his pain.

He slides one hand under my pajama shirt and cups my breast. I draw in a sharp breath of pleasure as my nipple buds against his palm. He caresses me slowly, his mouth still devouring mine, his long fingers gently twisting and rubbing my nipple.

My urgency fires up like a pressure cooker. Through the haze of pleasure, I'm aware that he would barely have to touch me, and I'd come right now, right here, hot and hard.

I pull my mouth away from his and grab his wrist, stopping his delicious caresses. He lifts his head, his eyes darkening—not with torment this time, but with consternation.

Easing away from him, I pull my shirt down and try to quell the lingering ripples of need.

"Nell, I—"

"No." I shake my head, thinking I'm either doing the right thing or making a big, stupid mistake. I'm pretty sure there's no middle ground. "You know I want you. That hasn't changed. But not like this."

I rise to my feet, pushing my messy hair away from my face. "You should get some sleep."

His guilt is starting to return—I see it in the tightness of his jaw. I grab his hand and pull him up, then lead him over to sit on the bed.

I get him a glass of water, noticing the shadows like bruises lining his eyes. He takes a few gulps of water, then sets the glass down and lies back on the bed, throwing one arm across his face.

I spear my fingers into his hair, stroking it slowly. "When we make love, Darius Hawke, we're both going into it totally aware of what we're doing. Open. Willing. There will be no excuses, no reluctance. No shadows. With us, there will only be bright, clear light."

He doesn't take his arm away from his face. His chest rises and falls with uneven breaths. I continue stroking his hair. His body finally settles into the steady rhythm of sleep.

I take my hand from him and sit down on the sofa, intending to watch over him until dawn breaks.

CHAPTER 14

Darius

GOOD SMELLS FILTER into my sleep. Things like blueberry muffins, cinnamon, an ocean wind. Images push upward, struggling to surface. I shove them back down and snap out of the haze. Open my eyes.

A heavy, drugged feeling weights my limbs. I haven't felt this way since—

I sit up, my heart kicking into gear, my breath suddenly too fast.

"Here." Her voice falls over me like a stream of sunlight.

No. No fucking way.

She holds out a glass of water. My throat is parched. I down the water in three gulps. She takes the empty glass and moves out of my peripheral vision.

Swiping my forearm across my mouth, I struggle to grab the memory, even though I know it's gone—shattered, demolished, obliterated. It belongs to me, but I will never find it.

Does she have it?

The idea is enraging, horrifying, embarrassing, unbearable—all at the same time. Nell's memories of me are her own creations. She'd once seen me as "heroic." I'm not even close, but until four years ago, there had never been a reason to destroy her illusions.

Then in Grenville—my heart slams against my chest—she'd seen too much, more than I'd ever wanted her to. And she'd still thought I was admirable. Worthy.

The best of men.

Now she knows the truth.

I pull my legs over the side of the bed and rub my eyes. The back of one of the dining chairs is broken. A picture on the opposite wall is missing. There's a rip in the sofa that hadn't been there before. I sense there was more, but she cleaned up whatever she could.

A cupboard door closes in the kitchen. I can't make my voice work to tell her to leave. Instead, I grab clean clothes from my suitcase and drag myself to the bathroom. After locking the door, I pull off my pants, step into the shower, and stand under the hot spray for a long time.

I can't even grab a sliver of the goddamned dream, nightmare, flashback...whatever the fuck it was. My doctors and therapists had given me plenty of resources for how to deal with the PTSD. Between that and my own methods, I'd battled away the worst of the aftereffects not long after I returned to the States.

Underground fighting had worked better than anything else. Getting into a ring, using nothing but my fists and my instincts, had forced me to rebuild my strength and control my mind. Facing the horrors of the world had made my own internal shit insignificant. I was done with it.

Was.

I press my hand against the shower wall and let the water pound the back of my neck. It's the *not remembering* I hate the most. If I can see it, confront it, I can fight it again. But I don't have the right weapons anymore. And I don't know how to battle something that's gone before I even know it's there.

After getting out of the shower, I shave, brush my teeth, and dress, forcing myself to at least look normal. The fogged mirror reflects my blurred, indistinct face.

Her, I remember with blistering clarity. The press of her mouth, feel of her body, scent of her skin...she had eradicated the bleak, empty darkness and filled it with everything good and pure.

Not long ago, that realization would have crushed me with shame. Now I'm not sure what it does. I just don't want to imagine what happened in the minutes before she was in my arms.

She's still out there. She's not going away.

Ever.

My heart starts beating too fast. I grip the bathroom door handle.

I don't want to do this. Open up to her. Let her in.

But I have to.

I don't want to know what she witnessed.

But I have to.

I push open the door. She's still in the kitchen, her back to me, her hair long and loose. I still feel those thick strands wrapped around my hand like a ribbon. She turns.

Tension shoots down my spine. I don't know what I'll see in her—pity, wariness, disgust...god forbid, *fear?*

"Good morning." She smiles slightly. Her eyes are warm gray, like smoke.

I can't form any words. She doesn't seem upset. If anything, she's looking at me with concern.

"How are you?" She tilts her head up, searching my face.

I swallow hard. "I'm okay."

"Good." She indicates the coffee maker. "Would you like some coffee?"

"No. I…"

Fuck. I've never had to talk about this with anyone but a medical professional. The fact that I have to talk to Nell is like a hurricane in my chest.

As much as I'd like to forget last night ever happened, I can't do that to her. I can't ignore, suppress, or hide the truth. Not anymore. Not when she's seen how bad it can get.

"Last night…" My voice is rough. I flex my hands, smothering old, jagged humiliation. "I'm sorry. I haven't had…when I first got back, I—"

"Darius." She steps closer. Her gray eyes are so earnest, so transparent. "Don't apologize. I'm the one who's sorry."

I frown. "What for?"

A shadow falls across her face. "I didn't even realize…when you first got here, I believe I was justified in reacting the way I did. We'd been estranged for so long, and then New York just seemed to make things worse, so having you show up out of nowhere was unsettling, to say the least. But obviously no one anticipated the lockdown…well, except for you knowing something else was going to happen…no, wait."

She shakes her head when I start to speak.

"The thing is…" She reaches out and takes my hands in hers. "I didn't think how hard it must have been for you to come back to Krasnovar at all, much less to the northern part of the country."

My jaw tightens involuntarily. Nell's eyes darken.

"I should have thought of that, but I didn't," she continues. "And then when we found out we were stuck in a lockdown, I didn't make the connection between the PLF attacks and the fact that you're *trapped* again in Krasnovar with no way out." She twists her mouth in regret. "But this time, because of me."

"Because of you?"

"You wouldn't be here if it weren't for me."

"Nell." I let go of her hands and move back before I haul her up against me. "Would I have come to Varaz if you hadn't been here? No. Would I ever have come back to Krasnovar? I don't know. But none of this happened *because* of you. None of it is your fault. I could have called other people to see what they could do to help you get home safely. I didn't have to be the one to do it...except that I did. Because even though years can pass without us talking to each other, I'm always aware of you in the world. I always know you're here. And I will always drop everything and run to you if I think you need help, even if you don't want me to. Maybe that's overstepping or whatever you want to call it, but it's the truth. I will always come to you."

Her eyes glitter. "But look at what that does to you."

Darkness pushes up inside me. "It doesn't do anything except make me batshit crazy when I fail. Whether I'm here with you or covering a war in the Caucasus, I still have the same fucked-up psyche."

"Stop talking about yourself like that. Surviving torture and its impact does not make you fucked up."

I sigh heavily. "I've dealt with most of it, but the nightmares and flashbacks are an unpredictable and shitty part of the PTSD. I'm sorry you had to see it."

"I am too, but for you, not me." Her forehead creases. "How long has it been since you've had one?"

"A long time." I hesitate, then give her the truth. "I haven't had them since the first year I got back. But I knew they weren't gone, just dormant. Anything could trigger them back to life. I knew that when I crossed the border into Krasnovar last week."

Last week. Feels like a hundred years ago.

I drag a hand over the back of my neck and force myself to keep going. "I don't remember what happened."

A flush rises to her face. "During the nightmare?"

"Sometimes I remember bits and pieces, but never anything

concrete. It's like a self-protective thing, a shutting off of memory. The biggest…" I take a breath, my shoulders tensing. "The biggest fear I have is that I'm going to hurt someone."

"You didn't hurt me." She looks at me for a long moment, her eyes grave. "You tore your apartment apart, and when I got here, you were in the corner, like you were about to lunge out fighting someone. Then you went for a gun that was underneath the sofa."

I jerk my head up, my heart slamming against my ribs. "I went for the fucking Glock?"

"Yes. Then you pulled me behind you, like you were protecting me from the threat. I started talking to you, hoping the sound of my voice would help you out of it. I managed to get the gun away from you, and that was when you said my name."

My throat constricts. "I…I don't remember any of that."

"I do." She moves closer. "Even in the middle of a nightmare, you're brave and protective, which means that your most basic instincts are *good*, not fucked up. I wasn't afraid of you. Not even when you were holding the gun. Not for a second. I knew you wouldn't hurt me. Because even now, even after all we've been through, I know to the depths of my soul that you're safe. Always."

When she'd told me that four years ago, the confession had hurt. I hadn't known she'd thought of me that way. I'd never been *safe*, least of all when I had her spread out naked on the bed.

Heat suddenly flickers through me. I shove it down and turn away from her.

When we make love, Darius Hawke…

I don't have to wonder if I'd heard her right in the aftermath of the darkness. Every one of her words, both gentle and deter-mined, had seared into my chest. They still burn somewhere near my heart.

"You don't scare me." She puts her warm hand on my arm. "And you don't have to be afraid of hurting me. You *won't*. Even though you leaving Grenville and being away from you for four years was painful, I know everything you've done was meant to protect me— at least, in your view—even when I didn't want or need protecting. You came here, back to Krasnovar no less, for the sole purpose of getting me to safety. There is no situation, no circumstance, no nightmare in which you would ever *ever* deliberately hurt me."

Nell feels. Right down to her bones. I've always known that, but only now does it take shape into an actual realization.

I've spent most of my life forcing myself not to feel anything. If I suppress both the good and the bad, smother it, bury it deep, I can do my job without getting too involved. Stand apart. Pretend like it doesn't burn me up, twist my insides, deaden my soul.

Not Nell. She feels everything. Even if she hasn't expressed it, it's all there, right at the surface of her skin, in her gray eyes.

She tightens her hand on my arm. "I feel badly enough about this whole situation. It will be even worse if you shut down again. Maybe we both just need to be done with guilt. And maybe it's finally time for you to start trusting yourself."

The knot tightens. I've always trusted my instincts in the field —I have no choice, if I want to stay alive—but I left Grenville and stayed away from Nell because I no longer trusted myself with her.

But still, even now, after she saw me gutted down to my worst, her trust in me hasn't wavered. I can't get my head around it—that this young woman who has battled her own demons isn't afraid of the legions still clawing in my subconscious. She might even be stronger than them.

"And, Darius…" Nell lets go of my arm and steps away. "Maybe it's also time you start trusting *me*."

I look up. She's watching me—direct, unflinching. I want to tell her I do trust her, that I always have, but that would be a lie. I haven't trusted her feelings. I haven't trusted that she knows what she wants. That she knows herself.

A faint sense of unreality shifts the ground under my feet. It's almost impossible to believe she's here, standing less than five feet away. She's appeared in my mind so many times. For four years, images of Nell have torn me apart, filled me with shame, driven me farther into darkness.

But now...her physical presence, close enough that I can see the dusting of freckles on her nose, is a kind of unlocking. A release, like she's reaching inside me and unfastening the old, frayed knots gripping my chest.

I walk to where she's standing. My heartbeat increases like a roller coaster inching up a hill. I lift a hand and brush away a strand of hair clinging to her cheek. She parts her lips on a slow intake of breath.

She'd fit so perfectly in my arms last night. Like a little sparrow settling into a nest. I'd wanted to hold her forever.

I bring my hands to either side of her neck, my thumbs against her cheeks. Her face is a painting—lovely, smooth, harmonious—but *she* brings it to vibrant life. I could live an eternity and still see something new every time I look at her.

Against my palms, her pulse increases. I lower my head and brush my mouth across hers. It's barely a touch but tension lances through me—an instinctive guard against the waves of shame, self-disgust, and wrongness that have lived alongside my desire for her.

But the waves are silent.

I angle her head upward, press my lips harder against hers. A sigh spills from her throat into mine. I breathe her in. Her body heat flows through the scant few inches separating us. I feel her soften the instant before she closes the distance, fitting herself up against me.

My heart swoops down the hill in an exhilarating rush. She

slides her arms around my waist. Her lips are warm and smooth. Sunlight. Flower petals.

Though the press of her body alone is enough to fire up my lust, I keep the kiss restrained. Sweet. I don't even know if I've ever experienced a *sweet* kiss before. But this one is.

At first she doesn't move, like she's hesitant about what she should do. Then she responds tentatively before tightening her arms around me and increasing the pressure of her lips.

I move my hands to the back of her head, driving my fingers into her thick hair and tilting her head back to settle my mouth fully over hers. The taste and feel of her heats my blood, thaws the ice in my bones, quiets the storm.

So *good*. This woman in all her warmth and gentleness. There is no battle to fight, not right now, not with her in my arms, not with her lips moving against mine as if she doesn't want the kiss to stop.

I don't want it to, either. The memory of her naked body is emblazoned in my mind, all soft, ripe curves and heat. Though I'm burning to see and touch her again, right now this kiss is enough to ease the darkness. To make me want to let in some light.

Only when the urge for *more* becomes too much do I reluctantly break the kiss. I lift my head. Her eyes are luminous clouds. The sight of her flushed cheeks and reddened mouth intensifies my lust. I force my hands away from her and step back, disliking the separation, the loss of her body heat.

She brings her hand to her mouth. Faint wariness shadows her face, as if she's expecting the battle to start again, as if she's steeling herself against my inevitable guilt and self-recrimination.

But the waves are still silent. Now there's only need, heat, and the knots all unraveled and loose.

There are a thousand things I should say to her, but the only words I can manage are, "I hate that you had to see me…like that, but thank you."

"You said you'd always come to me." She takes her keys off the counter and starts toward the door. "And I will always be here for you."

She stands on tiptoe and brushes her lips across mine before leaving. The door clicks shut behind her.

I stand there for a long minute, not sure what to do with the chaos of warmth mixing with the still-lingering shock of the flashback and the inevitable fear that it could happen again. And if it did, Nell wouldn't flinch.

I shove away the thoughts of what, exactly, that means. My distorted psyche can't matter right now. My goal has to be the same—I need to get her out of the country.

After retrieving the Glock, I shove it into the waistband of my jeans and walk down to my car. My attempts to get past the barricade through bribes and quid-pro-quo promises have been futile. The soldiers stationed there finally threatened to arrest me if I tried again.

So I spend another few hours scouring the still-deserted areas of town for anything useful—a cell signal, another way out, a CB radio, even a place that would work as a bomb shelter, if it comes to that.

And it might.

At one, I return to the square and cross to the museum. Life is going on, as it always does, no matter how bad the circumstances. Brian and a group of workers are lined up on the scaffolding of an old theater, repairing pieces of crumbling masonry. The twins Jacob and Tomas are playing ball with three other kids in the park, and a utility worker is fixing a broken streetlamp.

The museum is still officially closed, but the doors are always open to anyone who wants to stop in. I enter and walk through the empty galleries.

"Let's put the pieta between the St. Sebastian painting and the triptych." Her voice drifts from one of the galleries farther back. "It will draw people's eyes right when they walk in, but it won't dwarf the triptych."

"Agreed, but that does not work chronologically," Alexei replies.

I stop in the doorway to the gallery, which is filled with crates, boxes, and pedestals. Paintings are leaning against the empty walls, waiting to be put on display. Several other people are milling around with ladders and tools.

Neither Nell nor Alexei notice me as they continue talking. Nell pauses to consult a blueprint, looks at another painting, takes out a pencil to make some adjustments. She walks over to direct the placement of a small statue. Another worker asks her a question in English. She responds in broken Krasnovian, which makes them both laugh.

I can't stop looking at her. Though I've noticed how different she is from four years ago—how she's become more confident, self-assured, accomplished—I haven't seen her at work. I've never seen her interact with colleagues or even really her friends. It seems stupid, but watching her is like seeing all the pieces of Nell click and fit together into a polished whole.

Into a woman who's changed from the one I've been battling for over four years. I want to drag her into my arms, wrap myself around her, hide her inside me. I can't—won't—think about the blunt fact that she deserves far more than a battered, scarred war photographer who has nothing to offer her but protection.

She looks up, catching my gaze.

My heart slams against my ribcage. She puts down the blueprint and crosses the room.

"Hi." She stops in front of me, her eyes warm and a faint smile curving her mouth. "I was hoping I'd see you soon. Did you get my note?"

I shake my head.

"I put a note under your door before I left for work this

morning," she says. "You must've been gone already. It just said that I hope you're okay and that you know where to find me if you need anything."

I swallow hard, shoving my hands into my jacket pockets. "I'm…I'm okay."

"Good." She gestures to the scattered artwork. "If you're looking for something to do, we can always use another set of muscles."

"I'm going to listen to the transmissions on the old radio scanner I found, in case anything useful comes across." I back up a step. "But maybe another time."

"Okay. I'll see you later, then." A slightly quizzical look rises to her eyes. "Was there something you wanted?"

I want…

"No." There's suddenly a strange, rolling sensation in my abdomen. I have no idea what it is. "Uh, do you want to grab dinner tonight?"

She blinks. "With you?"

"Yeah."

"Sure. I'd like that."

"Okay. I'll come get you around seven."

"Great."

I turn, sensing her gaze on me as I walk away. Only when I step outside do I realize the source of the antsy feeling. I was nervous.

Because I just asked Nell out on a date.

CHAPTER 15

Nell

I THINK this might be a date.

Yesterday, I wouldn't have imagined Darius capable of dating. Actually, the idea of him even asking a woman out is weird. I've always assumed his relationships happened without any effort, as if all he had to do was look at a woman and, *boom,* she was his.

But this feels like a date. Or something close. Something different, at least.

Especially following *that kiss.* In all my fantasies of him, I've never imagined him giving me a kiss as light and delicious as spun sugar. I've pictured plenty of hot, hard, demanding kisses, and I've relived a thousand times our mutually possessive kiss the day he left Grenville, but this morning's kiss had been... gentle. Tender and complete. I hadn't sensed a war raging inside him or even any resistance. Instead, it had felt as if he'd finally let himself just enjoy the pleasure of kissing.

Of kissing *me.*

The pleasure, of course, had been enthusiastically mutual. But though I've been thinking about the kiss all day, I haven't cluttered the memory with questions or speculations. It's simply something good to have, like a four-leaf clover that brings you luck and happiness.

It's all the more precious because I know how differently the aftermath of Darius's flashback could have gone. In fact, I'd expected him to retreat even farther away from me or lock himself up behind his barricade again.

Instead, he'd kissed me.

So regardless of whether or not this is an actual date, I'm exceedingly grateful that we're finding our way back to being friends again, which we could never do if he refuses to even be here.

I shower and start to dress in my usual jeans, then I pull them off and take a jersey dress out of my suitcase. It's the only dress I brought—thrown into my suitcase last minute since I had no idea if I'd ever have a need to wear a dress in Varaz.

But this "maybe date" seems like a more-than-worthy occasion, so I wiggle into it and study myself in the mirror. Back in New York months ago, my dancer friend Cecily had convinced me to buy the dress during a shopping excursion.

The smooth fabric skims over my breasts and hips—clingy but not skin-tight—and the maroon color is a nice complement to my hair and skin. I leave my hair loose, put on silver earrings, and apply a light coating of powder and lipstick.

Pleased with the result of my efforts, I feed Poe his dinner and make sure my purse has all my necessities. When there's a knock on the door, right at seven sharp, my heart jumps with anticipation.

I shouldn't be too excited—I don't know *for sure* that this is a date—but when I open the door, my whole being floods with sparkling light.

He is heart-wrenchingly gorgeous in black trousers, a black

jacket, and a navy-blue dress shirt that makes his eyes the warm color of copper. His thick hair is brushed away from his forehead, and he smells fantastic, like spice and citrus.

"Nell." He smiles, his eyes crinkling at the corners. "You're beautiful."

I open and close my mouth. Darius Hawke all dressed up is a sight to behold, but Darius Hawke all dressed up and *smiling* is enough to both weaken my knees and render me speechless.

But since gawking and jelly-kneed are not great qualities in a dinner companion, I manage to return his smile. "Thank you. So are you."

"I'd have worn a tie, but I forgot to pack one."

"Understandable." I chuckle and step back to get my purse and a lightweight sweater. "This is the only dress I packed. Thanks for giving me a reason to wear it."

"My pleasure. I didn't want to pick any of the flowers in the square, so I got this for you instead." He extends a plastic-wrapped gingerbread flower, decorated with pink and yellow frosting.

I smile, touched that he remembered how much I love gingerbread. I'm also not surprised that he wanted to protect the gardens for the enjoyment of all the townspeople—*protection* is an essential part of his nature, encompassing everything he cares about.

After thanking him, I put the flower in the kitchen to save for later. Poe follows us outside and lopes off to sniff and explore. Darius guides me toward the maze of streets to the once-affluent neighborhood situated along the eastern wall close to the castle.

The large brick-and-stone houses are all boarded up, but a few retail shops are still open on the narrow street curving around the quarter. Though most people frequent Ivan's café, a bar, and a few coffee shops, several dedicated restaurants have reopened in recent months. Il Posto, which was a renowned Italian fine dining establishment before the war, is a lovely glass-

and-stone building with a big picture window framing a view of the mountain.

Darius pulls the door open for me, and I step into the gently lit, brick interior. White-clothed tables and chairs sit in precise, neat rows, but there are no diners or waitstaff anywhere to be seen.

As the door clicks shut, a short, balding man with a wide smile hurries out from the kitchen.

"Mr. Hawke, welcome!" he says in Krasnovian. "And Nell, our town's favorite volunteer. We have not yet had the pleasure of meeting, but I have heard such good things about you. I am Mr. Becherov. Welcome to Il Posto."

He leads us over to a window table—the only one holding a little rose in a blue vase.

"Sit, sit." Mr. Becherov pulls out the two chairs. "I will start to bring you food. It has been so long since I have cooked for anyone else, I hope I have not forgotten how."

Beaming, he lights a half-melted candle on the table and hurries back to the kitchen.

"I ran into him a couple of days ago when I was looking around over here." Darius waits for me to sit down before draping his jacket over the back of the chair and taking his own seat. "He's been struggling with the business and trying to stay open. This afternoon, I asked him if he'd be available to cook dinner for us. I thought you might like something different."

An Italian fine-dining experience in the middle of locked-down Varaz...with Darius, no less...yes, that definitely qualifies as "different."

"Did you come here the last time you were in Varaz?" I ask.

He nods. "You had to make a reservation to get in back then."

As Mr. Becherov brings out wine and appetizers, it becomes even more evident how much he misses hosting guests. He enthusiastically describes each dish, adding a story about its national origin, before hurrying back to the kitchen for more.

The food is delicious, made all the more so by the company and the glowing view of the mountain.

I spear an olive on the salad and hold it up. "I still can't believe you remembered the olives."

Darius smiles slightly. "I can't believe you don't remember you used to love olives. Whenever I brought you some, you'd sit down and eat them right out of the jar."

I chuckle. "Isn't that funny? You have a memory that I've lost. You've held on to it all this time. I wonder if I have any memories about you that you've forgotten."

He taps the side of his head. "Steel trap, baby. You'll never find one."

"A challenge, huh?" I pop the olive into my mouth. "Lemme think. I have a little stone elephant statue that you brought me from India, and you said you'd gotten it at a temple in the north."

"Where I was photographing a territorial dispute in Kashmir." He reaches for a piece of focaccia. "The statue was the Hindu god Ganesh, and it had been blessed by the temple's priest."

"Okay, fine." I roll my eyes. "What about the time you took me to that carnival in San Francisco and—"

"You ate two cones of cotton candy and decided you wanted to be a trapeze artist."

I laugh.

"Let me give you a list, and you tell me if you can't remember any of them." I set my fork down and start ticking items off on my fingers. "Tide pools, shrimp boil from the Water's Edge, you and Dad fishing in the creek before it dried up, bike rides along the coast, that time you were in town for Christmas and took me and Mom to see the Nutcracker ballet...Oh, and the old drive-in movie theater where we saw..."

My voice trails off. What the heck did we—

"The Creature from the Black Lagoon," Darius supplies.

"All right, you win." I shake my head at him in amusement. "You're the keeper of memories."

Though it's lovely to know that he hasn't forgotten all of our shared adventures, I can't help thinking of all the other countless memories he has stored away—many of them too horrific to imagine. He'd once told me that the people he's met and everything he's experienced never go away, which means his "steel trap" must be terribly crowded. I don't know if I'll ever fully understand why he keeps going back for more.

I push the thought out of my head as Mr. Becherov arrives with a platter of gnocchi and more wine. Darius asks me about my art, and I'm happy to tell him about all I've done over the past four years.

"So you were looking for a job in New York." He forks up a piece of pasta. "But what's your ideal career?"

"I don't know yet, honestly. Before I graduated, I thought I wanted to make a living as an artist, but I knew I wouldn't like the instability. Art galleries and museums were the next logical step, but those turned out to be much more competitive than I'd anticipated."

I shrug and take a sip of wine. "So I ended up casting a wide net in the hopes that I'd find an avenue I hadn't considered before. Obviously, that didn't work out, which is how I ended up in Varaz. And though I wish the situation were different, I still love what I've been doing here. After we leave, I might look into jobs with other volunteer organizations."

When he doesn't respond, I glance up to find him watching me, his eyes both warm and speculative.

"What?" I ask.

"I wasn't happy when you turned down my offers in New York," he admits. "For job help and the apartment...I thought you were just being stubborn. But now I get why you wanted to do it on your own. You wouldn't have found your own way if you'd let me get all heavy-handed with you."

"It's funny, because when I left Grenville—which I once never imagined I'd do—I thought that was it, that I'd broken free and was charting my own path." I swirl a ravioli into the sauce. "But the path doesn't always stay the same. It veers off in different directions or gets blocked...or sometimes it just disappears altogether. So you have to find it again or make a new one. It took me a while to learn that lesson."

"Some people never do."

He's not one of those people, though. I gaze at his face—so achingly familiar—and the way the candlelight plays across the angles of his cheekbones.

There never was—never will be—a way I could completely carve him out of my life. If I did, it wouldn't be my life anymore, the only one I've ever known. And I don't want a life devoid of Darius Hawke, no matter how challenging it might be.

"You've probably forged a new path most days of your life," I say.

He shrugs. "I've had to."

"What did your father want you to do?"

He looks up, as if the question almost startled him. Though I don't want the shadow of Conrad Hawke to infringe on the evening, I've never before had the courage to actually ask Darius about him. I've wondered over the years, especially after my father told me I was lucky that I'd never know "what kind of man" Conrad is, but I've never heard the truth from Darius.

"I just remember you once told me he'd been against you pursuing a photojournalism career," I explain. "But you did it anyway. Kind of like how my father wanted me to go to Evergreen College, and...I mean, not that I'm comparing what I did to what you did, but—"

"Nell." He reaches out to put his hand on my arm, his expression darkening. "Your father is nothing like Conrad Hawke. Nothing. Henry might have been misguided, but everything he's done, he's done *for you*. Conrad is incapable of caring about anyone but himself. To him, other people are disposable."

Even his son? The question sticks in my throat.

"What he wanted was for me to be a prodigy, his scion." Darius releases my arm and sits back. "But to do that well, I had to respect and trust him. I never did."

"Why not?"

"I learned at a young age what kind of man he is." He picks up his fork, then puts it down again. "I started to fight him then and never stopped. And he learned that his son would never be what or who he wanted."

"When did you cut off contact with him?"

"After I returned to the States."

After his hostage ordeal. I remember a short clip I'd seen of a press conference when Conrad Hawke had said how pleased he was that his son was home safely again. Darius hadn't been present, and there had been no further news about the two men. That must also mean that Conrad wasn't involved in Darius's recovery.

I restrain all the questions I still have when Mr. Becherov bustles over with dessert—a decadent tiramisu—and coffee.

After Darius pays the bill and we thank Mr. Becherov profusely, we start walking back home. A chill cuts through the air, and Darius drapes his jacket around my shoulders. I slip my arms into the too-big sleeves, loving the warmth and scent of him clinging to the material.

"This was a lovely evening," I tell him. "Thank you."

"Thank you for being so..." He shrugs, but I don't need to hear what he left unspoken. A momentous shift is happening between us, as if my seeing him stripped raw has laid fresh ground for us to cultivate something new.

We start down a sloped hill leading back to Harmony Square. Poe approaches us from the direction of the Koroleva Café, where he was no doubt filling up on table scraps. He greets us with much tail wagging and falls into step beside me.

"So." I nudge Darius's elbow as we enter the apartment building and go up the stairs. "Was this a date?"

"I don't date."

"Yeah, sure. I'll bet you dress nice and bring gingerbread flowers to all your dinner companions."

He throws me a faint scowl. "That was an accident."

"Mmm. Like the way your lips landed on mine was an accident?"

His scowl deepens, even as heat flashes in his eyes. "You were in my way."

"Lucky me."

A laugh rumbles through his chest. He stops and turns toward me. I back up. He advances, crowding me up against the door of my apartment. His wide shoulders practically block out the rest of the hallway.

He skims his gaze over my face. "You're in my way again."

"No place I'd rather be."

He cups the side of my face in his hand. I could be anywhere in the world—in a desert, on a mountaintop, in the middle of the ocean—and all I'd have to do is close my eyes to remember that gentle touch, like he's holding something valuable.

"You could be right." He brushes his thumb across my lips.

"About what?"

"This might be a date." He moves his other hand behind me and gathers the length of my hair in his fist.

I lift my eyebrows. "You said you don't date."

"I don't." He lowers his head, his lips touching mine. "So thanks for being my first date."

"My absolute pleasure."

He kisses me harder. Everything in me goes soft and hot. I wind my arms around him, pressing my hand to the back of his neck. He tightens his grip on my hair and deepens the kiss, urging my lips apart, sliding his tongue across mine. My breasts rub against his chest, the friction creating a surge of heat straight to my core.

The whole of my being, everything I am, everything I feel,

centers on the touch of his mouth, the endless strength of his body that I have longed to explore. I murmur his name, aching for him to come inside with me and continue this delicious seduction.

"Ah, Nell." With a half laugh, half groan, he lifts his head. "That was meant to be a polite good-night kiss."

"It doesn't have to stop at a kiss." I run a finger down the buttons of his shirt. "Honestly, Darius, if you haven't gotten the message by now, you need to find a new mail delivery system."

His eyes crinkle with amusement. "My sweet, beautiful Nell. I want you more than I want to breathe, but that's not what tonight is about."

Though disappointment nudges at me, I note that he said *tonight*. That leaves open the possibility that tomorrow night...or any night in the future...just might be about what we both so obviously want. What we've wanted for years.

"All right, then." I smooth my hand over his torso, shivering at the sensation of his hard, ridged abdomen through his shirt. "I've gotten pretty good at waiting. I can wait a little while longer."

His eyes darken. He brushes his lips against mine one more time, then backs up to his apartment across the hall. "See you tomorrow."

"Yes, you will." I give him a cheeky smile and go inside.

I feel like little lights are twinkling through my veins. Despite these very odd circumstances, I'm *happy*. The reality of Darius Hawke, his everlasting presence in my life, is so much better than the flimsy dreams that have sustained me for four years.

No matter what happens between us, he will always be there. He will always come to me.

CHAPTER 16

Nell

MAY HAS MELTED AWAY the spring chill, and the trees in Harmony Square begin flourishing with wavy, green leaves. Two days after my now-official date with Darius, Alexei and I make another trip up to Bram Castle to bring down a truckload of boxes, though it's astonishing how much artwork is still packed away in storage.

"When the war started, all neighboring towns and villages brought their treasures to be stored here." Alexei closes the huge wooden doors to just one of the many rooms, which spread like a maze through the lower part of the castle. "Then a convoy transported more from Telina when the city was attacked."

We walk back to the truck at the loading dock. I've only been up here a few times, and though the main part of the castle remains closed, Alexei has given me a tour of the grounds.

The whole compound is like a layering of time itself—the original twelfth-century fortifications surround interior courtyards, which contain later structures like a Romanesque tower and a sixteenth-century Gothic-style chapel. The views from the outward-facing walls span miles in every direction with an especially spectacular panorama of the surrounding forests and lake.

"One day, I will show you the frescos and mosaics on the interior walls," Alexei assures me as we make the bumpy, precarious trip back down the narrow mountain road. "The chapel has very beautiful scenes of the Old Testament. I am hoping Global Rebuild will have funds to help us restore them. Though the castle was spared during the war, both it and the artwork have suffered neglect. We must help it all to breathe again."

I smile. "That's a nice way of putting it."

"Today is especially poignant." He steers the truck slowly around a sharp turn. "It is the day of what used to be the Friendship Festival, when we celebrate the fourteenth-century unification by King Braslov of Krasnovar's three provinces. The Friendship Festival always had much dancing, feasting, traditional crafts, and many activities inside the castle. We had a big parade through the entire town. Many people came to Varaz just to enjoy the festival. But it has not been celebrated in many years."

"Was it ever celebrated outside of Varaz?"

"No. Only here. We had to stop during the war, then the castle is closed, then not enough people or tourists to celebrate." Alexei shrugs as we pass through the eastern stone gate leading into town. "And it cost money, of course. But when traditions fade, it is difficult to revive them."

"It doesn't have to be a huge festival with tourists, though. Can't it still be done on a smaller scale just for the people of Varaz?"

"I suppose, but I think everyone in town is occupied with getting their lives back rather than celebrating."

"Maybe celebrating should be part of getting one's life back."

He chuckles. "A valid point."

He parks at the museum loading dock, and several people come out to help us unload the truck.

"Can we go inside the castle before it's open to the public?" I ask as we guide a cart toward the freight elevator.

"I have the keys, so maybe one day I will show you." Alexei punches the button for the basement. "We plan to open by midsummer. After our work at the museum is completed, the next step is to transport artwork back to other towns, then organize the castle interior before opening to tourists. Who will hopefully begin to arrive by then. If all is well."

Surely all will be well by then.

It's not until I'm at the computer, logging in the items we brought back, that I realize the date. May 20. The day I was scheduled to leave Krasnovar and return to New York. I was supposed to be gone long before midsummer.

I'm suddenly cold. Though my changing relationship with Darius—not to mention just his being here—has eased my fear, the fact is that we're still trapped in a country that, by all accounts, appears to have tipped back into outright war.

Since our source of information is mainly limited to the TV and radio news, we've only heard about attacks, skirmishes, and riots. My father continues to bombard the State Department with demands to take action, but we have no messages from either the embassy or Global Rebuild about how they're going to help us.

At lunchtime, I go in search of Darius and find him standing at the bar in the café, one booted foot on the barstool rung and his gaze fixed darkly on the TV.

Despite our much-welcome détente, he's increasingly frustrated by the lack of answers and his inability to find a way out. In fact, since the Krasnovian military banned him from the roads, he's handling the lockdown like a tiger handles being trapped in a too-small cage. The only blessing is that he hasn't had another flashback—at least, not one he's told me about—although that doesn't mitigate his irritation.

Most of the time he either paces through town growling to himself and arguing with the municipal workers about the Wi-Fi, or he's holed up listening to transmissions on the radio scanner. I'm pretty sure he's about ready to start digging an escape tunnel through the mountain, even if he has to use a plastic spoon.

The townspeople are mostly unfazed by him—a big, grumpy American is annoying but of little concern given what's happening to the country. Ivan always has a beer ready for him, the bookstore owner challenges him to chess matches, and the construction crews recruit him to help work on exterior building restoration.

Keeping busy gives him a physical outlet, but I know his impatience stems from more than just the volatile situation. He's running out of ways to take action.

"Hey." I sit on the barstool next to him, noting the set lines of his face and an edge of anger that hadn't been there when I saw him this morning. "What happened?"

"You should be on a plane right now."

"I know, but I'm here." I put my hand on his arm. "What happened?"

"I managed to get ahold of my old friend Savko. He's the one who held on to my camera when I was a hostage." Darius narrows his gaze on the TV. "He gave me more information about what's going on. The PLF attacks are spreading, and they're only allowing emergency flights out of the airports. The embassy has evacuated."

"The US embassy?" I shake my head. "In Saldem?"

"They brought in helicopters to get the officials across the border to Moldova."

"And everyone left?"

"According to Savko, yes. There's no US presence in Krasnovar anymore."

"But…"

"There's a chance they're still planning to try and get you out." A bitter tone underscores his voice. "But I'm not counting on it. Given their limited staff and lack of response, I never was."

I've known that, since it's the reason he came to Varaz himself instead of leaving it up to the officials. But now he hates even the idea that the government hasn't just failed to help, they've apparently abandoned me.

Though I'm not thrilled about that either, there's no question I trust Darius far more than I trust any embassy official—even when the road out keeps getting blocked.

"So there's no one we can contact?" I finally ask.

He shakes his head. "Even though I didn't expect their help, having US personnel in the country offered some degree of support. Now it'll be tougher to get to the border since we can't use the embassy as a safety net anymore. But it's not the first time I've been stuck in a country without a US presence."

I slide my palm down his arm to his hand. "I might not have said this two weeks ago, but it's the truth now. Selfishly, I'm really glad you're here."

He tightens his fingers around mine. "I'd intended for you to be back at home long before now. But Savko knows we're here. He's putting word out across the newswire and is working with several foreign journalists. I don't know what they can do at this point, but they'll try."

He looks at his watch, as if there's a deadline he has to meet. In his mind, he's already missed it.

"Did you bring your camera with you?" I ask.

He frowns. "You mean here?"

"Yes, when you came to Varaz. Did you bring your camera?"

"Yeah, it's still in the car."

"Go get it."

"Why?"

I poke his arm. "Just go get it."

With a faint scowl, he strides outside to where his car is parked in the square. I follow, waiting as he takes his old camera bag from the trunk. Then I lead him into the section of town that climbs toward the mountain—a crisscrossing maze of narrow streets, sharp corners, and topsy-turvy houses that are still abandoned, boarded-up, and waiting for repair.

"Don't you have to go back to the museum?" he asks.

"I have Monday afternoons off. There." I stop in front of a building and point to the pediment, where an old, faded fresco is etched against the peeling plaster. "That was painted in the fourteenth century. There are dozens more like it throughout town."

"Interesting."

"Take a picture of it."

He affixes a lens to his camera and adjusts the focus. After snapping a shot, he lowers the camera, peers at the fresco, and takes a few more pictures. "What are these for?"

"Your job is to document what's happening in the world, right?" I continue up a steep incline to the Holy Trinity Church where Alexei and I work on Thursdays. "To tell real stories and raise awareness of situations that people might otherwise not pay much attention to. Well, this is one of them."

I spread my arms out to indicate the town. "Varaz is a historic town that's been badly affected by a war and is struggling to rebuild. It has an astonishing, complex history of its own. So why don't you use your talent to tell the story of Varaz and the people who live here?"

He squints at a half-timber house with a sloped roof that probably dates back to the town's origins. "I'm not that kind of photographer."

"Darius, you can take amazing photos of *anything*. Just because you've focused on war doesn't mean that's all you're capable of seeing."

Just the opposite. He sees so much. He's the first person who ever saw *me*.

He studies the camera, a crease between his eyebrows. The afternoon sun gleams against his thick, dark hair. His long fingers move with comfortable assurance over the camera body and lens.

A longing so familiar that it's become part of me rises to my chest. I still vividly recall the day I saw him holding his camera in the house on Dearborne Street.

I hadn't known at the time that he'd been battling his inability to take another picture, that his captivity had twisted and crushed that vital part of his identity. I hadn't known about the promise he'd made to himself in his cell—that the next photo he took would be of "something good."

All I'd known was that I was enraptured by the way he cradled his camera, as if it were shaped for his hands alone. And I'd wanted, deep down in a place I hadn't even acknowledged yet, to know what it would feel like if he focused on *me* with that same intensity. As if nothing else existed for him in that moment.

"When was the last time you took a picture that wasn't related to a war?" I ask.

He doesn't answer. The lines around his mouth deepen, but a flame flickers in his eyes.

You. In Grenville.

The unspoken words fall like leaves between us. I don't know what happened to the photos he'd taken of me that night, but I remember every detail of how I'd looked and who I'd been in Darius Hawke's eyes. I will never forget that I'd been his *something good.*

"Listen." I approach. "I know this is tough for you, but you're going to drive everyone crazy unless you channel your energy into something more productive. I've found so many interesting things to draw around here, and it would be wonderful if the town had a photographic documentation of its history. Especially as it's right in the middle of rebuilding. I know we'll be leaving soon, but you can still get started on it while we're here."

He finally agrees, though he's not exactly brimming over with enthusiasm. We continue walking, and he shoots images of the art and architecture, as well as the kids playing in the schoolyard, a few shopkeepers, two nuns heading toward the square. We climb the stairs to the top of the wall that encloses the town, and he takes pictures of the views from all angles as the sun begins to descend on the other side of the sky.

Though "getting out" is always at the forefront of his mind, by the time we start back to the apartment, he's spent several hours focusing on something else. I know he's sharply aware that the nightmares could ambush him again, so putting that fear aside even temporarily is a small victory.

"You haven't gotten a new camera?" I indicate his old Nikon. It's the same camera he had four years ago—even long before that. I'd know it anywhere.

He shrugs. "I haven't needed a new one. This camera and I have been through a lot together."

"What was your first ever camera?"

"An old Polaroid. I'd found it in the garage when I was nine. Your mother and I used to take pictures of each other making faces."

"Did she put any of those pictures in her album?" I glance at him, feeling an old ache of longing for a tattered photo album I hadn't known existed until he'd mentioned it back in Grenville. "Do you remember telling me about it? You said she'd filled it with pictures of you and her as kids, and of her and Odette. My father said you couldn't find it."

He shakes his head slowly, regret darkening his eyes. "I'm sorry, Nell. I did look for it. I can't imagine your mother would have left it behind after she married Henry."

"Maybe Odette took it with her back to Russia." *Or maybe my mother burned it, like she did all our other family photos.*

"Maybe, although she knew it belonged to Katherine."

"Did she take the pictures?" I ask.

"Some of them. Others were taken by friends, maybe some distant relatives. I took a lot of photos of Katherine and Odette."

"Sounds like your interest in photography might have started long before you were in high school," I remark.

"You're probably right. Have you kept up with photography?"

"Not really. I took a photography class at the Art Institute… not nearly as good as yours, by the way…but mostly I've taken pictures in connection with my paintings or for a collage. I've done a few drawings based on photographs, though. Drawing is still my first love."

"Given your talent, it obviously loves you back."

My breath catches. His remark is casual, almost offhanded, but also strangely poetic—and he's always been far too grounded in hard reality to have time for poetry.

As we start back to the town center, faint music drifts toward us. I assume it's coming from a radio nearby, but it gets louder the closer we get to Harmony Square. There's also an increasing abundance of voices and conversation.

"What's going on?" I ask.

"I don't know." Darius slows, putting his hand out in front of me as if the noise might pose a threat.

We turn the corner to the square, and I stop in surprise. String lights gleam and twinkle from the trees around the plaza and decorate several shop windows. A five-piece band is playing beside the fountain, and people are setting up tables and spreading blankets out on the grass. Children are racing around, laughing and chasing each other.

It looks as if everyone in town is either gathering in the plaza or approaching with baskets and boxes. I spot Brian helping to put lights up around the fountain, and Hazel and several others setting up folding chairs.

"Alexei!" I wave as he hurries across the street from the pharmacy. "What is all this?"

He stops and spreads his arms out, giving me a wide grin. "You said we should celebrate getting our lives back, yes? You were right. So welcome to the new Friendship Festival, with small numbers but big heart."

With a laugh, I hug him. "This is wonderful."

"I told Sofia, and she and her father sent out grapevine to announce the plan." He returns my hug, his eyes sparkling. "Everyone rushed to help make it happen tonight, the exact day the king signed the unification papers. We will have music, dancing, food, and even a small parade. Come, come."

Waving for me and Darius to follow him, he heads to the plaza.

The hastily organized festival is an absolute delight. A group of women staff several long folding tables piled with traditional Krasnovian dishes, from cabbage rolls to sausage stew and pickled peppers. Mr. Becherov's contribution includes lasagna and *pasta alla carbonara*.

After all the dishes are set out, people line up to serve themselves buffet-style. Ivan brings out bottles of cold beer and soda. There are ball games, relay races, and a version of "capture the flag." An expanse of grass illuminated by the overhead string lights turns into a dance floor, and people alternate between eating, drinking, and dancing.

At first, I think Darius might decline to participate in the festivities, but he helps with the last-minute setting up of tables and chairs and brings several crates of soda over from the café.

After making our way through the buffet, we join Sofia and Alexei at a picnic blanket near the cathedral steps. The food is delicious and plentiful, though it's not long before Sofia's twin boys corral Darius into refereeing a game of soccer. He amiably accompanies them to the makeshift field, and again I'm pleased that he has something else to focus on—for a short time, at least.

"Nell, Alexei tells me this was your idea." Sofia finishes her soda and gives me a smile.

I chuckle. "He's exaggerating. I made an offhanded comment, which he and everyone else turned into this amazing event."

"But you were the one who inspired it." She takes my hand, pulling me to my feet. "You must be a part of the celebration."

She leads me to the pharmacy, where a dozen women ranging in age from ten to seventy are busy getting dressed in brightly colored skirts and vests.

"The Friendship Festival always has a big parade through town, usually with horses, hay carts, bands, so many things." Sofia picks up a black skirt decorated with vivid red and yellow ribbons. "So this year we are just a few, but we have traditional Krasnovian folk costumes, and we will circle the square three times in honor of the three provinces. This looks like it will fit you."

"You want me to join the parade?"

"Of course." Sofia laughs. "Why would you not? You are unofficial resident of Varaz now. An honorary Krasnovian."

The designation strikes me with unexpected force. My chest constricts.

Sofia holds the skirt up to my waist, then catches my eye. "Nell, what is the matter? You do not wish to participate in the parade?"

"No, I..." I clear my throat. "I would love to. Thank you so much for asking me."

"Put on this skirt and this blouse." Sofia hands me a white blouse intricately embroidered with bright red, yellow, and green floral designs. "I will help you with the sash and your headband."

The other women are also delighted and enthused about helping me. They tell me all about the symbolism of the costume, which is a strikingly colorful outfit that includes an embroidered vest, a red sash with gold tassels, and a floral headband with long, trailing ribbons. The skirt is worn over a longer white petticoat with a band of flowers sewn around the hem, and one of the women finds a pair of embroidered slippers that fit me perfectly.

"We also have some musical instruments." Sofia hurries over to a corner of the pharmacy where the supplies are organized. "You can use *trimal*. I think in English it is called tambourine."

She brings me a tambourine decorated with ribbons and pom-poms. The men are getting ready at the bookstore, and we all go outside to meet them at the corner of Dandelion Street.

They are resplendent in black pants and vests, red sashes, and white shirts—all embellished with the colorful floral designs. Josef, the bookstore owner, is carrying a large Krasnovian flag, and the others have smaller flags or instruments.

I catch sight of Darius taking pictures of the festivities. For such a tall, well-built man, he moves with surprising stealth. Almost no one glances his way, as if he's not even there. It's a quality he must have spent years honing.

"Everyone, get in line, please!" Sofia calls.

She corrals us all into a parade-like formation as the crowd quiets down. The band begins to play a few notes of the Krasnovian national anthem. Everyone stands, and the men take off their hats.

An air of solemnity falls over the square as the parade begins, Josef leading the way with the large flag rippling in the dusk. People begin to sing, the lyrics and music suffused with both pride and a touch of sorrow.

As the anthem draws to a close, the crowd applauds. The band strikes up a livelier tune, and the parade turns into an energetic celebration of laughter, waving, and lots of impromptu dancing and gymnastics.

It's so much fun. We dance, skip, and sashay our way around the square amidst applause, cheers, and catcalls. I alternate between shaking the tambourine's cymbals and striking the drum, though the music becomes more of a rambunctious cacophony rather than any particular tune.

The men weave around the women, pausing to grab us for a quick twirl before showing off with cartwheels and backflips. By the time we make our way around the square the first time, I'm already out of breath.

Several children run alongside the parade, and other people join in the back as we start our second circling. I'm so busy playing the tambourine and keeping up with the energetic pace that I don't think about Darius...until I glance over and see him. He's standing with one shoulder against a tree trunk, his camera in his hands and his gaze fixed on me like a key turning in a lock.

All the breath escapes my lungs. Around me, people keep whirling and shouting, but the slice of time and earth where I'm standing goes quiet and very still. As if the place inside me that has always been reserved for Darius Hawke, the place of utter certainty that survived even when I fought against it, is expanding into the world itself. Making room for both of us.

He lifts the camera to his eye and focuses the lens on me. A smile flies up from my heart and spreads across my face. A smile meant only for him.

Someone bumps into me from behind. With a quick apology, I tear my gaze from Darius and keep moving. My heart is racing, but a sense of peace spreads through my blood and into my bones.

For months now, nothing has gone as I'd planned, as I'd expected, as I'd hoped...but everything *has* unfolded in a way that led to this. Both of us forced to confront the very things that caused us pain, but also to do it together. Maybe even to finally let those things go.

I don't see him again as the parade makes its way around the square two more times. Halfway through our last circle, almost everyone else joins in for the final march to the fountain, where the band is still playing. Cheers and laughter fill the air as we pile our instruments on an empty table and disperse in search of drinks and more food.

Darius steps in front of me, holding out a cold bottle of soda.

"Thank you." Gratefully, I tip my head back and let the bubbly drink flow down my throat.

The bottle is half gone before I stop to take a breath, wiping my mouth with the back of my hand. "I had no idea when I woke up this morning that I'd be playing the tambourine in a parade celebrating a medieval king's unification of the country. Actually, I didn't know that two hours ago."

"From where I was standing, you look like you were made for tambourines, parades, and unification." A warm, golden heat rises to his eyes as he skims his gaze over me. "Not to mention that outfit. You're stunning."

I smile, ridiculously pleased by the compliment. "Thank you."

He inclines his head toward the area where people are dancing under the twinkling white lights. "Come dance with me."

My heart drops. "Oh no, I…I can't dance."

"You were just dancing in the parade."

"That wasn't dancing. That was following along."

"Then come follow along with me." He puts his camera on a table and closes his hand around mine, engulfing my fingers in his palm.

I accompany him across the plaza—more because I don't want him to let me go rather than any desire to attempt dancing.

"Wait a sec." I stop, tugging him to a halt. "*You* can dance?"

He lifts an eyebrow. "You thought I couldn't?"

"Well, I guess I've never really thought about it. I've never seen you dance."

"I'm actually pretty good at a lot of things you've never seen me do."

Heat flickers through me. I have no doubt that I've seen many of those "things" in my fantasies.

He reaches out to straighten my floral headband before leading me over to the grassy dance floor. The band is playing Krasnovian folk and dance music—lively, upbeat songs accompanied by bells, flutes, a kettle drum, a hurdy-gurdy, and a guitar. Some of the older couples are mirroring each other's steps in sync with traditional folk dances, while others look like they're just winging it. Now that the parade and dinner are over, the dance area is expanding throughout the square and into the streets.

"Follow my lead." Darius slips his arm around me, settling his right hand under my shoulder blade and tightening his left hand on mine.

"Okay, but I'm sorry in advance if I step on your toes."

He chuckles, his breath brushing against the hair at my temple. "I won't even feel it."

He pulls me closer, guiding me into what should be a simple two-step movement. "Nell, relax. I promise it's easy."

"Where did you learn how to dance anyway?" I force myself to look up at him rather than down at my feet.

"My stepmother Odette. She taught me when I was ten or eleven. She believed every man should know how to dance." He leads me slowly into a circle in time with the music. "Then in high school, I had a girlfriend who was on the dance team. Between the two of them, I guess it stuck."

"Have you had a lot of opportunities to dance since then?" I step on his toe and wince.

"A few." He moves forward and to the side, his sense of rhythm effortless. "Usually at a fancy shindig put on by some press organization. Haven't been to one of those in years, though."

Given what I know about his immersion in war, this might be one of the few times in a while when he's actually doing something carefree and pleasurable. The realization eases my self-consciousness, and slowly I relax and go wherever he takes me.

His guidance is smooth and confident, and it's not long before I'm enjoying the way we're moving in sync.

He spins and twirls me easily, keeping us both out of the way of other dancers and making sure no one bumps into me. He has always moved with an assured, masculine grace, but watching him move to the rhythm of music makes me breathless from more than just exertion. Our bodies touch, retreat, touch again.

I'm filled with exhilaration, both from the sheer fun of the festival and this intense new energy coursing between us. In all my thoughts and fantasies about Darius, I'd never imagined we would one day *dance* together.

We step away from the main crush and into the street where there's more room. My shoes click against the cobblestones. Perspiration trickles down my spine, and my hair sticks to my neck.

The music gets louder, bolstered by whoops and clapping from the crowd. The joy of the festival-goers is palpable as the men begin a heavy foot-stomping dance that seems to shake the earth.

Ivan saunters past, giving me a wink before grabbing my hand and whirling me away from Darius. With a laugh, I let him spin me into a circle. He leads me back over to the plaza, but we don't make it halfway there before Darius steps between us and takes possession of me again.

He gives Ivan a narrow look. With a good-natured harrumph, the café owner departs in search of a more available partner.

Darius pulls me to him. A scant column of air separates us. Flames rise in my blood.

"Hmm." I slide my arms around his waist. "If I were a gambler, I'd bet you were jealous."

"Ante up, baby." He tightens his hold on me, his breath stirring my hair. "You'd win the whole pot."

Pleasure billows through me, light and airy, unweighted by shadows. I drink in his smells of shaving cream and clean sweat.

He slows, spreading his hands over my lower back, our bodies so close my breasts brush against him. Heat radiates through his T-shirt. Another raucous cheer rises from the crowd in the plaza as the band launches into a popular folk song.

But for me, the noise recedes. The thump of my pulse fills my ears. We're underneath a streetlamp. The light encloses us in a circle. Darius is still holding me, but hardly moving anymore. The exhilaration in my veins shifts into a heavy throb.

I slip my hands under his shirt and rub the warm, taut skin of his lower back. He tenses slightly in reaction. Emboldened, I glide my fingers up his spine, tracing the perfect structure of his vertebrae before closing the distance and pressing our bodies together.

Though he is so much bigger than me, all of my curves find places to settle, shaping easily against his powerful frame. I can feel the blood coursing in his veins, the energy seething relentlessly through him.

My breath shaky, I look up. He's watching me, his expression shuttered but his gaze dark and intense. He will always be impenetrable on the surface, but I've learned to read what is written in the depths of his golden-brown eyes.

Tension laces his shoulders. A low curse breaks from his throat. Then he anchors his hand on the back of my neck and brings his mouth down on mine.

Hard.

CHAPTER 17

Nell

HEAT EXPLODES in me like fireworks, sparkling and popping. I rise to my tiptoes to meet him. My breasts crush against the wall of his chest. He locks his arm around me and urges my lips open with his mouth.

My blood surges, rolling like the tides as our tongues slide together and his breath fills my throat. A haze of arousal descends over me, so all-consuming that I'm barely aware of the dancing and revelries still bursting across the street. I spread my fingers over his back and sink into the kiss.

I inhale, absorbing him into me all over again, filling my veins with his closeness, his touch, his strength. His lack of restraint.

Though tension still lines his body, it's not from the tortured battle of his conscience that I've confronted in the past. This is different. This is the stifled force of desire breaking free and rising to the surface. This is Darius *allowing* it to.

A haze of urgency descends over me. He lifts his head and

steps forward. I back up against the side of a building. He wraps the length of my hair in his hand, holding me captive.

I want to tell him he doesn't have to—I am bound to him by a thousand invisible, unbreakable threads—but his grip is strangely exciting, as if for the first time he won't let me go even if I want him to.

Which I absolutely do not.

"Kiss me again," I breathe.

His gaze slips to my mouth. He doesn't just kiss me. He owns me. He tilts my head back and slants his mouth over mine in a hot, compelling possession that unbinds all my pent-up need and lust.

As I'm sinking into the pool of heat, he stills suddenly, flexing his hand against my lower back. A sharp disappointment clouds my urgency the instant before I hear someone calling our names.

With a resigned, choked laugh, Darius presses his lips to my temple and eases away from me. He takes my hand, and I struggle to catch my breath as we join in the group national dance that marks the closure of the Friendship Festival.

Later, after we've helped clean up the plaza, two of the women pack up several containers of leftover food for us and Poe. Darius hefts the box into his arms, and I retrieve his camera from another table.

He follows me into my apartment and sets the box on the kitchen counter. Though I'm still all worked up with adrenaline and unfulfilled desire, I think the heated moment has passed.

Then I turn and find him watching me, his eyes glittering with golden flames. My breath catches. A lock of his dark hair clings damply to his forehead, and a five o'clock shadow darkens his jaw.

I'm still holding his camera. It's far bigger and heavier than any camera I've ever used. The casing is badly scarred, the strap worn and frayed. Slowly I take the lens cap off and lift the camera to my eye.

I fix him in the lens. He doesn't move, doesn't smile. His gaze is pensive and direct. I snap the shutter, securing the image of him on the microcard even though it's not necessary. This is the first photo I've taken of him, but I know every angle and plane of his face. I've drawn him countless times, my pencil etching the shape of his mouth, his thick eyelashes, the column of his throat. I almost know his face better than my own.

I set the camera on the counter. The air is warm and heavy, and faint guitar music still drifts through the open window, as if the musician is saying goodbye.

Darius steps closer, reaching out to straighten the floral headband I'm still wearing. He slides his hand down the side of my face and rests his palm against my neck. His thumb brushes my clavicle, the slow, rhythmic movement quickening my pulse. I settle my hand on his chest. He lifts one of the ribbons trailing from my headband and twists it around his forefinger.

This time, we meet each other halfway. Our lips fit together seamlessly. Against my palm, his heartbeat increases, resonant as a drum.

He brings his hands to the back of my head, sliding his fingers into my hair and holding me in the way that feels both possessive and protective at the same time. He could be the only man I've ever kissed, and I would still know to my soul that he is without compare. His kiss is so skilled, so easy, as he alternates both gentle and firm pressure, each touch lighting a new fire inside me.

In my response, I give him all the good things I've ever felt for him. Love, hope, adoration, need. There are so many kinds of kisses in the world, and it feels as if this one contains them all. As if we're the only people ever to discover the sheer pleasure of exploring each other with our lips. As if I'm the first woman in the history of time to be kissed.

I slide my lips to his jaw, breathing him in and rubbing my cheek against his stubble. He brings his hand under my chin, spreading his fingers across my cheek. I pull his head down, locking my gaze to his, willing him to believe in the truth of this bond we share.

But now, finally, I don't need to wish for anything. He knows. He's always known; he just hasn't let himself acknowledge it until this moment.

I fumble to unfasten the laces at the front of my vest. Before I can even get the first one loose, he lifts me into his arms, then takes three steps forward and lowers me onto the bed. He looks at me for a long moment, his eyes as dark and fathomless as the ocean. Seeing me in ways that no one else ever has or ever will.

He runs his hand through my hair, taking off my headband before cupping my neck and kissing me again. I open for him in utter submission. Part of my mind is still stunned that this is happening, that Darius is kissing and touching me with growing urgency—*finally*—but the disbelief is overcome by my deep, abiding certainty that we have always been inevitable. *This* was meant to happen.

He trails his lips across my cheek and down to my neck, flicking his tongue against the hollow of my throat. My clothes are too heavy, pressing against my skin. He moves back to pull my shoes off, skimming his fingers up my legs and body as he returns to unfasten the intricate laces of my vest.

Easing it from my shoulders, he strips me slowly, like he's unwrapping a gift. He presses his mouth to every exposed inch of skin, and by the time I'm down to only my underwear, I'm trembling with need.

He puts his hand over the ladder of thick, raised scars on my thigh, tracing the lines with his fingers. A fresh shiver rattles through me. He's the only other person in the world who has touched my scars.

"You are so damned beautiful." His voice is a low, husky rumble against my bare breast.

A wild tendril of love and lust blooms through me. I have

wanted this for so long. I have dreamed of him on top of me, inside me. I've imagined us touching, kissing, exploring each other everywhere. But my fantasies could never come close to the reality of *him*.

He is an eclipse, overtaking my body, my soul, my heart. Heat courses through my veins as he caresses my breasts before sliding his hand down between my thighs. He brushes his fingers against my cleft through my underwear, murmuring a noise of pleasure in his throat.

"Take them off." I squirm under his touch, my breath coming faster and faster. "I want to be naked."

He tugs the panties over my hips and drops them to the floor. Four years ago, I'd wondered if he'd like how I look, if he'd compare me to other women. As much as I'd loved him touching me, I'd hated how it made him feel.

But now...his dark gaze is filled with pure want. He strokes his hand from my breasts to my thighs gently, as if he's trying not to startle an anxious kitten. I want to be the one to undress him, to finally explore all the intricacies of his powerful body, but my need is taking over, swift and intense.

I tug the front of his T-shirt. "Take this off too. And before you ask, you don't have to worry. I've been on the pill for a year because of period issues, and I've been waiting for you a lot longer than that. I also trust you with every part of me and my life. Hurry."

I pull at his shirt again, and he slowly hitches it over his head. My mouth goes dry. His chest is a landscape of hard planes and ridges covered with taut, bronzed skin and a perfect pattern of hair arrowing straight down into his jeans.

He is not flawless. His body is marked by scars from bullets and God knows what else—I can't bring myself to think about the scars on his back—but the brutal evidence of his ability to survive makes him even more unfathomably beautiful.

I urge him down to me, drawing in a sharp breath at the

sensation of his chest against my breasts. My nipples tighten even more from the delicious abrasion. He glides his fingers to my sex, his groan muffled against my neck as he discovers how wet and ready I already am.

I close my eyes, clutching his biceps. Arousal spins inside me, and I want the tense anticipation to both end and to last forever.

"I lost track of how often I thought about this." His whisper is smoky and guttural, his fingers stroking me with slow expertise. "The way you arch your hips and your whole body trembles when you come. Let me feel it again."

I'm helpless against the gentle command, not to mention the precise circling of his thumb and fingers. The tension breaks into a firestorm of sparks. I cry out his name, digging my fingers into his arms as he urges the sensations from my body.

I fall back, panting and hot. It's not enough. I'm not sure anything will ever be enough.

His eyes smolder. He moves away from me to kick off his shoes and socks before shedding his jeans. The bulge of his erection strains against the front of his boxer briefs. Though I've dreamed for years about seeing him naked, the sudden proximity of his size and hardness gives me a flicker of trepidation.

Darius rests his hands on the bed on either side of me, his gaze locking to mine. I know exactly what he's asking. I curve my hand to the back of his neck and press my lips against his.

"You," I whisper, "are every *yes* I've ever had. All the *yeses* I've kept locked inside me, waiting for the moment I could give them to you. Waiting for now."

He lifts his head, a shadow of disbelief crossing his expression —not because he doesn't believe me, but because of who he is. Before any doubts can take hold, I settle my hand against his groin. My heart leaps into a frenzy of lust, emboldening me to slip my shaking hand into his briefs and—

Holy god.

It's like nothing I've ever felt before—a hot, hard column of flesh with veins pulsing just beneath the surface. With no small degree of fascination, I run my fingers over the shaft to the smooth, damp crown.

"You're so..." I clench my thighs together, both unbearably excited and nervous at the idea of him pushing his full length into me. "Um...large."

A laugh chokes out of him. "And you're so impossibly sweet. We don't have to—"

"Oh, yes, we do." I wrap my arms around him. "I want you. I want this. I want *us*. Yes, yes, yes."

I pull him down to me. The shock of his near-naked body on top of mine wrenches a gasp from my throat. He is everything I've ever imagined and more—a powerful, unbreakable fortress, his muscles both tense and pliable. His erection throbs against my thigh.

Stripes of light from the streetlamps come through the shutters. Voices still rise from the square, but my world distills to the press of Darius's lips and the weight of his body. Fresh arousal winds through me as his kisses fall like rain on my neck, my breasts, my belly. His stubble scrapes my skin like the finest sandpaper.

I pull at his briefs, and when he finally takes them off, I stare in breathless shock at the length of his cock. I touch him again, mesmerized by the size and shape of this purely male shaft that will somehow fit inside me. When I tighten my fingers around him, his low groan releases something deep in my soul, eliciting a surge of both power and pleasure.

I urge him on top of me again. Though I ache to touch his sculpted body, I've been waiting so long and wanting him so desperately that I'm too impatient for slow explorations right now. I lie back, lifting and parting my thighs. My nerves are stretched taut, like violin strings humming and vibrating.

He is locked with restraint, his breath hot against my lips, his big hands stroking downward to open me wider—first with a light touch, then one finger, then two. I feel myself softening in readiness, like he's priming me to take him. He eclipses me again, his hips between my legs as he starts to press slowly into me. I grip the bedcovers.

He pauses, dragging in a breath, his eyes fixed on mine. "Tell me what you want. If you need me to stop—"

"God, no." My whole body is aflame, everything centered on the sensation of him partway inside me. "Don't stop. Never stop."

He edges his hand between us and strokes my clit, loosening the tension winding through my lower body. Somehow I relax enough to let him in another inch, and then he's moving into me with a slow, stinging glide that has me alternately arching up against him and retreating.

I bite my lip. I'm burning, my mind and heart wanting this with the whole force of my being, and my body tempted to resist the invasion.

His control is unyielding. He stops, gazes down at me, waits for me to adjust to him. Unspoken questions flick through the heavy air. In response, I slide my arms around his back and hug my legs to his hips. My thighs already ache. I can't possibly open up for him any farther.

"Ah, fuck, Nell." His voice echoes through me like thunder, his powerful frame resonating with tension and self-control.

"Keep going." My fingers press against the scars on his back. "Oh, please…"

He pushes forward, breaching the last inch, and then he's completely inside me. I'm stretched full, my blood pounding, sweat rolling down my temples. Though I know there's more, my brain refuses to believe it. This is too much.

For an eternity, he doesn't move, his arms braced to hold his weight off me. I feel his shaft pulsing, sending heat directly into my veins. Then I know exactly what to do. Certainty and an instinct as deep as the earth's core prompt me to lift my hips in silent entreaty.

He presses his forehead to mine. I stare into his eyes, oceans deep. If we are given only one certainty in life, one inviolable truth, then this is mine. He is mine.

Holding my gaze, he eases back, then forward, creating a smooth, slow rhythm that begins to feel both effortless and increasingly intense. Somehow my body knows how to respond —arching, flexing, gripping. The discomfort fades as my urgency builds, each heavy stroke pushing me ever closer to the pinnacle.

Then we're moving together in an increasingly fast cadence, our bodies rocking and thrusting. The world spins. Sensations overwhelm me—the push of his cock, the power of his body on top of mine, the friction of our skin. Everything in me goes tense and bright the instant before the glittering thread breaks, suffusing me with a bliss almost too intense to bear.

"Darius..." My eyes flood with tears.

His mouth descends on mine. I grip him harder as the wave ripples through me, as his thrusts increase in pace. Then he stills, his muscles stiffening. His rough growl heats my neck. A gasp breaks from my throat at the shockingly intimate sensation of him shooting inside me, filling me with his essence.

With a groan, he rolls to the side, pulling me up against him at the same time. The ragged sound of our breath fills the air. He pushes my hair away from my forehead and strokes his hand through the tangled length.

I experience a feeling of simultaneous sinking and floating as my body absorbs the lingering aftershocks. As my mind tells me this happened. This is real.

I rest my head on his damp chest. His heart is racing. After a few minutes, he eases away from me and gets a warm, wet towel. He wipes the stickiness off me before tossing the towel aside and getting back into bed beside me. I nestle closer. He wraps his arms around me, locking me to him.

Warmth slides through me, like a ribbon unlacing from its bonds. I've spent so long fighting and trying to smother my feelings for him that setting them free is both a relief and a little scary. He is not, after all, an easy man to love, and our relationship contains far too many twists and turns to be smoothly navigated.

But somehow here, in the middle of a country under siege, the north star might finally be visible through the clouds. A bright, shimmering light in the darkness.

CHAPTER 18

Nell

HE'S GONE when I wake in the morning. My body feels both sated and charged, sore and healed, wild and peaceful. No part of me thinks that what happened last night was in any way a dream. He is imprinted on me forever.

I sit up slowly. Early morning sunlight slants through the window, and the smell of coffee drifts from the kitchen. The sheets and pillow beside me are cold.

Pulling on my robe, I move to the side of the bed. The mild aches and twinges of soreness feel good, like deep echoes of him still in my body. Though he's always been inside me, sometimes taking up more space than I'd like, I've craved this physical union for so long. I've wanted to give him all of me, everything I am.

And I've wanted him to take it without punishing himself and thinking it's wrong. Even more, I've wanted him to feel good about our desire and need for each other.

The door opens. My heart bumps against my chest. He comes

in, looking edible in track pants and a navy T-shirt washed so many times that the material shifts and tugs over his shoulders and chest. His face is flushed with exertion and sweat, his dark hair messy from the wind.

He closes the door behind him, meeting my gaze. "Morning. Didn't know if you were awake yet."

"I just woke up." A flush heats my neck. Not only have I never experienced a morning after, until recently I hardly dared hope I'd ever have one with him. And given our history, I'm not sure what to expect. "How was the run?"

"Good. Just a short one." He crosses to me and runs his hand over my hair, bending to press his lips against the top of my head. His voice lowers to a husky rumble. "You okay?"

"More than okay." I breathe in his scents of wind and sunshine.

"I'll get you some coffee."

"Thank you." I place my hand on the sheets. "I slept so well. I didn't even wake when you got out of bed."

When he doesn't respond, my heart sinks a little. He didn't sleep here. Given the intensity of his nightmares, I'm not surprised, but I don't want him to have any more barriers with me. Especially not traumatic ones.

He brings me a cup of coffee, then sits on a chair close to me. He skims his gaze over my face as if he's looking for something I'm not showing him.

An old apprehension starts to rise past my lingering warmth. His battle over our attraction had almost wrecked him four years ago. If he regrets it now that we've finally crossed the line, my heart will break all over again. And I can only try to fix my heart so many times before the damage becomes irreparable.

"Are *you* okay?" I take a sip of coffee. "Because if you give me any indication that you regret having sex with me, I'm going to develop a complex that's bigger than the Rock of Gibraltar."

He smiles faintly. "I don't regret it. Just the opposite."

"But now you're thinking very hard about it. You're remembering what we've always been to each other."

"I've never forgotten." He puts his hand on my knee. "That's just one of the reasons it's been this seismic chasm I've fought like the devil not to cross."

"And now that you have? Are you upset with yourself for giving in?"

"No." He strokes his hand up my thigh. "You're beautiful, Nell. And you know who you are. You always have. It just took a while to get that into my head."

I rest my hand on top of his and tangle our fingers together. Everything is still fragile, spiderweb-thin, but there's a deep settling inside me, as if I've found something that had been missing for too long.

Darius rises and presses his lips against mine. "Let's get dressed, and we'll go over to Ivan's for breakfast."

He returns to his apartment to shower and change, and an hour later, we head out into the bright sunlight. Spring is in full force now, the flowers in the square blooming in bursts of color and the trees all flourishing with green leaves.

If anyone senses something different between me and Darius, there's no indication. Ivan greets us warmly, as always, and we exchange the latest news before he brings us plates of pancakes and sausage. We eat in silence for a while before Darius reaches across the table and rubs his thumb between my eyebrows, like he's erasing a line.

"Now you're the one who's thinking," he says.

"There's a lot to think about." I put my fork down and take a sip of coffee.

He glances at me with a slight frown. I pat his thigh under the table.

"Not *us*, you big oaf. I mean, yes, I think about us, but only in a good way." I hesitate, trying to figure out how to explain it. "Sometimes I think I should feel guilty for wanting you so badly when there's so much horrible stuff happening, but I can't. If anything, I'm even happier, as if it's a huge win to have something good in the midst of all the bad."

"Something good is the biggest win." He looks at me, his eyes warming. "And you are always my *something good*."

My heart rises like a balloon. I understand our truth—that a future for us is still an impossibility. Our desire is honest and real, but it can only exist here, in this strange reality where the conventions and practicalities of life hold no power. But I also know we exist inside each other in ways that not even time or distance can erase.

"Mister Darius!" Jacob darts into the café, carrying a soccer ball.

We both greet him, and Darius pushes a chair away from the table. "Sit down and have some pancakes."

Jacob shakes his head and says in breathless Krasnovian, "Mister Darius, you have to show us that trick again. What did you call it?"

"The stop and go, you mean?" Darius puts his cup down.

"Yes." Jacob nods vigorously. "Stop and go. Will you come now?"

Darius glances at me, as if he's not sure he should leave me alone. With a smile, I squeeze his arm.

"I'm going to catch up on writing some wall text for the exhibitions," I tell him. "I'll see you later, okay?"

"Yes, you will." He leans over to kiss me and gets up to pay Ivan for the breakfast before following Jacob out to the square.

Through the window, I watch them—the tall man and the little boy turned toward each other, Darius bending lower as he listens to Jacob's animated chatter.

What would a life with Darius be like if he didn't seek out war and violence? If he sought peace...or at least had it for himself?

In this strange time-outside-of-time, I can't—won't—put a

name to the breathtaking new intimacy of my relationship with him, but for the next few days, I revel in its sheer existence.

Though my wish to close that final distance between us has been pulsing beneath my heart for years, I've also feared that it would never happen. That my life would always have a carved-out space, a vast absence where he should be. I've been afraid I would never know what it feels like to be uninhibited and free with the man I've loved for so long.

And now, finally, I know. I *am*.

If I'd had any concerns about being self-conscious with him, those misgivings dissolve so fast it's like they never existed. I'd once frozen up whenever a man tried to touch me beyond the most rudimentary kissing, but all Darius has to do is look at me, and I melt.

Though I'd love to spend every minute with him, we separate during the day so I can work and he can continue planning and plotting. For several days after the festival, he's waiting for me outside the museum when my shift ends at five. We stay together all night, and though the pleasure is more than I'd imagined, I don't think even forever would be enough time for me to do all the things I want to do with him.

On our third night together, I straddle his lap as he sits on the sofa in my apartment. I touch him without hesitation, satisfying years of fantasies about what he both looks and feels like. He has an infinite patience for my curiosity, letting me touch him wherever and for as long as I want to.

His body is an endless source of wonder and fascination. I trace the slopes of his shoulders, the cords of his thighs like firewood, his beautiful back with its architecture of bones and tendons. I map the landscape of his chest over and over, trailing my fingers across the ridges of his breastbone and stacked abdominal muscles.

I'm captivated by all his involuntary movements—the flex and pull of his muscles under my fingers, the pulse of his thick erection, the way he can't stop himself from fisting my hair or curling his hand around my nape.

"Are you ticklish?" I touch his naval and rub the line of hair that disappears into his jeans.

"I don't feel like laughing right now, if that's what you mean." He skims his gaze over me, and the sweeping, predatory glance makes me shiver with anticipation. I'm only wearing my bra and underwear, but even the flimsy pieces of cotton are too confining.

"What do you feel like doing?" Lifting my eyebrows inquiringly, I sit back on his thighs and circle my finger over the button of his jeans.

He gives a pained laugh. "If I told you all I wanted to do right now..."

"You can." I look him in the eye, wanting him to *know*. "You can do anything you want with me."

"Ah, Nell." He slides his hands up and down my bare thighs. "Nothing I've thought of in four years has ever come close to the reality of you."

"Same here." I cup the heavy bulge of his erection pressing against his fly. "I've fantasized about you so much, but it's like the difference between a raindrop and the ocean. You're the ocean, by the way."

"You're the whole fucking universe," he mutters as he strokes his hands up to my breasts.

His palms are rough, his fingers callused. I've been aroused since stripping off my clothes less than half an hour ago, and sitting on his lap like this with my legs spread, not to mention touching him, has driven up my need in slow, tantalizing bursts. The friction of his rough hands against my skin almost sends me over the edge.

He reaches behind me and unfastens my bra with one flick of his fingers. I shrug the straps off, and it falls like a piece of dandelion fluff, dropping soundlessly to the floor. His breath escapes him in a rush. His eyes darken, smoke-like and hot.

He cups my breasts as if they were made to fit his hands, rubbing his thumbs slowly over my hard nipples. Heat courses through my blood and pools in my lower body. With a little moan, I wiggle against his thighs.

"I'm ready," I whisper.

"I know you are." His voice is a deep rumble.

He presses one hand between my spread legs, his finger probing into my cleft. I'm already so wet it's embarrassing, but his husky murmur of approval prompts me to lift my hips and allow him easier access. Pressure tightens inside me. I brace my hand on his shoulder, not wanting it to be over and yet unable to stop the wave.

It's astonishing—the way he touches me. As if he knows exactly how close I am, and when I'd like to be teased, and when I'm edging toward desperation. The movement of his fingers aligns perfectly with the rhythm of my body, like he's turning the key of a clock.

"Darius…" Strain laces my voice.

He puts his other hand on my nape and pulls me down to him, covering my mouth with his the instant before I start to come. I shudder violently, digging my fingers into his shoulders. He swallows my cries of pleasure, then grabs me around the waist and rises to his feet. In three strides, he crosses the short distance to the bed and lowers me onto it.

I'm still trembling, shockwaves rippling through my nerves. Tension compresses his muscles, and his eyes burn as he pulls off his jeans and briefs. With a low growl, he enters me, a swift push that jolts me against the headboard. I gasp and wrap myself around him like a vine.

"More," I beg.

He pauses, his jaw tightening. Sweat glistens on his chest. He eases back, then forward again. His thrusts shift into a measured cadence, deep but slower. I arch my hips in a silent plea, trying to tell him with my body that he doesn't have to be gentle, that not only am I no longer sore, I'm craving all of his power, everything he can give me. I want him to fuck me *hard.*

But only seconds pass before that thought falls away, and I lose myself in the rhythmic rocking and thrusting that ignites my arousal all over again. Sensations consume me—the rasp of his chest against my breasts, the slick heat of his skin, the power simmering underneath his control.

This time, somewhat to my shock, I come without him having to touch me with his fingers—my need rises and breaks, and I convulse uncontrollably around his cock. He murmurs low, thick words of encouragement, still buried deep inside me.

Only when I fall back against the pillows, sweaty and gasping, does he give in to his own release. I love it all, crave it—the sensation of him filling me with his heat, the sight of his tightening features and the muscular arch of his body. Knowing he's surrendering to *us.*

He rolls to the other side of the bed, putting his arm over his eyes, his chest heaving. I curl against his side and smooth my hand down his abdomen. While he has no hesitations about me touching him as if he's the most fascinating creature on earth—which to me, of course, he is—there's still a restraint in him, as if he's not letting himself be completely unleashed. As if I might break if he gets too rough.

As if he doesn't trust himself.

He moves off the bed, turning to lift me into his arms before carrying me to the shower. He turns on the water and washes me thoroughly and deliciously. Within minutes, I'm panting and clinging to him as he urges me to another orgasm that buckles my knees.

When we go back to bed, he pulls the covers over me and reaches for his jeans. Dusky moonlight slants through the shutters and illuminates the planes and angles of his body. It's our third—or fourth?—night together, and he still hasn't literally slept with me.

I rise to one elbow. "Stay with me."

He sits beside me and strokes a hand through my hair. "I'll stay for a while."

"Are you ever scared?" I ask.

He glances at me, his eyes opaque.

"Sorry, that came out of nowhere." I pull the pillow closer under my head. "I've just thought a lot about the situations you're in, and then it also sounds like you had it rough with your father, so I was wondering if anything scares you. Because you always seem so fearless."

He's still silent for a moment before he says, "I don't often get scared, no. I've learned how not to be. How to stifle fear. But the flashbacks scare me because I'm not..."

His voice trails off.

"In control," I finish.

He nods. The need for control is one of the reasons he was driven into war zones. With his camera, he can control even the most chaotic and violent of circumstances. Sometimes he even changes the way things happen; his camera itself can make people react or behave differently.

"The other night..." He pauses and clears his throat. "It's been years since I've had a flashback, and they were rarely that bad. You were right. Being back in Krasnovar triggered a bunch of crap I'd thought I was done with. But I can deal with it. That doesn't mean it won't happen again, but I know how to lock it down."

I have no doubt. *Locking down* is one of the things he does best. I want to tell him I'll be here no matter what. That I want him to lock me *in*.

I settle my hand on his knee. "I meant what I said. What I've been saying all this time, even back in Grenville. I'm not scared of you."

He slides my hair through his fingers, his expression shuttered. A buzzing noise breaks the quiet. For a second, I almost don't recognize the sound.

"What…"

"My phone." Darius strokes his hand down to my shoulder.

I ease away from him, knowing he has to answer the call even though I don't like the sudden intrusion. The Wi-Fi might only last for a few minutes.

He reaches for his phone and unlocks the screen. Tension stiffens his back. Before he even says anything, my heart plummets.

He lifts the phone to his ear. "Henry."

My father's voice comes through, the words indistinguishable. My chest constricts. Though I've established my own life away from him, one in which he has no say, he's still my father. I don't want to hurt him, and of course I would do anything to protect Darius.

Darius listens for a minute before saying, "Good to know. Yeah, I heard…no, not since they shut down the borders…no, an old radio scanner. I got it working again, just local police frequencies. The police officers go down to talk to the soldiers at the barricades."

They converse for a few more minutes before Darius turns to look at me. I extend my hand.

"She's here," he says into the phone.

He hands me the phone, then gets up and strides to the kitchen.

I take a breath. "Dad?"

"I'm so glad Darius is there with you, especially since I'm having such trouble getting through." He sighs heavily. "You're okay?"

"I'm fine, and I'm…um, keeping busy."

"I was telling Darius that I finally got a response from the state senator about your situation." He tells me all the details of their correspondence, which includes a promise from the senator to try and arrange assistance.

"If Darius doesn't get you out first," he adds. "I'd put my money on him rather than the senator's office."

So would I, though I don't tell my father that. After another few minutes of catching up, I end the call.

I glance at Darius, who is leaning against the kitchen counter with his arms crossed. I set the phone on the coffee table and go to slip my arms around his waist. "I'm Nell. Not *Henry's daughter.*"

"You're both, and that's a compliment and a blessing." He folds his arms around me, though his body is still tense.

"But one phone call from my father has you upset again."

He sighs. "Because I promised I would get you out of here, and I'm doing a shitty job of it."

"No, you're not. And the only promise I ever wanted from you was to stop thinking our feelings for each other are wrong." I pull away to look up at him. "And I wanted *this*, Darius, right here. You unlocked. Taking what I've desperately been offering you. Wanting it as much as I do."

"I'm incapable of resisting you. Of *not* wanting you." He settles his hand on the side of my neck, his eyes dark. "But that doesn't make it enough."

"This is more than I ever thought we'd have." I wrap my fingers around his wrist, feeling the everlasting beat of his pulse. "Yes, I've wanted you, but I haven't been wishing for a fairy tale. We both know life is the opposite of a fairy tale. And I know *you.* Even if we did figure out how to be together outside of this, you would never be okay with leaving me to go work in the most dangerous places in the world. And I would never be okay with being the reason you stop. So this isn't about me dreaming of some unworkable future. I meant what I said—I will take whatever you can give me. In fact, I'll grab it greedily with both hands and hold on for as long as possible."

Though a faint smile tugs at his mouth, a shutter comes down over his eyes, concealing the warm tenderness I've seen so often over the past week.

"This..." His throat works with a swallow as he rubs his thumb against my neck. "This is all I can give you, Nell. We're still in a war zone and—"

His voice breaks off abruptly. He detaches himself from me, brushing his lips across my forehead before going to pull his shirt on. I hug my arms around myself, trying to contain a new wave of unease.

...and nothing good ever happens here.

CHAPTER 19

Nell

I SIT on a bench in the square, sharing my lunch with Poe. The sky is pale blue, sunlight filtering through the tree leaves. The construction workers recently completed repairs on the fountain, and water trickles down from a statue of Poseidon holding his trident aloft.

On the other side of the fountain, Jacob and Tomas are racing handmade boats in the water, alternately cheering and groaning depending on the race's outcome. Alexei is helping them make boats from leaves and scraps of tree bark, and Sofia is spreading a picnic blanket on a patch of sun-filled grass. She catches my eye and waves, urging me to join them.

I wave back and shake my head, making a few hand motions indicating I have to get back to work soon. But the truth is that I don't want to intrude on their idyllic family time. Alexei had told me he wants to marry Sofia next year, but their devotion to each other and the boys runs so deep it's hard to believe it could be any more profound.

But maybe that's the point of vowing to walk through life together. You discover all the different nuances and challenges of love while knowing the other person isn't going to leave. Just the opposite, in fact. You'll hold hands and figure it out. Weather the storms. Bask in the sunshine. Be grateful for the past and have faith in your shared future.

Alexei's booming laugh carries across the square. Jacob is jumping up and down over an apparent victory, and Tomas is doing some sort of dance. Shading her eyes from the sun, Sofia tries to cajole them over to eat. All four of them have suffered such darkness, and yet their joy of life—of living it together—has overpowered their pain.

Maybe that's why. The dark makes the light shine even brighter.

Poe nudges my leg. I break off a piece of my sandwich and hold it out for him. He gobbles it down and gives me a hopeful look for more. I let him have the rest of it and start to pack up my lunch things.

It's been almost two weeks since the lockdown began. Two weeks of the PLF waging a war across the country to wrest control of the government. Two weeks of no forthcoming aid or attempts to get us to safety. Darius had said we might be in lockdown for a few days, maybe a week, but now there's no telling how long this will last.

Would he and I ever have crossed that line if we hadn't been trapped in Varaz together? The question brings a tangle of emotions I can't unravel. Obviously I wish this new war hadn't happened, but if I hadn't come to Krasnovar, Darius and I might never have seen each other again. Much less finally given in to this desire that's lived for so long.

And now, though I don't want the war to continue, I can't help hoping that he and I will have just a little more time together. If we can't have a lifetime, I want *now* to last as long as possible.

I rub Poe's head. I've asked Alexei and Sofia to look after Poe when I leave, and though they'd agreed without hesitation, the brief discussion had been sobering. Because I'll be leaving behind more than I'd ever expected to. Including me and Darius.

I return to the museum and work on inputting artwork into the collections management system. After Alexei comes back, we make another run up to the castle to transport a truckload of sculptures, then spend the afternoon organizing their display.

When I leave the museum at five, I see Darius coming out of the police station. I assume he's asking them about the transmissions he's been listening to over the radio scanner he found. As far as I know, he hasn't heard anything useful. At least, nothing about the movements of the PLF or any talk warning of a potential threat to Varaz.

I watch him cross the street. His gaze slips appreciatively over me from head to toe, and his eyes crinkle with a smile. It is such an amazing pleasure to be the recipient of his unconcealed admiration.

"Hi." I start to reach up to kiss him, then hesitate. There are plenty of other people in the plaza, and I'm not sure if he wants us to be public with our affection.

He curves his arm around my shoulders, tugging me against him before planting a warm, hard kiss on my lips. "How was work?"

"Really good." I squeeze him around the waist. "We're on track with the exhibition timeline, which is great given everything that's been happening."

"If you want me to—"

"I figured it out." Hazel's voice suddenly breaks into the air.

Darius and I both turn. She's standing by the fountain, her hands on her hips. Though I like Hazel and her commitment to

Global Rebuild, her abruptness and faint hostility toward Darius is getting on my nerves.

"What did you figure out?" I ask.

She points her chin at Darius. "I thought your name was familiar, and I've been racking my brain trying to remember where I'd heard it. Now I know. You were in the news because you were taken hostage."

My spine tenses. "That was a long time ago, and it has nothing to do with why Darius is here now."

"But you were taken hostage in Krasnovar weren't you?" She frowns. "It was a pretty big deal, from what I recall."

"At the time, yes," he replies.

"Did you tell anyone you were coming back here?" Hazel glances at me. "That you intended to rescue Nell?"

"I didn't intend to *rescue* her." His tone drops a few degrees.

"But did you *tell* anyone?" Hazel spreads her arms out. "I mean, not to poke at a wound, but you got a lot of press, right? There were all kinds of negotiations and whatnot, and you must've met with a lot of high-level people when you got back."

"Hazel, what's your point?" I ask sharply.

"My point is that he has connections. So why didn't he use them to help us?"

"In case you forgot, he warned us that the situation was going to get worse and tried to get us out before the lockdown," I remind her. "We're the ones who stalled. As it turns out, Darius was right, so if anyone's to blame, it's us, not him."

"No." He puts his hand on my arm. "No one is to blame. It was just bad timing and shitty luck. For what it's worth, Hazel, I contacted everyone I could think of on my way to Varaz. But there aren't many officials I trust to get anything done. Even if I did, they'd have to cut through miles of red tape. The friends I talked to are doing what they can, but with the situation getting worse and the embassy nonexistent, our best bet is still to find our own way out."

"What about your father?" Hazel asks. "Brian said he's rich, some kind of company owner. Can't he use his money to get us out of here?"

I almost gasp, shocked at her audacity. Beside me, I can feel Darius's defenses slamming into place.

"No." His features harden, the word snapping out of him like a deadbolt. "Don't ever mention my father again."

Hazel opens her mouth, then closes it and takes a step back.

Darius turns and strides away. After throwing Hazel a withering look, I hurry after him.

"That was incredibly rude of her." I fall into step at his side as we approach our building.

"I've dealt with worse." He opens the door and moves aside to let me enter first.

As we go into my apartment, I push aside an unwelcome barrage of speculation over just how much "worse" he's endured.

He returns to his apartment to check the frequencies on the radio scanner, despite the lack of useful information. Instead of going to the café for dinner, I heat up some soup and toast thick slices of bread. We eat at the table by the window, then watch the latest TV news reports.

I still have trouble reconciling the PLF soldiers in their dark green uniforms and red bandannas with the group of men who took Darius hostage. I can't—don't want to—imagine how he feels knowing they've instigated another war.

I nestle closer to him on the sofa. "Can I ask you something?"

"Sure."

"It's about your captivity."

He looks at me. "Go ahead."

"Ivan said that one of the PLF's goals is media attention." I stroke my palm in circles over his abdomen. "I remember there were a ton of news reports when you went missing, and even more when the PLF released a statement that they were holding you hostage."

The words crack in my mouth, dredging up unwanted images of Darius tied up, beaten, locked in a cage. "I'm sorry. You don't want to talk about this."

He settles his hand on my knee. "I'll tell you whatever you want to know. Yes, the PLF wanted attention. They had me record a lot of videos to release to the media. Asking for help and stuff. For all the good it did."

"But why did they take you? What else did they want?"

His mouth twists. "You know my father owns Hawke Financial. His personal net worth is well over six hundred million."

I look at him in surprise. "That much? I mean, I know he's wealthy, but...wow."

"Yeah." He's silent for a second before continuing. "My captors knew who I was. They'd targeted me because I was high-profile and had published a bunch of stories about the Krasnovian war with Russia and the civil war. They also knew the owner of Hawke Financial was my father. They thought negotiations would be straightforward. They'd get the ransom money, have their other demands met, and release me. That would be it."

I frown, processing that revelation. "They asked your father for the ransom?"

"My father's wealth was one of the reasons they targeted me."

"But why didn't..." A slow, dawning horror creeps into my mind, turning my insides to ice. "He refused to pay, didn't he?"

Darius's silence is taut like a wire.

"Oh my god." The horror expands, mutating into shock and rage toward a man I've never even met. "You were his *son*."

"Company policy." He shrugs, like it was just a clinical decision. "He had hostage insurance for his top executives and himself, but the hard line was that Hawke Financial didn't negotiate or pay ransom. He refused. That threw the whole plan off. One of the reasons I was held for so long was that the PLF had to come up with a new strategy. If I hadn't escaped, I'd probably still be there."

"But what about your father's personal wealth? You weren't even associated with his company, so that *policy* shouldn't have applied to you."

"Yeah. That's what I thought too." He drags a hand through his hair. "But Conrad Hawke doesn't negotiate with terrorists. He later told me that if he'd given in, he'd have left both himself and his company open for further threats and abductions. So he held the hard line."

"I can't believe this." I press a hand to my chest. "I had no idea. I'm so sorry."

He shrugs again. "It was what it was. I guess he has a right to do what he wants with his own money."

"How much had your captors asked for?"

"Five million US dollars."

Five million. A significant amount of money by most standards, but not even a drop in the bucket for a man of Conrad Hawke's wealth.

I shift a little closer to Darius, nudging him with my elbow. He lifts his arm, and I settle myself against his side. The warm, strong sensation of his body eases the pain constricting my heart.

Despite my rage and resistance over being sent to a youth psychiatric institution when I was fifteen, I always knew deep inside that my father had been trying his hardest to help me. He would move mountains to ensure my safety and well-being.

Darius's father, on the other hand, had abandoned him. Left him to die.

"No wonder you cut off all contact with him," I mutter.

He gives a humorless laugh. "He and I were done long before that. But yeah, it was the nail in the coffin. So to speak."

I close my eyes against a surge of anger. Conrad Hawke could have spared his son a year and a half's worth of torture and pain, but he'd chosen not to. Between that knowledge and the horrors Darius has both seen and endured, it's no wonder he has an armor thicker than steel. It's no wonder he finds safety in the dark—he knows hope is unreliable at best and useless at worst.

I tighten my arm around him, not knowing what to say except, "I'm so sorry."

"Forget it." He strokes his hand down my side and pats my hip. "It's over. I survived and moved on."

I turn, shifting to my knees so I'm eye level with him. Though tenderness softens his eyes as he looks at me, I know his pain is a part of him, embedded in his bones.

I lean in to kiss him, warmed all over again at the press of his lips against mine. He tightens his hand on my hip. I have no words to express my aching sorrow for all he has endured, and there is not enough time in forever for me to tell him everything in my heart. But at least we have this...and I not only want to take whatever he's willing to give, I want to give him as much as I possibly can in return. I want him to know he has all of me.

With my lips still locked to his, I move around to straddle his lap. I've learned to read the subtle movements of his body, the growing tension of his arousal, and it sparks an incredible feeling of power, awe, and pleasure in me. Sometimes I still have to remind myself that this is real, that Darius is touching and kissing me back without a fight.

I lift my hand and trace the edge of his cheekbone, rubbing my palm over his scruff. The friction elicits a shiver of arousal as I think about the delicious roughness of his stubble against my breasts, my belly, my thighs.

Slowly I unbutton his shirt, pressing my lips to each exposed inch of taut skin. He spears his hand into my hair as I trail my tongue down his abdomen and flick open the button of his jeans. Before I unfasten the rest of the buttons, he pulls me up to him and rises to move us both over to the bed.

I lie back and watch as he sheds his jeans and boxer briefs. I love the sight of him looming above me—all hot, dark, revved-up male. He's already hard, his shaft pulsing, and my insides clench in response. It takes no time at all for me to be *ready*, as if my body is automatically attuned to his. But now—

I sit up and reach for him. My heart thumps. I've fantasized about this, of course, but I've never considered the actual logistics of taking him in my mouth. With his size, it won't be exactly easy, but the thought of sucking on him, tasting him, maybe even making him come...my blood fires with heat so fast I almost gasp. I take his shaft in my hand and draw him closer when he puts his hands on my shoulders, gently stopping me.

I look up at him in faint confusion.

"Don't you want me to—"

"You don't have to." He lowers himself on top of me. "Not now."

Before I can tell him that I want to, he's kissing me again and pressing his hands against my inner thighs to open me. The rest of the world disappears as we fall into a prolonged bout of love-making that has me twisting, moaning, and coming so hard that stars burst behind my eyes.

Afterward, he pulls me into his arms. I fold myself against him, burying my face in his neck. The rhythmic stroking of his hand against my side lulls me into sleep. When I wake, it's still dark outside, and he's gone.

I climb out of bed and push my feet into my slippers. I pick up my keys and cross the hallway, letting myself silently into his apartment.

He's in bed, his chest moving in the heavy rhythm of sleep. Light from the courtyard slants through the shutters and gleams off his smooth, bare shoulders and muscular back.

Lifting the covers, I slide into bed behind him. As soon as I settle my arm around his waist, he startles awake and sits up so fast the sheets slide off both of us. I retreat against the pillows, my hands up and my heart in my throat.

"What the..." He twists to face me, his eyes dark.

"I...I'm sorry." I take a breath and force my pulse to slow down. "I just wanted to sleep with you."

"Nell." He sighs, his shoulders slumping.

"I've been through a nightmare with you." I touch his arm tentatively. "I'll go through a thousand more, if I have to."

His jaw tightens. "I know you will. No matter how much I don't want you to. That's just one of the reasons why—"

His voice breaks off. He drags his hands over his face.

"Why you don't want me here," I finish.

He's silent for a second, his profile etched like stone against the whitewashed wall.

"Why I can't have you here," he says.

I climb out of the bed, deflecting a sting of hurt. Though he's the one who has to set the parameters of this part of our relationship—after all, it's not my business to tell him how to handle his trauma—his rejection is another reminder of how temporary we are.

"Nell." He grabs my wrist and pulls me toward him.

I stroke his dark hair and press my lips against his forehead. "It's okay. I overstepped. It's just that I really love your body and—"

You.

Somehow, I manage to grab the word right before it breaks free.

He knows the truth. I'd told him I love him four years ago. That I would always love him. But now I swallow the confession back down. In no circumstance do I want him to think my love is conditional or that it obligates him to do or say anything in return.

"I'm going back to my room." I smooth my hand down to his jaw and cup his face. "But my door is always unlocked for you."

I kiss him gently, then let him go and return to my bed alone.

CHAPTER 20

Darius

Everything has a sharper edge—the sunlight, the leafy trees, the worn cobblestones. Like a layer of grit has been scrubbed from the air.

I stop in front of the corner store and watch Nell cross the square to the apartment, Poe at her side. Her hair swings behind her in a high ponytail, like a golden-brown streamer.

She'll get lunch for herself and the dog, then come outside and eat it by the fountain in the middle of the park. She'll scatter bread crusts for the birds and greet whoever passes by before going back to the museum.

I will take whatever you can give me.

Her voice is a constant stream, like music. She's been under my skin for so long that it hadn't seemed possible that she could get any deeper. But if I let her, she'll become a permanent part of me. She could do it so easily, like slipping a thread through the eye of a needle. Even now, I have to block the images of a world in which Nell is completely mine.

She and Poe walk into the building, and the door closes.

I dig my fingers into my palms to stop myself from following her and catching her from behind. She'd let out a squeak of surprise before laughing and wiggling around to face me. Her gray eyes shining, she'd give me her heartbreakingly beautiful smile before lifting her face for a kiss.

One press of her perfect mouth, and I'd be hard as a rock. On fire to strip her naked and bury myself inside her for hours. And she'd let me. She'd be as hot and hungry for it as I am.

Christ in heaven. My subconscious has always known it'd be mind-blowing with her, even if I've gone to war with every fantasy that tried to surface. But now that I've crossed the line, I don't know how I can ever go back. I also don't know how I can't.

I twist my neck and roll the tension from my shoulders. There's no way to sort out my simultaneous belief and disbelief —*She's a woman who knows herself and what she wants. But why the hell does she want me?*

She'd hate that I'm still thinking like that, but it's impossible not to. There's a gulf of over twenty years between us. Why would she want to waste her youth and beauty on—

I shake my head, dislodging the thought. There's nothing permanent or long-term about what's happening right now. I won't insult her by assuming that her attachment to me is based on the volatile situation we're in, but we both know my goal is to get her out of Varaz. Which also means away from me.

The building door opens again, and she comes out with a paper bag and a water bottle. She glances in my direction and switches course to approach me. A breeze blows strands of hair around her face. Her smile is a sunrise.

Ah, Nell. I've made it rough on you. How could I do that to a girl like you? What kind of bastard doesn't realize what a gift you are?

"Hi." She squeezes my arm. "Have you eaten lunch?"

"Not yet."

"Come on." She holds up the bag. "You can share my sandwich and gingerbread, but I'm not giving up my pickles."

"I need to get some stuff done, but I'll meet you after work."

"Okay." She pats my chest and reaches up to kiss me. "Alexei and I might go up to the castle for another storage run or to the Holy Trinity Church in case you can't find me."

"I'll always find you." I stroke her thick, shiny hair, pressing my mouth harder against hers. My pretty sparrow.

I don't like leaving her, not even for a second. I want to tuck her away in my shirt pocket, right next to my heart. I kiss her again and let her go, watching as she crosses the plaza.

Though this situation is absurd—the last thing I should be doing now is sleeping with Nell, of all women in the world—*she* makes it okay. There is no darkness in her, not about this, no guilt or remorse. Nothing but delight, happiness, hunger.

I see it every time she looks at me, her gray eyes unclouded and bright. I feel it in her unbridled response, her breathy cries, the way she clenches around me and pulls me closer. I sense it in her constant touching—the stroke of her hand through my hair, the press of her lips, the way she takes my hand whenever we're walking.

She wants to bask in every nuance of us being together. She wants to learn everything. She wants to get close to me without constantly hitting the walls I keep putting up.

I want to let her. Even if the idea scares the shit out of me.

Pushing the thought away, I go back to my apartment to listen to and record police transmissions over the radio scanner. The talk isn't helpful—mostly casual conversations broken up by an occasional domestic altercation, the arrest of an inebriated resident, a confrontation with a couple of rowdy teenagers. The police officers often talk with the soldiers stationed at the barricade—most of whom are bored and glad for the company.

Despite the banality of the transmissions, I make the recordings and take notes in the event they might be useful. I try not to think about the fact that I'm killing time because I have no other plans. Because I've failed Nell.

When a weak Wi-Fi signal comes through, I manage to contact my old friend Savko with a video call, glad to hear that he's at least safe in his hometown of Polvik and that the PLF has retreated from the city—for now.

"You are well, my friend?" He squints at me through the blurry screen, his dark eyebrows pinching together.

"Yes, thanks. Just ready to claw our way out of here."

"You haven't plotted your escape yet?" He smiles faintly. He also knows something about escape—he'd narrowly escaped being abducted along with me. We were reunited at the hospital after I'd finally managed to get away. Savko brought me my camera and a thousand unnecessary apologies. I suspect he'll never rid himself of the guilt over having escaped while I was taken.

"I'm working on it," I assure him. "What have you heard about the border?"

"Not so good." He updates me about what he's heard, though the rumors are almost impossible to verify.

"I will be traveling to Telina to assist Michael Benoit...you know him, I think, from Agence France-Presse?" he says. "I will contact you once I arrive. I'll be of more help closer to Varaz, and I know several people in the media there. I am also trying to get a response from the US State Department as well as the Krasnovian government."

Though I'm grateful for his help and efforts, I have even less faith than before in any governmental action.

After we end the call, I pick up my camera and head back outside. I walk around town, taking pictures of both the architecture and people. Though I'm doing this for Nell, I've found a strange relief in photographing a fresco, a bunch of flowers, or two kids swinging in the park. I'm so used to focusing on violence and bloodshed through my camera lens that I'd almost forgotten that all the other dimensions of life—the peaceful parts—are also right there for the capturing.

Close to five, I walk back to Harmony Square to wait for Nell. Poe is pacing near the fountain, sniffing at the grass and nudging leaves with his nose. He glances at me and trots over for a greeting. His initial hostility toward me has waned, as if he's figured out that if Nell likes me, I must be okay.

"You're waiting for her too, huh?" I sit down on a bench and scratch him behind the ears.

He indulges me for a second before returning to his explorations. I lift my camera and snap a few pictures of him. He looks toward the museum, his ears perking up as Nell comes out. I keep shooting as he bounds over to greet her, his tail wagging so hard his whole body shakes.

Nell crouches to hug him, smiling at me over the dog's head. "Are you busy right now?"

"Only with whatever you're plotting."

"Excellent. I have a surprise for you, but we have to take your car."

I pull my keys from my jeans pocket as we walk to the car. Poe bounds toward the café, apparently uninterested in joining us. Nell directs me to drive to the eastern wall and the road leading to a fork that diverges in two directions—one past the deserted factory and down to the valley, and the other to the castle. At her instruction, I take the castle road, and within an hour, we're pulling into the round parking lot.

"What are we doing here?"

"You'll see." She gets out and waves for me to follow her.

As if she has to ask.

"Did you take a tour of the castle when you were in Varaz?" She starts searching in her bag.

I shake my head, looking up at the massive walls and turrets. "I guess I didn't have time. I heard a lot about it, though."

Nell stops beside a narrow wooden door under the main gate. "Well, then. Welcome to Bram Castle."

She takes a set of keys out of her bag and opens the door.

"Are we breaking and entering?" I follow her into a small room leading to a ticket booth.

"Oh, please. You're talking to a girl who doesn't even litter." She plucks a paper floor plan from the desk and opens it. "I've been hounding Alexei about letting me see the interior of the castle, and finally he gave me the keys. He's reviewing the restoration of a cathedral wall with Hazel tonight so he can't join us, but he said we can take a tour as long as we lock up after we leave. By the way, Hazel was looking for you earlier today. She wants to apologize for what she said the other day."

"No need." I didn't like Hazel's remarks about my father, but I know she's increasingly scared and needs an outlet for her fear. I just happen to be the most visible target.

"She knows it was entirely inappropriate." Nell unlocks another door leading to a long, carpeted corridor lined with iron-latticed windows. "This is the west gallery that should take us to the guardroom. Alexei said it's fine if you take pictures."

She consults the map as we walk. Dirt smudges the windows, and the carpet is covered with dust. We pass through the guard-room—rough stone walls, an ancient trestle table, a few swords on display—and into the other chambers and anterooms. Though most of the furnishings were put into storage, some of them are still in place—suits of armor in glass cases, velvet-upholstered chairs, tapestries, and huge oak tables.

The great hall is bordered by tall stained-glass windows and floor-to-ceiling columns. An elaborate fireplace with a carved stone mantel sits at one end of the vast room. I take dozens of pictures, aware that few people have the good fortune to be able to see a place like this in solitude.

"This is amazing." Nell looks at the vaulted ceiling with awe. "It's almost like Sleeping Beauty's castle. But so much more... well, real. Can you even imagine how many people have stood within these walls? How many ghosts must still be here?"

More than the ones in my head, at least. I also take shots of Nell throughout the interior. With her long hair and gray eyes, she could be a medieval princess.

"In all the places you've been, do you have a chance to see a country's monuments?" she asks as we walk out to the building that once housed the castle's kitchen and pantries. "Like important buildings and artwork?"

"I've seen a lot of them." I pause to snap a few pictures of the interior courtyards, shadowed by the watchtower and protected by the heavy crenelated walls. "Not as a tourist, but because they're such a part of a country's landscape. You can't escape seeing them, even in a war."

She turns her head, studying the chapel on the other side of the courtyard. The sun has set, and a twilight glow shadows her face. "I've heard about a lot of horrible things that happen to art during wars. Obviously, a lot worse things happen, but art is still important."

"That's why people try to save it when they can."

Nell sits on a bench underneath a tree. The breeze shifts her hair around her shoulders. "Have you ever done a story about people who save art during a war?"

I shake my head and sit down next to her. "I don't think I've ever seen that happen. I've done a series on the destruction of art, though. Terrorists who have bombed medieval mosques and ancient statues. Governments that've ordered the razing of historic or religious buildings. I was in the Caucasus when a riot broke out in a city center, and within minutes, people were looting the museum before it was set on fire. Not much of the art has been recovered, even to this day."

Nell lets out her breath in a long exhale. "But those were still somewhat *tame* reports compared to most of your others."

"True." I don't even remember all the events and wars I've covered, but I still see the people running through the chaos—bloody, burned, screaming, sometimes sobbing uncontrollably. "The world has a lot of..."

There's no word for what people do to each other.

Nell rests her hand on my knee.

Sometimes I think I've seen everything. Been through too much. Nothing can penetrate the thick, heavy walls of scar tissue and ice, the anvil weight.

Then she comes back. Slides right under the walls. Warm, melting, light.

"I once read about a city in Syria that was under siege during a war," she says. "In the midst of this horrific violence...snipers, attacks, bombs, and a total lack of food and medical help...a group of people salvaged hundreds of books from destroyed homes, then organized them all in a secret library in a basement. A fourteen-year-old boy was the librarian, and anyone who wanted to could borrow a book. They held book clubs and classes. They created a haven of poetry, novels, Shakespeare. Like an oasis. It made me think that even in the terrible places you've been, with all the violent things you've witnessed, you must have seen some good."

"Yes."

"Like what?"

I don't often think of the good. The violence breaks the good apart, and I have to work to put it back together. But for Nell...

Anything.

"I was in Syria a few times." I rub my thumb over the casing of my camera. "I asked both soldiers and civilians if I could photograph them in their homes. These were people who barely had enough to feed their families. But they wouldn't let me leave without giving me dinner. They'd put out their best tablecloths and plates, make incredible food with whatever they had—rice, meat, spices. Their hospitality was one of the most gracious and humbling things I've ever experienced."

I look across the courtyard at the castle wall. Let another good thing rise from the cavernous depths of my mind.

"Kids play all the time, wherever they can, with whatever they can. Kick-the-can on a bombed-out street in Chechnya. Soccer in a gutted field that used to be a village. Carom, checkers, cards. Even the soldiers would play games. Sometimes they'd ask me to join them. I played chess with an eighty-year-old man who'd outlived almost his entire family. He didn't fear death because he knew they were all waiting for him."

A strange tightness constricts my throat. Images, thoughts, memories start floating upward, breaking like bubbles through the surface.

"When there's no food, people try and grow gardens. There was a woman in Somalia who planted flowers next to her vegetables. A father walked his two children three miles to school through the front lines every day because he didn't want them to miss out on their education. A group of women in Lebanon started an embroidery circle in the hopes that one day they could use it to support their families. Doctors risk their own lives to save someone else's, and they keep trying, even when everyone knows the victim is going to die.

"Art is everywhere. Murals, graffiti, paintings. Even on buildings that have been shelled. Messages of hope. I've seen people reunited after long separations when they've thought each other dead...couples, parents and children, husbands and wives. Their joy and disbelief is otherworldly. I've listened to people create music with whatever they could find—wash tubs, broken guitars, metal spoons. And the minute a crowd hears the rhythm, someone always starts to dance."

I feel rather than see Nell smile. I remember the day she'd

asked me if I ever thought about the thousands of people I've photographed over the years.

All the time, Nell. They never go away.

She brushes her fingers through my hair and rubs my scalp. "Steel trap, baby. You hold on to a lot of good stuff up here."

I haven't realized that before now.

She rises and crosses the courtyard to the ramparts. Darkness has fallen, and a few stars peer down from the sky. I gaze at her outline against the vast stretch of land, the length of her hair gleaming in the pale light.

Maybe she doesn't slide under the walls. Maybe she's always been inside.

I push to my feet and join her at the rampart. I gather her hair in my hand and tug her head back just enough to lift her face upward.

"Thank you." I press a hard kiss to her mouth. "But we should get back. The military imposed a nine p.m. curfew for everyone to be back within city walls."

She lets her lips linger on mine for a moment before we separate and return to the car. I pull open the passenger side door and wait for her to get settled inside before closing it.

I walk around to the driver's side when a chill rattles through me. Several male voices rise into the darkness. A flash of red.

My blood freezes. Every single defense slams into place.

PLF soldiers? Here? How the fuck did they—

I back up to stand in front of the passenger side door, blocking it. Whatever good I'd remembered less than an hour ago dissolves. Now there's only a locked cell, a filthy concrete floor, a killer with a red bandanna pressing a gun to my head and pulling the—

Three men walk out of the shadows. Camouflage uniforms, caps with black visors, yellow insignia.

Krasnovian army. Probably stationed at the barricade. One of the men is carrying a red jacket.

I don't move. They continue walking, not glancing in our direction. After a minute, they disappear around the side of the castle wall.

"Darius?"

Nell's voice restarts my heart. She's rolled the window down slightly. I step away from the car door.

"What's wrong?" she asks.

I shake my head and wipe a trickle of sweat from my forehead. Inhaling a breath, I get behind the wheel and shove the key into the ignition. I can't look at Nell. I feel her confusion as if it's a living thing.

"Darius, what—?"

"Nothing." I push down the parking brake, hating the sudden claustrophobia closing in on me from all sides. Even hers.

She puts her hand on my arm. "But…"

"Nell." I shove her hand away. "It's nothing."

Her silence is like a blade. I struggle to find a way to explain, but there isn't one. I guide the car out of the parking lot to the narrow, winding road leading back to the town. Halfway there, I've managed to smother the shock. But my pulse is too fast. I'd reacted without rational thought. Let old fear take control.

I tighten my grip on the wheel as we approach the eastern gate. Almost fifteen days of inaction. Of failure. Of letting Nell in so fucking far I can't see past her gray eyes. Of forgetting my defenses.

I drive into town and park in front of the apartment building. As we get out, Poe lumbers up from his position by the door and trots over. He follows us inside and up the stairs. Nell opens her apartment door and glances at me in wary hesitation.

"Are you coming in?" she asks.

My shoulder muscles are knotted like frayed ropes. I should've gotten her on a plane the day after I first arrived. Instead, over two weeks later, I'm spreading her legs and pushing into her so deeply I never want to come back out.

And I want more of her. *For fucking ever.*

I shake my head.

She looks away, but not before I catch the flash of hurt in her eyes. Clenching my jaw, I step back. "I'll see you tomorrow."

I turn and head back down the stairs.

"Where are you going?" she calls after me.

"Out."

I stride down the stairs to get away from her. Like the coward I am.

CHAPTER 21

Nell

POE NUDGES his head against my hand. Without going inside, I close the apartment door and drop the key into my bag.

"Come on, boy." I ruffle the dog's fur and lead him downstairs and back out to the street.

Frustration tightens my throat. I'm not upset with Darius for not telling me about whatever caused his sudden shutdown—yes, I want him to trust me with anything, no matter how dark, but I will never know or understand all the lingering echoes of what he's both seen and endured. He doesn't owe me any explanations.

What's upsetting is the reminder that I'm the reason he's back on the defense, and not just because I took him up to the castle this evening. If he hadn't come to Varaz, he wouldn't have to confront his demons back on the battlefield.

If it was his demons that got to him.

The Koroleva Café is bustling with patrons eating and drinking. As usual, the TV is blaring with news reports of skirmishes and battles. The reporter relays information about the PLF leader, General Balakin, and his determination to seize power from the president, who is still in charge…for now.

I shake my head at Ivan's offer of a drink and ask around about Darius. No one has seen him since our return from the castle. Though more than likely he's either just walking or he's gone over to the deserted areas of town, his shutdown was so sudden and abrupt that I need to at least know that he's okay.

After leaving the café, Poe and I walk toward the school, which is situated a block away from the main street. The night and the moon throw long shadows over the cobblestones. I check a couple of restaurants and a coffeehouse to no avail.

The shops are all dark. The only lights and noise come from a hole-in-the-wall bar not far from the main walled entrance into town.

I stop across the street from the building. He's standing at the bar, his tall figure visible through the foggy window. I briefly consider going in, but reject the idea without much thought. He'll work it out however he needs to, and right now his strategy doesn't include me.

I start to turn away when he lifts his head and catches my eye. Even from a distance, I see his expression harden. He pushes away from the bar and strides out, crossing to me in seconds.

"You shouldn't be out here alone," he says.

I bristle a little at his sharp tone. "I wanted to make sure you were okay. You don't have to tell me what happened, but I think I'm entitled to worry about you when the situation warrants."

"There's nothing to worry about."

"Considering the turnaround you did on me, I beg to differ." I step back, clicking my fingers for Poe. "But I'm not going to argue. If you—"

Darius steps in front of me suddenly, blocking me with his body. A sudden burst of raucous male laughter breaks through the air. My heart thumps. I peer around his shoulder.

Two large, bulky men are walking up the hill toward the bar, their voices overly loud. They're in combat fatigues that display the yellow insignia of the Krasnovian army, but they don't appear to be carrying weapons. Though I've seen a few soldiers in Varaz getting food or supplies, they mostly stick to their duties guarding the barricades.

I'm not particularly alarmed since these two seem relatively unthreatening. They probably came up to get a drink and blow off steam.

But Darius goes on alert. Tension ripples through his large frame. Sensing his wariness, Poe advances.

I put my hand on Darius's arm. "Let's go home."

He doesn't move. His feet are planted apart, his muscles locking. A sharp unease lances through me. I tighten my grip.

"Darius—"

One of the soldiers calls out in Krasnovian. Then they approach us, their boots ringing against the cobblestones. Their eyes are glassy, and the bitter scent of alcohol wafts from them both. The older one, a man with a thick beard and deep grooves down his cheeks, flicks his gaze between us. His insignia bears the star indicating his status as an officer.

"What are you doing here?" he asks.

Darius responds in Krasnovian, his words too fast for me to understand. But from the tone of his voice, it doesn't sound like he's telling them we're out for an evening walk after dinner. Poe barks.

"Shh." I put my hand on the dog's head, not wanting this situation to escalate.

The men's voices rise.

"Darius." I tug on his sleeve. "Let's go."

The second soldier steps around to look at me. He's younger, with a thin mustache and a squat, heavy frame.

"Dovoro uchav?" he asks.

I start to tell him my name when Darius turns.

"Don't talk to her," he snaps.

The soldier holds up one hand, his eyes hardening. "Who the fuck are you?"

Darius's tension is winding tighter. I want him to walk away. We could do it right now with a few deferential words, an apology, a "have a good evening."

But *deference* is not in Darius Hawke's vocabulary.

The officer fixes his gaze on me and issues a few words. I shrug to indicate that I don't understand. He barks out what sounds like an order and snaps his fingers.

"Riet." Darius's tone sharpens. *"Vam polich—"*

The younger one interrupts. His voice is increasingly strident, his glassy eyes skimming over me from head to toe. He says something to the officer. They both laugh. Darius fists his other hand.

My unease turns into outright dread. I take his arm again and pull, trying to tell him to walk away. His muscles are steel. The officer takes my wrist and yanks me forward. Darius shoves himself between me and the soldier, breaking his grip.

The younger man shouts. There's a sharp, snapping noise, metal hitting metal. I turn. He's aiming a pistol at me.

My breath lodges in my throat. Darius stills.

"Dovay!" The officer grabs the front of my shirt and pulls me to his side. The stench of cigarette smoke and alcohol fills the air.

Time stops. A half second. Then Darius moves.

I once saw him fighting. The match had been brutal and bloody, contained within a roped-off ring.

This time, there are no boundaries. He lunges at the younger man, knocking the gun out of his hands with one swift kick. The officer shouts. Darius swerves, his fist connecting with the other man's face.

Poe starts barking in a frenzy and racing around the three men as if looking for an opening to join the fight. The soldier kicks him. Poe yelps.

My heart racing, I grab Poe's collar and drag him away from the fighting. Grunts and yells echo through the deserted street. Men stream out of the bar and gather to watch.

Darius is a blur—throwing right hooks and undercuts with sharply targeted efficiency. Though the other men are dulled by the alcohol they've consumed, they're trained soldiers whose fighting instinct comes out full force. Poe strains against my hold, barking ceaselessly.

The younger soldier catches Darius's jaw in a punch, snapping his head back. Darius advances. Blood trickles from his nose. They exchange a few swift jabs before Darius lands a roundhouse kick on the other man's torso. The guy careens backward and hits a lamppost so hard the crack echoes through the street. He falls like a deadweight.

"Stop!" The officer has gotten ahold of the fallen pistol and is pointing it at Darius.

For a terrifying instant, I wait for the blast, the firing bullet. But before he pulls the trigger, Darius plows forward, tackling him to the ground. The soldier's head smashes against the street, the gun clattering to his side.

A second of silence descends over Darius's heavy breathing and Poe's barks. Then the men gathered outside the bar break out into raucous cheers and whistles, pumping their fists in the air.

Darius drags his arm across his face. Blood smears. He turns toward me, his eyes black and features hard as granite. Sweat dampens his forehead, and there's a bloody abrasion on his cheekbone.

My throat aches. I dig into my bag for a tissue and hand it to him. Poe leaps forward, clawing at Darius's leg. Darius picks up the fallen pistol and rubs the dog's head, his gaze on me.

"You okay?"

Oh. My. God.

I turn and stride away from the main street. Tears burn my eyes.

"Nell." He catches up to me, his voice rough. "They were—"

"No." I stop and turn toward him, holding up my hand. A flame of anger rises in me. "They didn't even notice us at first. You could have walked away. I asked you to. But you were looking for a fight, weren't you? You wanted to throw some punches and get into a brawl. Because that's how you deal with your shit when you can't find another way."

He clenches his jaw. "You shouldn't have come looking for me."

"Don't you put this on me!" I stalk away from him, wiping angrily at my tears. "Of course I was going to look for you after you shut me out. How could you think I *wouldn't* be worried about you? And still you'd rather fight than just *talk* to me?"

"I have *talked* to you," he snaps, his voice so sharp it cuts through the air like a blade. "That's the fucking problem."

I stop and stare at him. He spreads his arms out, the street-lamps casting harsh shadows over his blood-smeared face.

"You make me forget what I'm even doing here." He paces a distance away, his hands clenching and unclenching. "I want to talk to you and be with you, and God knows I want to fuck you every chance I get, but—"

"Don't you dare say that's not why you came here," I interrupt. "I know it's not. Especially after you told me in New York that you couldn't *be around me* ever again. So now that you've finally let yourself want me and…and *have me,* you need another reason to feel like shit about our relationship?"

"I don't feel like shit about it," he retorts, his eyes blazing. "Just the opposite. You make me want to stay here because I know the second you leave, it's over."

Though his words about wanting to stay echo what I've secretly thought, a chill runs down my spine. "The second *I* leave?"

It's over.

He stares at me, and an instant passes before the pieces click.

"You...you're not coming with me?" I almost can't get the words out, even as part of my brain thinks, *Nell, you fucking idiot. Of course he's not coming with you. That was never his plan. It's still not his plan, no matter what happens between you two.*

"Well, that was a stupid question." I force a humorless laugh. "We're in a war, right? This is where you belong."

He steps back, his mouth compressing. "Did you think I'd ever belong anywhere else?"

A wave of pain courses through me. I'd told him—told myself —that I would take whatever he could give me. But I've been unable to stop the tiny seedling of hope that maybe, somehow, *this* war would be enough for him. That maybe we would—

God. I *know* better than that.

"No, you won't." My voice is tight, on the verge of breaking. "And that's one of the reasons I fell so hard for you, because you know where you belong. Because you're so good at what you do. But working in war zones does not mean you need to keep one alive inside you."

He flinches, an almost imperceptible movement in the yellow glare of the streetlight, before his eyes harden in defense. "Is that what this is about? You wanting to fix me?"

"Oh, stop it." I swallow another upwelling of angry tears. "I'm not the one who needs to fix everything. I will always take you exactly as you are—scars, demons, and all. But I will not keep pounding on the door, begging you to let me in."

"I came here to get you out, not to *let you in,*" he snaps.

"If I'm such a distraction that you need to stop being with me and fucking me, then fine." I turn away, dragging a hand over my eyes. "Go find someone else to beat to a pulp and see if that helps you refocus on your goal."

I stalk away from him, my blood at full boil. Only when I'm locked back in my apartment do I start to cry.

CHAPTER 22

Nell

AFTER A SLEEPLESS NIGHT, I drag myself out of bed to shower and dress for work. When I take Poe outside, I stop and knock on Darius's apartment door. My brain is overworked and foggy, but I have one clear, rational thought: No matter how fraught and tangled our relationship still is, it's ridiculous for us to fight with each other when the country is being overrun by a war.

He doesn't answer my knock. His car is gone too, which means he's either scouring the deserted neighborhoods in search of equipment, or he's gone down to the barricades again.

I make lunches for myself and Poe and pack up my book bag. Maybe it'll do me and Darius good to be away from each other for a day. God knows we've spent an inordinate amount of time together since the festival. A short break will give us both time to decompress and defuse our anger.

Poe and I head outside, where the bright morning sunshine and blue sky lift my low spirits. Every Thursday, Alexei and I work at the Holy Trinity Church, the parish chapel tucked against the rocky mountainside. Though the neighborhood itself is sparsely populated and in the midst of renovation, it's a priority for both the town and the museum to bring their historic and religious artworks back to where they belong.

Alexei drives his scooter up the steep, crisscrossing streets, and I always decline his offer of a ride in favor of making the challenging trek on foot. I enjoy looking at the mishmash of architecture that speaks of the town's lengthy history and finding little gems, like an intricate mosaic decorating a pediment.

Today the exercise feels especially good, and I imagine seeing Darius later this evening, both of us sheepishly agreeing that our argument was silly and finding ways to make it up to each other. Poe trots along beside me, pausing to sniff at various things along the path.

The church is a lovely stucco building with a nave and two narrow side aisles situated around the pews. The walls are embellished with frescos of biblical scenes, and Global Rebuild is working with the local administration on a timeline to start a structural reinforcement of the walls and roof. Alexei and I are in charge of cleaning and returning the statues, crucifixes, paintings, icons, and stained glass to their original locations.

He greets me with his usual warm smile, which quickly fades. "Nell, what has happened? You are looking so sad."

His genuine concern makes my throat tighten. I put my bag on a wooden pew and attempt a smile. "I'm fine. I just...um, Darius and I...we..."

"Ah." He nods, his forehead furrowing. "There was a quarrel?"

Grateful that I don't have to explain, I nod. "A quarrel, yes. It was silly."

"Nothing painful is silly." He studies me, his dark eyes both pensive and understanding. "There is much love between you and him."

I look away and try to shake my head, but my body refuses to lie. I've never *not* loved Darius. And I know he cares deeply for me. He's never said he loves me, but his feelings go beyond mere affection. What he feels probably lies between like and love. Maybe there's not even a word for it.

"This is the thing with love," Alexei says gently. "We fight both with and for each other. This is how we know the love is strong. That it survives and becomes everlasting."

"Oh, Darius and I aren't..." I brush a lock of hair away from my forehead, trying to keep my voice from trembling. "I mean, it's not that kind of love."

Alexei frowns. "What other kind could you and he possibly have?"

I laugh suddenly and cross the stone floor to hug him, wishing I had his untarnished view of the world. Of love.

"I don't even think I know what it is," I admit. "But it's definitely not easy."

"The things in life most worthwhile are often the most challenging." He returns my embrace. "And now you find I am truly a philosopher at my heart."

His warmth and friendship lift the cloud a little more. He moves away to get a foil-wrapped box from his backpack, which he presents to me with a flourish.

"This is good timing," he says. "Sofia makes *kilfie* yesterday, the sugar cookie with raspberry jam, and she put these aside for you before the boys devoured them all. You and Darius share them this evening with coffee and brandy. Quarrel is...*poof.* Gone."

He waves his hand like he's performing a magic trick.

I take the box with a smile. "I will definitely share them, then. Thank you."

After I put the box in my bag, he and I start cleaning and organizing the statues. As we work, we continue listening to the radio, but sometimes Alexei turns it off to give us a short reprieve from the bad news. Then he entertains me with Krasnovian folktales about enchanted pigs and magical birds, always starting with, "Once upon a time, these events happened, or there would be no story to tell."

He's a great storyteller; he uses different voices for the characters and animated gestures that bring the details to life. When I tell him it's impressive, he smiles abashedly.

"My sister and I acted stories all the time when we were younger," he says. "No television, and we had no money for movies. So we made performances for our parents and other children."

"That's really nice. I was always too shy to get up in front of other people to perform."

"But you perform with your art, yes?" He indicates my leather satchel, where I keep several sketchbooks. He's asked to see my work and was gratifyingly complimentary. "That is how you express yourself."

"Very much so."

"Where will you go when you leave Krasnovar?"

I push down my lingering despair from last night. I can't even pinpoint when I just assumed that Darius would be at my side when we finally get out of here. The thought goes against everything I know about both him and us.

"I'll go to New York or California," I tell Alexei.

"Ah, California. Right back where you—"

An enormous *bang* rocks the church on its foundation. We both gasp. Cracks snake up the stucco walls and across the roof. The rose window shatters in a hailstorm of broken glass.

"Earthquake!" Alexei grabs me and ducks underneath a heavy table near the apse and away from the side windows.

Growing up in California, I've experienced at least four or five earthquakes. I know before we even hit the ground that this shattering rumble is not a seismic tremor. This is something else, like a giant hand has grabbed the mountain and given it a single hard shake.

Not knowing what the hell just happened makes it even scarier.

Alexei's grip is tight on my wrist. My heart is racing. We're both breathing fast, tense in anticipation of a second…whatever it was.

"That wasn't a—"

Another ear-splitting crack jolts the building. Plaster and concrete rain down from the ceiling. The statues topple over.

An intense rumbling comes from deep within the earth, like a monster rising to the surface. Panic flares through me.

We scramble to our feet. But before we can even get out from under the table, an avalanche of boulders and uprooted trees crashes into the church.

The walls collapse, the noise a deafening roar. Dust fills our throats and eyes. Alexei and I cover our heads and pray for the table to hold. Mud pours across the floor. The roof caves in.

A massive weight crushes us to the ground, and the world goes dark.

CHAPTER 23

Darius

THE EXPLOSION REVERBERATED through the entire town. It's the realization of what I've been fearing—an outright attack too damned close to Varaz. No sign of aircraft, so likely a surface-to-surface missile. But why did the PLF aim it at the mountain?

Black smoke and dust rise from the mountainside like a volcano, twenty or thirty miles away. Rocks and trees tumble down the slope, shearing away an entire ridge.

I can't find Nell. A crowd gathers swiftly in the square, people streaming from buildings and running into the streets. Everyone is talking loudly, gesturing toward the mountain, arguing, embracing. Some of the women are crying, and the children are huddled together near a tree.

"Hazel." I shoulder through the crowd to get to her. "Have you seen Nell?"

"No." She's thin-lipped and pale. "But it looks like we made a mistake not going with you when we had the chance."

"It doesn't matter now. I need to find Nell."

"She should have been working at the museum." She lifts a hand toward Brian, who is making his way through the square. "Have you seen Nell or Alexei?"

He shakes his head. "They're probably up at the Holy Trinity. They work there on Thursdays."

Hazel's eyes widen. "The Holy Trinity is right at the foothills of the western ridge."

My terror is instant. I race toward my car, pulling my keys from my pocket. Brian follows and gets into the passenger seat.

Outside of the nightmares, I don't remember the last time I felt actual fear. I've spent the past six years smothering it under the scars and ice. But now it's a flash flood spilling into my bones, my blood. Hot and sharp.

I drive through the twisting streets to the old, deserted neighborhood. Rocks, uprooted trees, and broken branches are scattered over the cobblestones, blocking the roads.

Shoving the car into park, I get out. We'll have to run the rest of the way. I take off, veering around corners and navigating the debris. Alexei's scooter lies tipped over on the street.

I run toward the church, which is isolated on its own plot of land near the mountain.

"Holy shit." Brian careens to a stop beside me, his breathing fast.

We both stare at the remains of the church piled with massive boulders and chunks of stone and wood. There's almost nothing left of it save parts of three walls and the foundation with gaping holes where the windows once were.

"Call for help." I throw Brian the car keys and start toward the destroyed building. "If there's no signal, drive back to the square. We need an ambulance, the firefighters and police, and as many people as possible. *Hurry.*"

He runs. I climb over the pile, shoving rocks and tree branches out of the way. A thick layer of mud covers the ruins.

"Nell? Nell!"

Focus. Get closer. Move the stones. Dig.

I've done this before. Dug through wreckage, looking for survivors. I've pulled people out of the destruction caused by bombs and earthquakes. Some were alive. Some were dead. I'd been determined, sick, and angry, but I hadn't been scared.

I hadn't known until now how terrifying the search can be.

She's not here. She can't be. No way is Nell buried under tons of fucking rock and mud. She and Alexei got out, or they were at lunch, or she was wandering around with her sketchbook, far away from a goddamned landslide...

"Nell!" A rough edge of concrete scrapes my palm. "Alexei?"

Silence, except for the distant sound of sirens. I shove a broken branch aside. Seconds later, the police officers and half a dozen firefighters come running, followed by a crowd of towns-people on foot. One of the police officers uses a bullhorn to order unauthorized people away from the site, warning that there could be another rockfall or, worse, another explosion.

"We need lifting equipment," I shout. "A crane."

"They're coming," the police chief calls. "They have to clear the roads to get through. Fire trucks are on the way too."

Smothering a wave of frustration, I throw another branch to the side. Voices yell instructions. Several firefighters plunge into digging through the rubble, while the police officers take off to ensure no one else was hurt. The other buildings in the neigh-borhood—all deserted or abandoned—are damaged, but the church was the only one completely demolished, having been right in the landslide's path.

An hour passes before the crowd finally parts to let the ambu-lance through. Mechanics bring in some lifting equipment for the biggest rocks and branches, but the street is too narrow to maneuver in a crane.

There are a dozen men plowing through the pile. It's not enough. I want the whole damned town moving rocks.

The police chief makes his way over to me and confirms that a PLF missile launched from the valley sparked the landslide. Whether the missile was intended as a warning or the start of a full-blown attack on Varaz...no one knows.

It could happen again any second—and the target could be the town itself rather than the side of the mountain. Not only do I need to get Nell out of here, I need to *get her out of here*.

We haul rocks and branches, and shovel through layers of mud. An animal whine suddenly breaks through the noise. I run over and pull a plank of wood away from the source. A dog's black nose pokes out from under a branch. I yank the branch off and push smaller stones away.

Poe struggles to free himself from the rubble and stand. He's covered in mud and dust, but doesn't have any visible injuries.

To stay on the safe side, I heft him into my arms and stumble back toward the medics and ambulance. "Get him over to the vet. Make sure he's okay."

One of the medics nods and takes the dog from me. I hurry back to the church and continue shoving debris aside.

It takes forever, a fucking eternity. The sun starts to descend. Someone tosses me a bottle of water. I block images of her, trying to stay focused on the work. Crashes and the rumble of machinery fill the air as an excavator lifts and moves the heaviest rocks.

The worst of the wreckage is inside the church. The air is still thick with dust and dirt. I stumble, crawl, and climb over the pile, calling Nell and Alexei's names, my terror twisting into sick agony at the thought of them having been in the church when the landslide hit.

My eye catches a glint of silver. I shove at a heavy rock. It doesn't budge. I push it with my shoulder and manage to move it far enough to grab whatever's underneath.

God, no. No.

I pull Nell's bag out from under the rock. The leather is torn, the silver buckles broken.

Keep going.

My eyes burn. I taste blood. I wipe sweat from my forehead and push away another stone, leaving bloody handprints on the surface. I stop only once to briefly grip the piece of gray sea glass in my jeans pocket.

Finally, I get to the interior of the church. The landslide destroyed all the pews. Sharp, broken pieces of wood lie crushed under the rubble. Shards of colored glass crunch under my boots. The decapitated head of a statue stares at the sky.

Past the fear pounding in my head, I hear the rescue workers yelling Nell and Alexei's names. I half-listen for a shout of discovery.

Not "I found a body," God, please.

A heavy, black dread encroaches. Darker than anything I've ever known.

I shove it down and keep looking for her.

CHAPTER 24

Nell

THERE'S NO LIGHT. My throat is thick with dust, and searing pain rips through my shoulder. A scream tries to push through my chest, but I can't get it out. I'm entombed. Buried alive.

Tears burn. I'm lying in a cold, slimy puddle of mud. The wet stickiness of blood runs down from my forehead. I squeeze my eyes shut and flex my fingers, struggling to pull in a shallow breath.

Alexei. I move my hand carefully, my fingers encountering pebbles, mud, a rough piece of concrete.

"Alexei." His name is a choked, desperate whisper.

No response. Did he somehow escape? Or is he buried with me? I can't remember his position in relation to me. I have no sense of place, no idea where I am except trapped under tons of rock and concrete. We were at the apse of the church, close to where the altar would be. Had we moved or been thrown somewhere else?

What happened? First the massive blast, then the landslide…
but why? Was it a bomb? Is Varaz under attack? Did the PLF get
past the barricades?

I tell myself not to speculate because obviously I have no
answers. My shoulder is screaming with agony. My head pounds.
A metallic thumping noise that makes no sense—a machine, a
thousand hammers?—fills my ears.

I flex my other hand and my toes. I attempt to move my leg,
but it's pinned under a heavy weight. I peel my gritty eyes open
and try to focus on something, anything.

I shift and reach out for Alexei again. Fiery pain tears through
my shoulder and down my back. My stomach heaves. A strangled moan comes out of my throat, and then there's nothing.

CHAPTER 25

Darius

I STOP, swiping my arm across my forehead. The machinery is thumping, the echo loud and rhythmic against the mountain. Was that her voice under the noise? I strain to listen. Or am I so goddamned desperate I'm hearing things?

Brian gets past the caution tape barrier to help the rescue effort, and he assures me that Poe is okay and the vet is taking X-rays as a precaution.

The sun sinks into the horizon. The fire department hooks up floodlights and directs them onto the wreckage. The towns-people provide food, drinks, blankets. More volunteers join in the search. The fear of another landslide hangs heavy in the air.

The area of the rockfall covers several city blocks, but the other damage is to property only. No one else is reported miss-ing. Though the focus is on the church, the wreckage spilled far out into the streets, and we have no idea where Nell and Alexei might have been. With only smaller equipment and people working by hand, it's a prolonged, tedious job.

Right when every second counts. When another missile could destroy the town without warning.

The floodlights cast distorted shadows over the ruined foundation and the sinister bulk of the mountain. Cold snakes through the air.

We dig and shove rocks and move tree branches. The priest hovers nearby. The nuns pray with their rosary beads. I find a ruined book, pages torn and smeared, listing the church's inventory.

"We got something!" A yell comes from a group of three men near the far end of the church, followed by a bunch of Krasnovian that's too jumbled for my comprehension.

The other workers go on sudden alert.

Outside the building's foundation, the police chief snaps out a series of rapid orders. A man jumps into a bobcat and restarts the engine.

"What is it?" I shout.

A firefighter, Matthias, lifts his arm. "We think it's a hand."

A hand?

My gut roils. I climb over the mud-slick rocks, stumbling in my haste to get to the area. The three men are clustered around a boulder resting on a huge slab of concrete. More rocks and uprooted trees are scattered on top. Matthias is crouched down, peering through a crack under the concrete.

"Hard to see." He moves aside.

I grab a flashlight from my pocket. I'm shaking. I can't hold the beam steady.

Getting to my knees on the rough stone, I shine the light into the narrow opening.

A hand.

Holy fucking Christ.

Nell's hand. Lifeless and still, her fingers slightly curled.

My breath stutters. I guide the beam upward past her arm, her shoulder...her face. Dirt and blood cover her forehead and cheeks. Her hair and clothes are caked with mud. Her eyes are closed, her skin white.

A mixture of panic and relief floods me. I grip the flashlight harder. I can't tell if she's breathing.

"Nell." I reach into the opening and try to touch her. My fingers grab a fistful of gritty mud. "Nell, honey, can you hear me?"

I give the flashlight to Matthias and get flat on my stomach, straining to reach her. The boulder and concrete crashed onto a heavy wooden table, which is broken but still holding the deadly weight off her.

"More light."

The men crowd closer and shine multiple flashlights into the pocket. I can't see any sign of Alexei.

"They're bringing the excavator," Matthias says.

Impatience burns my throat. They still need to lift yards of wreckage out of the way before the machine can make its way over here.

I reach farther and cover Nell's hand with mine. The shock of touching her reverberates up my arm. Her skin is cold. Though I've seen too much horror to have an easy relationship with God, I send up a thousand silent prayers.

Then I slide my hand up and press my fingers against her inner wrist.

Please please please...

A pulse. Faint and unsteady, but there. Beating under her delicate skin. Sending blood to her heart. Keeping her alive.

I shut my eyes and heave in a breath. "She's alive."

"Excavator will still take time." Matthias crouches beside me and peers through the crack. "We can collect men and try to move the rock together. Use lever and pulley system. Risky, but faster than wait for machine."

I open my eyes and look at Nell. My chest aches. If we move the boulder and shift the pile off balance, the table and the concrete slab could fall and crush her. On the other hand, if the excavator takes too long to get here, she could—

I can't overthink this. We have to get her out. "Let's try and move it."

I start to pull away from her when her fingers twitch. "Nell?"

In the beam of the flashlights, her face is ghostly and shadowed. Her eyelashes flutter against the crust of dried blood.

"Nell, can you open your eyes?"

She opens her eyes slowly and stares at me. I tighten my hand on hers, swallowing past the sudden constriction in my throat.

"Hey." I almost can't speak. "We're going to get you out of here."

Her eyes are dazed, the pupils dilated.

"Was Alexei with you?" I ask.

"I…" Her voice is thin and hoarse. "He was. I can't…can't find him."

Her eyelids start to drift closed again.

"Nell, baby, stay with me, okay?" I fight the panic still churning inside me. "You're trapped under a boulder and a piece of concrete that we have to move before we can reach you. Can you move your fingers and toes?"

"Yes, but…" She shifts slightly and grimaces, her body spasming. "Hurts."

"I need you to lie as still as you can while we get the rocks out of the way."

"How long…?"

"I don't know. I hope just a few minutes." We'll be lucky if it's less than an hour. "Hold on, okay?"

I start to ease away from the ledge. Nell suddenly tightens her fingers around mine.

"Don't leave."

"I'm right here, sweetie. I've gotta help move the boulder. It's taking too long for the machine to get here, so we're going to do it manually."

"No." A plea cracks her voice. "Don't leave me. It's too dark."

I close my hand around hers and pull in a breath. My heart is hammering. I don't want to leave her alone, but she has to get medical care as soon as possible. She could have internal injuries.

"Nell, honey, I—"

Matthias puts his hand on my shoulder and lowers his voice to barely a whisper. "Stay. If collapse, you can pull her out."

My spine tenses to the point of snapping. If the slightest shift topples the pile, tons of debris will crash down on her. The chances of me being able to pull her out of the imploding rock-fall are slim to none.

But if there's *any* chance...

I nod at Matthias. "Go."

He hurries off with the other two to gather the men and prepare to move the wreckage. I ignore the noise, the shouting orders, the buzz of the crowd. I set the flashlight on the ledge, directing the beam away from Nell's eyes but close enough to illuminate the pocket.

"What else hurts?" I ask.

"Everything." Her mouth twitches slightly at the corner.

"Sorry. Stupid question." I rub my thumb against her wrist. "We found Poe. He's okay. The vet is doing some extra tests just to make sure."

She closes her eyes briefly and sighs. "How long have I been here?"

Seven hours and twenty-eight minutes. "A few hours. They're just getting the equipment to move the rock out of the way."

"Don't leave."

"I won't."

She's shaking, both from shock and the cold. I release her hand to take off my jacket and push it through the crack. I adjust it as best as I can over her. It's not enough but it's better than nothing.

The workers clamber over with pry bars, pipes, ropes, and a wooden sled. I can barely restrain myself from getting up to direct the whole operation. If this goes wrong—

The thud of metal against stone vibrates through the rubble. I tighten my hand around Nell's wrist.

"I can't move my leg," she says.

"Which one?"

"Right. It's pinned."

I shine the light toward her leg. A thick layer of mud coats a splintered tree trunk, but it's underneath the broken table. Which I pray will hold.

"It's part of a tree," I tell her. "We'll get you out as soon as they get the boulder off."

The hammering continues until they get a lever under the rock. The concrete slab shifts. The men shout out orders and instructions.

"Hey, remember the story of the hermit crab?" I ask in the hopes of distracting her. "He kept looking for the perfect home."

"I thought of you like that." She turns her gaze to the concrete slab above her. The echo of the noise must be excruciating in the pocket. "But you just took your home with you...never had to look for one...oh..."

She winces, her face draining of more color.

"Nell? What is it?"

"Shoulder." She bites her lip, pain and fear darkening her eyes.

Rocks bang against each other as the men push smaller ones away. Bits of dirt rain down onto Nell's face and hair. She turns her head, closing her eyes. All I can do is hold her hand tighter and rub her wrist.

"I was...when I met Lindsey, I was kind of envious." She takes a deep breath, like she's steeling herself. "All that adventure and excitement like...like you. But this is overkill."

"Agreed." I manage a hoarse laugh. "Thankfully, not all adventure and excitement is this dangerous."

One of the men shouts, and a flurry of Krasnovian follows. Nell flexes her hand against mine. "What are they saying?"

"I think they found Alexei." I straighten, a twinge of hope pushing past my fear. "I'm going to let go of your hand for just a few seconds while I find out what's going on, okay? I'll be right back."

Letting go of her is like ripping part of myself off. I get to my feet and move to where I can get a better view of the firefighters. They're clustered a short distance away, shoving at a broken tree trunk. Matthias suddenly lets out a whoop of victory.

"He's here!" One of the men waves. "He's good."

They scramble to move the trunk and widen the opening. Two of them reach in and haul Alexei out. He's covered in mud, his face marred with scratches and cuts. His left arm is bent at an unnatural angle, but he's alert. With two men supporting him, he's able to shakily stand. He catches my eye.

"Nell?" he asks.

"We found her," Matthias assures him in Krasnovian. "We're trying to get her out."

The men help Alexei navigate the wreckage to the side aisle, where two medics are waiting with a stretcher. The others resume the task of freeing Nell.

I return to her and relay the good news. "They're taking care of him now."

"Thank god." She breathes out.

I close my hand around hers again. "You're next, so get ready."

"I was born ready, tough guy," she murmurs, then chuckles hoarsely. "Actually, I totally wasn't, but I'm ready now. More than ready."

The noise gets louder—hammering, shouts, the hideous

screech of metal against stone. More dirt and pebbles spill down. My heart is about to burst out of my chest.

"What should I do when the rock is moved?" She eyes the concrete slab warily.

"Just lie still. I'll take care of you, I promise."

If only I could squeeze through the damned crack and get in there with her, I could protect her. Cover her up.

Matthias shouts. The concrete slab shifts. The table creaks. I try not to grip Nell's hand too tightly so she won't sense my fear. A huge crash sounds from above—the boulder rolling against the rocks below.

The concrete tips.

"Hurry!" The yell escapes before I can stop it. I can't get in there. I can't pull her out either. Her leg is pinned.

The men scramble and shout, turning their attention to the concrete slab. Another massive shriek of metal on stone, the heaving noise of moving rock, voices rising like crows.

"Hold on, baby." I get to my knees, ready to shove my way under the fucking concrete if I have to. "It's almost over."

Her eyes are squeezed shut, her breathing shallow.

The table starts to tilt off-balance. A thin slice of artificial light rains down from an opening at the edge of the concrete. One of the men shoves a crowbar under the slab and shouts for the others to help him. Another scramble, a shower of dust and dirt, and they heave the slab up. With an enormous crash, it topples to the side.

Light floods the pocket. Nell opens her eyes and stares at the six men standing on the rubble above her. Matthias and two others reach down to pull the table out of the way. Relief weakens every part of me.

I climb into the opening, feeling my way down Nell's leg until I find her calf pinned under the tree trunk. Matthias shoots rapid-fire Krasnovian at his crew, and two of them clamber down to help lift the wrecked tree. When a few inches are clear, I ease Nell's leg out from under it.

I turn back to her. She's still conscious, her eyes dark with pain and her teeth digging into her lower lip. The jagged cut on her forehead has started to bleed again.

"You're safe." Forcing my voice to remain steady, I bend down and tuck my arms under her back and legs. "I'm taking you out now."

I start to lift her into my arms. Her shoulder hits my chest. She gasps—a choked, strangled noise of agony. Tears flood her eyes and fall down her cheeks. I stop, gesturing for Matthias to shine another flashlight down. I take my jacket off Nell, my stomach pitching. Her shoulder is out of position.

I take a breath and try to pick her up again. She cries out sharply and starts to sob. I lower her back to the ground and drag my arm over my forehead. She's close to passing out again. If I move her, she'll go under. I can tell her what I'm going to do, but the anticipation will make it worse.

I kneel beside her and gently run my fingers over her shoulder and upper arm. She moans, her face twisting with pain. I ease her arm out gently to a forty-five-degree angle. Steeling myself, I pull her arm firmly, pushing her upper arm bone back into the socket joint.

Her scream stabs me to the bone. She goes limp, but stays conscious.

"I'm so sorry." I press my lips against her blood-streaked forehead.

Her breath whooshes out on a heavy sigh. She's still in pain, but now it won't be as severe. I gather her into my arms and climb out of the opening. The other men grab hold of me, hauling us the rest of the way.

I stumble over the boulders and branches to the medics. Her hand fists into my shirt. One of the medics reaches for her to get her onto the stretcher.

"No." Her grip on me tightens. Her eyes are dark, her pupils dilated to pinpoints.

I move past the medic and lower her onto the stretcher. "Honey, you need medical care. You have to let them treat you."

Her gaze searches mine. "Where are you going?"

"Nowhere." I squeeze her hand. I don't want to leave her, but the medics need to ride with her in the ambulance. "I'll be right here. I'm just staying out of the way so they can take care of you. Alexei will want to see you too."

"Where is he?"

"He might be at the hospital already." I stroke my hand over her mud-caked hair. "I'll meet you there."

Though it physically hurts, I detach her fingers from my shirt and nod at the medics to take the stretcher away. They hurry off. Beyond the barrier, the crowd erupts into cheers and applause. Within seconds, they load the stretcher into the ambulance and drive off, lights on.

The instant Nell is out of my sight, all the strength drains from me. I sink onto a boulder and drag in a breath. Someone pushes a bottle of water into my hand.

"Come over and we will look at you." Another medic stops at my side.

I wave him off and gulp the water. "I'm fine."

"You do not look so fine."

I shove to my feet. Nell is alive. I don't need anything else to be *fine*.

No, that's not true.

I need *her*, the woman whose entire life is woven into the loops of my memory. My heart can't beat without her.

CHAPTER 26

Nell

A DOCTOR and two nurses are waiting for me at the four-story stucco hospital near the watchtower. As they take me out of the ambulance, they explain that Hazel drove down to alert them as soon as the firefighters found me under the wreckage.

They whisk me in for tests, scans, and X-rays. I'm put on an IV drip and given painkillers. The doctor closes the gash on my forehead with stitches and checks my shoulder and leg, both of which are sore but not broken. He puts my arm in a sling to keep my shoulder in place.

A nurse helps me take a shower to wash the mud off, then she cleans the cuts and abrasions on my face and arms. I have a concussion, bruised ribs, and plenty of aches, but no internal injuries. I am extremely lucky.

The doctor wants me to stay at the hospital overnight, and a nurse brings me bread and a bowl of soup. As I'm eating, Alexei comes into my room. A bandage covers a cut on his cheek, and his left forearm is in a cast.

The instant I see him, tears fill my eyes.

"No, no." He stops beside my bed and bends to give me a careful embrace with his good arm. "We are not sad. We are happy that we are alive."

"Most definitely." I wipe my cheeks with a napkin. "Happy and relieved. How do you feel?"

"Like I was crushed in landslide."

We both laugh. He pats my uninjured shoulder. "The doctor tells me you are not badly hurt. For that, I have utmost thanks. So will everyone else. The nurse already updated Hazel and Brian, and Sofia will come to see you with the boys after you have had a chance to recover and sleep."

"Is Darius here?"

"Yes, he was pacing outside like he cannot stand waiting one more second." Alexei glances toward the corridor. "I saw him from my room. But I think he left, for some reason. I will go find him for you?"

"No, you need to rest. I'm sure he'll come back soon."

He nods. "When we are both out of hospital, we will celebrate being alive with champagne or whatever drink Ivan will give us for free."

"Agreed."

We hug each other again, and he returns to his room. I finish half my dinner and settle back against the pillows. The medicine has eased my pain, but I'd asked the doctor not to give me a sedative. Though it would soften the edges of the trauma, I have such bad memories of being sedated both right before and during my stay at the institution that I have no desire to experience the fuzzy effects again.

"You up for a visitor?" Darius's deep voice filters into my ears. I open my eyes. He's standing in the doorway, his broad shoulders blocking the light from the corridor, his warm, brown eyes fixed on me. Relief and an aching, intense need flood me, as if the sight of him has turned on a faucet full blast.

"Always," I whisper.

He pushes the door open farther, and Poe trots into the room, his ears perked and tongue hanging out.

"Poe." I start crying again in earnest.

The dog jumps onto the bed, snuffles around at my blankets, and licks my hand. I wrap my arms around his neck and sob into his thick, soft fur. Darius unhooks the leash and sets it on the table. He bends to press his lips against the top of my head.

"He's just fine," he says gently. "A few bumps and bruises, but he gobbled down a steak dinner and couldn't wait to leave the vet's office. I brought him back to your apartment so I could pack you some clothes, and he was about ready to claw through the walls looking for you."

I chuckle and hug the dog harder, wiping my tears against his fur. He squirms, his tail thumping against my legs, and flops down next to me.

"The doctor said you'll make a full recovery." Darius hands me a few tissues and sits in the chair next to the bed. "You just have to rest and not overdo it for the next week or so. How's your shoulder?"

"Sore, but a heck of a lot better than it was." I put my hand out, and he clasps it between both of his.

"Thank you," I whisper.

"You…" He pauses and clears his throat. "I told you that you don't have to thank me. Not for anything. And the whole town rescued you, not me."

Oh, Darius, no. You rescued me. You've been rescuing me my entire life.

When I'd heard his voice through the haze of pain and confusion, I hadn't thought I was dreaming or hallucinating. Of course it was him. Of course he'd come to me when I needed him, no matter what's happened or how out-of-sorts we are with each other.

"I don't even know how to thank everyone." I squeeze his hand. "It's amazing, what they did."

"Your recovery is all anyone needs or wants." He rubs his thumb across my inner wrist.

"What happened, exactly?" I shift to put another pillow behind my head, and he reaches over to position it for me. "Alexei and I were unpacking some artwork like always, and we heard this massive bang, like an explosion. He thought it was an earthquake. We got under a table for cover, but seconds later there was this deafening noise, like the earth was cracking open. We couldn't get out before the landslide hit."

Darius's jaw clenches. He tightens his hands around mine. "It was a missile. Launched from the ground."

A sick dread pitches my stomach. "The PLF?"

"A faction is targeting Varaz. Likely a show of power rather than for destruction."

He doesn't believe that. The threat of destruction is the reason he came to Varaz in the first place. The reason he tried so hard to get me out before things took a turn for the worse. He knows better than anyone how brutal the PLF can be.

I press my other hand against Poe's head. "But if the PLF wanted to destroy Varaz, why didn't they aim the missile at the castle or at the town itself?"

He shrugs, but the tension in his shoulders belies the casual gesture. "Try not to worry about it. I'm getting all the information I can, and I'll tell you what I find out. There's a good chance the Krasnovian army will take down the barricades if they have to reinforce their troops, so we might see an end to the lockdown soon."

My chest constricts. "And we'll be able to leave?"

"That's the plan." He smiles faintly and squeezes my hand. "I'll take care of it. I'll take care of you. Your only job right now is to get better."

Poe stretches, pushing my legs to the edge of the bed. I pet his neck, thinking that if Darius hadn't had to come to Varaz to get me, he'd be out in the world doing his life's work, like always.

"Nell."

I sigh. "I just wish it hadn't come to this."

He presses his lips against my knuckles. A warm shiver races up my arm. "None of it is your fault. There is nothing you could have done to predict or stop any of it. Please remember that."

I untangle my hand from his and turn his palms upward. Two of his fingers are bandaged, and a crisscross of scrapes and cuts line his palms.

"Did a medic look at these?" I touch a bruise on the pad of his thumb.

"I'm fine."

I run my fingers up his arm to his shoulder. Dark shadows ring his eyes, and there's another scratch on his jaw. I can feel the energy leashed inside him still, even after God knows how many hours of digging through all that wreckage.

The door opens and a nurse bustles in. "How are you feeling, Nell?"

"Much better, thank you."

Darius moves back to give the nurse room to check my vitals and the monitoring machine. She makes notes on my chart and takes my dinner tray before leaving.

Fatigue settles heavily over me. Darius bends to press his lips against my forehead. "Get some sleep."

I tighten my fingers around his. "Please stay."

Regret flashes in his eyes. "I promise I'll be back as soon as I can. Poe will be here with you."

He kisses me again and untangles his hand from mine. As soon as he leaves, Poe shifts and paws at the blankets before settling heavily against my side, his nose resting on my shoulder.

I wrap my other arm around him and let myself fall into a shadowy sleep.

The doctor keeps me for observation for most of the next day before releasing me in late afternoon with pain medication and instructions to return for a follow-up. Darius drives me back to the apartment, with Poe in the backseat. To my surprise, balloons, streamers, and flowers decorate the front of the building.

"Courtesy of your friendly neighborhood Krasnovians." He shoots me a smile, his hand on my arm as we climb the stairs. "Hazel and Brian were getting so many inquiries about you that they had to make an announcement at the café just so they could go home and sleep."

He helps me get settled again and leaves only to buy some groceries, check in on Alexei, and let people know how I'm doing. When an unsteady Wi-Fi signal comes through, we contact my father and give him a version of events so sanitized it's practically sterile.

But I see no reason to stress him out even more than he already is, and it's not exactly comfort food to hear that your daughter was trapped by a missile-triggered landslide in a foreign country where a sudden war has broken out.

Darius gets stew and bread from the café for dinner, which we eat sitting at the table by the window. Poe gobbles down his portion and settles into his nest of blankets beside the bed.

After dinner, Darius brings me a doughnut with sides of blackberry jam and sour cream. He tells me that Ivan sent it over because he knows how much I love them.

I eat the dessert with both enjoyment and a touch of disbelief. I've been in Varaz for less than two months, and the people of this town have treated me like one of their own since the day I first arrived. I hadn't even felt this sense of home and community in Grenville.

I finish the doughnut and nod toward the square. "More soldiers."

Darius follows my gaze to the group of half a dozen Krasnovian army soldiers walking toward the police station. "A few of them helped up at the church, but the landslide blocked the eastern road. They've been trying to move the debris and open it back up."

"What about the lockdown?"

"The barricade was still up when I went down there this morning." He sits back and folds his arms, his gaze narrowing on the soldiers. "Wouldn't tell me anything, but they were bringing in reinforcements."

"That's good, right?"

He doesn't respond. Of course it's not *good* that the Krasnovian army sent in more units to protect Varaz right after a missile attack. Because that means the threat of the PLF is getting worse.

"The air feels different, doesn't it?" I push my plate away. "Almost alive, like it knows it could be torn apart any second."

He's silent. I feel the weight of his gaze, that unwavering scrutiny.

"Is this what it's like in all war zones when there's no actual fighting?" I ask. "Quiet and terrifying at the same time?"

He nods slowly. "But sometimes it's strange because everything is heightened. The light, the sounds, how things taste. Whatever you're doing—brushing your teeth, eating, checking your phone—some part of you knows it could be the last thing you ever do. You notice every breath. You feel your blood moving. Everything is sharp, like a razor's edge."

"That's one of the reasons you keep going back." I skim my gaze over his hard-edged features. "To feel that way."

His jaw tightens, as if I've spoken a truth he doesn't want to acknowledge.

"Do you remember telling me about the Greek village that's your favorite place in the world?" I reach across the table and put my hand on his.

He glances at me, faint warmth rising to his eyes. "Arkenos."

"Did you feel that way there? Like everything was heightened, but in a good way?"

He nods. "The sun is brighter. The water is so blue it's like a painting. And don't even get me started on the food."

I smile. "You still haven't returned?"

"No. It's been almost fifteen years, I guess."

"Do you want to go back one day?"

"I don't know." He rubs his thumb across my knuckles. "It was incredible when I was there, but I'm sure it's changed. I have too, obviously. Everything would be different."

"Change isn't always a bad thing." I want to tell him to look at how we've changed, but we're not exactly the best example of positive, uplifting change at the moment. We are, however, a damned good example of survival.

Darius detaches his hand from mine and rises to pick up our plates. "You should get some more sleep."

"I'm not tired yet." I stand and stretch carefully before moving to sit on the sofa. "Did you see Alexei?"

"He went home earlier too. Sofia and the boys are with him." Darius returns from the kitchen and sits beside me. "Anything else you need?"

I need *him*—always—but I shake my head. My emotions have been hovering right at the surface all day, which is likely both an aftereffect of the trauma and an incomprehensible gratitude. I've experienced terror before, but never has it been followed by a feeling of grace and awakening.

"What happened to those soldiers from the other night?" I ask.

"The captain told me they were fine, aside from having to take some crap about losing to an American." He shakes his head, shifting his gaze away from me. "You were right. I was looking for a fight."

"I know." I settle my hand on his knee. "I'm glad they're okay because no one else needs to get hurt. But the reason I hate seeing you fight is because I don't want *you* to get hurt anymore. I told you that in Grenville. You've seen enough pain. I don't want you to inflict it on yourself or anyone else. And that flashback...if you're even fighting like that in your nightmares, you don't need to go looking for it when you're in full control of your senses."

"Yeah." He drags a hand down his face. "For what it's worth, sleeping with you...it wasn't about me not trusting you to handle the flashbacks. I knew you could. It was that if I let you in too far, I'd never be able to let you go."

My heart constricts. "I never wanted you to."

He stares at the opposite wall. A strange tension lines his body, but it's not like the usual locks and defenses that have always been so much a part of him. I shift closer, tucking myself tentatively against his side. He puts his arm around me and presses his lips to my temple.

"I've hurt you." His voice is rough. "The one person in the world I want to protect. But I couldn't protect you from me."

"I never wanted you to do that either. I've only ever wanted to get as close to you as I possibly could." I rest my head on his chest. Something small and hard pokes into my hipbone from the side pocket of his jeans. "What is that?"

He reaches into his pocket, then holds out a gray stone. I take it from him. Not a stone. It's a piece of gray sea glass, resting in my palm like a tiny cloud. The interior looks swirled with fog, as if it contains a stormy sea.

He and I had found the sea glass on the beach at Volkov Bay years ago. The last time we were there, I'd told him to take it as a good-luck charm when he left Grenville. But I hadn't thought he actually would.

"I didn't know you took this with you." I look up at him. "Much less that you've had it all this time."

"I've never *not* had it." He picks up the glass. "I always have it in my pocket, no matter where I am."

"I'm glad you kept it. Good luck can be a light in the dark."

"Good luck isn't the light." He studies the smooth surface of the glass. "Not for me."

A slight ache pushes at my heart. I don't know if he has any light at all.

"Then what is?" I ask.

He looks at me almost pensively for a long moment.

"Nell." He lets out his breath slowly. "*You* are my light."

I shake my head, certain I didn't hear that correctly. "I don't understand."

"No." He closes his fist around the sea glass. "I never told you. I couldn't. But this sea glass is the exact color of your eyes. No matter how bad things got, it reminded me of you, of everything you said to me, of how good you are. Remembering all that made me want to keep going. Because even though parts of the world are absolute hell, there's also a girl who looks at the stars and draws superheroines and loves butter pecan ice cream. If I stayed alive, maybe I could see her again."

My heart is thumping like a bird trying to escape a cage. I'm still not sure if I heard what I think I heard. What I *wanted* to hear.

"That's lovely," I manage to say. "Did you *want* to see me again?"

"More than anything."

"But you thought being attracted to me was wrong."

"Yes, I did. Once." He shakes his head, his mouth compressing. "I've seen the worst part of humanity. Lived through it first-hand. Sometimes I've thought it couldn't get any worse...and then it does."

I curl my fingers into my palms, all my old pain for him breaking open again.

"I've seen whole villages massacred." Shadows darken his features. "Children forced into becoming soldiers. So much brutality and killing. I've spent my life documenting war and its effects, but it never gets any better. People constantly find new ways to terrorize and hurt each other. I still haven't accepted the fact that I can't stop it. That it will never change."

He pauses. I want to touch him, but I don't want to give him a reason to stop talking.

"I've thought a lot about what drives people to such extremes." He stares at his hands, rubbing an abrasion with his thumb. "Sometimes I've even understood it, which is its own kind of nightmare. It's all so fucking *wrong*. I've seen wrongness. I've done and felt more *wrong* things than I can count. But what I feel for you has never been one of them."

My breath stops in my throat.

"In fact..." He lifts his head to look at me. "It's the most genuine, pure thing I've ever known."

I press my hand against my eyes. I can't contain all the sudden emotions spinning and rolling through my heart.

"Nell." He takes hold of my wrist, pulling my hand away from my face. Lines of regret bracket his mouth and eyes. "I thought I was going to lose my mind when I was looking for you. I've never been so fucking terrified in my life. And I'm so sorry. I'm sorry I made you think you were a problem and not my...my *answer*. I'm sorry I couldn't admit that you're so much a part of me that I don't even know how I existed without you. I'm sorry it took so long for me to admit that you've always been my light in the dark. That you're the reason I still know what *right* feels like."

"Darius Hawke." I press my hand to his cheek and look into

his eyes past a blur of tears. "When I told you I would always love you, I meant it. I've been loving you from a distance for the past four years. I love you still."

A deep, almost painful tenderness fills his eyes. I lean forward and press my lips against his, not wanting him to think he has to say the words back and not even sure I want to hear them.

Though we will always be part of each other, we both made no promises beyond the time we have. Our reconciliation still feels fragile, like a newborn chick struggling to break through a thick eggshell. Right now, I just want to treat it gently.

When he moves to ease away, I take hold of his forearm and pull him closer. After a brief hesitation for fear of hurting me, he lifts me and carries me over to the bed.

He lowers me onto the mattress with infinite gentleness before bringing his mouth down on mine. Warmth floods me, erasing any lingering pain. He stretches out beside me, and our bodies lock together.

The kiss is unlike anything I've experienced before, even with him—slow and gentle at times, then more intense as he slides his tongue into my mouth and bites my lower lip. After soothing the mild twinge with a sweep of his tongue, he eases back to gently kiss my cheek, my jaw, the secret hollow above my chin. Every touch stokes the flames burning low inside me, even as I know he won't move past these slow, tantalizing kisses.

My breath grows quick and shallow, my head filling with the mouthwatering scent of him—cloves and citrus and spice—and the sensation of his powerful body, a fortress in which I have always been so safe.

I sink into the pleasure of it all—the gentle, teasing game of advance and retreat, the way even a slight change in intensity elicits a new sensation, the thrill of learning a rhythm that belongs to us alone.

After what feels like both forever and an instant, our kiss

slows into a soft-edged haze. I rest my head against his chest and close my eyes, my whole body filled with a bright, clear peace.

He gathers me against him, pressing his hand to the back of my head and folding his body around mine. There is an almost audible click, like pieces fitting into place, a door closing to keep us both inside.

I sleep dreamlessly, submerged fathoms deep. When I wake, he's asleep at my side, still holding me in his arms as if he'll never let me go.

CHAPTER 27

Darius

I DON'T WANT to let Nell out of my sight, but I force myself to watch her walk to the museum alone the next day.

She needs and wants to get back to work, and I can't both stay with her and figure out what the hell is going on now. I've failed before, but with the new PLF threat and increased military presence, my determination to get her out of here is going nuclear. There's little time left...if any.

I take a pair of binoculars up to the watchtower on the city wall and scan the horizon. Everything looks calm and still, no sign of smoke or gunfire. But I didn't expect there would be. A surprise attack was how the PLF started this invasion, and they're not going to abandon a tactic that worked.

I can't get any official information. The soldiers either ignore me or wave their guns and tell me to back off. They are immune to monetary bribes. The local police officers are equally close-mouthed. Rumors are flying among the residents, but no one can verify any facts. Some people are making hasty plans to evacuate, despite not having anywhere else to go.

I turn and stare at the mountain, the looming presence of the castle. Over the past few weeks, I've analyzed a thousand ways to navigate an exit route over the mountain range and even to make it all the way to the border of Moldova, but the jagged cliffs and vast, uncharted forest have stopped me from attempting it with Nell.

But now, there's a possible way out via the eastern route. The military abandoned the barricade after the landslide blocked the road, and they're still working to clear out the rocks and debris. A car or truck can't get through yet, but a person might be able to. Then they could follow the road down, if it's passable.

Getting off the mountain is only the first step. Aside from what I've heard on news reports and through rumors, I don't know what's going on outside of Varaz. Nothing good.

If I were alone, I'd have taken the mountain route first thing. But with Nell, especially now, my risks have to be calculated and deliberate. It's not enough just to get her out of Varaz. I also have to get her safely out of the country—and with as few incidents as possible. Which also means protecting her from all the unthinkably brutal ways she could become a target.

The Wi-Fi is out again. I scan old messages from friends and contacts updating me on what they know—which changes every two seconds. The media knows about us, but the sheer chaos is preventing anyone from being able to offer assistance. In his last message, Savko told me he made it to Telina. If I can get Nell there, he might be able to help us with transportation across the border.

Back in my apartment, I listen again to the radio scanner. The police chatter is about the explosion, the chances of another missile or a full-out PLF attack on Varaz, and what kind of defensive strategy the Krasnovian army intends to deploy. I record the transmissions on my cell and take notes, transcribing a few lines verbatim.

"Darius?" A knock comes at my door and the knob turns. Nell peers in, her face lit up with excitement. "Get dressed. Put on your navy dress shirt and black trousers. You have time to shower, if you hurry."

"What for?" I set the pen down. Though I love her unexpected pleasure, I can't think of a reason for it.

"You'll see." She claps her hands. "I'll meet you at my place. Fifteen minutes, max. Bring your camera."

She hurries out. I take a quick shower and get dressed—navy dress shirt and black pants—and cross the hallway to Nell's apartment. She's changed into the maroon dress that skims her gorgeous body, and she's in front of the mirror, trying with one hand to put her hair into a ponytail.

"You look incredible, but you should be wearing your sling." I close the door and approach her.

"I'm being careful," she assures me. "And my shoulder mostly just hurts when I lift my arm."

I take the brush and an elastic band from her and start to brush her hair. The thick strands fall like a river down her back. Though I could spend hours touching her hair, we apparently have somewhere we need to be.

After gathering her hair in my hand, I tie it into a ponytail— high on the back of her head, the way she likes to wear it. She gives me a black velvet ribbon. I fasten the ribbon into a bow over the elastic band and adjust the ends to make sure they fall evenly.

"Perfect, thank you." She smiles at me in the mirror, and my heart thumps in response. "Let's go."

"What's going on?" I hold the door open for her as she picks up her handbag. "Is this another festival?"

"Of a sort." She slips past me. "Come on. We don't want to be late."

She grabs my hand, and we head downstairs and across the street to the plaza. The cathedral doors are open, and people are climbing the steps—some dressed up, others still wearing their everyday clothes. Inside, music from the old organ is drifting through the air, and the priest is at the altar, skimming a black book. Lara from the Gingerbread House is scattering flower petals over the aisle.

"You can sit here." Nell indicates a seat in a front-row pew. "Take pictures. I have to do something, but I'll come join you soon."

She rushes off. I look around. Some of the men have put flowers in the buttonholes of their old work shirts. Mr. Becherov is holding a bottle of Italian wine, and three women are arranging bouquets in vases at the altar. The organ music changes to something resonant and ceremonial. Everyone moves into the pews and remains standing.

I stand and turn toward the doors. Sofia's twin boys, Jacob and Tomas, enter the church, both dressed in rumpled suits and ties, their dark hair combed and still wet. They walk to the altar, hiding self-conscious giggles behind their hands. I lift my camera, adjusting the focus as I snap shots of them approaching.

Then Alexei walks in, beaming so widely his smile looks as if it's about to lift him off the ground. His cast is decorated with Jacob and Tomas's colorful drawings. He joins the boys at the altar, pausing to give each of them a fist-bump.

The music changes again. Nell walks in next, her radiance erasing the lingering bruises on her face. She winks at me and stops on the opposite side of the altar from Alexei and the boys.

A palpable anticipation ripples over the crowd. On the arm of her father, Sofia enters the church. She is a luminous vision in a pale ivory dress and a short veil that enhances her aquiline features. She's carrying a small bouquet of flowers wrapped in a pink lace ribbon. The crowd becomes a sea of happy smiles and sighs of admiration as she passes.

At the altar, her father, Marcus, kisses her cheek and steps back, discreetly wiping away a tear. Nell takes Sofia's bouquet as the bride turns to her groom.

Sofia and Alexei reach for each other's hands. They're so caught up in staring at each other that the priest clears his throat to get their attention before starting the ceremony.

Nell sits beside me as the wedding begins. The ceremony contains the familiar exchanging of vows and rings along with Krasnovian cultural elements. Alexei doesn't let go of Sofia's hand for the next half-hour, and when they face each other and recite their vows, sporadic sniffling rises from the guests. The sniffling grows louder when Jacob and Tomas step forward to stand with their mother.

Alexei takes a lit candle from the priest and kneels in front of the twins. In Krasnovian, he says, "Jacob and Tomas, you are, individually and together, all that is good, mischievous, and energetic in the world. You are made of joy and curiosity. I promise to you that I will strive each day to keep your mother safe and happy, to let her know she is loved, to prove worthy of her. And to you I promise the same. I thank your mother, your father, and you for entrusting you to my care. I will be there for you both and love you for all of my days."

I put my camera down and take a clean handkerchief out of my pocket, passing it to Nell. She hiccups softly and wipes her eyes.

The priest gives Sofia, Jacob, and Tomas each a taper candle, which they light with Alexei's. Then all four of them place their flames on the wick of a larger candle on the altar, creating one big, bright flame.

After a final closing from the priest, the new family walks back down the aisle together, the twins in the middle, and Sofia and Alexei on either side, all holding hands and smiling. Thunderous applause, cheers, and whistles fill the air.

Nell tugs my sleeve, her eyes still damp. "If you can take some photos of them all outside, I'm going to run over to Ivan's to help him get ready for the party."

We go out to meet the happy couple and their boys in the plaza. I take pictures of them in different settings—some posed shots and some spontaneous. I've never photographed a wedding anywhere before, least of all in a war zone.

Ivan and Nell have put flowers on all the tables at the café, and he and several other men are popping champagne corks and setting out glasses. Platters of food are spread out over a long table.

Nell hurries over to me, still glowing. "Isn't this fantastic? Alexei and I were working on writing wall text for some paintings, and he said he had to run an errand. He was gone for an hour, and when he came back, he was beaming from ear to ear. He told me to take off early because we both had a wedding to attend. Of course, everyone rallied to help. Let's get some champagne."

Krasnovians know how to party, and soon both the café and the street are filled with people dancing, eating, and drinking. I take pictures of the festivities before Sofia brings me a plate of food and tells me to sit down and eat.

I find a table by the window, setting my camera on an empty chair. Alexei comes over, his face flushed with exertion and joy.

"My friend, I cannot thank you enough for the photographs." He pulls out a chair and sits beside me. "They will be treasured."

"I'll put them on a flash drive for you later tonight." I pick up my beer bottle and salute him. "Congratulations. I wish you all much happiness."

"If I have more happiness, I might explode." He grins. "I did not ever imagine I would marry and have two sons on the same day, but this is...abundance of riches, yes?"

"Yes." I set the bottle down and study him. "What made you decide to get married right now? Nell said you planned to wait another year."

"Plans cannot be counted on." He indicates his cast with a rueful shrug. "When I was under the rocks, I made promise to God that if he allowed me to live, I would no longer push love and honor away into the distance. I would make it number one on my to-do list every day. So this afternoon, it hits me, you know? *This* is every day. Right now. What am I waiting for? If there is another bomb, a landslide…whatever…I want to face it as Sofia's husband, as the father of her boys. So I run to pharmacy to ask her, and she is so happy she starts to laugh and cry at the same time. Now I am married man and father of twins. My life truly begins."

"You're all very lucky to have each other."

"That is why I could no longer wait. How can I postpone such great fortune?" A pensive look descends over his face, his forehead creasing. "I did not lose consciousness in landslide, like Nell did. I remember every second of noise and the crush of rocks. The pain like fire in my arm. The darkness. The whole time, I am thinking I have to survive for Sofia and the boys. And that Nell has to survive for you."

My heart bumps against my ribs. "For me?"

"Of course." He chuckles. "One needs only to see the way she looks at you to recognize how deeply she loves you. As for you…"

He shrugs, as if he's about to tell me a foregone conclusion. "There is old Krasnovian saying that everything rotates around a center. Like earth around sun, or spinning top and gravity. Same with people. When one is in chaos, one must always look to center for harmony and peace. This is how it seems Nell is for you. It is a rare gift. Do not abandon it for an uncertain future."

He claps me on the shoulder and pushes his chair back. As he walks away, I see Nell talking to the bookstore owner near the bar. Strands of hair have escaped her ponytail and flutter around her neck. Her face is bright, and the sound of her laughter rings out over the noise of the crowd.

She catches my eye, and her smile widens. After saying something to Josef, she weaves around the tables to me.

Before she can sit down, I grab her hand and pull her onto my lap. She gives a little gasp of surprise before softening like warm caramel against me.

"Well, hello there." She winds her arm around my shoulders, her eyebrows lifting. "Are you having fun?"

"I am now." I stroke her hip, wanting to keep her nestled against me forever. "You?"

"It's wonderful." She runs her hand over my chest. "A wedding in the midst of all this fear. You can add it to your list of good things."

"You're at the top of that list."

She smiles. She's so fucking beautiful.

"Are you feeling okay?" I ask. "Both you and Alexei should still be taking it easy."

"No better medicine than a party like this." She kisses my chin and wiggles off my lap. "I'm going to help Lara bring out the cake. Will you get some pictures of it?"

"Sure." I reluctantly let her go and pick up my camera.

After the cake-cutting and more dancing, the festivities begin to wind down. Waving and laughing, Alexei and Sofia get on his scooter and depart for his house in a shower of cheers and confetti. Sofia's father Marcus corrals the twins back to his place, and everyone pitches in to clean up.

It's past midnight before Nell and I make our way back to the apartment.

"Thank you so much." She indicates my camera as she closes her apartment door behind us. "They'll be thrilled to have memories of this day."

"I'm glad I could do something."

She slides her arms around my waist, settling her lower body against mine. "Let's make our own memories of this day."

I rest my hand on her collarbone. I love that hollow, the soft, secret juncture where her neck meets her shoulder. "You should get some rest."

"I'll rest later." She slips off her shoes and rises onto her tiptoes to kiss me. "Right now, I want you."

I have no defenses against her. I no longer want any. With one breath, she brings me to my knees.

I slide my hand to her nape, angling her face so I can deepen the kiss. The lust is instantaneous, a fire spreading through my blood. She tastes like chocolate frosting. Her luscious body presses against mine—all soft curves and heat.

I bite down on her lower lip and slide my tongue into her mouth. She murmurs a husky noise of encouragement, stroking her palm over my abdomen to my groin. I'm already half-hard, and it only takes one squeeze of her hand to bring me to a full erection.

I step back far enough to pull her dress off, locking my gaze onto her cleavage. Flashing me a smile, she unhooks her bra and tosses it aside, then wiggles out of her underwear.

The sight of her naked body hits me like a lightning bolt, setting my blood on fire. I undress and tug her onto the bed. I love the way she opens without hesitation—everything. Her arms, her legs, her heart.

I lower myself on top of her and kiss her again. She winds her arms around my neck, arching her hips up. I move between her thighs and sink into her. So hot and tight. My mind goes blank. Lust takes over. She gasps and grabs the sides of my head, pulling me down closer.

She pushes her tongue into my mouth. I thrust into her. Need boils through me. She hugs my hips with her thighs and bucks upward. It won't last long, not for her or me. I brace my hands on either side of her and pump harder. My head spins with the sensation of her clenching around my shaft. My whole body tightens with pleasure.

"Darius." Her fingernails rake my back.

I slide a hand down to her clit. She moans, digging her fingers in harder. She tenses, her breath catching in her throat, and then she sinks her teeth into my shoulder and comes hard and fast. Her body vibrates around mine so intensely that my control snaps. A hot, blinding wave courses through me as I shoot deep inside her. Wanting to stay there forever.

She clutches me, wrapped so close it's like she's fused to me, her breasts rising and falling against my chest. I press my mouth to hers and reluctantly move my weight off her. I get up to dampen a washcloth and clean her up before getting back into bed. With a sigh, she folds herself against me, every curve fitting just right.

"Stay," she murmurs.

I ease my hand through the length of her hair. "I'm not leaving you—"

Ever.

I bite back the word before it breaks free.

CHAPTER 28

Nell

POE'S BARKING wakes me first. I reach for Darius, but he's not there. A siren splits through the night—a high-pitched blast rising and falling like a scream. I sit up. He's at the window, pulling a long-sleeved shirt on over his T-shirt.

"What is it?" I almost can't speak.

He turns, his features rigid and his eyes pitch-black. "Stay right here. Lock the door and don't open it for anyone but me. Keep Poe close. I'll be back as soon as I can."

Before I can get another word out, he pulls on his boots and heads out the door. Poe is on full alert—ears back, tail pointed, his incessant barking a clear warning. I scramble to get dressed in jeans and a shirt, then peer cautiously out the window.

Illuminated by streetlamps and flashlights, the police and Krasnovian army soldiers are running through the square, yelling orders. I can't understand what they're saying. Men are boarding up shop windows and unloading trucks filled with sandbags. The siren continues to wail, drowning out Poe's bark.

I grab my phone and search frantically for a signal. Dead air. Where did Darius go? *Why* did he go? What the fuck is going on?

Outside, Alexei's tall figure suddenly crosses under a streetlight. He breaks into a run toward the museum.

I don't know what to do. I don't want to disobey Darius, but if Alexei is going to the museum, then I should be there too. God knows he and I have been through a lot together. If he needs help, I can't hide away up here. I won't.

I pull on my sneakers and scribble a note for Darius in case he comes back before I do. I don't want to put Poe at risk, but he'll lose his mind if I keep him locked inside. He makes the decision for himself, sticking unerringly to my side as I leave the apartment.

Heart racing, I hurry downstairs and open the front door. The siren has stopped, but the shouting is louder. The police chief is yelling out commands through a bullhorn.

I quicken my pace, darting across the plaza. An airplane whooshes overhead. Not until now have I heard an airplane fly over Varaz. Poe spooks and starts barking again.

"Come on, boy." I urge him into the museum and shut the doors firmly behind me. The noise is muffled but vibrating through the walls. "Alexei!"

"Nell?" He appears at the top of the stairs, his hair disheveled and eyes frantic. "What are you doing here? Where is Darius?"

"I saw you come in, and I thought you might need help." I run over to him. "Darius left, but I don't know where he went. What's the siren? What's going on?"

He closes his eyes briefly and mutters something in Krasnovian that could either be a prayer or a curse. "That is emergency siren. Warning to prepare."

"For what?"

"Usually storm or flood." He looks past me to the doors. "Now it is for siege."

Siege.

Holy shit.

Darius's voice echoes in my head. *They are ruthless...I know how fast violence can spread...It's only a matter of time before they strike somewhere else...I do not want you in this country when they do...The shit has hit the fan.*

I press a hand to my chest. "Where are Sofia and the boys?"

"I took her to her father's. The boys are there." He turns and heads into the largest gallery. "Marcus has bigger house with large basement. Concrete walls. They will hide."

"What do we need to do here?"

"Nell, you go back." He waves his good arm sharply. "Go to Marcus's house. Safer that you stay with Sofia."

"I'm not leaving." I hurry after him. "What do we need to do?"

With a frown, he picks up a battery-powered screwdriver from a workbench. "I must get the most valuable art back downstairs. If the PLF comes into Varaz, they will loot all the art, if they don't just destroy it. In storage, it will at least be locked up. Not enough time to transport it back to the castle."

He certainly can't do all of that by himself, especially with his left arm in a cast. I grab another screwdriver, and we get to work opening display cases and vitrines.

"You take the paintings and the psalters." Alexei removes several icons from one of the cases. "We can only be careful, no time to follow all protocol."

I climb the ladder to take down the smaller paintings we so painstakingly organized for display. The siren starts up again, and shouts ring from outside as people rush past.

Alexei and I work as fast as we can—running back and forth between the galleries and the basement, returning art and artifacts to the storage crates from which they were just liberated.

After putting away a medieval manuscript, I pause by the

window on my way back to the gallery. The square is a seething mass of Krasnovian army soldiers running and shouting orders. Some are crouched behind trees and cars with their guns drawn.

Another plane swoops overhead, the screech of the engine rattling the windows. Alexei stops beside me and pulls open the door. We edge cautiously onto the portico, staying behind the shelter of a column.

A blast shakes the earth—the horrific thunderous crash of an explosion. The reverberations shock me to my bones, knocking me off my feet. Alexei grabs my arm and pulls me upright.

We stare at the mountain. Bram Castle, the fortress that has steadfastly overlooked Varaz for hundreds of years, is on fire. Black smoke billows upward from the smoldering mass.

Another plane dives toward it. A second bomb drops. The left section of the castle crumbles.

"Quickly." Alexei leads me back toward the door.

I turn just as a military truck rolls over the hill from the main entrance of town. Men jump out, rifles clutched to their chests, harsh yells rising like a flock of crows. A gun goes off. Someone screams.

We duck back into the museum and bolt toward the basement. I grab Poe's collar, pulling him down the stairs. My brain frantically tries to process what just happened.

The People's Liberation Front has invaded Varaz.

And with the landslide still blocking the eastern route, there's only one road in.

Only one road out.

CHAPTER 29

Darius

FUCK. Fuck. Fuck.

A barrage of gunfire bursts through the air. Soldiers are hit before I even get out of the police station. The siren is incessant. The bombed castle is a blur of fire and smoke.

And this is just one PLF platoon.

"How many total?" I yell at the police chief.

"We don't know." He clamps on a helmet and face shield. "They came in from the west. Why the hell didn't the Krasnovian army take the offense and stop them before they got close? They gave us a fucking warning with the missile attack."

"That wasn't a warning," I snap. "That was a distraction. The warning was the first attack on Saldem."

I grab the Glock out of my waistband and put my finger on the trigger. Keeping close to the buildings, I run back to the apartment, yelling at a few residents to get back inside and barricade the doors. They sure as hell don't need to be risking their lives piling sandbags and boarding up windows.

I take the stairs three at a time back to Nell's apartment. The second I shove open the door, I know she's not there.

Dragging in a breath, I read her note. I should have known she wouldn't be okay with doing nothing. No matter the risk to herself.

A plane roars overhead. God knows what their next target is.

Not the museum.

I shut down the thought and run back outside. I can't get her out via the main road. I have no idea how many PLF troops are mobilizing against Varaz.

The air is thick with gun smoke and yells. A bullet zips past my head and hits the wall. I pass a Krasnovian soldier who is crouched behind a Humvee.

"The eastern road." I stop, my fingers tight on the gun. "Is it clear?"

"Don't think so." He narrows his eyes at the PLF soldiers breaking the windows of the stores across the street. "You want to get out, you're too late."

The fuck I am.

Ducking low, I sprint across the plaza to the museum. The doors are locked, the windows dark. I run down to the loading dock and punch the code into the entrance panel. Only a matter of time before the PLF cuts the power supply.

A shout comes from behind me. My stomach roils.

I turn and face the PLF soldier. Combat gear, helmet, heavy boots. Bright red insignia like a spray of blood on his shirt.

He waves his rifle at me. "Get away from there!"

There is no fear. No freezing up. Not this time.

I lift the Glock and pull the trigger. The shot lands in the other man's chest. He falls. Blood spreads from the bullet hole.

Shoving the gun back into the waistband of my jeans, I grab

his M4 carbine and another pistol from his holster. I punch the code into the panel. The gates open.

I yank open the side door and barrel up the stairs to the main floors. "Nell? Nell!"

The galleries are empty, some of the artwork gone from the walls and display cases. Underneath the noise from outside, I hear the faint sound of barking.

I race downstairs. "Nell?"

"In here." A door to one of the storage rooms opens, and she flies out, straight into my arms.

Relief surges through me. I drop the rifle and crush her against me, giving myself two seconds to absorb the feel of her. "Are you okay?"

"We're fine." She untangles herself from me and pulls me into the storage room. "We were concealing as much art as we could. Are *you* okay?"

I nod, glancing behind her at Alexei. "You both need to get out of here. I don't know what their plans are, but if they bombed the castle, they might be targeting the main buildings next. Cathedral, town hall, museum. The police are telling people to stay sheltered or to go over to the deserted neighborhoods on the west side."

"Can we even get safely over there?" Nell wraps one arm around Poe, who is shaking and whining. "We need to get Sofia and the boys too. Marcus and Ivan. Lara lives alone, so we need to make sure she's all right. And what about Hazel and Brian?"

I smother a burn of frustration. I learned a long time ago that it's impossible to help everyone, no matter how much you might want to. And my focus—my *center*—is Nell. I can't let anything or anyone else get in the way of her safety. I failed her once. I fucking refuse to fail her again.

But she won't save herself before anyone else. Which means I have to do it.

"Okay." I pick up the M4 and indicate for them both to go up the stairs. "Where is Sofia?"

"Marcus's house, on Centennial Street."

We return to the loading dock, Poe close to Nell's side. She stops when she sees the dead PLF soldier lying near the entrance. I grab her hand, steering her and Alexei down a narrow alley away from the plaza.

A haze of yellowish light hangs in the air. Several bodies lie sprawled on the streets around Harmony Square. The smell of smoke is rancid and thick. The gunfire has lessened to intermittent bursts.

"It's quieter," Nell whispers.

"Not for long," Alexei mutters. "That PLF platoon was sacrifice, to gauge defense. They are preparing larger attack. They have learned lessons from the war."

Nell tightens her fingers on mine. Her skin is clammy. I squeeze her hand in a futile attempt at reassurance.

The side streets appear to be empty, but we stick to the shadows. Marcus's house is a large stone building not far from the school.

Alexei pulls a key from his pocket and opens the wooden door. The interior is dark and silent. He gestures for us to follow him down the narrow stairs to the basement.

"Alexei, thank god." A teary-eyed Sofia and the twins crowd around him in an embrace. "We heard the fighting and were so scared."

She turns to hug Nell. I take Marcus aside. He's a solid, level-headed man who will understand the necessity of subterfuge, if it means keeping family members safe.

"I need to go back out," I tell him in a low voice. "Nell has to stay here with you. She won't want to, but she has to. It's critical."

He runs his hand over his beard. "You need my help?"

"Just to keep her safe. Please."

He nods gravely and pats his jacket pocket. "I have key that locks door from inside. Will use, if necessary."

"Thank you." I head toward the stairs, unable to stop myself from pulling Nell against me for a quick, hard kiss.

Her eyes widen. "Where are you going?"

"I'll be back soon, I promise."

"But—"

Before she can weaken me with a plea, I stride upstairs and close the basement door behind me.

Gripping the rifle, I run through the streets spiraling out from the square. Noise continues to rise from the town center, like a molten core still burning.

As I approach New Street, I pause and hide the M4 and the Glock behind a garbage can in an alleyway. Taking a chance, I keep the pistol in my waistband, pulling both my T-shirt and long-sleeved shirt over it.

Forcing myself to walk slowly, I approach the PLF truck parked in the middle of New Street. Two soldiers are standing beside it, the stocky one speaking into a radio. The other, a tall, skinny guy, lifts his rifle.

"Halt."

I stop and put my hands up. In Krasnovian, I say, "I am an American. I'd like to talk to your commander."

He eyes me suspiciously, his gun aimed at my chest. "You speak Krasnovian."

"Some. I'm a journalist. I've worked in Krasnovar."

"What do you want with the commander?"

"To talk. I have information he can use."

He elbows the other soldier, and they converse. The second soldier speaks into the radio before giving a shrug. The tall guy unclips handcuffs from his belt and tosses them to the other one. He cocks the rifle and fits the barrel into his shoulder, this time pointing it at my head.

"No funny business," he says in English.

I keep my hands up. The shorter soldier approaches and barks out an order. I put my hands behind my back. The clamp of metal around my wrists sounds like a cell door slamming and locking shut. The soldier pats me down and grabs the pistol out of my jeans. With a smirk, he shoves it into his belt.

"Get in." He jerks his head toward the truck.

I climb into the back. My heart starts to race. I force my brain to stay focused. I came to Varaz to get Nell safely back home. I'm going to succeed if it fucking kills me—which it might very well do.

The soldiers get into the front seat and guide the truck back toward the road. It's darker without the streetlights, and dawn hasn't yet broken. The truck's headlights illuminate the military jeeps and trucks making their way into town.

My muscles tighten to the point of snapping. The truck winds around the twisting road to the base of the mountain. The Krasnovian army barricade is gone, replaced by PLF tanks, Humvees, and dozens of armored vehicles. Soldiers swarm like cockroaches over the road.

The truck comes to a stop beside a field littered with makeshift tents. They order me out of the back and lead me past the tents. Generator-powered floodlights cast a harsh white light. Hard stares follow us. I'm acutely conscious of being surrounded by PLF soldiers.

A massive, gray-haired man wearing a captain's insignia on his combat fatigues steps out of a tent and narrows his eyes at me. "This is the American?"

Though the chances of him recognizing me are slim, I stay in the shadows. He's barrel-chested but shorter than me, so I make an effort to sound nonthreatening.

"David Smith." I meet his cold gaze. "Journalist."

"Lenkov." He takes a drag of his cigarette. "Captain. What do you want?"

"Captain Lenkov, I came to Krasnovar to write a story about the wine-making industry."

He chuckles and sucks on the cigarette again. "And how did that go?"

"Not well." I shrug abashedly. "But clearly, the strategy of the People's Liberation Front worked very well. The Krasnovian army forced me to stay in Varaz during their lockdown. My hope is that you will be generous enough to allow me to leave."

He drops the cigarette and grinds it with the heel of his boot. "Why would I do that?"

"Because I'm in possession of something you can use."

"Does it have a pussy?"

The other soldiers laugh. Lenkov's eyes gleam. Cold sweat trickles down my spine.

"I have information." I force my voice to stay even. "I know the defensive strategies the Krasnovian army and the town officials plan to deploy."

Silence falls. The two soldiers look at each other. Lenkov's mouth thins.

He steps closer to me. "Where did you get this information, *David Smith?*"

"Intercepted police and military transmissions. The soldiers at the barricades got bored and careless. They talked to the police about their plans in the event of numerous scenarios. I have their conversations transcribed in notebooks and recorded on flash drives. I'll give them all to you."

"You think we do not have our own intelligence?"

"I know you do. But military communications are bound by operations security and subject to deception. These recordings, on the other hand, could provide you with information—human intelligence—you'll never get through other channels."

He squints, studying me hard. "And in exchange, you want me to allow you to leave Varaz."

I try not to clench my teeth. My heart is punching my ribs. "Me and my wife."

He lifts his eyebrows. "Your wife."

"She came to Krasnovar with me."

"She is also journalist?"

"No. She just wanted to see the country."

"Where is she now?"

"She's safe in town. I want to get her home, but I can't without your help."

He purses his lips. "Who else knows about these recordings?"

"No one."

"How can I trust they exist, then?"

"I have no reason to lie." I let out my breath and make my shoulders slump slightly. "The Krasnovian army is made up of incompetent assholes. I have no loyalty to them. Why would I when they refused to help us? We should have been allowed to leave the second the PLF showed its strength."

Lenkov lets out a short laugh. "You are good sycophant, David Smith. Where are these notebooks and drives?"

"In my apartment."

"And how do you expect me to help you?"

"I have a car, but I need a PLF escort to help us get past the checkpoints to Telina."

"I cannot spare an escort."

"Two soldiers, max." I nod toward the two men who drove down in the truck. I'm still not sure I want a PLF escort, but they will be insurance on the road. "One truck. It will take less than three hours to reach Telina."

"And back." Lenkov's frown deepens.

He hasn't refused.

"Then halfway to Telina," I offer. "To the village of Kolchava."

If they haven't knocked out the cell towers near Kolchava, I can try to reach Savko from the village.

"And if not that," I add, "then you can simply allow us to leave

Varaz. We will fend for ourselves. Whatever you choose, you will have all my notes and recordings of the radio transmissions. Hours of them."

He studies me for a long minute, his gaze sharp and assessing. He's not stupid. He knows I'm lying about who I am, but he can't figure out why. And he's not sure if he should bother caring.

"All right, David Smith." He smooths a hand down the front of his fatigues. "Lieutenant Reiter and Private Tarek will take us to your apartment. You will show me these documents and recordings. If advantageous, I will consider your offer."

My spine feels like it's about to break. I want his agreement now, but the bastard holds all the cards, and he knows it.

I nod. "I would be most grateful."

With a snort, he snaps his fingers at Reiter, who hurries to get back into the truck and start the engine. I indicate the handcuffs.

"I have no weapons," I tell Lenkov. "Your private saw to that. I have no reason to be insubordinate."

Lenkov raps out a few quick words in Krasnovian. Tarek unlocks my handcuffs and nudges me in the back with his rifle. I climb into the truck. Lenkov gets into the passenger seat, and Tarek sits on the bench across from me, his gun pointed at my head.

As the truck makes the bumpy, twisting drive back up the mountain, I silently hope the private doesn't have a jittery trigger finger.

"Where is your wife?" The captain twists around to look at me. "In your apartment?"

Shit.

My plan was to convince them to let us meet them back at their camp. I could pick Nell up and leave right away. I don't want Lenkov or the other two anywhere near her. I also don't want them knowing Marcus's address or the fact that there are five other people in the basement.

"I told her to stay in the apartment." I give him a man-to-man laugh. "But she's a woman. Not prone to obeying orders."

Lenkov grunts.

The truck rolls into town. With the second wave of units, the fighting is spreading again, as if the PLF is throwing fuel onto the fire. Soldiers are running through the side streets, and a building burns in the distance, adding a choking smoke to the air.

Tarek prods me in the back with the barrel of his rifle. I lead him and Lenkov up the stairs to Nell's apartment and open the door.

"Anna isn't here." I look around, as if she might be hiding in a corner. "I'll have to fetch her."

Lenkov frowns. He's losing patience. "Where is she?"

"Probably with a friend." I edge into the hallway. "Please, wait here. I will return shortly."

I expect him to send Tarek with me, but instead he snaps an order in Krasnovian. Tarek goes into the kitchen and starts rummaging through the cupboards.

I run back down the stairs. They know I have no choice. No other plan. And I'm on thin ice. If Lenkov decides this is a waste of his time, he could either leave or kill me. Or take me prisoner.

I sprint toward Marcus's house, stopping to grab the Glock I'd hidden in the alley. Can't take the carbine. I'd left the front door of Marcus's house unlocked, and I bang on the basement door. He answers it, alarmed.

"My friend, what has happened?"

"Darius!" Nell bolts up from her position sitting against the wall and hurries over to me. Her eyes are red, her hair a disheveled mess. "Where did you go?"

"I'm sorry." I clamp down on a stab of regret. "Come with me. Leave Poe here for now."

"But what about them?" She indicates the others. Alexei and

Sofia are sitting with the twins, playing a game of checkers—no doubt to distract the two boys.

"We'll come back." One more lie won't send me to hell. I'm going there anyway.

I grab Nell by the wrist and back toward the door, keeping my gaze on Marcus. "I'll return soon."

He nods, glancing at his daughter and grandsons. He's lived long enough to know a lie when he hears one.

Still holding Nell's wrist, I head outside and back to the square. She stumbles after me. Her pulse is racing under my fingers.

"Darius, what..."

I stop and turn to her. "Nell, you once said you would follow me anywhere. I need you to do that now. I need you to trust me."

She stares at me, searching my face. "What are you talking about? Of course I trust you."

"Promise me you'll go along with whatever I say and do."

"Darius, what's going on?"

"Promise."

"Yes, but—"

There's no time to explain. For all I know, Lenkov and his men have written this off as a wild goose chase and left already. I stride back to the apartment building and go upstairs.

They're still there—Lenkov by the window, and the two soldiers standing near the kitchen, rifles at the ready. Lenkov frowns.

"You are trying my patience, David Smith," he snaps.

I feel Nell stiffen in surprise. I tighten my grip on her in warning.

"Apologies, Captain." I let go of Nell so it won't look like I'm coercing her. "My wife was with a friend. This is Anna."

Nell's gaze sweeps over the three men. A visible shudder goes through her. She moves closer to me.

"Your wife, hmm?" Lenkov approaches, lifting his eyebrows. "Young one, isn't she? Nice and ripe."

He pinches her cheek. I want to slam the fucker's head against the wall.

Nell recoils, her skin draining of color. Lenkov chuckles.

"Lucky man, David Smith." He skims his gaze over Nell's body and licks his lips. "Watch out for her. Maybe you should stay in Varaz. Lock her up like princess in tower, huh?"

A red mist descends over my eyes. Somehow I manage to take a breath and keep the rage contained. "Your admiration is well founded, Captain. Now would you like to see the documents?"

"Yes." He glances at the clock. "I'm losing interest in your little game."

Leaving the apartment door open, I cross to my room and grab two flash drives and several notebooks from my desk. I hand them to Lenkov and return to Nell's side.

She's still standing near the door, her arms wrapped around herself and her face pale as paper. I move slightly in front of her in the hopes that the other men will forget she's here.

Lenkov spreads the notebooks on the table. Reiter and Tarek peer at them from the other side of the table. Reiter puts one of the flash drives into a cell phone and hands it to the captain. They converse in low tones, a mixture of Krasnovian and occasional Russian.

Finally Lenkov lifts his head and looks at me. "Until my intelligence officers review this material, I will not know how worthy your information will be. However, you are somewhat amusing, and this is an unusually interesting offer that I am prepared to accept. Captain Reiter and Private Tarek will accompany you as far as Kolchava."

Relief eases some of my tension. I won't relax until Nell is on a plane to Frankfurt, but now, finally, she's closer.

I nod. "Thank you, Captain. We just need a few minutes to pack."

He makes a sharp gesture at Tarek, who starts to sweep the notebooks into his arms.

I hold up my hand, phrasing my next words carefully. I don't want the captain to think I expect him to take off with the material and leave us behind. Even though that's exactly what I expect.

"We will bring the books and flash drives with us." I indicate the apartment across the hall. "I have more there, in my workroom."

"Insurance, huh?" Lenkov barks out a laugh. "Reiter will wait outside and ensure you give us all your materials. You have ten minutes."

He strides to the door, Tarek at his heels. Reiter cocks his rifle and stands in the hallway. Nell shuts the door on him and locks it.

She spins to face me, her eyes suddenly blazing. "Darius, what in the everlasting *fuck* is going on?"

I grab her backpack from beside the bed and unzip it. "Take only what you need. Give me your passport and travel visa."

"I'm not giving you anything until you tell me the truth," she snaps. "You're making a deal with a PLF captain? Did I hear that right or am I having a nightmare?"

"I'm getting you out of here." I throw her sketchbooks into the backpack and open the closet. "Pack your stuff, or I'll do it for you."

"You arranged for PLF soldiers to take us halfway to Telina?" She spreads her arms out, her voice rising in anger. "Since when did you become so chummy with the assholes who *took you hostage*? The ones you've been trying to take down for the past four years?"

A thousand curses split through my brain. I point to the window. "Nell, there is a fucking *war* happening out there. When you're in a war, you do whatever the hell it takes to survive, to escape, to come out of it alive. Even if that means cutting a deal with the enemy. Morals and ethics don't exist when people are getting killed and maimed. When you could be next."

"Bullshit. You've been in more war zones than a combat veteran, and no man on earth has a stronger moral compass than you do."

"Right, that's why I caved and started fucking a girl half my age."

"Oh, shut *up* with that crap." She strides over and shoves me in the chest, hard enough to make me back up a step. Her eyes glitter with angry tears. "And don't try and change the subject. You're giving the captain the radio scanner reports in exchange for his help getting us out of here? Did I get that right?"

"Yes, dammit." I stride over and yank open the dresser drawers. "We don't have time to pack all your stuff. Where's your passport? Just take essentials. Everything else is replaceable."

"Not everything." She curls her hands into fists. She's sparking with righteous fury. "You're giving the People's Liberation Front details about Varaz's defensive strategy. What if they find out the officials have been stockpiling food and medical supplies in the warehouses? What if they learn people are evacuating to the west side? They could decide to bomb the warehouses and all those other neighborhoods. What if they find out that Dr. Petrov wants to move patients to another location to keep them safe from shelling? Then what if the PLF attacks the new hospital? God only knows how many people could die."

I clench my teeth. "The recordings don't have that level of detailed information. And the PLF won't have time to listen to them all and then form a strategic offense."

"You don't know that! But you're giving them a fucking map." She paces to the windows and back, her body trembling. "You're selling the town out and putting our friends in terrible danger. Why would you do that? *How* could you?"

"Because of you!" I whirl around, a tortuous mix of rage and frustration surging in my chest. "I would do anything...

anything...to get you to safety. I can't fucking stand that you're still in this hellhole, that I've failed to get you out. If you being safe means I have to be a traitor, then fine. I'll take it. I don't give a fuck about anything or anyone but you."

She presses her hands to her face. Tears roll down her cheeks. "That's not true."

I open her travel bag and start searching for her passport and visa.

"Darius."

I can't look at her. My insides are about to break in half. "Nell, please, just—"

She puts her hand on my arm. "You care too much. That's why you keep going back, why you're working with the UN. It's why you've been investigating the PLF. You want to help people. You need to. Which is why turning over the army and police intelligence is so totally antithetical to your nature. It's not who you are. Not even close."

I can't respond past the sudden constriction in my throat. I dump the contents of her bag on the table. "Where the fuck is your passport?"

She pulls open a desk drawer, then turns and throws her passport at me. It hits me in the chest. I grab it with one hand and point my thumb at the door. "Let's go."

She crosses her arms, her features tight and her eyes as bright and luminous as twin moons.

Fucking hell.

"I said I would follow *you* anywhere." She wipes her cheek with the back of her hand. "But this is not you. Not the Darius I know and love. And I can't be the reason you're forced to betray the people of this town. Please. I'm begging you not to go through with it."

"I don't..." I swallow hard. My chest almost cracks. "I don't have another plan, Nell. I came here for *one reason*. To get you home. Not only have I failed, I've put your life at risk. All the things I've done, the lives I've lived...and I can't do this *one* thing for you, of all people. I would enlist in the goddamned PLF if it meant you could be safe."

"Oh, my guardian angel, I know you would." She crosses the room and slides her arms around my waist, pressing her forehead against my chest. "But you haven't failed. You've done more for me than anyone else could do in a lifetime. That's just one of the reasons you have my whole heart, every part of me. I'll promise you anything. And I promise we can figure this out together."

I wrap my arms around her. Give myself five seconds to absorb her softness and warmth. The feel of her takes the edge off the pain clawing at me like razor blades.

I let her go, dropping her passport into her backpack. "We need to hurry."

Her eyes darken. "Darius—"

"Stay back." I open the door.

Reiter looks up from examining his fingernails. "What the hell is taking—"

I pull out my Glock and fire. The bullet hits him in the chest. He staggers and goes down, his rifle clattering to the floor.

I turn back to Nell. She's staring at me.

"Come on." I hold my hand out to her. "We're getting out of here."

CHAPTER 30

Nell

DARIUS TAKES fifteen seconds to throw all of the radio scanner notebooks and flash drives into the incinerator chute. I grab his camera from the kitchen counter and shove it into my backpack.

He picks up the rifle, and we run down the stairs leading to the garage. The garage door exits onto the deserted back alley. Dawn is starting to break, stealing our cover of darkness.

I follow him as fast as I can, fueled by both panic and relief. Gunfire blasts through the air. Another plane swoops overhead, engines screaming. A Humvee turns the corner and barrels toward us.

Darius jerks me into an alleyway, shoving me behind him. I grip his arm. I'm sweating and shaking, but his presence is a grounding force, like gravity. After the truck passes, we keep going—sticking close to the buildings. He carries the rifle with natural facility, as if he's used such a weapon countless times before.

The chaos has reached the far end of Centennial Street. The gunfire is a wall of sharp, metallic noise. PLF soldiers are smashing in windows with the butts of their rifles. A spray of bullets scars a row of retail shops.

Darius swears, dragging me to the narrow alley behind Marcus's house. We go into the back door and downstairs to the basement. Marcus, Alexei, and Sofia hurry over to greet us, though for the sake of the twins, they keep their fear contained.

Poe leaps all over me, licking my face and thumping his tail. I hug him tightly, unable to think about what happens next.

"The eastern route past the factory is the only way out." Darius speaks in a low voice. His features are set like stone, his eyes glittering with determination. "I don't know if they've cleared the landslide debris, but we'll have to take the chance."

"How will we get there?" Marcus asks.

"Walking, for now." Darius takes out his phone and unlocks it. "I don't want to be out there in daylight, but they're going to start looting houses next. We can't get to my car. I have an offline geological map that might help."

Alexei turns to talk to Sofia. I tug Darius's hand. "What about Hazel and Brian?"

"Her house isn't far from here. We'll stop there."

Sofia gathers Jacob and Tomas as we start back upstairs. Darius pauses at the front door, crouches in front of the two boys, and speaks to them in Krasnovian.

I can't make out all of what he's saying, but I catch the phrases *spy books, secret agent*, and *bad guys*. He's telling them his job is to navigate our way out, and their job has something to do with staying close to their mother and Alexei.

Jacob and Tomas listen to every word before they both nod solemnly.

We start out via the alley again, hurrying toward Hazel's house near the Global Rebuild office. Poe lopes along at my side, flinching at the sound of gunfire. Hazel and Brian, as pale and shaken as the rest of us, are both at her place.

"If they hurt us, it would be an international incident." She waves her passport.

"They're not asking nationalities before shooting," Darius replies somewhat dryly. "If you choose not to come with us, that's your call. But I've seen the number of platoons the PLF is mobilizing. I guarantee this is your last chance."

This time, Hazel quickly gathers her essential possessions, and she and Brian follow us outside. We make our way to Ivan's café. The glass windows are shattered, the interior dark. Tables and chairs lay overturned and broken.

Darius goes in to search for the café owner and returns with a shake of his head. "He's not here."

"He might have gone to the west side," Marcus says. "Many people tried to escape there and hide."

"We have to keep moving." Darius gestures for me to stay behind him. "We'll go around the plaza to avoid the worst of the fighting. The more stops we make, the bigger a target we'll be."

We keep walking. I remember that every single person in Varaz survived the five-year-long civil war. Not only that, they were determined to rebuild their lives after it was over. I have to believe they'll survive this too. I have to believe we will.

Darius leads the way over the winding streets, past the demolished Holy Trinity Church, and along the town wall. Though we stay in a single file and away from high-traffic streets, even I know that traveling in a group makes our situation even more dangerous. We will not find safety in numbers.

A series of explosions bursts from the cross street ahead. Poe spooks and retreats, too scared even to bark.

Darius stops, putting his hand out. Several PLF soldiers run forward, rifles pointed. Two start firing. Another breaks the window of the Gingerbread House with the butt of his rifle. He throws a handheld explosive into the shop and runs.

Darius shouts. He spins around and flings himself at me. I hit the ground with a thud that knocks the air from my lungs. He lands heavily on top of me the instant before the bomb goes off.

Stones and glass shatter and fly onto the street. He wraps my head in his arms, covering me with his body. I can't breathe, can't see. I pray Lara wasn't in the shop.

The boys? Sofia?

The ground stops shaking, but the noise is incessant. Darius levers himself off me, pushing his hands under my arms to haul me to my feet. Dust and smoke clog the air.

The others are crouched in doorways, Jacob and Tomas shocked with terror but physically unharmed. Brian and Hazel are running away from the blast, yelling for us to hurry.

Darius says something to Marcus that I can't hear past the ringing in my ears. They start after Brian and Hazel. Darius takes my hand. I stumble after him, coughing against the billowing smoke. If nothing else, I can follow him.

When we're farther from the blast site, I get my bearings. We'd been heading for the eastern wall and the gate leading to the castle, but the bomb forces us to go in the opposite direction, back toward the town square. Poe is nowhere to be seen.

Engines roar. Darius yells for Hazel and Brian to stop, but they're too far ahead. A convoy of half a dozen military trucks crests a hill and speeds toward us. The beds are filled with PLF soldiers carrying assault rifles. Shots fire into the air, as if in warning. They could mow us down in three seconds flat.

Darius spreads his arms out, herding us all between two buildings, a space too narrow to be an alleyway. The smells of garbage and dampness cling to the stone walls. Jacob is crying, his sniffles muffled against Alexei's shirtfront.

The convoy rumbles past. Darius stands blocking us at the entrance, his back to the street, his wide shoulders almost touching either side of the passage. Guns fire again.

My heart jams into my throat. The stone walls vibrate with

bullets, but none of them reach us. I close my eyes and send up a silent thanks to the medieval town builders who crammed the buildings so close together.

"We need to separate." Marcus's face is gaunt, peppered with dirt and grime. "We are going to attract too much attention. I will take Sofia and Tomas and follow your American friends. Alexei, you stay with Darius, Nell, and Jacob. If we are not at the eastern gate when you arrive there, we will meet you in Kolchava."

Darius hesitates, but Marcus is already picking Tomas up and heading out of the passage. Though Marcus is a pharmacist, after his family had fled Varaz, he'd spent years fighting in the civil war. This is not new territory for him.

"We cannot leave…" Sofia reaches for Jacob, her eyes red-rimmed with fear.

"I will protect him." Alexei pulls his wife into his arms and whispers something in her ear.

Marcus issues an order in Krasnovian. Sofia hugs Jacob tightly and follows her father back out to the street. They hurry in the direction Hazel and Brian had gone.

"We'll go the other way." Darius wipes a trickle of sweat from his forehead. He grazes his eyes over me in a swift assessment.

"Mama!" Jacob launches himself away from Alexei and races after his mother.

Darius grabs him before he gets even a few feet.

"I want Mama!" Jacob kicks at him, his scream high-pitched and his face streaked with tears.

Alexei tries to reach for him, but Jacob throws a punch and kicks harder. Darius locks his arms around the boy, stilling his frantic movements. After a minute, Jacob's screams devolve into hiccuping sobs and whimpers.

Darius sets Jacob on his feet and gets down in front of him. He puts his hand on the boy's shoulder and speaks to him in Krasnovian, his tone low.

Jacob scrubs his face, his chest still heaving with sobs. Darius reaches into his pocket, still speaking gently, and holds out the piece of gray sea glass.

Jacob hiccups again and peers at the object. Darius takes his hand and puts the sea glass in his palm, closing the boy's little fingers over the good-luck charm. Jacob nods, dragging his sleeve across his eyes.

I pull a water bottle out of my backpack and unscrew the top. After Jacob takes a few swallows, Darius gets to his feet.

"We'll take Birch Alley," he says. "It's closer to the square than I want, but it leads to the eastern gate."

Alexei readjusts his sling over his cast and holds his uninjured arm out to Jacob. The boy's fist is closed so tightly around the sea glass that his knuckles are white. But he's calmer. He takes Alexei's hand, and we continue our fraught journey.

Darius tries diverting us away from the square, but we are stopped by a group of Krasnovian army soldiers. He gestures for me and Alexei to stay back as he approaches one of the soldiers, his hands up and rifle in view. The soldier points him toward another man who must be in charge.

Something nudges my leg. *Poe.* Swallowing a cry of relief, I bend to hug the dog around his neck. "I knew you'd find us."

He licks my face and ducks his head as Jacob hurries over to greet him. Poe is tense with fear, his fur matted with dirt, but thankfully he appears unharmed.

Darius continues speaking to the soldier, who finally waves us through.

"Can he help us get to the eastern gate?" Alexei hurries to keep up with Darius's long stride.

Darius shakes his head. "He says they're bringing in reinforcements, but I don't know how they'll get through the PLF blockades."

We keep going on a strange, winding route—through alleys, past the bookstore, into a park. Poe walks between me and Jacob, his ears flattened against his head and his tail pointed. He gives three short, sharp barks of warning.

Another massive explosion breaks the air. Alexei drags Jacob closer. I grab a lamppost as the concussion reverberates into the sky. My bones feel as if they're about to shatter.

Smoke and fire erupt from the vicinity of Harmony Square. My gaze collides with Alexei's. First the castle, now possibly the museum.

I touch his arm and whisper, "The boys."

He nods, holding Jacob tightly. The artwork may be priceless, but nothing is more important than our lives. The clarity is like the eye in the chaos of a hurricane.

We reach the crest of a ridge overlooking the town square. The police station is engulfed in flames, but the museum and cathedral are both still standing. The bomb created a temporary lull in the gunfire as the noise of the fire takes over.

Alexei pauses, his chest heaving. His hair and beard are caked with dust and sweat. He squints at the plaza where we celebrated both the Friendship Festival and his wedding. Military trucks clog the streets, and bodies litter the grass. Some of them are wearing civilian clothes.

I take out the water bottle and hand it to him. The sun is halfway up the sky. My chest burns, and my skin feels scorched. Poe sits at my feet, panting.

Darius is still striding ahead, his booted steps forceful enough to stop the earth from rotating. He could have walked through the explosion and come out of it alive. The rest of us do not have his apparent invincibility.

Alexei gives Jacob a drink and returns the water bottle to me. I slip it into my backpack and adjust the straps over my shoulders.

"We're getting closer." I try to sound reassuring, though my voice is as rough as sandpaper.

"Yes." Alexei turns to look toward the city wall. "If we take the—"

Poe barks. Alexei's eyes widen in shock. He convulses, his face slackening.

"Papa!" Jacob screams.

CHAPTER 31

Nell

I HAVE no time to process what happened. I grab Alexei as he staggers. He falls against me. I stumble, trying to absorb his weight and keep us both upright. I grip the back of his shirt. The warm wetness of blood coats my hand.

Terror seizes me. I open my mouth to shout for Darius, but he's already running back to us.

"Shit." He hauls Alexei into his arms. "Nell, quick."

Clutching Jacob, I hurry after Darius as fast as I can. He bolts across the street into the relative shelter of a doorway. He sets Alexei down, his expression grim. A red bloodstain spreads over Alexei's left shoulder, seeping across his chest and through his sling.

Still swearing under his breath, Darius tears off the long-sleeved shirt he's wearing over his T-shirt. He binds it around Alexei's left shoulder.

Jacob wrenches away from me and drops to his knees at

Alexei's side. Alexei's face is pallid, his breath shallow, but his eyes are open. He struggles to give the boy a faint smile of reassurance.

"What...what happened?" I battle back a wave of dizziness and nausea.

"Sniper." Darius narrows his gaze at the watchtower jutting upward from the city wall. "Fuckers aren't wasting any time."

How the hell are we going to evade *snipers*? How are we going to get Alexei to medical care? Where are the others? Are they even still alive? What if Alexei—

A heavy despair hits me so hard my knees buckle. I sink down onto the doorstep next to Poe, struggling against the sudden impenetrable cloud.

Darius moves in front of me, crouching to my eye level. He puts his hand on my nape, his grip tight and heavy. His face is streaked with smoke and grime. Deep brackets edge his mouth, and sweat rolls down his temples. Beneath the steely hardness in his brown eyes, a fire of determination burns. Like candle flames in ice.

He presses his forehead to mine. I close my eyes and absorb the weight of his hand on the top of my spine.

"Hold on," he whispers.

I nod and pull in a shuddering breath. He detaches himself from me slowly, sliding his hand over my neck before turning back to Alexei.

Somehow I gather the strength to stand. Darius speaks to Alexei in Krasnovian, while Jacob hovers anxiously at his father's side. Darius lifts Alexei's right arm and hooks it over his shoulders as he helps the other man to his feet. Jacob slips his hand into mine.

I can't hear anything past the thundering of my heartbeat. Edging alongside the buildings, ducking behind trees and parked cars, we make painfully slow progress toward the eastern gate.

Poe is quiet, as if he knows we need to be invisible. Every second, I expect a bullet to scream through the air.

Alexei stumbles and grimaces. We stop, and Darius helps him sit on a bench concealed behind a row of trees. I hold the water bottle to Alexei's mouth so he can drink the last few drops. His skin is waxen, his eyes glassy.

Darius scans the street, every muscle locked and on alert. His shirt and hands are stained with Alexei's blood. The blaze from the police station is still eating into the sky.

A PLF truck swerves around a corner and skids down the ridge. The bed is concealed by a canvas cover, but appears to be empty. A soldier in the front seat is firing rounds of ammunition at the buildings, shattering the windows and scarring the facades. As the truck nears, he points his AK-47 out the window.

Right at us.

In a split-second, Darius fires his rifle. The bullet lodges in the man's chest, throwing him back against the driver. The truck veers to the left. The fender crashes against a lamppost, bringing the truck to a halt.

Yelling in Krasnovian, Darius advances on the driver, his rifle aimed. Another blast comes from the interior. A bullet zips past me, so close I can almost feel it.

Darius fires again. Bullets hit the truck and strike the driver. Darius runs forward, yanking open the driver's side door. His rifle in one hand, he hauls out the driver and throws him onto the ground. He grabs the other soldier, tossing him out. The two men crumple like rag dolls.

"Get in." Darius opens the canvas flaps at the back of the truck. His eyes are black, his features like rock.

I toss my backpack into the truck, then scramble to climb in with Jacob. It's empty, with just two long benches on either side. Poe jumps up, heaving himself in after two tries. Darius lifts Alexei, and together we manage to get him in.

"Keep pressure on his wound," Darius orders, slamming the tailgate and closing the canvas flaps. "Stay under the canvas."

I crouch beside Alexei on the bed of the truck and press my palm against the makeshift bandage. Jacob kneels on his other side and holds his hand. A few seconds later, the truck lurches into motion with a crunch of metal.

Being in a military vehicle—a PLF one, especially—allows me a faint relief. We could be stopped at any time, but at least we're marginally less vulnerable than we were on foot.

The truck swerves and careens over the streets, the stench of exhaust mixing with the smoke and dust. I lose my sense of direction and stay focused on Alexei. He's still conscious, but his pupils are dilated and his breath increasingly raspy.

Then, through a narrow opening in the canvas cover, I glimpse one of the city towers. We're passing under the gate leading to the castle road.

Please. Let the eastern route be open.

If we can't get out that way, crossing the mountain itself is the only other option. With its massive cliffs and forests, we'd have to do it on foot, which would be brutal in normal circumstances and impossible with Alexei so badly wounded.

The truck screeches to a sudden stop, slamming Jacob and Poe against the benches. I manage to steady Alexei.

Darius shouts, his voice rising over the engine's rumble. The canvas flaps open, and Hazel clambers into the truck, followed by Brian.

"Thank god you found us." Hazel starts over to hug me, her gaze skidding to Alexei lying on the bed of the truck, his shirt stained with blood. "Oh, no."

"He's alive," I say. "Where are Sofia and Marcus?"

"We thought they were with you."

Jacob's chin trembles. I attempt to smile at him in reassurance. "They've just gone a different way. We'll meet them in Kolchava, like your Deda promised."

"What can we do?" Brian kneels on Alexei's other side and opens his backpack. "I have extra water."

I lift Alexei's head so he can drink, then Brian turns to give another bottle of water to Jacob. The truck jerks forward again, slower this time, the gears grinding.

I've been on this road enough times with Alexei to recognize the sharp twists and turns leading to the fork, where one path goes up to the castle and the other winds down miles to the valley.

The truck stops again. Male voices rise, barking orders. I peer through an opening in the tarp. Krasnovian army. Better than the PLF, but still not exactly a reassurance.

I hear Darius speaking, his tone measured. A soldier pushes open the tarp and looks at us before letting the canvas drop back into place.

Darius starts the engine and keeps driving. A steep incline. A hairpin turn…and then the slow, laborious descent down the road leading away from the castle.

The truck rattles over rocks and grooves. He slows, easing around a turn. Another bump jars Alexei and makes him groan in pain. Jacob whispers to him, his face sheet-white. He holds the gray sea glass against Alexei's chest. The truck stops.

Darius cuts the engine. A door slams, and he pushes the canvas aside. "There's some debris ahead I need to move before we can get through. Who can drive a stick shift?"

Brian and Hazel shake their heads.

"I'll do it." I scramble to the other side of the truck, gesturing for Brian to take over the compression of Alexei's wound. "I learned how to drive on a stick shift."

"Nell." Jacob closes his hand around my arm, his dark eyes wide and terrified.

I pull him into a tight hug. "I'll be back soon, I promise."

The boy clings to me. I hate having to pry myself away from him, but we have to hurry. I whisper for him to take care of his father, then detach his arms from me and make my way over to Darius. Hazel settles her hand comfortingly on Jacob's shoulder.

"Do you need our help?" she asks Darius.

"No, the rest of you stay here." He grabs my waist and lifts me over the tailgate, then reaches for my backpack. "Don't get out, and keep the tarp closed. We can't draw too much attention."

Poe jumps down and follows us to the driver's side, lumbering up into the passenger seat. Darius puts my backpack on the floorboard.

I climb behind the wheel, fighting a surge of nausea and fear. Though he wiped down the interior, the seats and dashboard are still smeared with bloodstains.

I take a breath and focus on the controls. An old Volvo sedan is a very different kind of stick shift than an Eastern European military truck. But surely the basic mechanisms and gears are the same.

"I'm going to move some rocks and tree branches aside, and you just keep driving forward, okay?" Darius closes the door, keeping his hand on the open window. "It'll be slow going, but I'll guide you around any obstacles. Once we're past this stretch, hopefully we'll have a clear path the rest of the way down."

"Ten four." I give him a shaky smile.

He leans in and presses his mouth hard against mine. I let the brief kiss reverberate all the way down to my soul. Then he lets me go and runs down to the wreckage still cluttering the road.

For the next hour, I inch the truck forward every several feet while he moves away rocks and tree branches and guides me around boulders and piles of mud. The left rear tire gets stuck in a low ditch, and he maneuvers a branch underneath it so I have enough traction to drive out.

The cliff above us is unnerving, the entire side sheared away by the landslide. Another explosion or rockfall could happen without warning.

I try not to think about Alexei bleeding in the back of the

truck. I focus on shifting the vehicle into the proper gear, applying the right amount of pressure to the pedal, watching for Darius's hand gestures and instructions.

Poe is a welcome presence, sitting in the passenger seat with his head halfway out the open window, his ears perked and his tongue lolling.

Then, finally, the debris starts to lessen. Darius waves at me to stop.

"I'm going around that bend to make sure it's clear," he calls, pointing to a sharp turn in the road. "Follow slowly. If it looks good, I'll take over the wheel."

I give him a thumbs-up and shift into first gear. Poe barks, his ears flattening. I reach over to scratch his neck.

"It's okay, boy. We're almost there."

He barks again, his body tensing with sudden agitation.

Unease simmers in my chest. I wipe my sweaty palms on my jeans and grip the wheel. I release the clutch and press the gas pedal, easing the truck forward.

Aside from the destroyed section of the mountain, the other side of the road drops off into steep cliffs dotted by trees and brush. Only a flimsy guardrail protects vehicles from going over the edge.

I tighten my grip, my breath shallow. I'll feel much better when Darius is driving again.

Cautiously, I ease the truck around the curve. Poe's bark becomes a loud, steady stream, like the blasts of a foghorn.

"Poe, quiet, please...oh, *shit*."

I hit the brake, jerking the truck to a hard stop. I shake my head, almost unable to make sense of what's in front of me.

Lined up on the other side of the road, at the entrance to the deserted cheese factory property, are two trucks and a jeep emblazoned with the People's Liberation Front insignia. A dozen armed, helmeted soldiers are crowded around the vehicles, holding their rifles at the ready.

Darius is standing in the middle of the road. Blood trickles from a cut on his forehead. In front of him is Captain Lenkov.

CHAPTER 32

Nell

MY HEART PLUMMETS like a rock falling into an endless black pit. The captain is flanked by several other soldiers in combat gear and red bandannas either around their necks or showing under their helmets.

Poe's barking and the rumble of the engine catch their attention. One of them strides toward me, his finger on the rifle trigger. He gestures sharply for me to get out.

I turn off the engine, trying to breathe past the gut-wrenching fear. There is no fucking way the captain will let us pass his blockade.

I climb out of the truck, forcing myself not to look at Darius. Poe scrambles over to the driver's seat, barking and baring his teeth.

"Shut him up." The soldier aims his rifle at Poe.

Shaking badly, I put my arm around the dog and try to keep my voice calm. "Quiet, boy. It's okay."

I stroke his head and murmur comforting words. He barks a few more times. I brace myself for the crack of the rifle, but then Poe appears to recognize the need for silence. His bark shifts into a low whine, and he nudges his nose against my shoulder.

"Name!" The soldier shouts at me in Krasnovian.

"Anna...Smith."

Two others approach, rifles in front of them. I feel Lenkov's cold stare like a burn.

Another soldier yells something I don't understand. I shrug and try to look cooperative. He gestures to the back of the truck with his gun.

My stomach churns. I walk to the back, and he pushes open the canvas flaps with the barrel of the rifle.

"They are..." I struggle with the Krasnovian word for *civilians*. "Friends."

"We are no threat to you." Darius's voice cuts through the air, sharp but calm. "There is a child, two Americans, and a badly injured man who needs medical care."

The soldiers peer into the back of the truck. I catch a glimpse of Jacob huddled next to Hazel. Their faces are white with fear. Brian is still beside Alexei. He catches my gaze and nods slightly.

I let out my breath. Alexei is still alive. That at least means the bleeding has stopped.

One of the soldiers whom I recognize as Private Tarek snaps out, "Names!"

Hazel responds, pointing to each person in turn as she relays their names.

"Do not move," Tarek warns.

He closes the canvas before striding back to Lenkov. The other two soldiers stay on guard. Not that any one of us can go anywhere.

I follow Tarek back to the driver's seat, where Poe is waiting quietly but on full alert. I shut the driver's side door to keep him contained.

Darius and Lenkov are still standing in the middle of the road. I sense Darius's leashed energy as if it's a catapult about to be launched.

"Wait." Tarek points to the front of the truck. I stop beside the fender. He stays close, his rifle ready but not aimed at me.

Behind the jeep, the deserted factory is spread out on a large plot of land, the industrial brick architecture a stark contrast to the beauty of the rest of Varaz. Dozens of PLF trucks are parked outside, and soldiers are guarding the doors, like they've taken it over as their temporary headquarters.

Lenkov walks away from Darius and speaks with the private. There are at least six rifles pointed at Darius. The terror is a thick, oily mass spreading through my entire body.

Lenkov starts toward me. He's big and stocky, his face greasy with sweat. Just the memory of his hand on my cheek makes my skin crawl.

"Anna Smith." His English is clipped and precise. He moves his gaze over me from head to toe. "It seems you and your husband are in a bit of a dilemma. Are you the reason he betrayed me?"

I shake my head. I don't know what to say or what he wants to hear. I don't know how to diffuse this situation.

"Captain, we…I'm sorry if we insulted you."

He gives a short laugh. "I'm sure that you are sorry *now*. I doubt you were before."

I struggle to speak in Krasnovian in the hopes that my effort will soften him. "We love this country. But we have…this is a frightening situation, and we want to be back at home with our families."

He points toward the truck. "So what are you doing transporting Krasnovians out of Varaz?"

"They are friends. The man…Alexei…is father to the boy. He is wounded. He needs a doctor."

Lenkov strides past me to peer into the truck. He snaps out questions in Krasnovian, likely to Jacob.

I look at Darius, swallowing a sob when he meets my gaze. His features are set, every muscle straining against the urge to fly into action. He nods slightly, a quick reassurance that somehow gives me a bit of courage—even though I can't imagine any way out of this.

A plane swoops overhead, the engines echoing against the mountain. I tense in anticipation of another explosion before it darts toward the town.

Lenkov returns, jerking his chin at Darius. "You are an idiot, David Smith. Instead of taking my escort out of Varaz, you burden yourself with women and children? A dying man? A *pirank* such as you deserves to die."

The earth tilts under my feet. Darius could be dead in less than a second. So could the rest of us.

"Captain Lenkov, please." I take a breath and curl my fingers into my palms. "Allow us to pass."

"Anna, don't—" Darius steps forward. A soldier fires his gun at the ground near Darius's feet. He stops, his jaw clenching.

Lenkov glares at the man who fired the shot and shouts a few words at the soldiers before approaching me.

"I already agreed to help you leave Varaz." His eyes harden to pieces of ice. "You rejected my kindness. One of my men was killed, and your husband has destroyed the documents he dangled before me like a carrot. You made me a fool. Why would I allow you to escape again?"

Good question.

"I'm terribly sorry." My chest is so knotted up it hurts. I see Darius out of the corner of my eye, his full attention focused on me and Lenkov. "It was my idea. Not my...my husband's. He intended to give you the documents and fulfill his end of the bargain."

Lenkov purses his lips. "And for what reason did he listen to you?"

I don't think it's wise to reveal our loyalty to Varaz and its people, so I shrug and attempt to smile. "It is a good man who listens to his wife, yes?"

He chuckles and glances down at my body again. "A wife like you, yes. As I said, he is a lucky man to have you. But perhaps he has not cared for you as well as he should have."

He flicks his hand against my cheek, a sharp tap meant to sting, then trails his forefinger down my neck to the V of my shirt. Nausea curdles my stomach.

"Captain." Darius puts his hands up to chest level and comes toward us. Metallic clicks fill the air as the soldiers cock their rifles, but no one fires another shot.

Darius stops beside Lenkov. His expression is a mask concealing his hatred, his tone forcibly measured. "We've just been through Varaz. We have seen the destruction caused by the PLF. We know the Krasnovian army is close to complete surrender. You are assured of great success. And we are nothing. We have no power. We ask only for your mercy."

Lenkov grabs a rifle from the soldier beside him, ramming the stock into Darius's abdomen so swiftly I almost don't see him move. With a grunt, Darius doubles over.

I gasp and reach for him, but Tarek yanks me away.

"Do not," he warns in English.

Though his tone is not harsh or threatening—or maybe because of that—I obey the command and go still.

Another soldier shoves Darius, making him stumble. Darius holds out his hand to me in an *it's okay* signal. He pulls in a breath and straightens, his eyes blazing.

"I said before your husband is a good sycophant," Lenkov tells me. "What about you, Anna? What are you good at?"

He issues an order to the man beside him. The soldier lifts his rifle and moves closer, putting the barrel flush against my temple.

My legs start to buckle. I steady myself on the hood of the truck. I've known this kind of terror once before in my life, on a Tuesday afternoon when I opened the garage door in search of my mother. It's impenetrable. A terror that can stop time and swallow you whole.

Lenkov grips me under the chin and forces my head back. His breath is foul. I want to spit in his face. He pushes me against the hood and grabs my breast, shoving his body up against mine. Bile surges in my throat. From the passenger seat, Poe starts barking frantically.

I feel Darius moving, hear the feral, animal-like growl erupting from his chest. I want to tell him to stop, to not put himself in further danger, but I don't dare speak.

Watching my face, Lenkov gropes my other breast and twists my nipple so hard I gasp in pain. He chuckles and slaps his hand between my legs.

Every cell in my body screams in revulsion. The barrel of the rifle knocks against my head. My vision blurs.

There's a sudden commotion to the left, but Lenkov's grip is immobilizing. I can't turn my head. Yells fill the air, all in Krasnovian.

I hear Darius's voice. His shout rises above the noise.

Three words that turn my blood to ice.

"I'm Darius Hawke."

Lenkov pauses, his mouth twisting. He glares at me, as if processing what he just heard. Then he pushes away from me.

I gulp in heavy gasps of air. The soldier holding the rifle to my head backs off, still pointing the weapon at me. Tarek moves closer.

I rub my forearm over my eyes. Darius is on his knees in the middle of the road, his hands behind his head and every part of him tense with rage. Six soldiers stand in a half circle, all aiming their guns at him.

Lenkov strides over. "You lie."

"No." Darius's voice is a hiss of hatred. "My passport is in my back pocket."

Lenkov snaps out an order. A soldier steps forward and digs into Darius's jeans pocket. He retrieves the passport and brings it to the captain.

Lenkov pages through the battered passport with its countless stamps and visas. He studies the photograph, looking up at Darius several times. Then he stuffs the passport in his own pocket and approaches.

He kicks Darius in the jaw with his heavy boot, jerking his head to the side.

A scream lodges in my chest. Lenkov kicks him again, then punches him on the temple. Darius grunts and staggers, putting one hand on the ground to stop himself from losing balance. Lenkov grabs Darius's hair and yanks him to his feet.

"You are a traitor to our cause," Lenkov snarls.

"A traitor is someone who betrays you," Darius retorts. "I'm the worst enemy of your fucking cause."

Lenkov shouts in Krasnovian, most of his words too fast for me to comprehend, but I catch the words *criminal* and *Conrad Hawke*.

The sound of his father's name seems to fill Darius with fresh rage.

"My father gave you nothing then," he snaps. "He'll give you nothing now."

Lenkov barks out a laugh. "Your father has interests far greater than you."

"He's not the one who knows who's funding the PLF." Darius yanks himself away from the captain. "He doesn't know about the PLF structure and operations. But I do."

"You lie." Lenkov's mouth thins. "How would you obtain this information?"

Darius responds in Krasnovian, his body lined with a fury so intense it almost reverberates in the air. I steel myself for more of Lenkov's attacks. The captain's voice is a cold stream of what sounds like warnings and decrees. Darius indicates the truck, looking as if he's forcing his voice into a more even tone.

Lenkov releases him. His eyes are narrowed to slits. The soldiers crowd closer, guns still aimed. Two of them accompany Darius to the truck, where he rummages in the cab and returns with my passport. He gives it to Lenkov, who studies it.

Darius speaks again and gestures to me. Trying to convince the captain of something. Negotiating.

No. No.

My suspicious are like needles poking just beneath the surface of my chaotic thoughts. I don't want to acknowledge them. Can't.

I don't know much about the PLF, but Darius is legendary among their ranks...and not in a good way. He's the American hostage who escaped their guard and became renowned for his victory. He bested the entire People's Liberation Front, and the world knows it.

Because of Darius, the UN officially designated the PLF as a terrorist organization. He's been working with NATO to establish technologies and capabilities against the PLF. He's been investigating their structure and funding channels for the sole purpose of taking them down.

A man of Lenkov's rank will not pass up the chance for revenge.

Which, I think with a despair blacker than tar, is exactly what Darius is giving him.

Finally, Darius steps away from the captain, taking my passport back. He returns it to my backpack in the truck.

I watch through blurred vision, seeing him move almost in

slow motion as he comes toward me, his tall figure diminishing the trees on the mountain behind him, his wide shoulders blocking out the soldiers and their weapons.

His features are set in hard lines of determination, his face streaked with dirt and blood, but his gaze is unerringly fixed on me.

I brace my hand on the hood of the truck. I can't pull a breath into my tight lungs. He stops in front of me.

For the first time in my life, I don't want to read what is written in the depths of his brown eyes. An ache claws out from the center of my heart, pushing up into my throat.

"Please..." The word is a choked whisper.

"Nell." He closes his hands on my upper arms. "Listen to me."

"Maybe we...we can still contact the embassy or the ambassador or...there has to be something..." I can't get the words out. My head is spinning.

"Lenkov is going to let you go." Darius looks at me steadily. "You, Hazel, and Brian. Not because he's being generous, but because he wants to use you for media attention. He'll be the captain who helped three Americans get back home when not even the US embassy or anyone in the Krasnovian government bothered trying."

I stare at him. "What about Alexei and Jacob?"

His mouth compresses. "A wounded man and a child are of no use to Lenkov. In fact, they'd be a liability. I asked him to let them go with you so Alexei can get medical care. I don't know if he'll agree. Listen."

He tightens his grip on me as if he's willing me not to break. "You're going to drive to the PLF camp. Lenkov will radio down so they'll know you're coming. They'll want you to record a statement praising the PLF. Do whatever they ask. You'll have to find another vehicle, but they'll give you a pass that should get you through the checkpoints."

"What...what about you?" I stammer.

"As soon as you get a cell signal, call my friend Savko. I programmed his number into your phone. He'll help you get to Telina."

"Darius." I curl my fingers into the front of his shirt. *"What about you?"*

"I'll be okay." He glances behind him at Lenkov, who is watching us impatiently. "Their general isn't far from here. Balakin. He's the one who ordered my abduction and made the ransom demands. Lenkov will probably earn a promotion by turning me over to him. He has a score to settle. I'm going to let him."

"No."

"Nell." He pulls me closer, a dark pain rising to his eyes. "Alexei needs a doctor. Both he and Jacob need to be with the rest of their family. Hazel and Brian should have been back in the States weeks ago. You all need to get out of this hellhole."

"So let them go." I struggle to swallow past the pain in my throat. "I'll stay here with you."

"You need to lead them. You're the strongest."

"No, I'm not! I'm fucking terrified. And what if Lenkov is lying? What if he has us killed as soon as we reach the camp? Or sooner?"

He shakes his head. "He doesn't want your blood on his or the PLF's hands. You're more valuable to their cause alive, especially after you make a statement that you won't be able to deny once you're back in the States."

My heart twists with anguish and guilt. Darius shouldn't even be in Krasnovar at all, much less trying to get me and four other people, not to mention a dog, out of a deadly war zone.

"Let me talk to Lenkov," I say. "Maybe I can reason with him."

"No." His jaw clenches. *"Reason* is not what he wants from you."

A sick feeling surges through me. "So you're planning to…

what? Join their ranks? Become their translator or their liaison to the United Nations?"

Let them take you hostage again?

I can't stand it. My insides are as cold and brittle as ice. There has to be another way. *There has to be.*

"I'm going with them." Darius nods toward the factory. "They'll want to know about my work, the details of the counterterrorism initiatives, what I've learned about them through the investigations. Names, contacts, intelligence. They want information."

I shake my head. Even I know the PLF wants more than just *information* from Darius Hawke. They want his surrender.

"Please." Tears flood my eyes. "Don't do this. Don't go with them. Don't leave me."

"I'm not leaving you." Pain and regret etch deep lines across his face. "I didn't come here to leave you."

But he will sacrifice himself for me. A thousand times over, if necessary.

"My beautiful girl." He puts his hands on either side of my head, brushing his thumbs across my cheeks. His eyes glitter. "You are the only thing that makes perfect sense in this world."

The tears spill over and course down my cheeks. I grip the front of his shirt harder, my knuckles whitening. He gazes at me as if he's memorizing every detail of my face.

"I love you, Nell." His voice roughens. "I love you so much. More than I knew it was even possible to love someone."

A sob breaks from my throat. He spreads his hand over the back of my head and pulls me against his chest. I squeeze my eyes shut, unable to contain my tears. His heartbeat, as strong and eternal as time itself, reverberates through me, sinking into my blood. An everlasting part of me.

He wraps his arms around me, locking me to him. I fill myself with the sensation of his body against mine, his breath stirring my hair, his stream of low murmurs. He puts his hand under my chin, lifting my face. A thousand emotions darken his eyes—love, torture, regret.

He presses his mouth to mine, imprinting every part of himself on me. I slide my hands into his hair as his kiss breaks open the ice inside me, letting in rays of warm, multicolored light.

My mind can't process what's happening, how we came to this, but my soul still knows that truth—our truth—is stronger than any force that would conspire to keep us apart.

What we have is made of starlight and birdsong. Through all time, any distance, we are bound by unbreakable golden threads.

I press my hand to his heart. "I love you."

"I'll find you again, I swear." He tightens his hold on me, his arms like iron bands. "I will always come to you."

Lenkov's harsh shout cuts through the air. Darius pulls away from me. Our separation feels like the plates of the earth breaking apart.

"Go," he says. "Don't stop. Don't look back."

Fresh tears fill my eyes. "I—"

"Hurry. Stay safe for me."

He kisses me again, a hard, swift kiss of possession and promise, then turns and walks back to the captain and the other soldiers.

An anguished cry takes root deep inside me. I press a hand to my mouth.

Tarek approaches, shouting something in Krasnovian to the other soldiers. He catches my eye and points to the truck. Holding his rifle, he climbs into the back to accompany us down to the camp.

Forcing myself to move, I get into the driver's seat and start the engine. I'm shaking so hard my teeth rattle. Poe clambers anxiously back to the passenger seat, whining.

I can hardly see past the tears. I scrub my face with my sleeve and manage to shove the truck into first gear. I let out the clutch and start forward, half expecting a spray of bullets to hit the windshield.

But the soldiers only watch as we pass, their rifles ready but not aimed. Dragging in a hard breath, I tighten my hands on the wheel and keep going. There's another bend in the road up ahead. Once I turn, we'll be out of the soldiers' sight.

I'll no longer be able to see Darius.

I glance in the rearview mirror. He's walking down the incline to the factory, his spine like steel. A soldier prods him in the back, forcing him to walk faster.

Lenkov disappears through the building's heavy metal doors. Flanked by the armed soldiers, Darius follows.

The doors slam shut.

My vision blurs again. Two planes split through the clouds and dive low.

I maneuver the truck around a fallen rock. Poe circles in agitation, whining and scratching at the door. I reach to pet him.

He puts his front paws on the open passenger window and barks. Before I can settle my hand on his back, he jumps out the window.

"Poe!" My shout is lost in the screech of the plane engines.

I hit the brake and look backward. Poe is racing up the road back to the factory, his legs a blur and his body a streak of black.

"Oh, no…no." I fumble to open the door.

Then Darius's order penetrates my anguish. If I go back now, there's no telling what Lenkov will do. If not to me, then to Darius or the others. To Jacob, who has already been through untold trauma in his seven years. He has to know that his good-luck sea glass will protect him.

I grip the wheel. Tears spill in rivers down my cheeks.

I start forward again, easing the truck toward the sharp bend in the road. Gunfire suddenly resounds from the soldiers stationed near the factory. In the distance, close to the eastern gate of the city wall, an explosion rips through the air.

Don't stop. Don't look back.

I shove the truck into gear, navigate the turn, then speed up.

I wipe my eyes with my sleeve again. Fixing my gaze on the road, I keep driving as my pain turns into single-minded determination. I will get us to safety. For all of our sakes…but especially for Darius.

I'd once thought I would always be trapped by him. I was a bird, and he was the cage. He had imprisoned my heart. Captured me.

I know differently now. Because of Darius, I've learned that the world is not a place to be feared. Though there are sins, dangers, and untold risks…there are also good-luck charms, exuberant dances, and kisses that taste like sunshine. There are blackberry-jam doughnuts, gingerbread flowers, and dogs who choose you. There are friends who become family.

Above all, there is a man whose protective instinct runs deeper than the ocean. A man who locks his body and soul around the woman he loves.

No, Darius has never trapped me. He's the one who set me free.

I press the pedal harder and guide the truck down the mountain to the valley.

∼

Nell and Darius's story concludes in *Wishes & Wings*, the final book in The Birdsong Trilogy.

ABOUT THE AUTHOR

Born and raised in California, *New York Times* and *USA Today* bestselling author Nina Lane now lives in Wisconsin where the winters are freezing and the cheese is exceptional. Mom to two teens and a neurotic dog, half her life consists of laundry, Girl Scouts, horses, and football, while the other half is filled with hot, swoony alpha heroes and the women who bring them to their knees.

Nina is a fan of popcorn, print magazines, working out, and checking the weather daily with her meteorologist husband. She holds a PhD in Art History and an MA in Library and Information Studies, but considers writing epic, emotional romances her one true calling in life. Thus, she is grateful to be able to bring the stories in her head to life for all her amazing fans.

www.ninalane.com

facebook.com/ninalaneauthor
instagram.com/ninalaneauthor
amazon.com/author/ninalane
goodreads.com/ninalane

ALSO BY NINA LANE

~

— THE SPIRAL SERIES —

From an exhilarating crush to the intensities of marriage, Liv and Dean West embark on a passionate lifelong journey together, with an everlasting romance and a love to end all loves.

AROUSE

ALLURE

AWAKEN

ADORE

ALWAYS

~

— THE STONE BROTHERS BILLIONAIRES —

Starring hot, hunky billionaire brothers who run a candy empire…and the women who bring them to their knees.

THE DEAL MAKER (LUKE & POLLY)

THE RISK TAKER (EVAN & HANNAH)

THE RULE BREAKER (TYLER & KATE)

THE GAME CHANGER (GAVIN & MIA)

~

— THE WHAT IF SERIES —

Two reunited lovers confront the demons and heartbreaking aftereffects of their tortured past.

IF WE LEAP

IF WE FALL

IF WE FLY

~

— THE DARING HEARTS SERIES —

In bustling, colorful Victorian London, powerful lords and unconventional women battle scandal and secrets as they risk everything for love.

A STUDY IN SEDUCTION

A PASSION FOR PLEASURE

A DREAM OF DESIRE

'TWAS THE NIGHT BEFORE CHRISTMAS

— THE STARTING OVER SERIES —

Three unforgettable couples. Three second chances at life and love. Standalone spin-offs from Nina Lane's beloved series.

BREAK THE SKY (ARCHER & KELSEY)

THE SECRET THIEF (EVE & FLYNN)

BECAUSE OF YOU (JULIA & WARREN)

WRITTEN AS NINA LINDSEY

Enjoy my sexy-sweet, heartwarming romances in Bliss Cove, where love sweeps in on the ocean breeze.

WE FOUND LOVE

After Trevor's meteoric rise to fame in the chef world tears them apart, Kate escapes to a small seaside town to heal her broken heart. Determined to prove they belong together, Trevor seeks Kate out in Bliss Cove and risks it all for a second chance.

THE MOMENT WE KNEW

Shaking off her past mistakes, Aria Prescott is determined to start a new life with her latest venture, the "Meow and Then Cat Café." Then property developer Hunter Armstrong swoops in to take over the whole district. Who will win this war of both homes and hearts?

ALL WE'LL EVER NEED

An expert on the hot, wild tales of mythology, Callie Prescott leads a tidy life. And that, thank you, is exactly how she wants it...until action hero Jake Ryan arrives in town and wants some close-up action with the brilliant, beautiful professor.

EVERYTHING WE HAVEN'T SAID

Rory Prescott and tavern owner Grant Taylor make a deal — she'll be his date to his brother's wedding if he'll let her stay short-term in his cottage. But what happens when this fake relationship becomes passionately real?

THIS TIME WITH HER

When chirpy reporter Brooke Castle gets trapped in a snowstorm with grumpy bookstore owner Sam Donovan, the fire isn't the only thing heating up the cabin.

COMING HOME TO HER

High school literature teacher Grace Berry has no time for romance. But when sexy, award-winning author Lincoln Atwood comes into her classroom, Grace is eager for his lessons in love.

IT'LL ALWAYS BE HER

Disgraced physicist Adam Powers comes to Bliss Cove to debunk a haunting, but the town's scrappy librarian, Bee Delaney, makes him question everything he believes. Bee is determined to save her crumbling library by proving a ghost lives there—until falling for Adam puts her heart at risk.

www.ingramcontent.com/pod-product-compliance
Lightning Source LLC
Chambersburg PA
CBHW051952240626
47153CB00005B/1732